THE YEAR OF YES AND NO

Sara Sartagne

FE3 LIMITED

Copyright © 2024 by Sara Sartagne

All rights reserved.

No part of this publication may be reproduced, distributed, or transmitted in any form or by any means, including photocopying, recording, or other electronic or mechanical methods, without the prior written permission of the publisher, except as permitted by U.S. copyright law.

The story, all names, characters, and incidents portrayed in this production are fictitious. No identification with actual persons (living or deceased), places, buildings, and products is intended or should be inferred.

Book Cover by Jen Moon

First edition 2024

Contents

Acknowledgements and historical notes	VI
Chapter 1	1
Chapter 2	10
Chapter 3	18
Chapter 4	27
Chapter 5	37
Chapter 6	45
Chapter 7	52
Chapter 8	61
Chapter 9	70
Chapter 10	80
Chapter 11	88
Chapter 12	94
Chapter 13	104
Chapter 14	112
Chapter 15	121
Chapter 16	131

Chapter 17	141
Chapter 18	151
Chapter 19	161
Chapter 20	173
Chapter 21	183
Chapter 22	193
Chapter 23	203
Chapter 24	213
Chapter 25	221
Chapter 26	229
Chapter 27	239
Chapter 28	247
Chapter 29	256
Chapter 30	265
Chapter 31	274
Chapter 32	282
Chapter 33	292
Chapter 34	302
Chapter 35	312
Chapter 36	321
Chapter 37	332
Chapter 38	341
Chapter 39	351

Chapter 40	362
Chapter 41	371
Chapter 42	376
Epilogue	380
Other Duality novels	384

Acknowledgements and historical notes

As usual, I owe an incredible debt of thanks to all my writing buddies who've helped to make this a much, much better book – Jilly Wood, Jan Page Jackson, Natasha (who keeps me current!), Katharine Edgar, (whose advice on being a historical detective has been invaluable), Jane Roberts, and of course, Fiona.

You're all bloody superstars.

Thanks also to the Malton writing group *Monkeys with Typewriters*, the Allerthorpe *Write Now* ladies, and the *Beverley Novelists Group*, for providing critique on early drafts, enthusiasm and encouragement.

Also as usual, this is historical fiction, rather than historical fact. I've played fast and loose with some of the dates used in Harriet's story for the sake of the book, although I've tried hard to create the environment that buffs of Georgian and Regency history will recognise. These include, for the first time for me as a writer, some real people.

John Hoppner was a popular painter, famed for his pictures of children, and Richard Cosway is one of the era's renowned miniaturists. Richard Cosway is mentioned in several letters as being a little eccentric, with outlandish dress sense.

ACKNOWLEDGEMENTS AND HISTORICAL NOTES

Lady Arabella Porter-Hume is very loosely based on Sarah Sophia Child Villiers, Countess of Jersey, who inherited bank shares from her mother and as a result, was a senior partner at Child & Co bank. She was also a patroness of Almack's, but for my story, I only needed her banking credentials!

Miss Mary Berry (not the well-loved UK chef!) held a regular and well-attended salon from her London home. Salons in eighteenth-century Britain gave women the opportunity (mostly only allowed to men) to mix with actors, poets, artists and politicians. I've based some of Mary's dialogue in the book on her letters and journals, particularly her travel journals. With her sister, Agnes, Mary Berry travelled in the latter part of the 18th century and, as mentioned, even met Napoleon.

Anne Seymour Damer was a sculptor and did indeed exhibit at the Royal Academy, but she created the bust of Princess Caroline in 1814, not 1803. She was the goddaughter of Horace Walpole, who described her as 'a female genius'. Her rumoured preference for women and her odd manner of dress has been well documented, as has the prenuptial agreement that allowed her to sculpt after the suicide of her husband. She was great friends with Mary Berry and I've based some of their conversations on letters that remain.

The performance of Mozart's *The Clemency of Titus* at His Majesty's Theatre with Mr John Braham and Mrs Nancy Storace took place in 1806. So did the debut of Angelica Catalani

David Lang was a long-time conductor of clandestine marriages in Gretna Green and obviously charged for his services.

All the books mentioned here exist; A *Description of Latium* by Mrs Knight, was released in 1805.

The book is set in England, has English characters, and so is written and edited to follow British English spelling, grammar, and punctuation.

Chapter 1

COLCHESTER HALL, DECEMBER 1802

Harriet felt the room sway as the attorney finished speaking. Augusta, her mother-in-law, gasped and there was an indrawn breath from Alexander Richardson, her husband's close friend. Harriet realised her mouth had dropped open. She closed it swiftly and swallowed.

"Me?" she said, stupidly. She tried again, attempting to force some steel into her soft voice. "I'm sorry, did I hear correctly? John left it all to me?"

Augusta jumped to her feet. "Preposterous! Our family fortune? Built up over long years of careful business dealings? Surely there's some mistake! Give me the will!" she demanded, her dark eyes snapping and meagre bosom rising with agitation.

Mr Bessiwick, from Bessiwick, Stamford and Jones, peered at Augusta over his spectacles, reminding Harriet of a cross owl. "Yes, perhaps I should repeat it." He ran his finger under the lines on the page as Augusta leaned over his shoulder. "'Unto my dear wife, Harriet Colchester, I bequeath my whole estate to and for her absolute use and disposal during the term of her natural life.' It's quite clear, Mrs Colchester," he said to Augusta. "There are some small gifts, but other than your annual allowance and his bequest of the York house to you, Harriet is his sole beneficiary."

Augusta swung away, her hands clawed tightly. Harriet focused on the gilt decoration on the green leather inlay in the desk and the garnet signet ring on the plump finger of the attorney. Augusta's usually cream complexion turned more and more red as the news sank in: the Colchester fortune passing into the hands of her son's unworthy wife.

Harriet drew a breath. "I see, Mr Bessiwick. Thank you. Please go on."

Mr Bessiwick nodded and continued. John had bequeathed his pocket watch and a book to Alexander, a small sum to his valet. In truth, Harriet hardly heard him. The ground was still tilting, and she pressed her feet into the rug to steady herself. John's final wishes enveloped her like an ominous cloud. It wasn't that she doubted that she could manage Colchester Hall – she'd been doing that quietly for years – but managing the reactions of Augusta and the family now she controlled the family fortune was quite a different prospect.

Her gaze darted around the high-ceilinged room. There was, she knew, not a speck of dust anywhere, not an ornament out of place. Her energies, when she had been unable to ride or walk around the estate, had ensured Colchester Hall was immaculate, and John had often remarked how welcoming his house had become. The rooms were in the best style, classical, restrained – she was proud of her efforts.

"Harriet?"

Alexander's calm voice pushed into her reflections.

"Oh! I beg your pardon," she said, glancing up to see several pairs of eyes on her. "What did you say?"

CHAPTER 1

"He *said*, Harriet, that he would arrange for the banker to call and suggested that you sit down with John's man of business," Augusta repeated, the edge to her voice well known to Harriet. "It's obvious you're not fit to manage alone. You'll need someone with you. I'll send for Crewe, our man. He'll be able to explain to you what's to be done. And obviously, I will remain to support you while you consider your future."

Harriet, who tried to believe that somewhere underneath her sharp and dismissive manner her angular mother-in-law had a heart, was doubtful that Augusta had anything other than the protection of the family fortune in mind when she spoke of supporting her. And those words – 'consider your future' – made her uneasy. What fresh torture had her mother-in-law in mind for her now? And who might protect her? She glanced at Alexander, tall and imposing, his solid frame soberly dressed. His warm blue eyes were full of sympathy.

He seemed to read her mind and spoke. "I would be happy to stay a little longer, although I must return to London in the New Year."

Harriet gave him a grateful smile, despite Augusta's gimlet stare. "You are too good. Thank you."

Alexander in the house might deflect Augusta's more barbed comments. Her mother-in-law was better behaved in company, and, as John's closest friend, Alexander had been almost a *de facto* member of the household for all the time Harriet had been married. Harriet caught Alexander's wink as the attorney began to shuffle together the papers, and her heart lightened a little at the prospect of his presence.

She turned to Mr Bessiwick, a small man sitting low in the chair, and thought absently that she might have provided a cushion for him. "Thank you, sir. Is – is this an unusual situation?"

His watery blue eyes focused on her. "It is not unusual for a man to leave his estate to his wife if there are no children. Although to do so without conditions speaks volumes for his affections. Many a wealthy man would request that you remain a widow to enjoy the fruits of his labours, but there are no such constraints on you."

She heard Augusta tut and mutter something about 'sentimental claptrap!', and Harriet's eyes widened a fraction before she steadied her voice. "Is it sentimental that John cared for me?"

This was met with a profound silence. Alexander nodded at her words.

"He might have had a care for the rest of his family!" snapped Augusta, bristling and looking at her down her thin nose.

"But I am his family," Harriet said quietly.

"Aye, and thanks to you, his only family, more's the pity!" Augusta scoffed.

Harriet blanched. She had borne her heartbreak and distress at her inability to conceive in private, aware of the gossip behind her back from John's family, hearing their whispers of 'tainted stock'.

"You must make a will immediately, naming cousin Edwin as your beneficiary. Mr Bessiwick can draw it up!" Augusta added.

Harriet stiffened in revulsion. "I will take advice, Mama, but I shall do nothing immediately!"

Augusta looked ready to argue the point, but Alexander took a step closer to Harriet as if to protect her. Augusta shot him a look of intense dislike and bustled from the room, muttering.

Alexander turned to Mr Bessiwick, who was pursing his lips in disapproval. "Mr Colchester's will cannot be challenged, I take it?"

"Every will may be challenged, Mr Richardson. And as Mrs Augusta Colchester has noted, it is a little unusual to leave so large a sum without any conditions. I believe the will is firm, but I imagine some of the late Mr Colchester's relatives will feel unjustly dealt with." The lawyer sniffed at these unseen family members and then stood. "Mrs Colchester, I offer my deepest condolences on your loss, and I am at your service. I wish you good day."

"I will see you out," said Alexander.

After the diminutive attorney had left the room, Harriet folded into the nearest chair and put her hand over her eyes.

A month ago, John had fallen from his horse and broken his neck; there had been no long illness, no leave taking, no final words. There had only been shock, disbelief. The sense of quiet comfort, which for five years had wrapped around her, had been ripped away, leaving her bereft and vulnerable, as if she was naked in public.

And this! She had been hoping for an annual competence, nothing more. Certainly not twenty thousand a year!

She reviewed, as best she could remember, her interactions with her husband in the months before his accident. He would often reach over to pat her hand as they sat by the fire in the winter evenings when she would read to him. But he was not demonstrative in public, relaxing only when they were alone. He was kind to her, for which she was grateful, but this had never given her carte blanche to do what she wished.

Harriet remembered one of his visits to her bedroom. When he'd caught his breath and made to slip out of the bed, she had asked, tentatively, if it would be possible for her to visit her friend Anne in London the following month.

"You will be away during Mama's visit," he had commented, as he thrust his arms through his dressing gown.

"I know, but Mama has seen me a great deal this year," she said carefully. "I thought she might appreciate some time alone with her only son."

He laughed, blind to the faults of his mother. "She believes she is supporting you as best she can since your parents died. Please stay! The house runs so much better when you are here. You can visit Anne later in the year."

He kissed her cheek, wished her good night and left, whistling.

Now she stared at the jumping flames of the fire. Had he known of her yearning for more independence? He had known of her wish to travel, teasing her about her collection of travelogues, even though they rarely travelled further than Berwick, and for him, London meant business rather than pleasure. But now, his will offered her a different life, a life full of opportunities hitherto denied her.

She wished she had someone in whom to confide. Almost as soon as she was married and off their hands, her parents decided to explore the Continent. When she most needed the advice and guidance of her mother to navigate the sneers of her in-laws and John's endless cousins, Harriet was alone.

Her mother was an indifferent correspondent and sent only a few scrawled lines complaining about the food, or the heat, or relating how she had met agreeable company in Lord and Lady so-and-so. When her parents finally decided to return, their packet was caught in a storm and all aboard were lost. To Harriet's guilty surprise she felt as if she was mourning strangers. And then she was *truly* alone.

Restless with her thoughts, Harriet stood to stare out of the window. The weak December sunshine glinted off wet leaves in the shrubbery and she espied a rabbit hopping across the lawn. Part of her mind wanted the rabbit to flee, lest it find its way into a cooking pot. The other part wondered what had happened to Sophia, her sister, the cause of the family disgrace. Sophia's conduct and elopement had made contact impossible; Augusta would have been livid had Harriet attempted it. Harriet knew that Sophia was now a mother of several children; her husband Miles was a country parson. They lurked at the edges of Harriet's thoughts.

She heard the door open and close behind her and straightened her shoulders.

"Harriet? How are you bearing up?" said Alexander. She turned to him.

"I don't know what to think! I hoped John would treat me kindly, but I never imagined this largesse! It is rather overwhelming."

"My dear girl, why would John not treat you kindly? He held you in the greatest affection!" Alexander frowned, his dark brows pinched together.

She smiled ruefully. "He might have thought about how Mama would react to his wishes! She is horrified, and I have no doubt she will challenge the will."

"Or Edwin will," Alexander agreed, speaking of John's cousin, currently taking advantage of the uneasy Peace in Europe to conduct his Grand Tour.

Harriet nodded, pursing her lips. Edwin went through money like water. She would wager that Augusta was at this moment penning a letter to him, and didn't doubt that this would pull Edwin back to England post haste. But had John wanted to leave his fortune to Edwin, his mother, or any of his relatives, he would have done so. Instead, her shy, awkward husband had chosen to leave it to her.

"I had not thought until this moment that he held me in much esteem," she said softly.

"John was not the most demonstrative of men," Alexander said, looking at his fingernails instead of her. Harriet almost smiled at the understatement. "But what clearer communication of his feelings could he give you than this?"

She was not prone to tears, but at this, her vision became blurred, and she was unable to speak as the realisation of John's affection crashed over her like a wave. She owed him so much, and now, it was too late to thank him. She swung away from Alexander, her voice trapped in her throat as she struggled to control her emotions. Had John truly loved her? She had never looked further than his kindness.

"Steady, my dear." Large, warm hands curled around her shoulders. It was the first human contact she had received since the funeral, and she felt a sob rise to her throat. Alexander was such a dear friend. She gathered her composure and pressed his hand. She heard the intake of his breath, and after a pause, he squeezed her fingers and went to sit in one of the armchairs by the fire.

"You are very pale," he said, his blue eyes flicking over her as she sat in the chair opposite him. "Have you eaten today?"

She had not. The thought of the will reading had robbed her of her appetite for days. She plucked at the folds of her crepe dress with an amused twitch of her lips. "I look so ill in black."

"You look like Cleopatra with your dark hair. A pale one, I grant you. What will you do?"

"With Mama in the house? I will continue as before, while I grow accustomed to my new situation."

Alexander smiled. "I should make use of your inheritance before Augusta begins to cause mischief."

"I am still in mourning."

"Not forever," he responded firmly. "And in any case, custom does not dictate you should stay at home, just that you refrain from attending societal events. You are too young to rusticate in Colchester Hall; you should visit friends, get away from here a while."

Harriet shook her head. After Sophia's elopement, she had withdrawn from society, and except Anne, her few friends had disappeared. It was years since she'd visited London for her wedding trip, although the glittering amphitheatre and the grand masked ball at Ranelagh Gardens shone brightly in her memory.

She sighed. While she accustomed herself to her new situation, she ought to – she would – stay at Colchester Hall.

And watch for her mother-in-law to cause trouble.

CHAPTER 2

CENTRAL LONDON, JANUARY 2023

I thanked the art courier and signed my name. Gabriella Sullivan, assistant gallery manager. Such dizzy heights of responsibility at the age of twenty-seven. I smiled slightly before examining the paperwork for Gerrard's latest acquisition. 'Two miniatures of Harriet Colchester,' said the delivery note. Gerrard had been a little mischievous when I saw the amount go out of the business account and asked him what it was.

"Twin treasures," was all he'd said, twinkling at me. So, face to face with his purchase, my curiosity was now aroused.

I pulled on gloves and reached for the screwdriver to release the outer wooden frame of the small, flat case, the size of an old portable record player. I unscrewed the fixings and put the tool to one side. I paused. The clock on the wall said two-thirty-five. Gerrard was not yet back from lunch and might not be back for another hour. I wrinkled my nose. If I didn't open the case, any damage to its contents would go undetected and it would likely be Monday before any action could be taken.

I peered into the gallery. I ought to get back onto the floor, really, rather than deal with the new piece.

CHAPTER 2

But I'd done almost everything on my to-do list for today, and unless a customer strolled in, all that would keep me entertained would be to leaf through the trade magazines.

There was a buzz from my phone.

Or, I thought, I could speak to my mother, currently calling my mobile. Doubtless she was trying to arrange our regular trail around the shops. I sighed. Mum enjoyed it, I reminded myself. The phone went to voice mail, and I relaxed.

Outside the gallery, a movement caught my eye. A potential customer? A woman in a bright red raincoat paused in front of the window, and I watched as she pressed her nose close to the glass. She was sheltering from the freezing January rain. No doubt she would gaze for a few seconds at the landscape that held centre stage and then move on. The paintings displayed by Gerrard Williams, Art Dealer, were not casual pieces, bought by those with a couple of hundred or so pounds to spend. The cheapest piece in the shop (a particularly ugly portrait, in my view) was nearly five thousand pounds, and so, while the shop didn't sell hundreds of pieces in a year, what we did sell kept the accounts bubbling nicely. There were a few prices in the window, on my insistence. Some indication was essential if you were not going to embarrass potential customers or make them feel small. It had been quite a battle: Gerrard held the view that if you had to ask the price, you couldn't afford it. Thankfully, another dealer at an art fair had agreed with me, and grudgingly, Gerrard had allowed me to put tiny and discreet pricing against some of the smaller items displayed in the window.

As I had predicted, the woman in the red coat moved away, and I returned to the new arrival. I eased up the lid of the packing to find a battered green leather case. I placed it gently on the table and released a brass catch. Two small ovals were sunk securely into the velvet cushioning, the fronts concealed by a black silk cover. The ovals could have fitted into the palm of my hand, and I frowned, puzzled. Gerrard liked large, rather aggressive modern pieces – abstract or intense realism, blocks of colour and slashes of paint. This box looked cracked and stained with age.

Carefully, I lifted the silk to reveal two miniatures.

I blinked at the immediacy of the small pictures. From the past a composed young woman surveyed me with cool grey eyes. Harriet Colchester was by no means a looker, but she had... something. Her chin was perhaps a little firm for beauty, but her skin was porcelain and her dark brown hair looked thick and lustrous. Her mouth was well shaped. The grey gaze from the portrait seemed to indicate that Harriet Colchester knew her own mind, even if she kept her counsel.

"A determined lass," I said to myself. In the first portrait she wore a pale blue dress, white lace tucked over a rounded bosom. She was against a dark background. The fine gold frame of the miniature had a hook, presumably so it could be hung on a chain or ribbon around someone's neck. Harriet stared out at the painter, and he or she – who was this by, again? I slipped off my cotton gloves and went back to my desk to look at the documentation. The painter was Richard Cosway. Hmm. So, painted in the late 18th century. Yes, the first of the miniatures was painted in 1797. And the other...?

CHAPTER 2

I returned to the second portrait. Harriet Colchester was painted in a black dress edged with ribbon. I put my head on one side and took in the details. Was she in mourning? Possibly, but what a change in expression! The fine eyes sparkled back at me, the firm mouth was tilted upwards at the corners, her dark hair arranged away from her face, which was now shown off as heart-shaped. Her skin had less pallor, the tint of a blush in the cheeks. Almost as if she was daring the viewer to engage in some mischief with her. Still not a typical beauty of the period, but arresting, vivid.

"Wow, a very merry widow," I said, grinning. "What happened to you, girl?"

My phone rang and I glanced at the name on the screen. Mum, again. It flashed through my head that I wished my mother recognised that my job was indeed that – a job, which meant I was engaged during working hours in the day except for emergencies. From long experience, I doubted this was an emergency. Tearing myself away from the fascinating Harriet Colchester, I answered the call.

"At last! I've already left one message!" said my mother.

"Mum, are you all right?"

"Yes, of course. Why shouldn't I be?"

"Well, I've told you before that unless the house is falling down or someone is dying, you shouldn't call me at work!"

"But surely you can find two minutes for your mum? I bet there's no-one in the gallery, is there?"

"No, but that's beside the point!" I said, trying to keep my patience. "Would you phone Liam in the middle of the working day?"

"Of course not, he's always busy, and why would I call him with a message about a treat for you?"

I dropped my head into my hand. Realising my mother would hound me until we'd had this conversation, I said, "Now you've got hold of me, what can I do for you, Mum?"

"You might sound a bit more welcoming, Gabs!"

My parents had christened me Gabriella. But they considered it a bit of a mouthful after a few months and resorted to the current ugly, diminutive form. After a couple of attempts in my early teens to persuade them to use my real name, I remained Gabs. I gritted my teeth, and my mother continued. "I've booked you in for a styling session with Francine! I thought you could do with smartening up, particularly as your birthday is coming."

I had mentioned styling as a potential gift some time ago, but my birthday wasn't for another four months. "Um... thanks. When is this?"

"Next Thursday, five o'clock!"

"Sorry, Mum, I've got plans to see a film next Thursday." I had. I'd waited weeks for the film to come to the local cinema and bagged myself a prime seat.

"Surely you can rearrange. Her website says she can work wonders!"

"Really?"

"Don't sound like that! Don't you trust me, Gabs?"

"But this is the last night that the film is showing. Can't we rearrange?"

"We can't rearrange! Francine's moved things about especially for you!" Mum sounded shocked. I felt a flash of annoyance. How could Francine move things about for my convenience when I knew nothing about the appointment? I smothered my irritation and hesitated, searching for words. And you know what they say about those who hesitate. Mum pounced. "Come on, Gabs! We need some mother-daughter time! I wish you would move back home. I've got all this space, and it would save you a lot of money, with your mortgage and everything!"

Moving home had been mentioned at least once a week since I'd bought my flat three years ago. Thank God for Gran's legacy, otherwise I'd still be with Mum, plotting her murder. It was less than two weeks since I'd seen her, but nonetheless, guilt prodded at me, making my blooming headache worse. Perhaps unconsciously, I *had* been avoiding the family. I'd felt tired lately, and all the little jobs they usually asked me to do just seemed beyond my reserves of energy. I was glad to be useful, but I'd just felt... well, that I'd rather *not*, at the moment.

As for living back at home... As if my moribund love life would get any better if I lived with Mum.

But, after all, she depended on me, even more so since Dad had died. And she was trying to do something nice for my birthday.

"I'll see where else the film is showing," I said, pinching my nose. "But, Mum, can you please check with Francine if she could schedule in another time?"

"Of course! But if she can't, and I do think she's very booked up, I'll meet you there!"

I rang off, wondering how I could have handled that better. I looked at the miniatures and felt Harriet's gaze quizzing me.

"Yes, I bet you would have told my mother to find another date, wouldn't you?" I said to the portraits.

I supposed it was nice that Mum was so organised for my birthday. I was hard to buy for, she often told me.

I focused again on the miniatures. The sitter looked so different, considering the short passage of time between the portraits – only five years, according to the paperwork. One portrait was demure, determined, watchful. The other full of life, almost devil-may-care.

The doorbell tinkled and I glanced through the doorway to see Gerrard shrugging off his coat as his long body strode across the polished concrete floor. His greying shoulder-length hair was curling, so I deduced it was raining. He pushed long fingers through his mane, and I had to hide a smile.

I got on well with Gerrard, who appreciated my financial and organisational skills, which had helped him transform the gallery. But even I recognised he was a walking cliché with his silver-fox good looks and Oxbridge voice, white gold cuff links and Mont Blanc ink pen.

"Your miniatures have arrived," I said.

"Good, you've opened the package?" He rubbed his hands together and I went to switch on the kettle. He placed the miniatures onto an easel in the back of the gallery and looked at them for several minutes. Wordlessly, I handed him a coffee.

"Extraordinary," he murmured. "Such precision, and the colours are so vivid."

"Not your usual purchase," I observed.

He nodded with a huff of laughter. "No, indeed. But they are gorgeous, nonetheless."

I waited. Eventually, if I kept quiet long enough, Gerrard would tell me more. He did.

CHAPTER 2

"They're for a new client, hopefully someone who'll come back to me for further commissions. I think he'll be delighted."

"Who is she, this Harriet Colchester?"

He glanced at me. "It's good to see you so animated. I've been a bit worried about you lately – you seem a bit low. I wondered if it was this job? Or man trouble?"

I steered away from my non-existent love life and the general malaise that I couldn't seem to shake off, and grinned. "You know I love my job! I'm lacking some sunshine. I'll perk up when the weather does. Tell me more about the portrait."

"Ah, yes – Harriet Colchester. The wife of a very prosperous businessman, John Colchester. He died suddenly and left her his fortune. She's not very important. But Richard Cosway, who painted these, is one of the foremost miniaturists of the eighteenth and early nineteenth century! He has quite the history!"

He went on about the artist for a few more minutes, talking about the Prince of Wales and the Royal Academy, but my attention remained with his sitter, Harriet. *She* was interesting in herself.

He retreated to his office to phone the collector and I looked at the miniatures for a long time. The change in her expression between young wife and widow fascinated me, and I wanted to find out what had prompted that. Had her husband mistreated her, and so when he died, she was free of his persecution?

I decided to do some digging.

CHAPTER 3

COLCHESTER HALL, DECEMBER 1802

Crewe, Augusta's well-padded man of business, shook his head sorrowfully as Harriet struggled to contain her irritation. The meeting in John's study had started promptly at nine o'clock and it was now nearly eleven. The stuffiness of the room had given Harriet a headache. Augusta had left after twenty minutes, when she was convinced Harriet was sufficiently cowed by Crewe.

"Mrs Colchester, your husband was an astute businessman, but truly, his sentiments towards his tenants last year were beyond all good sense!" Crewe said, and Alexander, who had joined them at Harriet's entreaty, raised his eyebrows. Harriet saw Peters, who had been John's man of business, clench his fists and put them quickly behind his back.

"Are you suggesting my husband had lost his mind?" she enquired calmly.

"Not at all, but that his generous nature had been taken advantage of! I hear tenants made approaches to Mr Peters, who, possibly due to inexperience, conveyed their complaints to Mr Colchester."

Peters sucked in a breath and looked ready to combust. Harriet stood up, finally losing patience. "Enough, sir! You question John's commercial sense and then the appointment of his most trusted adviser? You go too far!"

Crewe looked startled, and wisely kept silent. Peters' stiff frame relaxed slightly, the twitch in his pale cheek less evident.

Harriet drew a deep breath and continued. "And while *you* may be impervious to the suffering of your tenant farmers due to last year's bad harvest and the price of bread, John was not! Thank you for the time you have spent trying to educate me this morning. I'm pleased to have Peters as a support. I will consider further before making any decision on the rent. Good day to you."

So effectively dismissed, Crewe could only bow and gather his papers without a word, his face tight with suppressed emotion. Tugging his waistcoat down over his stout stomach, he lumbered from the room.

"Thank you, Mrs Colchester," Peters said quietly, red to the roots of his hair. He was indeed young, but his slight frame contained a sharp intelligence, and Crewe had obviously provoked him. "The people are still recovering from the rain of the past two seasons – and as you know, the French blockades sent prices too high for the common folk…"

"And even with the Peace, the price of bread and their situation may not improve," Harriet agreed. "Fear not, Mr Peters, there will be no immediate changes."

Peters withdrew and Harriet dropped her head into her hand. Alexander patted her shoulder.

"What an odious worm Crewe is," he commented, and she burst out laughing.

"I should not laugh, but, oh, how right you are! Speaking to me as if I had more hair than wit!"

"Indeed, I was mightily impressed that Peters didn't plant him a facer, after Crewe implied he was a babe in arms!" Alexander moved to the desk and sat in the chair opposite her. "You look haggard."

She smiled faintly and raised her eyebrows. "Pray, don't think to spare my feelings! I have the headache."

"Unsurprising, given you've been cooped up here for the past two hours. Ask the stables to saddle your horse."

Her heart leapt at the thought. A glance through the window showed the day was bright. It had been dry for a few days, perfect weather for riding.

"Will you accompany me?" He nodded. "Give me ten minutes to change into my habit."

In the end, it took slightly longer for her to join him in the hall; her habit was dark blue, but its gold braid was totally unsuitable for her mourning state, and Louise, her maid, had to take ten frustrating minutes to snip the stitches and remove it. A black veil around her hat was less troublesome, and donning black leather gloves, Harriet eventually skipped downstairs to find Alexander deep in thought, staring out of the hall window.

"I beg your pardon! I had not thought to amend my riding habit for mourning."

He turned and smiled. "It will give the stables time to saddle the horses. And anyway, I was happy to wait."

Harriet paused fractionally as the warmth in his eyes seemed to pierce her heart. It seemed so long since she had been held, comforted. Loved. The thought struck her powerfully and her cheeks grew hot. She gathered her composure and pulled the veil over her face. They walked in silence through the gardens and around the side of the house to the stables, Harriet for once

CHAPTER 3

tongue-tied in Alexander's company. He had been in her life almost as long as John, she reflected.

He had been groomsman to John, and Harriet, rather awed by his dark good looks and stature (he was generously built, towering over John by a good head), had taken time to relax in his company. But he was such a gentleman, so respectful in his manner, that gradually she had joined in the laughter that flowed so easily between the two men, bound together by business and then friendship. When she was with them, she forgot that she came from a disgraced noble family and had married to repair her family's fortunes. Alexander, too, would mourn John and must feel his loss keenly.

Her bay mare, standing patiently in the courtyard, whinnied with anticipation as Harriet approached. Harriet's awkwardness disappeared in a wave of guilt that she had been absent from the stables so long.

"Ah, Gaia! You must think I have forgotten you!" she said as the horse nuzzled her palm. "And here I am, without even a carrot! What a poor human I am!"

Gaia snorted in agreement and Harriet gathered the reins. The groom cupped his hands for her foot and threw her into the saddle. At first, Gaia objected, tossing her head, but Harriet continued to speak softly to her, and after a little retaliatory prancing, the horse subsided. Alexander, watching from his own black mount, chuckled.

"She needs the fidgets shaking out of her legs – as do you!"

Harriet grinned and urged Gaia into a trot. Before long, they were on the fields overlooking Colchester Hall, and without speaking, both gave their horses their heads. Harriet, who had seen little exercise for the past month, revelled in the rush of the sharp December air against her face and the thunder of the hooves on the damp ground.

At the oak tree in the small copse, Alexander began to pull up, and reluctantly, Harriet slowed Gaia's pace. Sensing Harriet's feelings, the elegant mare swished her tail and stamped in disapproval before lowering her head to nibble unenthusiastically at the sparse grass.

Alexander grinned at her. "Feeling more the thing?"

Harriet laughed, almost giddy. "I am! I feel liberated out of the house! Does that seem nonsensical?"

"Not at all. Women are often constrained by society's expectations."

She smiled. "You and your modern views," she teased. She slid from Gaia's back and threw up her veil. She breathed deeply, looking over the land and the hills of the estate, gently rounded like green cushions in the pale winter light.

"I am unsure if I will like society's expectations of a new widow," she murmured.

"You are wealthy," Alexander said baldly, jumping down from his horse to stand beside her. "Financially independent widows may be considerably more at liberty than you imagine."

"It is a daunting thought."

"To do as you wish, rather than follow the dictates of your husband, Augusta, or members of the family? That is what is daunting?"

"I suppose so. I am used to being biddable."

"You are young enough to learn new ways of being in the world, Harriet. John's bequest gives you the opportunity to try out a few."

CHAPTER 3

Harriet did not answer. She was still rocked by John's death; there was no other reason that the gentle way Alexander spoke would affect her so. She turned away abruptly, and after a brief pause, Alexander said, "I am sorry. It is too soon. I am a clumsy oaf. Forgive me."

She shook her head. "It is no matter. I know you mean well."

"Always, Harriet."

He sounded rather stern, and she looked at him, his fine lips in a straight line. She managed a smile. "I do not know what these past weeks would have been without you. You are such a dear friend."

His mouth twisted as if displeased, but at her puzzled look, he nodded. "Shall we return over the lower field?"

Grateful for a change of subject she agreed, and soon they were galloping across John's land – now her land, she realised. A mixture of panic but also agency rose in her, and from nowhere a sense of anticipation gripped her. Perhaps... perhaps all would be well?

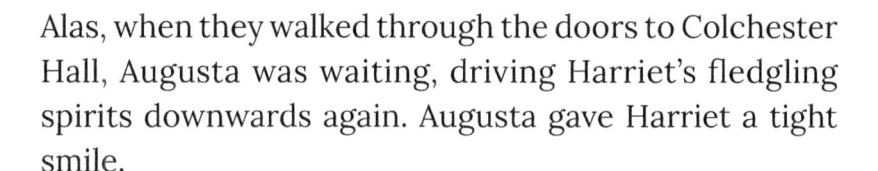

Alas, when they walked through the doors to Colchester Hall, Augusta was waiting, driving Harriet's fledgling spirits downwards again. Augusta gave Harriet a tight smile.

"At least you have respected John's memory in your dress."

Harriet paused before stripping off her gloves and unpinning her hat. "I was not aware that custom dictated no exercise during mourning."

Augusta ignored that. "I hope your meeting with Crewe was helpful."

Harriet was certain that in the hour or so she had been absent, Crewe had reported the contents of their meeting to Augusta. She smiled. "I am fortunate to have so much guidance at hand – Peters *and* Crewe!"

"Should you require it," put in Alexander.

"Indeed, should I require it." Harriet nodded at him. "I am grateful for your suggestion, Mama, and feel sure I will soon find my way. John was trusting enough to let me do some management of the estate and was pleased with my small contribution."

Augusta glared at her. "Quite. At least you know the *rudiments*, if you lack in other areas. We will have to hope you progress." She turned stiffly away, and Harriet stared at her retreating back.

"How supportive," Alexander said in a hard voice. Harriet made to speak, but found she had no words. Alexander shook his head in distaste.

"She is grieving," Harriet said quickly, unable to bear his expression of disgust, and then pulled him into the drawing room, away from the curious and all-seeing eyes of the servants.

"As are you, but *you* are not making disparaging remarks. Harriet, you *must* leave this place!" he urged.

"But they are all the family I have!" she protested, hating how weak she sounded, even to her own ears. Despite her uneasy and prickly relationship with Augusta and John's family, they were at least the devils she knew; she hesitated in her current state to take on the unknown.

"They are all the family you have for now, but you have friends, and can make more! Your wealth opens doors that might previously have been closed to you."

She smiled bitterly. "Those doors remained firmly closed when John was alive; I am not sure they would be unlocked now. He cared little for the *ton*, and believed most of them could barely tie their own shoelaces. I share his sentiments."

He looked as if he wanted to shake her. "*Then* you were not in possession of twenty thousand a year! I believe that, together with your gentle manners, would make you welcome at any society event!"

She gaped at him. "And John's money is my only hope of an entree? Those people would be my *friends*? I rate myself rather dearer than that, Alexander!"

"Don't be so naive! You know how society works!"

"I do, but that doesn't mean I should kowtow to its petty rules!"

He drew himself up to his full height and took a deep breath. Harriet noticed the cloth tightening over his chest. "I see you are not in the humour for a sensible conversation," he said coolly. "I bid you good day."

He strode from the room and closed the door with a disapproving click.

She sat heavily on the sofa, clenching her fists. Irritation remained for a few minutes, during which time she resisted an uncharacteristic urge to throw something. When it finally ebbed away, she was left with an echoing emptiness. Wearily, she rose to change out of her riding habit and spent a dreary afternoon with manufacturing correspondence and the estate accounts.

Even balanced and neat accounts gave her little satisfaction, and she was closing the ledger when a tap at the door heralded the arrival of Snow, the butler. He handed her a package with a note. With a murmur of thanks, she placed the package on the desk and opened the note. It was from Alexander, his writing a little untidy as if scribbled in haste.

Forgive me. My desire for your happiness has made me impatient. Allow me to offer some inspiration for your future. I remain your affectionate A.

The package contained Maria Edgeworth's latest book, *Belinda*. Harriet's eyes widened as she realised that he must have ridden to Berwick, the nearest town, to procure it for her. Her fingers trailed over the fine embossed leather and her heart warmed at the effort he had made. She found herself lost in the memory of their ride, and jumped when Augusta bustled in.

"There you are," her mother-in-law said, narrowly observing that Harriet hugged the novel to her. "Did Mr Richardson procure that for you?"

Harriet nodded, slipping the note between the book's pages. Augusta opened her mouth, but Harriet interrupted her. "Would you excuse me? I'm tired from the ride and would like to rest before dinner."

She left the room, relishing the astonished expression on Augusta's face.

Chapter 4

CENTRAL LONDON, JANUARY 2023

I rubbed the dust from my eyes as I peered at the screen in the British Library. It showed the barest information about Harriet. She was born in Oxford in 1780, the second daughter of Godfrey, Baron Chudleigh, and Clarissa, only child of Lord and Lady Sayers. Harriet's elder sister was Sophia. Information after that was very sparse.

Harriet herself was married to John Colchester in 1797, and from the parish records, his occupation was gentleman farmer. Harriet was identified on the record as a spinster, and I checked her age – yes, she had been barely eighteen. I wondered if the first miniature portrait had been a wedding present.

My phone buzzed and I saw a text from Aunt Mo.

I have a toasted teacake with your name on it. When are you coming over?

I grinned. Mo was Dad's sister and I loved her to bits. Organised, efficient, capable and the proud owner of a wardrobe full of what my mother declared to be unsuitable outfits, she couldn't have been more different from the rest of my family. When I called at her large, rambling, mansion flat, she never expected me to run errands, argue with the phone company or fix electrical items that she'd dropped.

I stretched my back, which was stiffening up from being hunched over the terminal in the records office. I could call in on the way back home. I texted that I'd be there about seven o'clock if that worked for her?

Splendid. Mx

I smiled and turned back to the screen. To my shock, John Colchester had died just five short years into the marriage. There was a link to the obituary in the British Newspaper Archive and I clicked through.

'The eminent Newcastle landowner and gentleman farmer Mr John Colchester died at the age of 37 on the 21st inst. at Colchester Hall following a tragick riding accident. Mr Colchester began life with small means but by his ingenuity and industry, exercised continuously for more than 20 years, he succeeded in amassing a fortune of some three hundred thousand sterling, which he leaves in whole to his widow, Mrs Harriet Colchester, along with his great estate which continues in his family name.'

My eyebrows disappeared into my fringe. Three hundred thousand pounds was a fair whack of money now, let alone then. I did some rough calculations and then sat back with a whistle. Twenty-four *million* pounds! And he left it all to Harriet? Did they have children?

I dug out my phone from my back pocket. "Do you just look happy because of the cash?" I murmured to myself, looking at the photo I had snapped of the miniature. Harriet's eyes seemed to dance as I regarded her, mocking my unknowing. "Or... did something else make you happy?"

CHAPTER 4

I continued to search for information but my mind was whirling, trying to imagine what it would be like to suddenly find yourself alone, independent and loaded. Harriet had still been a young woman when she lost John, not more than twenty-three or four. And overnight she'd become very, very rich. The men must have been around her like iron filings round a magnet. Had this huge change in her life been exciting or terrifying for her?

Another text pinged on my phone. It was from Joe, my neighbour, probably the most beautiful man I had ever met – and living in London, that was saying something, even if he was a model. We met on the day he moved next door and couldn't find the water stop cock. We'd had many a chuckle over a glass of wine at that first meeting, where I simply gawped at the vision on my doorstep. Now I counted him as a firm friend, and he asked me for advice over his torturous love life, although I was mystified at what I – who hadn't had a relationship in five years – could usefully offer.

Parcel being delivered tomorrow when I'm in Amsterdam. Would you be a love and take it in?

I texted back that of course I could. I rubbed my eyes and went back to the terminal.

I searched for another fifteen minutes but couldn't find any more information on the elusive Harriet, other than that she had all the makings of a very merry widow. Reluctantly, I closed the terminal and put the notes I had scribbled into my bag.

As I made my way towards the bus stop, I was thoughtful. Harriet's pictures and the fragments of her story had captured my interest in a way I hadn't anticipated. That I couldn't easily find further information was irritating and an indication of her status in her world. This in turn got me thinking about what might be said about me when I was dead and buried.

"Handmaiden of the Sullivan family?" I asked myself, smiling crookedly.

"D'you want a written invitation?" drawled the driver as he waited for me to notice the open doors of the bus that had pulled up. I scrambled aboard with apologies, but he winked at me, and I found a seat, feeling flustered.

Settled, I looked again at the portraits on my phone, one of a new bride who looked grimly determined, the other of a young woman who seemed to be daring me to do something... to be more Harriet?

Aunt Mo's road was coming up and I put my phone in my pocket and rang the bell for her stop.

"I can't tell you how nice it is to be here," I announced to Aunt Mo as she opened the door.

"Your mother getting up your nose again?" Aunt Mo presented her cheek for a kiss and held out her hand for my coat. I hugged her, smelling the Fiji perfume that she always wore.

"No. No more than usual. Something smells nice."

"Ah, well. I know I tempted you over with a toasted teacake, but I have a casserole that is enough for two – can I interest you in supper?"

This was another thing I loved Aunt Mo for – in addition to her general wit and intelligence, and that fact

CHAPTER 4

that she very rarely asked me for anything unless she truly couldn't manage it, she *cooked for me.*

"Perfect, I'll nip out and grab a bottle of wine from the corner shop, shall I?"

"Don't be daft. I have a rack full of wine. Choose a bottle while I start on the vegetables." She bustled off, her silk scarf fluttering around her shoulders. The bold geometric pattern in charcoal and scarlet emphasised her expertly cut short hair.

While I uncorked a Malbec, we exchanged views on last week's *Fake or Fortune* episode, where a man had insured a painting for thousands thinking it was an early Lowry, to find out its date was circa 1970. The presenters, egged on by the man's enormous ego, had been sympathetic in a nicely syrupy way, we thought.

An hour later, I placed my knife and fork together with a sigh of pleasure. "That was delicious, thank you."

"I understand from Theresa that you're off to see a stylist?" she said, as a gentle prod, and I shot her a glance.

"I haven't made up my mind yet. The new Pedro Almodóvar film is coming to the Picture House and it's on the same evening. I booked months ago." I folded my napkin neatly on the table and looked up to see Aunt Mo's eyes on me.

Her shrug spoke volumes. "I believe Theresa considers the date to be fixed. But if you want styling, Gabriella, we could go shopping together. I have a reasonable eye. Or, God help us both, we could go with Joe."

Her tunic top and scarf, tailored red trousers and funky hair were perfect for her – but would be disastrous for me, as unlike Aunt Mo, I was small, round and just generally less cool. Thank God Gerrard had needed someone who knew about accounting software, rather than a clothes horse. As for Joe – he regularly looked through my wardrobe and declared he wouldn't be seen dead with me in *any* outfit I had. It was astonishing to me that we were friends at all, but on the other hand, I was handy with a screwdriver when he needed something wiring. Aunt Mo was still looking at me.

She clicked her tongue in frustration. "If you don't want to go, don't go! I do wish you'd stand up for yourself for a change!"

"I've asked Mum to find a different date. It's for my birthday, and I'm grateful," I said, trying not to get into an argument. "But let me show you this!" I added, changing the subject. I explained about Harriet Colchester and pulled out my phone to show her the pictures of the miniatures. "It's a bit weird to be so stirred up about a woman I know practically nothing about, but the expression on her face after she'd been widowed is – well, don't you think it's fascinating?"

"She certainly looks free-er," commented Aunt Mo, enlarging the pictures carefully with scarlet-tipped fingers to get a better view.

I nodded vigorously. "Yes! That's exactly it!"

"How interesting. The money will have certainly made a difference, when so few women had control over their own destiny. Are you trying to find out more about her?"

"Certainly am, but it's come to a bit of a dead end. The last bit of information I've dug up was when she was made a widow. Naturally, I can find more about her husband than her, but I've got a few more sources to look at."

"I like the look of Harriet," she said, handing me back my phone. "She doesn't look like someone you would

CHAPTER 4

take for granted or who's constantly at the beck and call of her family! You're practically a second mother to the twins!"

She gathered up the plates. Aunt Mo was smart and fiercely independent, whereas my family had depended on me for so much, for such a long time, I could foresee a complete train wreck if I withdrew from their lives. When Dad died five years ago, I stepped in to support Mum in almost everything. I was sure she could pick up the threads of her life, but when I was on the edge of suggesting it, it always seemed a step too far.

I followed Aunt Mo into the kitchen. "I agree I need a bit more in my life," I said. "I have some thoughts about developing the gallery and my role."

"I've been telling you that since you were thirteen," Aunt Mo sniffed. "But don't you practically run the gallery anyway?"

I laughed. "Gerrard has given me lots of opportunities, certainly."

"More like he's taken your skills for granted, while paying you a pittance!" grumbled Aunt Mo, ramming a plate in the dishwasher.

"I'm going to tackle him about that, too!" She shot me a sceptical look. "I will! I promise!" I protested.

"Well, Harriet will be watching if you don't," she said darkly.

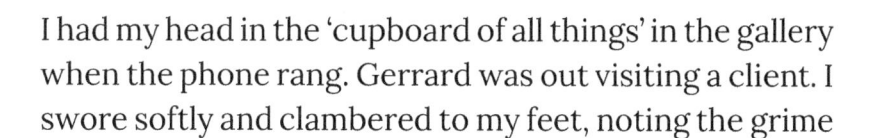

I had my head in the 'cupboard of all things' in the gallery when the phone rang. Gerrard was out visiting a client. I swore softly and clambered to my feet, noting the grime on the cuffs of my previously pristine shirt. I should have worn rubber gloves.

"Gerrard Williams, Art Dealer, Gabriella speaking. How can I help you?" I said automatically. No-one answered. "Hello?"

"Hi, I'm Hugo Cavendish. Is Gerrard there, please?" The voice made me feel as if my ears were being wrapped in silk.

"He's out at the moment. Can I help?"

Another pause. Then, "Thank you but it's fine. It's probably best if I talk to Gerrard, if you could ask him to call me back. He has my number."

"I'm the assistant manager at the gallery – are you sure I can't help?" I said, thinking that I might as well begin taking more responsibility in my work sooner, rather than later. If only Mr Hugo-voice-like-cream-Cavendish would let me. "Can you tell me what it's about?"

"Very well. I bought two miniatures—"

"Of Harriet Colchester?"

"Yes, that's right. You're very well informed."

"Well, it's part of my job to be aware of the art that comes into the gallery," I said, smiling.

"I'd like the miniatures to be brought to my home."

I was momentarily struck dumb as I realised I was going to lose the miniatures. Of course, the rational side of me knew that they would leave the gallery, but I felt a stab of loss that it would be so soon. Emotionally, the impact seemed disproportionate. I had wanted to be able to see the originals for a little longer. For my research, I said to myself. I reached for my pen and a pad. "If you'll give me your address, I can arrange for them to be shipped—"

CHAPTER 4

"I live in Berwick-upon-Tweed, and anyway, that won't do. I've had bad experiences with couriers before. I'd like Gerrard to bring them to me. Considering the price, I thought it was the least the gallery could do."

I wrinkled my nose, remembering the price of the miniatures. Gerrard never could resist a killing, and it was one of the reasons the gallery was so successful, but occasionally he went too far. Even so, personal delivery by Gerrard? Highly unlikely.

"It's quite unusual," I ventured. "We don't normally do this."

"Really? But I'm your customer. And really, these are such small items; surely it would be simple to organise."

"Yes, of course, but as I said, it's not our policy. We have an excellent courier service and most of our clients are perfectly happy."

"But I'm not most clients, and this is what I'd like." A note of steel threaded through the smooth tones. "So as *assistant gallery manager*," the stress on the title was tinged with sarcasm, "do you have the authority to arrange this with me, or do you need to check with Gerrard?"

"Well—"

"—in which case, I might have saved myself the time speaking to you."

"It's a shame you think that, because it's been so delightful," I said before my brain got into gear. There was a startled silence, and I closed my eyes briefly, as astonished as evidently he was. The silence stretched on, and I breathed in, ready but reluctant to apologise. Hugo Cavendish said nothing. I took a deep breath. "I will speak with Gerrard and get back to you."

"Thank you," he said coolly.

I put the phone down, feeling cross.

Chapter 5

COLCHESTER HALL, DECEMBER 1802

Just after Christmas, two letters arrived, one for Harriet and one for Augusta. Harriet, who knew she would be questioned about her correspondence, pressed down her impatience and slipped the letter into the novel Alexander had brought for her, to read when Mama retired for her nap.

Augusta carefully opened her letter and squinted at the single page, which was cross-written in cramped writing.

"Not distressing news, I hope, Mama," Harriet said, watching Augusta's scowl develop.

"Not at all," she said immediately. "Edwin has determined to continue his travels; that is all. He sends his condolences and should return to us in June, he writes."

Harriet observed her thoughtfully. Edwin was still in funds, then. Privately, she thought the disintegration of the fragile Peace in Europe was more likely to force him to return than any expression of support for his family.

Augusta, however, did not appear pleased by his decision, and pursed her lips as she gripped the letter.

"You must be disappointed that he was not able to attend the funeral," Harriet said, searching for the most charitable interpretation of Augusta's irritation. Augusta shot her a quick glance.

"It would have been unseemly to delay the funeral for Edwin to attend. Also, too disruptive to his party, and a needless extravagance."

At this, Harriet narrowed her eyes. Augusta was wealthy enough to enable this 'needless extravagance'. Edwin, her only nephew in a family of five girls, sponged shamelessly off her. If he had wished to return to see John interred, Harriet had no doubt that Augusta would have provided the funds.

Most of the time, Harriet dismissed Edwin as the over-indulged young man he was. When he was with the rest of his family, he treated her as an inferior and joined in with the general criticism of her. But away from this influence, he softened, and made her laugh. When the two of them were alone, they rubbed along well enough, but in company, he preferred to hunt with the pack. Her lip curled a fraction as she recalled the last occasion John's family had visited *en masse*. Yes, Edwin was young and easily swayed, but she also saw he had no backbone to speak of, particularly when Augusta was paying his bills.

Augusta rose from her chair, interrupting her musings.

"Are you going for your nap?" Harriet asked hopefully.

"Don't be ridiculous, girl. And even if I am, do I have to report my every movement to you?"

"I was going to send tea in an hour, if that was the case," Harriet said calmly.

Augusta huffed as she stalked to the door. "I can order my own tea in this house."

CHAPTER 5

The door closed. Harriet took a deep breath and moved to sit in John's favourite chair by the fire. She took out her letter. It was from Anne, and her lips curved into a smile as she began to read.

My dearest Harriet

How sincerely sorry I am to hear your news! Such a tragedy! How shocking that John should depart from your life so abruptly! How you must feel, I cannot imagine. I trust that Mr Alexander Richardson is with you to provide a little support, as I do not believe Augusta will be the comfort she should be. I am anxious for news of you, so please write to me with your situation as soon as can be contrived. I know that you held John in genuine affection, and you must feel his loss most acutely. And I have no doubt that Augusta will be organising you, as if you have not been perfectly in charge these last four years! I truly pity you and send you all my love.

As my dearest friend, you must wonder why I have not arrived on the doorstep of Colchester Hall before now. I would come to you if I could, but I have news that, knowing your own travails and your loss, I hesitate to give – but it will explain my absence...

Harriet looked up and gazed at the fireplace, where the flames leapt merrily. A flutter of anticipated pain ran through her.

"She is with child," she thought, dully. Reluctantly, she took up the letter again.

...I am enceinte and my love, nearly four months on, I cannot recommend it. I am horribly indisposed for half the day and awake with discomfort half the night. I would overcome all this for you, but Phillip forbids it – at the moment, I am confined to my drawing room, and my visitors are few so as not to put strain on my system. Dr

Thomas believes my sickness will ease after this month, and for all our sakes, I heartily hope so. So forgive my absence, Harriet!

That written, if you could bear to be with a pale, puking, listless creature and just be quiet, I would welcome you to stay with us at Grosvenor Square for the season. I know you are in mourning and so cannot gad about, but London will be thin of company anyway, and how wonderful it would be to see you. I could offer the comfort a friend should.

Re-reading that last piece, how unappealing that sounds! And in view of your own trials in conceiving, you may wish to be a million miles from me, but I do so hope not! Let me know your decision, and if you are able to visit, you will find the warmest of welcomes, dear, sweet Harriet!

Harriet drew an unsteady breath, folded the letter carefully and placed it into her book. Anne had been a good friend, steadfast in the face of the family's disgrace all those years ago. Part of her longed to see her again, although Harriet was affected more than she could put into words by the news of the baby. Perhaps it was just too soon after John's death. She felt too raw from his loss to be reminded of her childless state.

She sat for a long time, staring into the flames of the fire, memories and images flickering through her head. A soft knock at the door made her straighten her spine.

Snow arrived carrying a silver platter with a message. This was from Alexander, and it was short and to the point.

I must return to London next week. May I call on you before I leave? Please let my servant know, he awaits your response.

CHAPTER 5

Harriet's pulse faltered and then she silently berated herself. Of course he would leave! He had been in the locality nearly a month and would have business to deal with. He could not dance attendance on her for weeks on end. But, oh – she would miss him.

"I will reply," she said to Snow, who nodded regally. A few minutes later, she handed Snow a sealed letter that requested the pleasure of Alexander's company for dinner how at the end of the week. She might seek his advice about visiting Anne but knew what he would say. He would raise his eyebrows and smile, and ask what she was waiting for.

"What are you smirking at?" asked Augusta from the door, and Harriet pressed a hand to her thumping heart.

"You startled me! I had no idea I was smirking."

"Who has written to you?"

Harriet stiffened at the tone and forced herself to relax. "Anne has written to me with her condolences."

Augusta sniffed as she took her seat by the fire. "Now she's married an earl, she thinks herself above us! Where has she been in the past few weeks?"

"She has been indisposed," replied Harriet carefully, not wanting to add fuel to an already smouldering fire of ill-temper with news of Anne's pregnancy.

"Pah! You are simple-minded if you believe that. She is giving herself airs and graces."

"Anne is a good friend who is unwell! And as she cannot come, she has invited me to London," Harriet replied unwisely.

Augusta seemed to swell before her eyes. "To London? While you are in mourning? Out of the question!"

Harriet fell silent, feeling the chains of duty tighten around her. She had not intended to go to London, but now Augusta had objected, Harriet wondered how bad it would be. She could not attend balls, or parties, that would be unforgivable, but to visit a gallery, or have quiet dinners with Anne and Phillip – hardly scandalous. She straightened.

"I must go and write to her," she said quietly.

"Yes, you must refuse the invitation," Augusta repeated, her face implacable.

Harriet left without a word.

Harriet leaned against the door of her bedroom and sighed. She looked around the familiar room and felt her heartbeat slow. The house was of recent construction, designed and built by John Soane, and in the early months of her marriage, Harriet had found comfort in the regular, classical design and gently curved domes that graced the larger rooms. It provided order for her in a world where – at the age of eighteen – all order had been scattered.

A memory flashed into her head. On their wedding trip, John had taken her to Threadneedle Street and proudly told her that, after completing Colchester Hall, the architect was appointed to design the Bank of England.

On impulse, she opened the connecting door to John's bedroom. She gazed around, hardly believing that he would not walk from his dressing room, complaining that the valet had tied his cravat too snugly. Her eyes filled with tears and fell on a miniature portrait of her at the side of his bed. It had been painted by artist Richard

Cosway just after her marriage. Anne had been staying with them at the time.

Anne was Harriet's only friend to visit Colchester Hall. Harriet knew a little of the opprobrium Anne had endured. Anne was a Beauty and thought this sufficient armour to withstand the snide comments, but Harriet had worried for her. Thankfully, the addresses of Phillip, Lord Rochford, and his subsequent proposal, soon cemented Anne's position in society.

John had no sooner listened to Anne's declaration that all fashionable ladies had a miniature of themselves that their loved ones could carry, than he was making enquiries for a commission. Richard Cosway duly arrived at Colchester Hall.

Harriet had not immediately liked the slight painter, who reminded her strongly of a monkey. His eyes were dark and snapping, his mouth thin and petulant, and he had a prominent nose. He was extravagantly dressed, with pink heels to his shoes, and John had taken one look at him and retired to his study. As the afternoon continued, the artist scandalised and then delighted Harriet and Anne with tales of London society and tidbits of gossip from the Court, making sure they knew of his royal patronage.

Harriet believed she might be sitting for hours, but when Richard Cosway pronounced himself satisfied a mere hour and a quarter later, she was astonished. Anne clapped her hands when she saw the miniature.

"It's a perfect likeness! Mr Cosway has depicted your eyes exactly!"

Harriet, who knew all the shortcomings of her face, was astonished when she looked at it. The artist had made her elegant, and while her nose was no smaller, her mouth looked well shaped. It also looked a little stern, and her face was watchful.

"It is a likeness, no?" Mr Cosway said watching Harriet closely.

She nodded slowly. "It is. You have painted me as I am, Mr Cosway. I am grateful you did not flatter me."

His eyes narrowed. "I am sufficiently talented to ensure that my subjects are themselves but – more."

"More?" Anne said curiously.

"I try to show beneath the surface," he replied candidly. "I must bid you farewell, ladies. I will have the piece framed and returned to you."

Then he was gone in a flurry of lilac silk-lined coat.

Now, Harriet stared at the portrait, recognising what she had not seen then. Five years ago, she had been out of her depth, and apart from Anne, alone. But Richard Cosway had seen the strength in her jaw and the resolution in her eyes to restore her family's fortunes through this arranged marriage. She had determined to make the best of it, and said yes to John's offer. It was time, perhaps, to say yes to more than merely being a dutiful woman.

Quietly, she slipped out of John's room and sat at her writing desk. She pulled forward a sheet of paper and began to write.

My dear Anne,

Thank you for your love and best wishes. I should be delighted to visit and hope to do so in the coming months, when I have taken full control of the estate business, which now falls on my shoulders. But rest assured, I will come.

Chapter 6

NORTH LONDON, JANUARY 2023

Francine the stylist consultant threw me an embarrassed glance as, once again, she tried to turn the discussion to me.

"You're not tall, and I know your mum said you had a thing about your boobs, but with your small waist, you could certainly get away with tighter tops than you currently wear," she said with a smile. "You don't need to cover up with oversized shirts; they just add bulk."

I cast my eyes over my linen tangerine blouse, a straight up and down job that was one of my favourites.

"I told you that colour was more me than you," put in Mum. "I look great in all the citrus-y shades!"

"Do I need a belt?" I said to Francine. She nodded.

"Absolutely. Something to give it more shape. Or tie it around your waist," she said, leaping forward to show me. I glanced at the full-length mirror and was a little startled at the result. I wasn't tall – only five three – but my legs were good, and suddenly they appeared to stretch on forever, particularly when she bent and turned up the cuffs of my jeans, showing my ankles. She pointed at my leg and looked at me in the mirror.

"This gap here shows the thinnest part of your leg and gives the illusion that your legs are longer than they are."

"She gets her hourglass shape from me!" Mum said airily, draping a fuchsia cashmere scarf around her neck from the rack of jackets, accessories and jewellery that lined one side of the whitewashed room. "What do you think about this colour, Francine?"

Francine smiled tightly at me and rose to her feet to examine my mother. "I think it drains you, Theresa. You need something softer."

I stood uncertainly in the centre of the room. Regretfully, I'd cancelled my film tickets, and Mum had seemed truly delighted when I'd said I'd come. We'd been in the company of the elegant Francine for an hour, but in that time, the stylist had only spent about twenty minutes with me. We'd discussed my curvy frame, my short stature and whether my shoulder-length hairstyle really was the best cut, and then my mother had somehow inserted herself into the conversation. Helplessly, Francine had been swept away like a leaf on a fast-running stream.

"I'm singing a solo at a recital next week and although I have to be soberly attired, I did wonder if black was a little ageing," Mum said, holding a swatch of black fabric against her face. "What about navy?"

A light flicked on in my head. Mum had an Event to Go To.

"Um..." Francine's gaze flicked between Mum and me. She looked uncomfortable, and I raced in to save her.

"I thought this was supposed to be my birthday present," I said, forcing a laugh. "Perhaps you could have a chat with Francine at the end, if there's time?"

Mum's face froze for a moment before she threw herself into one of the deep, squishy armchairs. "Of course!

I'm sorry, just excited! You go ahead, Gabs. I'll just sit quietly and watch. You have fun."

I smiled apologetically at Francine. "So, what else can I do to update my look?"

To give her her due, Francine tried very hard to inject some jollity into the proceedings, but Mum's silences when she wasn't getting her own way have defeated stronger souls than the slender, young stylist, and the gloom from the corner spread through the room.

Francine advised me to try three-quarter sleeves and to wear softer fabrics. She gave me a fitted blouse that I wouldn't even have taken off the rail in a shop and encouraged me to try it on. When I emerged from behind the art-deco screen in the room, she moved towards me and tucked the front of the blouse into the jeans, leaving the sides loose. She also put a patterned amber and black headband around my hair and pulled it back from my face. I blinked at my reflection, feeling a different person. I turned to Mum, who was scrolling through her phone.

"What do you think, Mum?"

She glanced at me and then went back to her phone. "Very nice dear, although I'm not the expert. And as you said, it's your session – what do *you* think?"

For a long moment, no-one spoke. Francine hopped from foot to foot.

"Shall I get us all a cup of tea?" she asked, clasping her hands together.

"I'd love one. Mum, do you want one?"

"No, thank you. As a matter of fact, I may need to leave."

Anger flared in me, hot and surprising. "Okay, I'll call you a cab," I said promptly and proceeded to do so. After a shocked pause, Mum pulled on her coat and stood in silence until the doorbell rang, announcing the arrival of the taxi. She left without a word to me but told Francine that she'd book her own styling session because 'anyone who can make Gabs look halfway decent is obviously a genius'.

Francine returned with a pink face and smiled weakly. "Shall we continue?" she asked.

Half an hour later, my head whirling with ideas about tops, bottoms and dress lengths (just below the knee, which would make me look taller), and after discovering the joy of nude-coloured shoes, I grinned at her and rose to leave.

"That was wonderful, thank you! I'm sorry about Mum; she can be a bit demanding at times."

"I'm so pleased you found it useful!" she said, beaming at me.

I picked up my jacket and bag, and her smile faltered. I stopped. "Is something wrong?"

"Your mum booked the session but – she didn't pay me," she said miserably. My eyes widened, and swallowing a curse, I hunted for my wallet.

I walked slowly to the bus stop, my mind empty. Lately, I'd begun to be gently irritated by the same conversations – can you do this? Why don't you come back home? Oh, Gabs can handle that.

I was invisible. Work was the place I was taken seriously. Home – I was just convenient for awkward, tedious tasks, but other than that I felt sure Mum and Liam still saw me as the teenager I'd been, not wanting to go to university.

I reached my tiny sanctuary, a one-bedroom flat. Once inside, I leaned on the door, hunted for my tissues and blew my nose. I needed some tea. Strike that, I needed a gin.

I lit the wood burner in the sitting room and built up the fire until the flames burst into life and shadows danced on the walls. I sank into the corner of my sofa and cradled my extra-large gin and tonic.

I'd toyed with university but eventually decided that I could do without the student debt. So I'd remained at home, signed up for a business administration and accountancy qualification at the local college, worked at the local burger bar and squirrelled away money with the hope of getting a flat of my own. Dad seemed to approve; Mum hadn't expressed an opinion. I'd wondered at the time if there were issues about money in the house. I'd bet Liam a fiver he'd go through his term's budget in less than two months, and I heard the odd tense conversation between Dad and Liam when he returned occasionally at the weekend.

I took another sip of my gin and tonic, remembering. With my brother asking for more money at uni, Mum and Dad were relieved I wasn't going to add to their bills, and so not pursuing a university degree was more of a blessing to them than I'd anticipated. And they suggested I contribute to the house when I started earning, which was very soon after I qualified (with a distinction). With a natural administrative flair, I landed a job quickly, and gradually I began to develop my personal style. Mum and Dad told me how proud they were of me.

Liam had been the recipient of most of the limelight in our family, so to bask in the warmth of Mum and Dad's appreciation of the additional money that my job brought in, plus my cooking skills, was a novelty. Meals were delicious, the fridge was managed, bills were paid, cupboards tidied. My parents told me how much they loved me. I had developed the habit of helping and discovered just how flexible I could be, fitting my life around theirs. While Mum boasted about Liam going to university to everyone – the neighbours, those in her Pilates class, patently uninterested supermarket check-out staff, anyone who couldn't escape – I was her 'rock', I was the person she trusted with her life. I couldn't pinpoint when that had begun to grate on me.

I glanced towards the photo of my dad and mum at a do somewhere that sat at the end of my bookshelf, taken I think when I was twenty-one. She was looking adoringly up at him; he was laughing at the camera. When Dad died so suddenly of a heart attack, Mum was almost comatose with grief for months. Worried, I took over managing the parental house, sorting out probate, organising bank accounts, trying to get Mum to eat. I fell into the position that Dad had occupied.

When I told Mum that I was moving out to buy a flat with the money Gran had left me, there was a huge scene. But, desperate to leave, I'd laughed off her concerns.

"Don't be daft, Mum," I'd said. "You'll do fine on your own – you've got lots of friends and choir and the WI. You can always call me if you get stuck with anything. I'm moving to Haringey, not Hungary."

She called me often, getting 'stuck' with lots of things. I was determinedly patient, and she determinedly continued to lean on me. She missed me, she said, adding that I could live so much more cheaply with her.

On this, I had been adamant. Guilty I might be about leaving Mum alone, but I never wanted to live with her again. Our relationship changed.

CHAPTER 6

And tonight, I was angry, hurt. I wanted an apology. I took another swallow of gin.

Yeah, who was I kidding? I was uncomfortable with conflict, and Theresa Sullivan could win prizes for sulking.

I sighed, peering into my glass at the rapidly melting ice, and the portrait of Harriet flashed into my head.

"Be more Harriet," I muttered to myself, looking into the fire. I'd promised Aunt Mo that I'd speak to Gerrard, and I determined to do that. My family – I'd tackle them next, I vowed.

Chapter 7

COLCHESTER HALL, JANUARY 1803

Harriet held out her hands to Alexander as he strode through the door to the drawing room, and unexpectedly brushed her knuckles with his lips. Her eyes widened at his touch, but she swallowed her surprise and smiled. She gestured to the sofa and moved to John's seat by the fire. She patted her silk skirts into place and raised her hand to her hair, curled a little differently. He looked closely.

"I like your hair away from your face, Harriet. It suits you." She thanked him.

After he had a glass of madeira in his hand, he glanced at the door. "Is Augusta joining us?" he said, and she laughed at his carefully neutral tone.

"She is indisposed and has asked for dinner to be served to her in her room. She hinted quite strongly that I should cancel the dinner, for propriety's sake."

"But you chose not to?" His eyebrows rose and his voice had an edge to it she had not heard before.

She laughed nervously. "I wanted to say farewell to a good friend more than I cared about her scruples."

He looked at his wine glass for a moment and was thoughtful. "I am glad – you speak more freely without Augusta glaring at you."

"I expect I do," she smiled. "Although I am no Emma Hamilton!" she added quickly.

He laughed. "Indeed not! You are a model of propriety! But what do you know of Emma Hamilton? She seems to court scandal. I am surprised you brought her into your conversation!"

"I have a regular correspondent in Anne, who passes on the gossip," she responded. "It seems to me that Lord Nelson's affair with Lady Hamilton has only enhanced his reputation as a romantic hero."

He laughed. "Why, you are a cynic, Harriet!"

"Indeed, I hope I am not, but I like to consider all sides of a situation. I imagine the world must be wondering what powers he must possess to entice a woman to follow such a disastrous course which all adds to his fame."

Alexander's surprise flickered on his face at her words, and Harriet was relieved when Snow announced that dinner was served. She had spoken too freely. While she sincerely pitied Emma Hamilton, she also envied her the depth of love that obviously existed – like Sophia's relationship with Miles. Harriet could not imagine anything further from her own experience, and keenly felt that absence of knowledge.

As the footman placed her soup in front of her, Alexander spoke again. "Can I observe that, speaking of Lady Hamilton, a lady mired in scandal, you sound almost wistful? Considering the lady's situation, surely you cannot envy her?"

Harriet paused and gathered her thoughts. Alexander frowned at her face.

"I have made you uncomfortable! You are not obliged to answer me, you know. I am a rough fellow."

She smiled awkwardly. "As my old friend, I hope you will forgive me my vulgar fascination with Lady Hamilton and Lord Nelson! What passion must exist between them to persuade her to conduct a relationship in the face of society's condemnation? It seems so full of fire and daring!" Unlike my own, she added mentally. Alexander's eyes narrowed as if he could read her thoughts, and she felt a blush spread over her cheeks. Thankfully, he merely nodded and applied himself to his lobster bisque.

Conversation became more general. Alexander would remain in London for the season; he had leased a house in Conduit Street and was in the market for a new carriage. He would go to Tattersalls, and Harriet, who loved to ride, was eager for the details. She could recall vividly the excitement of her first visit to the auction house with John, and her smile faltered.

Alexander looked at her shrewdly. "Did John take you there?" he asked, and she nodded, gathering her composure.

"He felt the prices too high, although he admitted there was some prime horseflesh among the showy pieces!"

Alexander laughed. "Aye, John knew his way around a bargain! I miss him and his innate business sense. How are you getting on with Peters?"

"Very well," she replied, pleased to move from her sad thoughts. "I believe he is astounded at my grasp of wheat yields, and the conditions that bring about a good harvest. Who would have thought a mere female could master such knowledge?"

"You are no mere female, you know," he said a touch impatiently. She laughed.

CHAPTER 7

"Why, of course I am! No-one expects me to understand, and therein lies my greatest weapon! I smile sweetly, profess ignorance, and any improvements I suggest come about not by any application of knowledge, but simply through chance! That way, no egos are overset, knowledge snubbed, or dignities offended! It is by far the easiest way of managing any male member of my household!"

He burst into laughter, and the pair of them were still chuckling when the next course arrived.

At the end of the meal, however, Harriet's mood became muted. As the footman pulled out her chair, she became aware how much she had come to rely on Alexander over the past weeks. And it was not just the practical support he had offered, but the feeling that she had a friend, someone who understood her.

"I should like it very much if you were to write to me," she said abruptly. "I know you will be engaged, but it would... be nice."

It would make you seem closer, she thought. She gazed at him, her throat tight.

"I hope that I may see you in town," he replied gently.

She shook her head. "Not for months yet, Alexander. I need to observe the proprieties, and in truth, I would feel awkward in company. By the time I arrive in London, the season is likely to be over."

He sighed. "I wish you would take my advice and visit friends. You need a change of scene!"

She told him of Anne's letter of invitation but did not mention the baby.

He threw his hands up in frustration. "If Anne is unwell, you will hardly be socialising, but you will have company to lift your spirits! And a purpose, if she needs you."

"I will visit her, but not yet," she replied firmly. She caught his eye. "Truly, must I remove to London to release you from my request to write to me occasionally? For shame, Alexander!"

He smiled and shrugged. "I am an indifferent correspondent, I warn you." He paused. "Of course I will write to you, but I do not guarantee entertainment from my efforts."

She beamed at him. "Thank you. Shall I leave you to your port?"

"I will be with you shortly," he promised.

Harriet left, her step lighter than it had been.

Augusta, hovering with inquisitive eyes, and the faltering February sunshine were enough to entice Harriet into the shrubbery. She wrapped a particularly handsome Norwich shawl around her shoulders and stepped through the drawing room door onto the terrace. In her hand, she clutched another letter from Alexander.

Harriet glanced down the length of the terrace, running for a hundred feet along the back of the house. It sported holly trees in massive urns at regular intervals, and their foliage was green and glossy. A few scarlet berries remained, unaccountably missed by the birds. The steps that led down to the lower lawn beckoned, and lifting her skirts with one hand, she skipped down them.

CHAPTER 7

The spot by the wall held an ancient oak bench, the wood curved by the bottoms of endless sitters. The wood was smooth and, catching sunbeams in the afternoon sun, warm to the touch. It was also completely hidden from the top terrace and sheltered from the wind by the plump bushes around it. She sat and carefully opened the letter.

He wrote of the races, of ambling through Hookham's Circulating Library and of riding his new mare around the Ring in Hyde Park. More soberly, he wrote of the recent execution of Colonel Despard and his co-conspirators, convicted of treason and hanged at Southwark.

It is reported that a crowd of 20,000 were there, watching this awful spectacle, conducted in awful silence. But this is hardly suitable content for a letter to a lady, so I will spare you the details.

Alexander was not a comfortable purveyor of society tittle-tattle, although his first letters had made a gallant attempt. She was astute enough to know that to relay an endless stream of gossip would irritate him, so she asked for news 'of the day' and left it to him to choose what he would. So far, his letters rejoiced at a win at Newmarket, described the debut of the soprano Angelica Catalani at the Kings Theatre and told her of new acquaintances. And in every letter, he suggested she visit London. This one was no different.

You must not doubt that I loved my friend. But I fear that you are the one entombed!

She hung her head and sighed. Her letters to him were full of her life at Colchester Hall. But because so little happened, and her days were so much the same, she had embarked on a gardening project to give her something to write about. She was aware of Augusta's disapproval, but in her outdoor exercise, Harriet had support from the vicar, who commented on the bloom in her cheeks. Harriet suspected that Augusta's disapproval was less directed towards her horticultural efforts and more towards her continuing correspondence with Alexander.

Augusta was a constant critic, but so far, Harriet had kept the rest of John's family from descending, pleading that she was too occupied with the estate. She could handle Augusta; the rest of the clan shortened her odds of holding her own.

The sun disappeared behind a cloud, and she shivered. Harriet stuffed the letter into her pocket and lightly ran back to the house. As she expected, Augusta was waiting.

"I have waited this age for you!" she scolded, gesturing to the tea tray, now, Harriet imagined, stone cold.

"I beg your pardon, Mama. I have been in the garden."

"Yes, I saw you career – in a very hoydenish way, I might add! – down the steps. Is that another letter from Mr Richardson?"

"It is. It is wonderful to have John's best friend as a regular correspondent," Harriet said calmly. Placing a hand on the teapot, she found that it was indeed cold, and she rang the bell.

"Has he found himself a wife yet?" Augusta asked, her beady gaze directed at Harriet's pocket.

Harriet blinked, and when Snow entered, she was grateful to be given a moment to gather her thoughts. While her mouth ordered more hot tea, her mind turned over Augusta's question. Alexander was looking for a *wife*?

CHAPTER 7

"He did not mention it," she said calmly as Snow left. She took her seat in John's chair and gripped her hands together tightly. Augusta sat back with the air of a cat playing with a baby bird, and Harriet's spine straightened automatically.

"He is probably being discreet. I imagine the fathers of many a titled lady will be eager to harness his wealth to repair their family fortunes," Augusta said sweetly.

As mine did, Harriet thought as she gritted her teeth. Her chin rose and she said nothing.

"Of course, he's in his prime and will be looking for heirs." Augusta looked at her dismissively.

In her head, Harriet counted to ten. Snow arrived with fresh tea and Harriet leapt to arrange teacups, while thinking furiously. Surely Alexander would have talked to her about his plans? They were *friends*, weren't they?

Wordlessly, she passed a cup to Augusta, who returned to the matter of Harriet's will. Harriet nodded as if in agreement and then talked of the crocus bulbs that were emerging, giving her mother-in-law little opportunity to reintroduce the topic of the will, or Alexander.

"It is little short of a miracle! The little flowers are heroic, considering the very sad weather we have had," she added, watching with satisfaction as frustration tinged Augusta's expression. "For as you will know, Mama, there has been more rain this winter than ever before! I know John used to track the rainfall, and he would agree with me..."

She babbled on until Augusta rose to her feet.

"I will be in my room, resting," she said. "I have the headache coming on."

Augusta stalked away, and Harriet waited until she heard the creak of the main stairs before she let out a sigh and sagged against the cushions on the chair. Alone, her mind whirled. Alexander could not be looking for a wife, could he? He was so young!

He was five and thirty, her brain corrected her. Her heart sank, and for a moment, the thought that she might lose their comfortable conversations almost overwhelmed her. She must look through his letters and see if he had mentioned any lady more than once.

She scurried to her bedroom.

Chapter 8

CENTRAL LONDON, LATE JANUARY 2023

Gerrard was in front of me, astounded.

"I'm sorry – he wants me to deliver the miniatures to him *in person*?"

"Someone needs to," I said, swinging my computer screen to show him that I'd found the transaction on the accounts ledger. "He certainly paid through the nose for them. He was very insistent."

And very unpleasant, I added in my head.

I'd compared Harriet's pictures with other miniatures of the same period by Cosway. It might have taken a while for Gerrard to source the miniatures, which would account for a premium on the price, but even so...

Gerrard sucked his teeth. I could almost hear his thought process. This would set a precedent, in his mind, and anyway, who on earth wanted to slog up to Northumberland? He hated the idea, but I had a solution.

I was about to test my new 'Being more Harriet' approach to life on Gerrard.

"Well, I wanted to talk to you about something anyway," I said mildly. "I want to do more in the gallery – perhaps develop some events to increase our footfall. I know the business and would appreciate the opportunity to grow my job. I thought we could look at developing the gallery as a corporate space."

Gerrard gazed at me and then his face grew thoughtful. "Tell me more," he said carefully.

"We have a terrific mezzanine, but very few people find their way up there, so it's essentially unused. With a bit of alteration, that could host lectures, artists speaking about their work, a few business events – and we could use it to sell to some of the smaller accountancy and legal firms around here."

A smile tweaked the ends of his mouth. "You've already got the quotes for the alterations, haven't you?"

"I got them last year," I confessed.

He chuckled. "What's this got to do with Cavendish?"

"I want to go to Edinburgh to see Justin about the mezzanine. I'm perfectly capable of dropping off the miniatures en route."

Gerrard beamed at me. "Ah – the lighting manufacturer? Splendid, splendid!"

I drew a deep breath, mentally stiffening my spine. What would Harriet do? I opened my mouth before I could change my mind. "And given the work I already do, and *am* going to do for you, I'd like to discuss a pay rise. I've been on the same salary for the past eighteen months, and that will need to change."

He stared, unsure how we'd reached this point. "Hang on a minute—" He stopped.

I said nothing and looked at him, holding my breath. I was prepared to walk away, I'd decided. The money my grandmother had left me, which had given me the deposit on my flat, was almost gone. I knew – because I'd checked that morning – what a business administrator with my experience might expect to earn. I told myself

CHAPTER 8

that Gerrard was lucky he was having this conversation with me, and not opening my resignation letter.

"The gallery was perfectly successful before you came. I thought you had more loyalty," he said with a sniff, and I laughed.

"Gerrard, if I'd have had less loyalty, I would have left a year ago! Have you any idea what I do for you?"

I ticked off on my fingers just what I'd accomplished in the last two years – a new accounts system, an up-to-date inventory process, a new website and a social media presence, the renovation of the gallery space (a horrendous three months that still gave me nightmares), rent negotiations, not to mention a few new customers from my previous workplace, an insurance firm. Oh, and the accounts.

He was silent.

"And anyway, without me you'd need to get onto a train to get to Northumberland. Do you truly think I'm not worth the money?"

"That entirely depends on what amount of money we're discussing."

I told him and watched as I saw the flash of relief cross his eyes. I'd been fair, I thought. But I wasn't prepared to be underpaid.

"You'll ruin me," he said.

"You old fraud – you know I won't," I replied with a smile. "Don't forget I do the accounts for this place."

He huffed. "You'd better start earning your increased salary and ring Hugo Cavendish."

I only heard the ring of the dial tone for a few seconds, but those seconds seemed to stretch for hours. And then Hugo Cavendish picked up.

"Hello, Mr Cavendish, it's Gabriella Sullivan—"

"Ah – the assistant gallery manager."

"Hello," I said formally. I picked up a pencil and began tipping it over and over while I gathered my composure. "You requested delivery in person of the Harriet Colchester miniatures, and I'm calling to arrange a date."

"Will it be you, rather than Gerrard?"

"I'll be en route to Edinburgh for another appointment."

"Excellent, I'm glad you're able to fit in the delivery," he said briskly. "I'm going to New York this weekend; perhaps you could come late next week?"

"Of course. How about Thursday?"

"That should be fine. Can I have an email, or a contact number?"

I gave him my mobile number and my gallery email, and he rang off, leaving me thinking that his mood hadn't improved much. I jumped when my own mobile rang on the desk. I grabbed it.

"Oh, Gabs! I'm so pleased to get you!" said my sister-in-law, Evie. "You so rarely answer your phone."

"Well, I'm at work, Evie," I said, gathering patience. I liked Evie in small doses. Her demeanour was always sunny, but also like candy-floss – after more than a couple of hours in her company, you walked away slightly nauseous.

Her laugh tinkled over the line. "Of course! I'll make this quick, then – would you like dinner tonight with us? Or tomorrow, if tonight isn't convenient?"

CHAPTER 8

Evie might be bubbly and positive, but those qualities weren't useful in making dinner. I hesitated.

"Any special occasion?"

"You sound so suspicious! No, no special occasion, just a family dinner. We haven't seen you in a while and the twins miss you!"

I had a firm understanding with Sam and Jasper, the two tiny tormentors who were my nephews – Aunty Gabs was *not* to be messed with on public outings, but in return, she would cover up breakages, dole out chocolate bars on the quiet, and let them stay up half an hour later than normal bedtime when she was babysitting.

I felt a pang. I hadn't seen them for nearly three weeks, an enormous amount of time for small children. Evie, who could be astonishingly acute, pressed her advantage. "C'mon, Gabs. Come and see your lonely family!"

That pulled me up short. Would Mum be there? There had been radio silence worthy of a World War II blockbuster since the styling session and I was gritting my teeth against calling. Perhaps this would be a way for her to break the ice?

"I can make tonight," I said. "What time?"

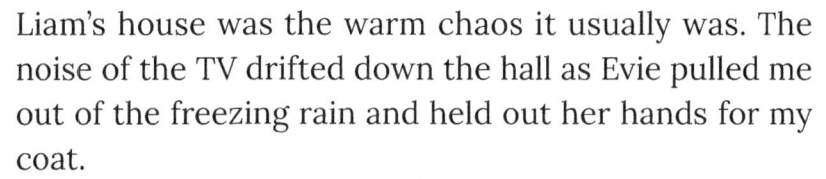

———◆O◆———

Liam's house was the warm chaos it usually was. The noise of the TV drifted down the hall as Evie pulled me out of the freezing rain and held out her hands for my coat.

"Gosh, it's perishing out there! Have you come straight from work? Did you come by tube?"

"Bus," I said, unwinding the scarf from around my neck. "You know I'm not keen on the tube. And yes, I came from the gallery."

She gave a theatrical sigh, looping a lock of ash blonde hair around her ear. "But the tube is so much faster!"

I shrugged. "I have a book."

To be accurate, I had a phone and had used it to search the internet for anything I could find about Harriet Colchester, unsuccessfully.

Rational conversation was suspended as one of the twins cannoned into me.

"Aunty Gaaaaabs!" yelled Jasper as his hot, plump arms wrapped round me. Evie protested, saying that Aunty Gabs needed a drink before she played with them, but I heaved him into the air. "Oof! What a lump you've become! When did you get this heavy? Where's Sam?"

"Watching cartoons!"

I carried him into the living room where his brother was in front of the TV. He jumped up, hugged me and then fixed his gaze on the screen again. I settled with Jasper on the sofa.

"Gin and tonic?" Evie called from the sparkling black and silver kitchen that ran along the back of their Islington house.

"Please! Is Liam home?"

"In the shower; he should be down in a moment. He's got a bit of a cold, poor lamb. Here you go."

Another ailment? It was a miracle Liam still walked amongst us. I took a thankful sip of the gin and tonic, made only slightly weaker than I liked, but with a twist of lime. I saw that the twins' attention would be on the cartoons until dinner and I went to the kitchen where I was amused to see Evie put one of *my* steak and kidney pies into the oven. She'd begged me for several for her freezer. Ah, well. At least the food would be good. She turned to see me propped against the door jamb.

"Great! You've escaped. Could you be a darling and put the broccoli on to cook? I just need to nip upstairs…"

Same old, same old. I sighed, rinsed the broccoli and set a pan of water on to boil. I was peeling carrots and slicing leeks when Liam bounded into the room. He hugged me.

"Hiya, Gabs! Evie told me you'd taken over the cooking."

She'd asked me; I hadn't taken over. And I'd got on with it, efficiently and with barely a murmur. What would Harriet do?

"Oh dear, how bossy of me! This isn't my kitchen. I probably don't do it the way she would." That was right enough, I thought with an inward grin. Evie *wasn't* a great cook. I picked up my glass. "I'll go and join the twins."

"I don't think she'll mind!" he added hurriedly, with an alarmed glance at the uncooked vegetables.

I hid a smile. The work as an IT consultant might pay well, but sitting on his bum all day was making it spread. His boyish good looks were still there. His teenage gawkiness had morphed into his slender five-foot eleven frame, and he still sported a too-long fringe that brushed into his eyes. His lovely smile remained. But in the harsh electric light, I could see lines around his generous mouth, and a bit of a jowl, arriving early.

"No, you're right. Better wait for her." I sniffed the air. "Mind you, you'd better check about the pie – is it burning?" I turned and went to join the twins.

Less than five minutes later, Evie was back, slightly pink and breathless and in a different blouse. Damp tendrils of hair told me she'd just stepped out of the shower.

"I hate to ask, but can you give me a hand?" she said brightly. "You know I'm not that great in the kitchen. We're even having one of your pies, so we can have something edible."

She beamed at me, and I reluctantly submitted.

Dinner was cheerful and the vegetables cooked perfectly. My pie pastry was slightly crozzled, but the meat was still juicy and tender, the gravy rich. The twins messed around a bit, demanding tomato sauce, and Jasper played imaginary football with his peas, but it was a nice meal. With the wine, I relaxed.

Liam spoke about his new and demanding director who brought on his migraine and was even pushing him to think about getting a new job, Evie described her latest commission, a house so glamorous she felt she needed to wear her Louboutin shoes to show it, and Jasper and Sam shared their latest school reports. I waited for someone to ask me about my job, but no-one did, so eventually I said, "I've taken on some new responsibilities at the gallery."

Evie smiled. "That's great news. What are you doing? Boys, bring your plates to the dishwasher, please."

In the hubbub of chairs scraping across the floor and the clattering of cutlery, I had to raise my voice.

"Developing new ways to make the gallery pay," I said, rearranging the plates in the dishwasher to my satisfaction. "We have an upstairs mezzanine and I thought we could host corporate events there. You know, rent it out for client entertaining, even sell some art!"

CHAPTER 8

"You're not really an event planner, though, are you?" said Liam, frowning.

I stared. "I do open days every month, Liam!"

He looked a bit shamefaced and Evie hurriedly offered me coffee. Liam disappeared to get the twins ready for bed and Evie apologised.

"He forgets... It all sounds very exciting!" she said, handing me a box of expensive chocolate mints. "Will you get to go to more art fairs, travel more?"

"Maybe, at some stage," I said, shaking my head at the mint. I would have enough to do to work off the pastry and booze from tonight's meal without adding chocolate.

Evie settled herself in the corner of the sofa and tucked her legs underneath her. "I wondered... Could you babysit next Wednesday? I won some tickets for a show in a raffle. I know it's a bit short notice, but you don't normally have anything on, so I thought I'd ask. You're so good with the kids."

Part of me rejoiced in the place I had in the twins' affections. Another part devoutly wished I could point to something in my calendar so I could say, 'No, sorry, occupied.'

I sighed. "Fine, but I'll need to let you know. I'm supposed to be visiting a client—"

"Oh, that's great!" Evie said at once. "Liam will be thrilled. Another glass of wine?" She leapt off the sofa and I trailed off.

On the bus, I mused that this was not a big deal. I loved the twins. I was free that night. It was Wednesday so it wouldn't interfere with my trip to Edinburgh, which would be the following day. It would be fine.

Chapter 9

COLCHESTER HALL, FEBRUARY 1803

Harriet woke with a start. Her face was damp with sweat, and with a grimace she pulled sticky hair away from her forehead. Her hand trembling, she pushed the covers back and walked unsteadily to the nightstand to light a candle and pour herself water.

She peered in the darkness at the clock. Nearly six. The embers in her bedroom fireplace had long died out and she shivered in the chill of the pre-dawn, casting around for her robe and her shawl.

She pulled on the bell, and ten minutes later the maid appeared, looking slightly flustered.

"Ma'am?"

"Louise, could you build a fire and bring me some tea?"

"Are you unwell, ma'am? Do I need to fetch Mr Snow?"

Harriet sighed. "No, it was a nightmare. Light a fire first, then make the tea."

Louise immediately set the fire as Harriet lit some more candles and then climbed back into bed, settling herself against the pillows.

A mere twenty minutes later, she was sipping tea thankfully in her armchair while the fire blazed, filling the room with heat and a flickering light. Weariness fell on her. She had thought that the nightmare had finally

CHAPTER 9

gone, but here it was, haunting her once more. In it, her sister, Sophia, stalked from her parents' drawing room, on the arm of her new husband, Miles.

That had been seven years ago. Harriet had not seen her since that final scene, which was branded into her memory.

Sophia's pelisse had been dark green and set off, as she would have known it would, her guinea-gold curls. Her hand was tucked through the arm of the tall, handsome man with whom she had eloped, his dark hair brushed into fashionable disarray. His eyes twinkled at Harriet, as if sharing some jest. Harriet stepped forward to embrace them.

"Sit down, Harriet." Her mother's voice snapped across the space like a whip, and Harriet faltered. Taken aback at the curt tone, Harriet sat with a thump on the chaise, and no-one spoke for a moment.

"What do you want?" Papa asked in a voice Harriet barely recognised. Sophia's eyes widened, and Harriet prayed Sophia's legendary charm would be in evidence more than her equally legendary temper. All she needed to do was apologise in her pretty manner. It should not be so hard; Harriet had seen her do it many times before. And although Harriet was not entirely sure what had happened in the London ballroom, it could not have been so bad, could it? After a breath, Sophia recovered her composure.

"I wanted to pay my respects to you as a married woman, Papa. And to properly introduce my husband."

Another silence fell as Papa looked them both up and down and then said nothing.

Miles seemed to wilt a little under Papa's unforgiving gaze. "Sir, it is an honour to meet you again," he said, bowing his head. Her father stared down his short nose, and his lip curled.

Harriet wondered when her mother would step in and pour oil – or rather tea – on these troubled waters. She wielded a teapot as a fencer would deploy a foil to enforce social niceties. But Mama stared straight ahead, her knuckles white as she clutched her fan.

Unease made Harriet's stomach churn. Sophia had always been Mama's favourite. That was, until she fell in love with Miles, a younger son of a baron and, while not penniless, not possessing the fortune Sophia had been expected to attract.

Sophia cried beautifully, and generally Papa was no match for the tears that fell from her large blue eyes. Mama had always readily forgiven Sophia for thoughtless and selfish behaviour, considering it a shame that so lovely a daughter should be banished to her room for youthful high spirits. Harriet watched for a repetition of the scene that preceded forgiveness.

"Mr Berkeley," said Papa in tones that could have frozen water. "You are not welcome in this house. I allowed you entry to tell you face to face and save myself the trouble of writing to you."

Miles' head jerked back in shock and Harriet gasped.

Two hectic spots of red appeared on Sophia's face. "Papa! I know you do not approve of the match, but I love Miles!"

Miles smiled mistily at her, and for a moment, Harriet wanted to slap him; there was a place and a time for such mawkish behaviour, but this was not it.

"So, your happiness is guaranteed by your marriage to a witless pauper?" said Papa.

CHAPTER 9

"Yes, it is! And he is not witless!" Sophia responded, hotly.

"But he is a pauper!" Papa said, pushing his reddening face close to hers. "I am glad you can find happiness so cheaply, because from the moment you enacted that disgraceful scene in front of all our friends, you were no daughter of mine. Have you any thought of the scandal you brought on this family with your wanton behaviour?"

Sophia, white to the lips by now, moved her mouth, but no words came. Miles stepped forward.

"That is enough, Sir Godfrey. We hoped for some reconciliation—"

"Bah! You hoped for her dowry!" Papa scoffed, almost spitting the words in temper. "I know the state of your affairs, Berkeley!"

Miles stiffened and moved away. Sophia sniffed and groped for a handkerchief in her reticule, and Papa snorted. "Don't think your tears will sway me, Sophia! You were too indulged as a child, and this is what becomes of it! You have not only ruined our family name and your life, but your sister's prospects – and she had slim enough chances to start with! Who would have her now, plain faced, and tainted as she is by your scandal?"

Despite the drama unfolding, at this, Harriet swallowed an exclamation. She was used to unfavourable comparisons with Sophia and was often discussed as if she was not present, but this was another blow to her already dismal self-esteem.

"Surely you would not disown me?" Sophia gasped.

"Your father might not," Mama said, rising to her feet. "But I would."

A silence fell that was so profound, even the clock seemed to attempt to muffle its ticking pendulum. Harriet gulped, feeling the ground shift beneath her as Mama's words sank into her brain. Sophia looked near collapse, and, alarmed, Miles placed an arm around her.

"Our hopes for you were high, after your come-out," said Mama, without expression. "We did not pressure you to choose a husband, as long as the match honoured our family and became your station. But no, you dishonoured our family name with your behaviour. Well, now I wish you the best of your choice. Your romantic notions of love will not clothe and feed you. And nor will we."

"But – but I'm your daughter!"

"You *were* my daughter," corrected Mama. "We are disgraced, and for that, I will never forgive you. From this day, I will never speak your name. Harriet is my only daughter."

Shuddering at the memories, Harriet stared at the fire, clutching her now-cold cup of tea. Her mother had been true to her word, but Harriet had only sensed resentment, rather than any transfer of maternal love. Yearning to indeed be a good daughter and make up in some small way for the disappointment of Sophia, Harriet had done exactly as she was told – but it never seemed sufficient.

And now she was a widow, she was still doing as she was told, only this time it was Augusta telling her what to do, rather than her parents, or John. She was four and twenty, for goodness' sake! High time for her to be making some of her own decisions. She poured herself another cup of tea and considered.

In the summer, encouraged by Alexander, John had talked with the rector about starting a Sunday school

CHAPTER 9

for the village. The idea was met with a variety of responses. Some people considered that no good would come of educating poor children to despise their lot in life. Others felt that to enable children to read the Bible could only bring good. Harriet, who was almost never without a book near her, could not imagine a life without reading, although she recognised that few children in the village would have the luxury of books other than the Bible.

No further talk of the school had taken place since John's death, the rector unsure now of the source of the funds that would be needed to run such a place. Well, that was now Harriet's responsibility.

She looked at the clock. Nearly seven. She was too agitated to return to sleep, so she rang again for Louise. The little maid came at a run.

"I will be visiting some of the tenants today; please lay out my carriage dress," Harriet instructed her.

"Yes, ma'am."

A thought struck Harriet and she paused. "And can you please trim my black velvet pelisse with some ribbon? Still respectful, of course, but something to make it less... severe."

"Will you need to visit the dressmaker, ma'am? For half-mourning?"

Harriet shook her head. No. It was far too soon. She would make do with the ribbon.

Harriet swung down from the saddle and patted Gaia. It had been an excellent morning's work – exercise *and* philanthropy. She smiled to herself and handed the reins to the groom, humming softly. She would write to Alexander about her progression of the scheme he had started with John.

After Augusta's insinuations, Harriet had carefully re-read all of Alexander's letters, looking for signs his attention had been caught. He had mentioned a Miss Johnson, and a Lady Worthington, but only once and their names did not reappear. After she had satisfied herself that an engagement notice was not imminent, she was relieved. And then she spent an uncomfortable ten minutes asking herself why she should feel so relieved that her husband's best friend was still unwed.

Deep in thought, she headed to the house.

"Good morning," said Augusta stiffly as Harriet was about to walk up the stairs.

"Good morning, Mama! I take it you have breakfasted?"

"Of course, but Snow tells me you were out hours before!" Augusta's stare was accusatory.

Harriet took a deep breath and gripped the banister. It was a lovely cherry wood, smooth and luxurious, and Harriet knew John had frequently admired it, caressing the warmth of the rail as he mounted the stairs.

"The perfect combination – strong and beautiful," he'd said. Harriet stood straighter and turned around to face Augusta.

"I have been continuing one of John's projects."

"What project?" In the gentle morning light, Augusta's face was sharp and pale, and Harriet regarded her thoughtfully.

"I should like to change my dress. Join me in the morning room and I can tell you all about it," she replied firmly and watched Augusta's eyes widen in surprise. Harriet walked steadily up the stairs and went to her room.

Augusta was at one of the writing tables, scribbling a letter, when Harriet arrived half an hour later.

"The tea is probably cold," she commented as Harriet sat on the sofa.

"No matter. I will call for more when we have finished our conversation. I went to see the rector about a Sunday school."

Augusta looked up, her lip curling. "Alexander Richardson's radical ideas! The common people are better without learning! Why, what possible use would reading and writing be to those who should know their place among their betters?"

Harriet had heard Augusta's views about Alexander's methods of running his business, at odds with the majority whose primary aim was profit. Alexander had wider goals. She shrugged. "John wanted it and had held initial conversations with the rector about furnishing such a school. I am simply fulfilling his wishes."

"And you intend to spend the family's hard-earned money on this frivolity?"

"John did not consider it frivolous, and I am guided by his view," Harriet said craftily, watching her mother-in-law struggle not to denigrate her son. A soft tap at the door announced Snow with a letter for Harriet. The handwriting was unknown to her. She glanced at Augusta, who was, she saw, thinking furiously. "I am sorry to be at odds with you, but I trust you understand my decision?"

Augusta looked down her nose. "I imagine you'll ruin us all with your preposterous schemes." She gathered her unfinished correspondence and swept from the room, leaving Harriet caught between indignation at such unfair castigation and gales of laughter at the ridiculousness of it all. She shook her head and rang for more tea.

With a cup of tea in front of her, she opened the letter. It was from Phillip, Anne's husband, and it was short and to the point:

Mrs Colchester –

Anne is now in her sixth month, and she is too low in spirits to write – hence my letter. As her husband, I give her what support I can, but what she yearns for is her best female friend. As she was your stalwart supporter through your family's own troubles, I had hoped that Anne's love and care would be reciprocated; I would be sincerely disappointed if, in her hour of greatest need, this was not to be the case.

Yrs, Rochford

The letter drifted to the carpet as Harriet covered her burning cheeks with her hands. How rightly he criticised her! How could she repay her dearest friend so poorly! Regardless of her duty here, she owed Anne so much!

She leapt to her feet and rang the bell so violently, Snow ran through the door.

"I will be leaving for London the day after tomorrow," she said, calculating that it would take at least a day to speak with Peters, pack her bags and deal with Augusta. Her heart sank. *That* was not a conversation to be relished. "I will ask Mama to remove to York, but doubtless she will make her own arrangements. Please return in half an hour when I will have a letter for the post."

CHAPTER 9

Not a flicker on Snow's face showed that he was in any way surprised by this news, and he headed in a stately way to speak to John Coachman. Harriet hurried to the writing desk to reply to Phillip that, all being well, she would be with them in four days, and that she intended to set out on Tuesday. She asked humbly for their forgiveness for her thoughtlessness and sent her love.

She read her brief lines through and nodded to herself in satisfaction. Snow had returned and was silently waiting at the door.

"Please ask Peters to attend me in the study at four," she said, and he bowed. After he had disappeared with the letter, she ran lightly up the stairs to her room. There was much to organise.

Chapter 10

NORTH LONDON, FEBRUARY 2023

Joe put his index finger on his chin and screwed up his nose as he looked at the rail of clothes. As he hmm-d and haa-ed, I began to feel alarmed. Surely my wardrobe wasn't that awful?

"This is what the stylist recommended," I said, stepping forward with the list of suggestions and sketches that Francine had given me. He plucked it from my hand and scanned it, clearly sceptical. As I watched, a look of respect dawned on his carefully made-up face. With his very short hair, there was nothing to detract from his face, but Joseph Delaney had no need to do that, with high cheekbones, almond-shaped dark eyes and immaculately sculpted eyebrows.

"Hmm. You certainly didn't waste your money. This is pretty much what I would have advised," he said in his soft Dublin brogue.

"Great – but do I need to go and buy all new clothes?"

"Don't be daft. But tell me – what's this all in aid of? You don't normally bother about what you look like."

I winced a little and he stretched out his hand, apologetically. "Sorry, I didn't mean it like that! But you're not precious about what you wear."

"I know, but I'm taking on more responsibility at the gallery and I have to go to Northumberland to see a client."

"Ah. All becomes clear. Okay, let's have a look. Take your clothes off and put on your dressing gown." I stiffened and he shot me a quizzical glance. "You're quite safe with me."

I laughed, feeling idiotic about my shyness. Joe's latest love was Steven, an electrician with arms like tree trunks. Joe adored him, and for once, it seemed as if the feeling was reciprocated. I had high hopes for the relationship. I was, if I was honest, also a tiny bit jealous of seeing Joe so happy.

Grinning, Joe opened the door to my voluminous wardrobe, and I used it as a screen while I stripped down to my underwear. I grabbed my cotton wrap.

Joe thrust a hanger at me without looking. It was an electric blue woollen dress I had bought and worn only once. Mum had said she thought it was middle aged, and so, back in the wardrobe it went. I held it up, and hesitated.

"Get it on you," Joe said, without taking his gaze from the rail. "And add this belt." He held out a black patent belt. "And these." He held out a pair of black patent heels, which again, I'd bought for a special occasion that had never arrived.

I put everything on and stood uncertainly. "Like this?"

He turned and pursed his well-shaped lips. "Not quite. Don't buckle up so tightly or you'll look like a string of blue sausages. Like this…"

He released a couple of notches on the belt, which rested gently on the upper curve of my hips. The skirt skimmed my shape, ending at my knee. He nodded to himself. "Yes, that looks great. See?"

I studied my reflection and was surprised. I looked elegant, up-together, as my Aunt Mo would say.

"You need some kick-ass earrings and a new haircut. We'll discuss that later. Now – off with that dress, and we'll look at something else."

Then began one of the most exhausting evenings of my life.

"That needs to go in the bin or to a charity shop; everything is wrong with it," he said of a bulky khaki sweater. "And this. And this. *This* is good." He held up a sundress that, again, I'd worn only once. "Why haven't I seen you in any of this? Actually – don't tell me, I know – you spend all day in jeans and sweatshirts."

"I wear suits for work!" I protested.

"Which should have been thrown out ten years ago!"

I opened my mouth to respond and then shut it again. Clothes shopping was a nightmare for me; I was never sure what would suit me, and as a result, I clung to what I already owned.

Joe looked at me and seemed to understand. He took my hand. "Sure, you need to update a bit, but that shouldn't be that hard," he said softly. "You've got a lovely shape; you just need to dress it better. You have terrific legs – it would be great to see them occasionally. Look," he added, diving back into my rapidly emptying wardrobe. "Try this on with this tee-shirt and this jacket."

I looked at the black and white dog-tooth skirt and rubbed my chin. "I always thought that was a bit short for me."

"Get it on you, girl."

CHAPTER 10

Minutes later, he grabbed me by the shoulders and turned me towards the mirror.

"Oh," I said.

"Uh-huh." In the mirror, Joe nodded smugly.

Silence fell as I gazed at my reflection, looking taller, *younger* than I recalled I was. As I watched, my shoulders went back, my chin rose a fraction, a sense of power spreading through me. I looked, finally, what I was – a professional woman, taking on responsibility.

"You're rocking that look, girl," Joe said with a grin.

"I am, aren't I?" I swung away from the mirror and hugged him. "You star. I feel like a different person. Are you free to come shopping?"

"After you've had the haircut," he said, whipping out his phone and thumbing a text. "I'll ask Sabi if she can fit you in tomorrow evening. You can be free from five-thirty, right?"

"Six is better."

"Okay, then we can hit the shops after that."

I doubted any hairdresser worth their salt would be able to slot me in at such short notice. I was eyeing the pile of clothes destined for the charity shop five minutes later, when to my surprise, a text pinged into Joe's phone.

He put down his tea to read it and grinned at me, his eyes twinkling. "She'll see you at six-fifteen. Don't be late; she's doing me a favour."

"When have I ever been late?"

"True, but perhaps you might want to cultivate being late! After I've finished with you, people will *wait*, love!"

I sipped my tea. "Yeah, right."

On Saturday afternoon, I was ruefully totting up my credit card purchases in my head from that Thursday night haircut and the shopping. I winced at the total and gulped my coffee.

At least I'd got a little more information on the miniatures, thanks to a local archive. Harriet had a sister who married the younger son of a baron. The marriage was shrouded in mystery, but apparently, Harriet's mysterious brother-in-law had been the rector of a parish in North Yorkshire. It wasn't Harriet herself, but it might lead somewhere.

The gallery had been busy that morning; we'd sold a small watercolour to a couple of newlyweds, and Gerrard was now discussing a series of mixed media collages with a slightly bored, but obviously well-heeled man. The prospective customer left the gallery after graciously declaring that he would think about it. Gerrard, never fazed by rejection, sauntered back to the counter and peered again at my hair.

"It's astonishing what a decent haircut can do," he said. "You look a different woman."

I ran a hand over my short, layered cut. I had gulped as Sabi had given me her recommendation to 'cut it all off'. I'd taken a breath and told her, yes – do it. The result was a glossy, pixie style that swept over my brow and round my ears. Even Joe was surprised, saying that it gave me cheekbones he'd never seen before.

Giddy with the success of my new look, I had then run riot in Selfridge's department store. Which reminded me…

"I've taken the liberty of increasing my salary payment for next month," I said. "Obviously, you'll need to sign it off, but it's in line with our agreement."

Gerrard grinned. "It's astonishing what a decent haircut can do," he repeated wryly. "Yes, of course I'll sign it off. Do you feel very different?"

"I do. And I never realised how much clothes could affect how I felt," I admitted, resisting the urge to pull the dog tooth skirt down my thighs. I'd teamed it with a black vee-neck cashmere jumper and a hip length jacket and black boots. I had dared to put on the red lipstick Joe had persuaded me to buy, hooked small gold hoops into my ears and felt like a film star.

This feeling influenced how I approached my work, too, it seemed. I'd sold a small abstract water colour landscape on Friday morning and an oil in the afternoon. At this rate, I reflected, I would have paid for my salary increase in sales.

My phone rang and it was a number I didn't recognise. I answered it and a rich chocolatey voice filled my ear.

"Is that Gabriella Sullivan? This is Hugo Cavendish. There's snow forecast for the end of the week, so perhaps it would be best to bring the miniatures earlier? Say, Wednesday?"

"Um, yes, I suppose so," I said, thrown slightly. "I'll need to rearrange my meetings ..." I stopped. Why was I explaining to him? He wouldn't be interested; all he wanted was the miniatures.

I said I'd let him know roughly when I would arrive. He thanked me and hung up.

Gerrard tweaked an eyebrow. "Don't forget Justin, although I suppose you could stay another night and look at some of the other commercial galleries."

I nodded, something else pecking like a bird at my consciousness. I went online and checked the weather. Yes, snow arriving Sunday. I sighed and changed my train tickets. Berwick-upon-Tweed was the nearest station to Hugo's address, and then I would travel onward to Edinburgh. I changed my Edinburgh hotel date.

I asked Justin by text if we could move our meeting forward, and grinned when he just sent a thumbs up. Having shifted everything forward, I sat back, unsettled by a nagging suspicion that I'd forgotten something.

I remembered on the bus home.

Evie and Liam! I groaned and hit my forehead, and for a moment I froze, wondering what to do.

Well, today was Saturday – they could probably get someone else to babysit. Let's face it, I thought, I could have been ill, run over by a bus, anything! Reluctantly, I dialled Evie's number.

"Hello!" she said gaily.

I took a breath. "Evie, I'm sorry, I need to see a client for work on Wednesday and I'll be going on to Edinburgh on Wednesday afternoon now. I won't be in London."

"What?"

I explained again.

"But – can't you ask your client to change it?" Evie said. "We've been looking forward to the show for ages!"

I bit my lip. "Impossible. He's paid a lot of money for paintings that I'm bringing to him."

"Can't Gerrard go?" Evie whined.

I paused. "Can I ask you a question? If Liam had something to do at work, would you expect him to cancel so you could see a show?"

"That's different! He's got a lot of responsibility!" I was silent. "I can't believe you're bailing on us! Liam, come here! Talk to your sister – she says she can't come on Wednesday night!" Evie called.

CHAPTER 10

He came on the phone, puffing a little. I explained.

"Can't you get back from wherever it is you're going in time?" he asked.

"No, I'm en route to Edinburgh. I had arranged a meeting the following day. Everything's moved forward."

He told me how disappointed they all were – him, Evie *and* the twins.

I wavered for one or two seconds. But then Hugo Cavendish's smooth, cold voice echoed in my head. "I can't make it, I'm really sorry."

"We were depending on you, Gabs. This is short notice for us to find someone else, you know. *Surely* you can rearrange?"

He wasn't listening. Something clicked in my head as if the final piece of a jigsaw puzzle had slotted into place.

"Look, Gerrard has given me responsibility for this delivery, it's an important client and I have a meeting in Edinburgh. Ask Mum," I said quietly. "Or one of your neighbours. Or a mate – you have plenty of those, don't you?"

"Mum told me you had been off with her," Liam said. "Sounds like it's our turn now."

At that, my flimsy resolve became concrete hard. "Perhaps if you didn't just expect me to be your chief babysitter, you'd have a few more options!"

He was still arguing when I put the phone down.

Chapter 11

COLCHESTER HALL, FEBRUARY 1803

Harriet smiled at the housekeeper, who had actually looked pleased to know the house would be vacated for a few weeks. Mrs Bessie Johnson folded her hands over a generous belly and recommended that a thorough cleaning of all the curtains was well overdue. Harriet solemnly agreed, although everything looked clean enough to her. Snow, the butler, nodded wisely and proposed the use of holland covers for the furniture to protect it during her absence.

Harriet laughed. "I will probably come home after a month, but I will send word in good time for my return."

Next was Peters, who was walking up and down outside the study in what Harriet perceived to be nervous agitation. So, she came straight to the point.

"Peters, I shall be in London for at least a month, possibly longer. I shall give you my direction and you must write to me with any concerns about the business or the estate. I put my trust in you, as did Mr Colchester. Do you have any immediate questions?"

He stared at her, his mouth dropping open in surprise, and he reddened. After a few seconds, he swallowed. "I shall write every day," he said earnestly.

CHAPTER 11

She shook her head. "Write to me if you are worried – I do not need you to write to tell me all is well. I may send to you, if I wish to know how you go on." She paused. "I have every confidence in your abilities to run the estate in my absence. John relied on you, as do I."

If Peters' face had been red before, now even the very tips of his ears were scarlet. He drew a deep breath and bowed. Harriet knew, as he left the room, that Peters would die in a ditch rather than let misfortune befall the estate.

The door closed and she sat in a chair, puffing out her cheeks. A glow began in her chest. She had been clear, her servants seemed content to do her bidding and her orders would be followed. While this had long been the case, this was the first time she had noticed that she was, indeed, in charge.

All that was needed now was to tell Augusta of her plans and to encourage her to return to York. A sigh escaped her, and on impulse, she went quickly to her room to find Louise almost hidden amongst boxes and Harriet's gowns. Seeing no calm to be had in her own bedroom, she slipped into John's room and sat in the window seat. There she assembled her arguments. She glanced at the miniature at the side of John's bed. The determination and the quiet steel of her expression – albeit for her survival in the Colchester family, rather than anything else – made her pause. She would find that strength again.

She rose and went to find her mother-in-law.

Augusta was quietly furious. Her face was white, and her mouth pinched. Harriet took one or two deep breaths and grounded herself, ready for Augusta's onslaught.

"How dare you?" was Augusta's opening sally. "How dare you disrespect John's memory by taking a pleasure trip to London – him barely in his grave!"

Harriet stamped on her indignation, and instead tried for a reasonable response. "A pleasure trip? To see my friend who is ill; someone who hasn't left the house for months, if her husband speaks the truth. I have few expectations that this visit will be unalleviated joy, Mama!"

"Pah! To dance attendance on a spiritless creature like Anne, who acts above her station! I thought you had refused her invitation?"

"I said I could not come at that time," Harriet said. Augusta strode around the room, her quick, jerky strides indicative of her irritation. "But that was two months ago, and she is still unwell. And so I must visit," Harriet continued.

Augusta seemed to take herself in hand and sat down on a chair. "But you cannot have considered what a strange appearance you would make, being still in mourning! I know Edwin would be very disappointed in you."

Harriet frowned. What on earth did her cousin have to say about the matter, from Italy, or wherever he was? Ah – of course – Edwin was the eldest male in the family, since John's death. Augusta caught sight of Harriet's face and again attempted to calm herself. "He wrote to me last week, telling me how much he had always admired you. I dread what this news will do to his regard."

CHAPTER 11

At this, Harriet's eyebrows shot up and she was then forced to stifle a giggle. Edwin would admire the family fortune regardless of the widow who accompanied it. When she felt she had control of her voice, she replied. "I had no idea his affections were so easily damaged or his regard for me was so high."

Augusta shot her a poisonous look. "The Colchester men are men of actions, not words. Do not expect to be romanced, Harriet! You are too old for all that anyway."

At this, Harriet did laugh. "I have no expectations of being romanced at all, Mama, least of all by Edwin, who is so much younger than I."

And who acts like a sulky boy, she added in her head.

Augusta waved a hand. "There are only five years between you, and I expect his Grand Tour to have given him a little polish," she said. "But your visit to Anne will have to be postponed – I have invited Clarissa and Jacob and their children to give you further support."

At the news of her sister-in-law, her husband and their five children descending without her permission, all traces of humour fled. "I beg your pardon?"

Augusta looked away, faint pink touching her cheeks. "They are your family," she replied defiantly.

"But this is *my* house and I reserve the right to invite guests. When do they arrive?"

"Friday."

"Then they will be able to accompany you to York on Saturday," Harriet said in a hard voice. "I am leaving tomorrow, and my plans are in place to close up much of the hall."

Augusta's eyes widened. "Surely you cannot leave your family to arrive to an empty house?"

"But it will not be empty, will it? You will be here to explain that you invited them without consulting me and that it was not convenient."

Harriet walked to the fireplace and rang the bell. Snow arrived very quickly, almost as if he had been waiting by the door.

"Snow, Mama will be here to greet my sister and brother and the family on Friday when they arrive. Please make them comfortable for the night. They will *all* be leaving on Saturday after breakfast, so they should not distract you from the tasks we discussed for the household."

Snow's face was completely impassive. "Yes, madam."

"Thank you. I know I can rely on you."

Snow nodded and left without a word. The silence that fell was thick, and Harriet could almost taste Augusta's anger. But Harriet was determined to be gone from Colchester Hall before Augusta could pull in reinforcements. Harriet had often struggled and failed to maintain her confidence and indeed her will against their combined force. Was she running away? Perhaps. But she was finding her feet with her new situation – she did not intend to be floored so early in her journey.

"So, you are determined to go to London and turn us out of our family home?" Augusta forced out between gritted teeth.

Harriet put her head on one side and regarded her coolly. "I am determined to visit my friend, who is ill and needs me – *has* needed me for the past two months or more. That she is in London is irrelevant. And this is my house now."

CHAPTER 11

Augusta sniffed. "Given your family's history, I suppose it would be something of a surprise if you cared about appearances, about behaving with propriety."

Harriet stood up abruptly, surprised at how enraged she was. "You need not insult me, or my family, ma'am. I have been a model wife and daughter-in-law, as well you know. I am going to see Lady Rochford, so accustom yourself to my decision. I expect you to leave on Saturday."

"But—"

"And now I must supervise my packing," Harriet added briskly. "I will be leaving at daybreak, so I doubt I shall see you at breakfast, and I intend to take dinner in my room, so I wish you a good journey back to York."

She turned to the door.

"I shall write to Edwin! He will be most displeased!" called Augusta shrilly. Harriet stopped and swung around to face her.

"Do! I tremble at the prospect!"

Harriet marched out of the room without looking back.

Chapter 12

BERWICK, FEBRUARY 2023

I peeked inside the holdall again at the miniatures in their green leather case, safely swathed in bubble wrap. I'd need to change trains at Newcastle. I struggled into my thick padded coat – it had turned very cold. The weathermen were talking enthusiastically about storms, but snow wasn't forecast until Sunday and I would be back in London by then. I settled to look at the bridges of the Tyne as they came into view.

A smile curved the corners of my mouth. The feeling of desolation I'd carried from London had lifted. I felt almost welcomed by the Tyne Bridge, and beyond that, the Millennium Bridge, its white curves glinting in the strange grey and yellow light of the late morning. I texted Hugo Cavendish to give him the time I was arriving at Berwick, then gathered my precious cargo and prepared to leave the carriage. I hoped he was in a better mood.

An hour later, I left Berwick-upon-Tweed's quiet red-brick station and looked about. A large man in navy corduroy trousers and a chunky moss-green sweater walked towards me and held out his hand.

"Gabriella Sullivan?"

CHAPTER 12

His voice was the rich baritone I had heard on the phone. "Yes, are you Mr Cavendish?" I put my hand in his, taking in thick, dark blond hair, dark eyes, a straight nose and a strong jawline. I swallowed.

"I am, but please call me Hugo. Come on, I'll take you to Cavendish Lodge. You must have been travelling a while," he said, and I smoothed my hair, wondering if I looked a mess.

"Since eight this morning." I held out the holdall with the miniatures. "But I have your purchase safe and sound."

He smiled unexpectedly, his eyes crinkling at the corners. "Excellent, thank you."

He took my large handbag and holdall from me and placed them carefully in the boot of his black car. To my surprise, he opened the passenger door for me, and with a murmured thank you I slid onto a leather seat.

He climbed in and started the engine, and I thanked him for coming to meet me.

"But of course."

I pulled out my phone and sent a text to Gerrard that I'd arrived in Berwick.

I was surprised to find myself heading out of the beige and grey stone houses, on a road following the river Tweed. I frowned and discreetly logged into a travel app, watching my progress as a little blue dot on the road.

"I'm about ten miles out of Berwick," Hugo said, not taking his eyes from the road. "It'll take about twenty minutes."

I nodded, taken aback that he'd seemed to read my thoughts. As we drove, I glanced up. The sky looked bruised and threatening. I was pleased I'd had the foresight to bring an umbrella.

We sped along narrow country roads, lined with bare hedgerows and dark ploughed fields, and finally turned left between some ornate black gates and began to climb a hill. At the crest of the hill was one of the loveliest houses I'd ever seen. It had two solid, square storeys, the golden stone of its walls shining softly in the gloomy midday light. It had, as Aunt Mo would say, 'windows round the doors' – in her view, an indication of the perfect dwelling. The gravel on the broad drive crunched beneath the tyres, announcing our arrival.

I climbed out to face a large, burgundy door with a shiny silver knocker. Hugo Cavendish locked the car and turned to face me. "Tea?"

"That would be wonderful, thank you."

I followed him into a large hall, my heels clicking on the black and white tiled floor. The noise echoed up into the high ceilings; the walls were painted duck-egg blue, the plasterwork white. I could be in an episode of *Bridgerton* or on the set of a Jane Austen movie.

His long legs ate up the narrow corridor; I had to trot to keep up with him and was slightly out of breath as we finally arrived in the kitchen. It was huge, with a large island in the middle of the room, gleaming dark blue and chrome. An Aga warmed the room from one side, and a microwave and complicated coffee-making machines filled another wall. On the other side of the island was a large pine table, bleached white with sun and use.

A petite, blue-rinsed lady in a pink overall was at the kitchen sink, washing out a cloth. She turned as we walked in.

CHAPTER 12

"Och, you're back. Did you want something?" she asked Hugo, a Scottish brogue flavouring the words.

"No, Birdie, I'm getting Miss Sullivan a cup of tea. She's come from London with the portraits. We'll be out of your hair in a minute." Hugo switched on the kettle and began putting cups and saucers onto a tray.

"I'll do that!" Birdie scolded and shooed him out of the way with a slender hand. Hugo smiled.

"If you must. We'll be in the library."

I wondered briefly how many rooms this splendid house had and followed him to a door a few steps from the kitchen. Abruptly, he turned, and I almost ran into him, stepping back with a gasp.

"Sorry. I just thought of something – do you have your train booked to go on to Edinburgh? We'll need to allow about half an hour to get back to the station."

"I have an open ticket, but the trains run quite regularly, don't they?" I said, and he nodded.

He opened the door to a room with floor to ceiling bookshelves. One large window showed the path to a garden, set in a wall painted royal blue. A huge red-hued desk that I guessed to be mahogany held a pile of correspondence. There was a ladder on wheels against one of the bookshelves, and in front of the fireplace there was a squishy-looking sofa and a wing back leather chair next to a low table. I compared this glorious place with my tiny flat, where most of my reading was e-books because I had no space to store paperbacks.

I found Hugo was watching me closely. His eyes struck me as the colour of bitter chocolate. He raised his eyebrows, and I realised I hadn't said anything.

"I'm sorry. I was just comparing your reading space to mine!" I apologised with a smile.

He nodded, and finally seemed to relax, his mouth turning up at the corners. "I'm very fortunate. Please sit down."

I hesitated. "I've just been on a train for four hours; would you mind if I stood up?"

He laughed, just as Birdie arrived with a tray of tea and what looked like fresh pastries. Before she'd even set it down, my mouth was watering. I was suddenly very hungry.

"There you go," she said, wiping her hands down her overall. "Och, and there's Mango," she said disapprovingly as a ginger cat shot through the door and sat expectantly by Hugo. "I bet you've walked in all over my floor, haven't you?" she scolded the cat. She turned to Hugo. "The kitchen floor is still wet, so be careful if you go in. I'll see you in a fortnight. Be careful with the weather that's coming."

He thanked her and she bustled out.

"I hope you're not on a diet?" Hugo asked, handing me a plate. I was continually on a diet, but I shook my head. "Excellent, please help yourself. I hope you don't mind if I look at the miniatures while you're eating?"

I dipped into the holdall and handed him the case. "They're fascinating – I'm glad I got to see them," I remarked as he took it and moved to the desk. Mango meowed. "Just a minute," he said softly to the cat as he pulled away the bubble wrap and reverently opened the catch. Sinking my teeth into a buttery *pain au raisin*, I heard his breath catch in his throat. I put down the pastry and wiped my fingers on a napkin. Mango stalked over to me, eyes on my plate.

"Don't think the pastries are for you," I said to the cat, and carefully moved the food before I joined Hugo at the desk. "They're wonderful, aren't they? What brought you to them?"

"Interesting that you put it like that," he said, his gaze still fixed on the miniatures. "What brought me to these portraits is that I'm descended from her sister, apparently."

"From Sophia?"

His head came up abruptly from his examination. "You know of Sophia?"

"I— er... well, I was really fascinated by the change in the two portraits, they look so different, don't they? I was intrigued," I said, flustered, "so I did a bit of research into the family and although I didn't find out much about Harriet, I found out about Sophia."

He stared and picked up the first miniature. "Yes, she looks much more alive in the later portrait. She looks a little grim here, doesn't she?"

"Yes! Like she was determined to do something she didn't really want to!" I agreed, nodding.

A smile spread slowly across his face. "It's nice to meet someone who's as captivated as I am! My brother and sister think I'm very odd, delving into the past to find out more."

"Why do they find it odd? Everyone should know where they came from." A thought struck me. "What do you do for a living?"

"I'm a consultant," he said. "I work with international banks to find operating economies." I must have looked a little doubtful, because he laughed. "And yes, some people might consider it dull, but it earns me an excellent living."

I felt heat run up my cheeks. "I'm sure you're very good at it," I said quickly, and he grinned.

"Yes, and I charge extortionate fees. But I'm worth every penny."

He said this in such a matter-of-fact way, I was reminded of all the times my family had introduced me as 'just an administrator' as if they were ashamed. I wasn't *just* an administrator. I was a very, very good administrator. And I wasn't *just* the assistant gallery director – I was a talented all-rounder, with a strong handle on the finances. I should rewrite my CV.

"Miss Sullivan?" Hugo said softly. I came out of my reverie.

"Please call me Gabriella," I said automatically. "Sorry, I was just thinking how nice it would be to describe myself like that – you know, worth every penny."

"Don't you?" He put his head on one side, and I laughed.

"God, no! I'm a woman – we don't praise ourselves, we hang around and hope that other people do it!" He looked at me curiously and I changed the subject. "I wasn't able to find out much about Sophia, but I'll gladly share what I found."

Hugo gently put the miniatures back in the case, and with a lingering glance at them, he sat next to me on the sofa. Mango jumped on his lap, purring loudly as I went through the notes I'd made from my session in the British Library.

Hugo looked thoughtful. "I've traced the ten of Sophia's twelve children who lived to adulthood," he said. "I found her son, Peregrine, who was a scholar at Oxford and was appointed a professor of divinity there. I found him from the university staff lists."

"Have you been able to find out anything more about Harriet?" I asked. "I can't imagine that a widow with that amount of money would go unnoticed."

"No, I was focused on Sophia. I didn't even know about Harriet before I began to investigate. I'm no historian," he said, smiling at me again, and I felt warmth spread down from my tummy right to my toes. "It took me forever to dig out just this amount of information about her from the ancestry sites!"

We talked, and I told him of some online archives that he would be able to access. Then we talked some more.

"Good grief, look at the time!" Hugo said with a start. "I'm so sorry, I had no idea I'd kept you here so long! What time is your train?"

I glanced at my watch. I'd been in Cavendish Lodge for more than two hours. "I'll just see what the next one is, but you might call me a cab, if that's okay?"

"No, I'll drive you." He left the room and I reached for my phone to check my train times. I had just navigated to the screen, when he returned. "Have you seen outside?" he asked.

"No— Oh!" The scene outside the window was a flurry of thick, white snow. Running to the window, I could see that it was already lying four or five inches deep. "Oh, God! I thought this was only forecast for Northern Scotland! Are you able to drive in this?"

"More to the point, are the trains running?"

I dropped my gaze to my phone to see a series of red 'cancelled' notices across the list of trains I could have caught. "Ah." I stopped, not sure what to say. There was a silence.

"If you can drive me to Berwick, I'll book a room," I said. "I saw a hotel when I was coming from the station."

I could see a couple of rooms available online, and decided I would call from the car. But as we reversed in the drive, the wheels of the car skidded in the thick snow. Quietly, I began to panic.

Hugo took a deep breath. "I'm not sure I'll be able to keep control of the car down the drive in this weather. I was going to grit it after you'd gone today, and obviously it's now rather late."

Wildly, I wondered what I was going to do – ski down? Sit on a dustbin lid and toboggan to the road? And then what?

Hugo continued. "I recognise this is awkward, but you should stay here. It's stupid to do anything else. I have plenty of guest rooms, and Birdie has at least cleaned everything!"

He waited for my response.

Oh, my God. Talk about uncomfortable. There were hotel rooms in Berwick, but did I want to end up crashing on his drive? No, I did not.

"That's incredibly kind of you to offer," I said. "You're right, I can't even walk to the town in these shoes!" I glanced down at my higher-than-normal black patents. "I can't believe I didn't notice the snow!"

"No, it would take you hours and you're not dressed for it. In this part of the country the weather turns fast," he said gravely. Hearing his tone, I felt a spark inside me that excited a shiver along my arms. We climbed out of the car, and he opened the door to the house. In the hall, he turned to me and smiled reassuringly.

"Let me start a fire. I'll get some more tea and then have a rummage in the freezer for dinner," he said. "Then I can show you to a guest room. But first…"

CHAPTER 12

He took out his phone and dialled a number. "Gerrard? It's Hugo Cavendish. The weather has turned pretty bad up here and the trains are cancelled. Oh, you too? Well, we've got a few inches already and I daresay it will get worse. So Miss Sullivan is going to stay here until it clears. Let me put you on to her."

He handed his phone to me and then took off his coat before striding away.

"Hi, Gerrard," I said, watching Hugo's tall figure disappear into a room.

"Are you okay? This is awkward! Are you sure you're going to be all right?"

"I don't have much of a choice. I can't believe how thick the snow is already, and the sky looks full of it!" I shrugged off my own coat with a sigh. "At least you know where I am, but if you could call Justin and explain, I'd be grateful."

"You should call people at home."

I agreed. Mum and I weren't speaking, but if Liam had asked her to babysit, and explained I'd stood them up for this trip, she might be worried if the trains were cancelled. I began to text.

Chapter 13

GROSVENOR SQUARE, MID-FEBRUARY 1803

Four weary days later, Harriet stared out of the window of the coach and wondered if London had always been the noisy, dirty place she saw now, or whether she had forgotten. She longed for nothing more than to stop moving. Louise was fast asleep in the corner, and Harriet envied the maid her oblivion.

Before she had left Colchester Hall, she had written to Alexander, telling him of her trip and Anne's direction. Then she had bespoken accommodation at The Old George in Newcastle, The Angel at Grantham, the Bell Inn at Stilton and the Red Lion at Welwyn. While The Angel was as comfortable as she recalled, The Bell's refreshments were indifferent and the chimney smoked. She'd been so exhausted by the time they stopped at the Red Lion, she would not have noticed if a brass band had played outside her door. The roads had been so rough in places, that even in a well-sprung coach her teeth felt as if they had been shaken loose. She could only be grateful that all the wheels were still on.

The rug around her legs had kept her warm during the journey, but the brick at her feet, placed there by the innkeeper at the last change of horses at Barnet, was now cold. She shivered, only partly from the temperature.

As the streets broadened, Harriet's thoughts turned to Anne and her welcome in Grosvenor Square. An endless spiral of thoughts churned through her mind. They combined a chilly reception, Harriet's lack of acquaintance in town and the wisdom of coming to London while she was in mourning and, it had to be said, woefully unprepared for any kind of society.

One part of Harriet was thrilled, despite her aching body and drooping eyelids, that she had dispatched Augusta and, for better or worse, was finally doing something she wanted. What the next step was, she was unsure.

Her hands clenched on her knee, and she speculated on the suitability of her gowns. She must be sadly outdated. Then again, she would not be in society, and if Anne was so unwell, she and Phillip would not be entertaining. Although doubtless family would visit. But then Harriet could hardly disappear into her room.

"Oh, be quiet!" she muttered to herself, trying once more to steady her whirling mind. She looked again from the window. The evening was fast drawing in, and Harriet saw the windows glowing golden in some of the grand houses in the fading light. Despite her decision to remain in mourning, she could not but feel a frisson of excitement. She was not naive enough to think the Colchester fortune would open any doors for her, but it would certainly make her stay more comfortable.

The coach was slowing down. Louise awoke with a start, and her hand went automatically to straighten her hat. Harriet threw the rug off her legs and found her reticule. John Coachman opened the door, and Harriet forced her stiff legs to move. As he handed her down, the door to the house opened and a footman in a splendid livery approached, carrying a lantern.

As Harriet straightened, Anne walked unsteadily down the steps, almost pushing the footman out of the way. Harriet bit her lip as she looked at Anne, thinner in the face than Harriet had seen before, her previously glossy blonde hair dull, her green eyes shadowed. Anne had indeed been unwell and Harriet's guilt soared.

"Harriet! It's so lovely to see you!" Anne cried, and Harriet burst into tears. Anne looked alarmed and Harriet attempted to pull herself together.

"I'm so sorry! I should have been here months ago!" she sniffed, searching wildly for a handkerchief.

Anne chuckled and pulled Harriet into a hug. "Don't be a goose! You're here now, and I wager you're exhausted, aren't you? Let's get you settled, and you can have some tea and go to bed. We can talk tomorrow."

"That sounds like heaven," Harriet said with a watery smile.

In the clear light of the morning, Harriet eyed her friend with some misgiving. Phillip had not overstated the case that Anne was unwell. Anne had lost weight, and her pregnant belly was obvious. Anne saw Harriet's stare.

"I'm not dead yet!" she scolded, passing Harriet a cup of tea. "I know I look as if I'm expiring, but although I don't feel well, I certainly don't expect to die yet."

Harriet swallowed and buried her nose in her tea. She noticed that Anne had taken a cup of weak tea with no milk and sipped it tentatively. "Has the sickness been with you all the way through?"

Anne nodded, screwing up her face. "Almost from the second month. My darling Phillip has consulted every doctor in London, but nothing they suggest seems to work. But I shall prevail, I'm sure! It's only a short time left, in any case."

Harriet blinked. How would Anne build her strength for her labour?

"I could write to Peters and ask him to enquire of one the women on the estate," she said slowly. "She is famed locally for her remedies. And I need to tell him I have arrived, of course."

"I'll try anything!" Anne said with a sigh. "But I refuse to be bled, or in bed, which are all Dr Thomas offers! He talks of balancing my humours – whatever that means! Indeed, my humour is most unbalanced after a visit from him!"

Harriet smiled and asked for pen and paper. It was the work of a few moments to write to Peters, and Anne rang the bell for the blue-liveried footman. He bowed as he took the letter and coughed before saying that Dr William Thomas had presented his card. Was my lady at home?

Anne looked alarmed. "Oh, goodness! Had I forgot his visit?" She chewed her lip and then nodded at the footman. "You'd better let him in, Coates. Harriet, you must stay and protect me!"

This didn't seem like a promising response to a man who was presumably dedicated to Anne's wellbeing, so Harriet settled into the corner of the sofa and prepared to do what she knew she did well – observe.

The first glimpse she had of Dr Thomas was not encouraging. He was almost as wide as he was tall and his cheeks were red from the exertion of climbing the stairs. He was dressed in what Harriet surmised must be the height of fashion. He sported a sombre coat of black superfine, fawn pantaloons and a dark green embroidered waistcoat. The points of his shirt collar had wilted slightly. After he had wiped the perspiration from his head with a voluminous handkerchief, he bowed to Anne. He barely acknowledged Harriet, which made her eyebrows rise and caused a smile to tilt the corners of her mouth.

"Lady Rochford, I am grieved to see you out of bed! You are too delicate for such exertion!"

"I will retire when I have welcomed Mrs Colchester," she promised. Dr Thomas cast a baleful eye on Harriet as the cause of Anne's departure from his instructions. Harriet returned his look coolly.

"Please sit down. I was not expecting you," Anne said, twisting her hands together.

"I saw your husband in Pall Mall, and we exchanged a few words," he said, lowering his impressive bulk into a chair that hardly looked up to the task of supporting him. Harriet watched the chair legs strain.

"And what did Lord Rochford say to excite you to a visit?" Harriet asked mildly. "Is he concerned for his wife in any way?"

"Obviously, I cannot discuss the details of my patient with you as a stranger," he replied, sniffing.

"Oh, Harriet is not a stranger! She is my dearest friend, and you can say anything you wish in her hearing, Anne said firmly. Dr Thomas looked very displeased.

"So, did Lord Rochford indicate his concern in any way?" repeated Harriet.

"He is obviously anxious," Dr Thomas said shortly. "Lady Rochford," he said, turning his back on Harriet, "perhaps I should examine you? I may need to bleed you. Lord Rochford is worried that any excitement," he flicked a glance at Harriet, "will be bad for your nerves."

I am obviously the excitement, Harriet thought. She made to rise from her seat, but an anguished look from Anne caused her to settle again. Dr Thomas' face darkened and he pursed his lips.

"How do you feel, Lady Rochford?" Harriet asked.

"Bleeding always leaves me feeling rather weak," Anne admitted. "Perhaps I might be allowed to miss this week?"

"But my dear Lady Rochford, bleeding is a sure way to rebalance your humours, which are sadly out of kilter, hence your lack of energy and appetite."

Anne and Harriet exchanged looks and Harriet saw a smile flit across her friend's face. The 'humours' had made an appearance.

"But do you have a lack of appetite, Lady Rochford? Or are you just constantly sick?" Harriet pressed.

"I could eat a horse," declared Anne. "But eating causes me to be unwell in the most appalling manner."

"So it is a digestive issue?" Harriet said. "Should we be looking to find something Lady Rochford can eat without being ill?"

"I should like that above all things!" Anne said devoutly.

"So perhaps bleeding is not the answer," Harriet said sweetly to the doctor, whose face turned crimson.

"Lady Rochford, I must insist my professional judgement be considered!" he spluttered.

"And so it will be, but not this week," Harriet said soothingly. She stood up, and a second later, Anne struggled to her feet as well. Faced with both ladies, the doctor stared at their obvious dismissal of him. He heaved himself up and pulled down his waistcoat, which had ridden up over his enormous belly.

"Thank you for coming, Dr Thomas," Anne said with a smile. "I do appreciate it."

He nodded briefly in farewell, and his huge figure appeared to roll out of the room. Both Harriet and Anne remained standing until they heard the front door slam, and only then did they sit. Anne caught Harriet's eye and then giggled.

"We joined forces beautifully, did we not? How glad I am you were here! I find it difficult to exert any kind of control with him. He bullies me into submission."

Harriet frowned. "But aren't you paying his fees?"

Anne waved a hand. "That is of no consequence to Phillip! He chose the doctor with the best reputation, and I'm condemned to submit to Dr Thomas' ministrations."

Harriet thought for a moment. From her brief surveillance of the doctor, she thought him a little too secure in his reputation, and so disinclined to do anything different from the actions that had brought him that reputation. Dr Thomas was simply applying treatments that had worked on other ailments – but not necessarily what ailed Anne. She leaned forward.

"Shall I remain until you have delivered the baby?" she asked.

Anne's pale face lit up. And then she bit her lip. "This is so hard for you," she whispered. "I know of all your efforts to become a mother. Are you certain? I would hate to cause you pain."

Harriet felt her heart swell. Anne had obviously forgiven her for not coming to London before now. Harriet swiftly crossed the room to kneel by Anne's side. "I can share in your joy. And I want – after you and Phillip, of course – the first cuddle!"

Anne clasped her hand and it was decided.

Chapter 14

BERWICK, FEBRUARY 2023

I left a message for Joe to say I was snowed in and where I was. I also texted Aunt Mo.

Joe responded a few minutes later.

Hey! Just started snowing here too. I'll watch the flat and get Steve to check your pipes aren't in any danger of freezing!

Justin sent a thumbs up in response to Gerrard's message and a cheeky text asking if I'd brought spare knickers. I had, of course; they were nestling in one flap of my bag, ready for my overnight stay in Edinburgh. Thank goodness for that, at least.

I caught sight of my reflection in the mirror over the fireplace and the image distracted me momentarily. The haircut had been a good idea, making me rather *gamin*, I thought, and my new soft red cashmere sweater brought out my hair's auburn tones. My new black wool trousers still had a crease, and although the charcoal jacket was a bit rumpled from being crushed under my thick coat, it was still elegant.

"At least the outside is respectable!" I breathed.

"What's that?" Hugo came in with tea, and I gave a self-conscious laugh.

"I'm hoping the clothes I'm wearing will do me for an extra day!"

He grinned, put the mugs down on the low table in front of the fireplace and began to feed the fire with chunky logs. I cradled my mug and watched his big hands place the wood carefully to catch the flames.

"My sister keeps some clothes here," he said. "Shall I dig out some of her stuff? I think she might be a bit taller than you, but there might be something to fit you."

I gulped. "That's – that's very kind of you. But I can manage for one night."

He shot me a glance. "The forecast is bad until Saturday."

"*Saturday?*" I said, pulling out my phone to look at my weather app. After a few minutes, I raised my eyes to him. "Good grief, I'm so sorry. This wasn't forecast in London! I imagine the last thing you needed was a complete stranger foisted on you for three days!"

He chuckled, and the sound of it made me feel rather hot. I moved back from the fire and took a sip of my tea. The silence stretched on for a couple of minutes longer than I was comfortable with. Hugo put his mug down and said, "Come on, I'll show you the guest room."

I followed his tall figure up the broad and curving stairs. There was a long, arched window at the first turn of the stairs, and the light from the white world outside reflected eerily pale on the walls.

The muffled silence prompted me to say to Hugo, "Snow always makes things quiet, doesn't it?"

He cast me an amused look over his shoulder. "I imagine the lack of traffic also contributes, but yes, snow dampens sound. I love it myself, inconvenient as it is – it smooths the landscape and makes it new. Like the earth was getting a makeover. Now - this is where I was thinking of putting you."

He opened the door to a room with a huge, canopied bed in the midst of pale blue and yellow striped walls. Although the other furniture – a table facing the window, a bedside cabinet and a tall wardrobe – was not antique, it looked perfectly in keeping with the room. The carpet was deep blue, and fawn and pale blue rugs were on either side of the bed. Through a side door I could glimpse a dark blue tiled bathroom. A little to my relief, I saw a lock on the bedroom door.

"It's lovely!" I exclaimed. "Thank you so much, I'm sorry to put you to this trouble."

"It's no trouble," he assured me. "And anyway," he added, dark eyes gleaming, "I'm counting on you helping me with my research into the Colchester sisters."

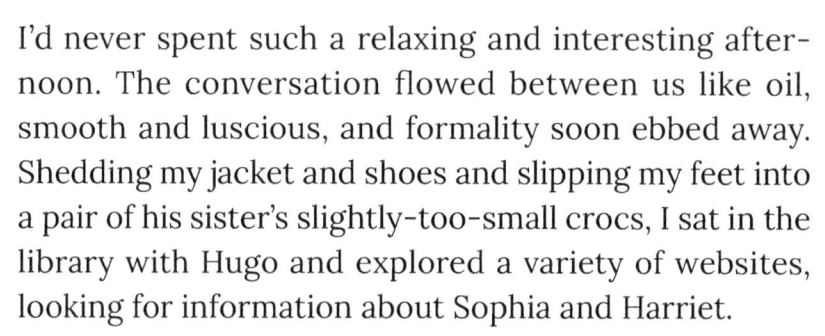

I'd never spent such a relaxing and interesting afternoon. The conversation flowed between us like oil, smooth and luscious, and formality soon ebbed away. Shedding my jacket and shoes and slipping my feet into a pair of his sister's slightly-too-small crocs, I sat in the library with Hugo and explored a variety of websites, looking for information about Sophia and Harriet.

Harriet watched our efforts from the corner of the large desk, accompanied by Mango. I felt sure Harriet's eyes mocked us gently. I made notes on my iPad of all we knew, and over dinner in the warmth of the kitchen, we speculated about Hugo's long-lost relatives.

CHAPTER 14

"So, we know when the sisters were born, who their parents were, and we think that the elder sister Sophia married a clergyman, although we don't have an exact date." I took a piece of bread and mopped up some of the delicious gravy on my plate as daintily as I could.

"He was the younger son of a baron before he was a clergyman," amended Hugo. "He was probably offered the living when he got married."

"But we don't know where or when they married, do we, Sophia and – what's his name?"

"Miles Grantley Fitzharding Berkeley."

"Quite a mouthful!" I laughed, and his eyes crinkled.

"I'll have you know that's my ancestor you're talking about," he said, leaning back from the table with a satisfied sigh and patting his mouth with a napkin. "Miles and Sophia set up home in a rectory in North Yorkshire. I found records of him taking up the living in 1795, so I presume they married that year."

"We don't know for certain when?"

He frowned. "I can't find out. Miles should have married in the family chapel, but I've searched the Berkeley records, and I can only find dates for the christenings of their children. So, wherever they got married, it doesn't seem to have happened in the normal way."

"I can't believe she had a dozen children!" I marvelled at the thought. The twins were exhausting enough. "Mind you, there wasn't much birth control then!"

"Only abstinence," Hugo agreed, standing to gather the plates.

Ah, of course. I don't have much of a problem with abstinence, I thought gloomily.

"Did you say something?" Hugo asked and for a wild, terrifying moment, I wondered if I'd spoken aloud.

I shook my head firmly. "Nope. But let me help with those." I rose and carried over the remaining dishes.

Hugo stacked the dishwasher.

"Hmm. It's strange, isn't it? No information on Harriet's side, either. I wonder…" I stared into space, thoughts whirling in my head. "How old was Sophia?"

"Well, she turned up with Miles at the rectory when she was barely eighteen, although that may not mean much. Harriet was just as young when she married." Hugo switched on the dishwasher and lights began to flash as it hummed into life.

And then it went dark.

I gasped and grabbed hold of the countertop. The kitchen was pitch black, and I heard Hugo swear softly and start to fumble his way along the cupboards using his phone as a puny flashlight.

"Just a blown fuse?" I asked hopefully. He grunted as he pulled an industrial size torch from a drawer and switched it on.

"More likely the weather; it's happened before," he said. "Stay here while I check it out. At least we still have the Aga, so we won't freeze to death."

"Will it work without electricity?"

"Battery backup." His smile gleamed at me in the dim light and left me. A couple of minutes after he had gone, I grabbed my phone, switched on the torch and looked for candles. He'd said this had happened before.

After a glance around the room, I headed for the old favourite – the cupboard under the sink.

"Bingo!" I said softly as I pulled out a box of thick, no-nonsense candles. Hunting around the Aga, I finally unearthed matches and opened another cupboard to find saucers on which to fix the candles. I was lighting the third candle when Hugo returned, looking resigned.

"None of the fuses are blown, and there's a message on the energy website that there's disruption due to the weather," he said, and I nodded. "We have a generator, which I'll get working in the morning – I don't fancy sorting it out in the dark. Good that you found the candles," he added with a smile.

I grinned. "Will we need them long?"

He grimaced. "No idea. Better save your phone battery, at least until I get the generator working."

I had a power pack in my bag but nodded and switched off my phone. There was an awkward pause. I hesitated, not ready yet to go to bed and lie awake wondering when I might get back to London.

"I need to get some firewood. Do you want to wait in the library?" He moved to the back door.

"I can help!"

"You have no wellies, no coat." He frowned at my black trousers and pink crocs.

"Don't you have anything I can borrow? I'm not going for a photo shoot."

He laughed, opened a side door and disappeared to return with a thick woollen coat and a pair of yellow wellington boots with blue flowers.

"Perhaps I *should* get a photographer on the phone!" I quipped.

Hugo pulled on his own black wellies and a sturdy-looking padded gilet and then pushed open the door against the drifting snow. The outside world was muffled, and large flakes of snow still drifted from an inky sky.

I breathed in, the cold air making my nostrils tingle, and stepping outside, the snow packed under my boots with a dull crunch. I lifted my face upwards to feel the cold kiss of the snow on my eyelids and cheeks. Hugo chuckled.

"You look like a kid," he said, and I could feel my cheeks heat with embarrassment.

"You don't see snow all that often in London," I mumbled. I pulled myself together. "Where are these logs, then?"

He led the way, but as I followed him, the snow grew deeper, and I found it difficult to pick up my feet. At one stage, I was fishing with my foot for my blue and yellow wellie firmly wedged behind me in the snow, swearing under my breath. Finally on the move again, I found Hugo in a lean-to log shed, stacking wood into a wicker basket about a metre wide. He glanced over his shoulder and nodded at the basket.

"Can you manage that?"

"Of course."

He turned back to the pile of logs and began to fill another basket.

I grimaced. It looked heavy, but I flexed my fingers and hefted it up, feeling the pull on my shoulders as I took the weight. I managed a couple of steps and had to pause. Then another. To my shame, it took me a full five minutes to retrace my steps to the back door of the kitchen and I was panting as I dragged the basket over the threshold.

I glared at the logs and decided to carry them into the kitchen individually rather than struggle further. As I was returning to the kitchen for the third time, Hugo was shutting the back door. He wiped a snowflake from the end of his nose. He ran his eyes over my basket, realising what I was doing.

"Good stuff. Thank you for your help."

I smiled. "Of course."

Twenty minutes later, he had built up the Aga and the fire in the library, and I eased off the boots with a sigh of relief, wiggling my toes to get the blood flowing again in my frozen feet. I stood, uncertain; it was now ten o'clock and I wondered whether I ought to be courteously withdrawing. He glanced at me and paused.

"Are you ready for bed?"

"Um…" I hesitated. I wasn't tired but didn't want to inconvenience him. Although how I could do that, when neither of us could go anywhere, I wasn't clear.

"Can I offer another drink? I was thinking of a brandy, myself," he said, pulling his jacket off his shoulders.

"Can we make tea?" I asked, and he gave a huff of laughter.

"On the stove. Take a seat; I'll be right back."

While he was gone, a text came through from Mum, telling me to take care, and asking when I'd be home. I said I would and that I'd let her know, but she could keep an eye on the trains.

"If that's not too much effort," I said to myself and then scolded myself for being childish.

I switched on some of the battery lights and carefully lit some candles on the mantelpiece, casting a golden glow around the room. I paused. It was too cosy for an assistant manager of a London gallery and *a client*. I stared into the fire, unnerved.

"You look thoughtful," Hugo commented as he kicked the door closed.

"It's not quite the delivery to a client I had imagined," I said, finally. He looked steadily at me.

"No, I recognise you would rather be at home. I hope that the situation isn't too uncomfortable for you?"

"You've been most kind," I said immediately. "I'm not sure where I'd be if it wasn't for your hospitality. But yes – it's a bit unconventional." I paused. "I'm a little worried that I'm in your way."

His brow cleared. "No, it's been a pleasure, and it isn't as if you've not worked for bed and board – clearing dinner dishes, lighting candles, hauling logs about – not to mention giving me some information about Sophia!"

He might be being polite, but I did feel a bit better. Relieved, I sat on the sofa and reached for my tea. He sipped his brandy, and we talked about ancestry sites, the gallery and our tastes in art. He had a stillness about him that I found very restful, and I was surprised to find it was nearly midnight. I exclaimed and stood up.

"I must go to bed, otherwise I'll never get up!"

"Not that there's a rush," Hugo observed. "The snow is a foot or so deep, and it's still falling, so I doubt anything will be moving tomorrow." He stood up too and gathered my cup. "Can you find your way to your room?" I nodded. "Take one of the battery lights to go upstairs with. I'll see you in the morning. We should have enough water in the tank for showers in the morning until I sort out the generator."

I went.

Chapter 15

GROSVENOR SQUARE, LATE FEBRUARY 1803

A week later, just as Harriet was reading a letter from Peters, which informed her blandly that the family had departed Colchester Hall and the covers were on the furniture, Coates stepped through the door of the drawing room and solemnly announced a new visitor.

"Mr Richardson has called, my lord, my lady. Are you and Mrs Colchester at home?"

Harriet dropped the letter with an exclamation and Phillip lowered the newspaper, casting a curious glance at his wife. Anne, watching Harriet scrabble on the floor for the sheets of paper, hid a smile and then winced as something pained her. She rubbed her lower back and took a deep breath.

"By all means, please show him up," she said to Coates.

Harriet sat up and blew a loosened curl from her forehead, looking flushed as Alexander walked in, tall and broad, wearing a smart waistcoat, his cravat snowy and modestly tied. Even after her note, she had not expected that he would call so soon, and now he had arrived, she found herself tongue-tied.

Alexander cast a swift glance around, saw Anne's pregnancy and paused, before bowing.

Phillip rose to his feet, and Harriet noted the difference between them. Phillip was medium height, had mid-brown hair and stood not more than half a head taller than Harriet herself. At first glance, one might think he could be cowed by the towering, swarthy Alexander.

But Phillip had thirty-two years of aristocratic upbringing and a quiet dignity. Alexander bowed in greeting, and to Harriet's enormous surprise, Phillip put out a hand.

"I'm pleased to meet you, Mr Richardson," he said, eyes flicking over Alexander's expertly tailored coat. Alexander smiled as he shook the manicured hand held out to him.

"Lord Rochford. I've heard a great deal about you from Harriet," he said, and Phillip turned to raise an eyebrow at Harriet.

"All good things!" she protested, laughing. "How are you, Alexand – Mr Richardson?"

He came forward and kissed Harriet's hand, and she was aware of his lips on her skin and Anne's sharp gaze on the interaction. There was a pause.

"Please, sit down," Anne said, filling the gap, and Alexander took a seat. Harriet reflected that while he seemed perfectly at ease, his energy felt too intense for this cool, elegant room.

For five minutes, they exchanged pleasantries. Phillip enquired about Alexander's stay in London. Alexander spoke of the races, and visits to the opera and the play, and listening to him, Harriet began to feel very dull. She could almost be glad when Coates arrived with another letter for her.

"Oh!" she said, recognising the handwriting of Peters. "Would you excuse me for just a moment?"

She hurried to the library. Tearing open the seal, she scanned the cramped lines from Peters and smiled as she found the information she wanted from Margaret, the cook from the estate, talented with herbal cures.

Well pleased with herself, she returned to the drawing room. As she opened the door, she could hear Anne laughing, and Phillip was looking on indulgently. Alexander looked up as Harriet stood on the threshold and smiled warmly at her. She waved the letter.

"I have a potential potion for you, Anne! Can I speak to your cook?" Barely waiting for Anne's nod, she turned and fled to the kitchen.

Cook approved of the draught, which featured mint, dandelion root and chamomile flowers, sweetened with honey. Harriet almost skipped back to the drawing room to find Alexander about to take his leave.

"Oh! Are you leaving already?" she said, dismayed.

"I have stayed the customary half hour," replied Alexander, smiling. "But if you are at home tomorrow, I would be very happy to call on you again."

Harriet frowned slightly, puzzled. It was true she had not been in town for five years, and she was not in her own house, but she was unaccountably irritated at the conventions being thrust on her. Anne glanced at Phillip, who gave an almost imperceptible nod, and she said immediately, "You are most welcome any time, Mr Richardson. I'm sure Harriet values your presence as one of the few people that she knows in London."

"I should be very happy to escort you both, should you wish to take the air – and perhaps we could ride in the Park at some stage, Harriet?"

"I'm not here to go jaunting about; I'm here to be with Lady Rochford!" Harriet protested, alarmed at the idea of going into the ton after such an absence and wondering what people would say about her presence in society while she was still in mourning.

"We are not joined at the hip, my dear!" Anne said with a laugh. "I'm sure you deserve an afternoon off occasionally!"

Harriet was unconvinced. With a tight smile, Alexander shook hands with Phillip and Anne, and again kissed Harriet's hand. She tried very hard not to think of the pressure and warmth of his mouth.

She felt rather flat after he had departed.

Then Coates arrived with Margaret's concoction. Anne wrinkled her nose at the smell and advised they retire to her sitting room, in case she was sick. Harriet took the tray from Coates; Phillip offered his arm to Anne, and she walked slowly to the sitting room. Once there, a bowl was found, and Anne took a small sip of the tea. Harriet watched anxiously as Anne screwed up her nose. After a minute, Anne took another sip.

"Margaret suggests you drink this before getting up and have thin strips of dry toast to begin the day," Harriet said.

"Anne has tried that previously with little success," Phillip said, his eyes never leaving his wife. "How do you do, Anne? Is it helping?"

"I still feel nauseous," Anne said apologetically, her hand rubbing her swollen stomach. "But at least I've not been sick."

"Margaret says to drink it very hot, but to be careful you do not drink too much, too quickly," warned Harriet.

CHAPTER 15

No-one spoke; they simply watched Anne sip and swallow.

Anne sat back, waited, and then leaned forward for another sip. After a few more minutes, she turned towards Phillip, tears in her eyes. "At least I have not emptied my stomach!"

He came swiftly to her side and clasped her hands, "It is a start! But you must try to build up your strength."

Anne beamed a watery smile at Harriet. "Thank you so much!"

Harriet shrugged. "As Lord Rochford says, it is a start. I shall thank Margaret when I return to Colchester Hall. We obviously need to take things slowly."

Over the next few days, Anne was still unable to eat much, but she drank more of the hot potion, and the more she drank, the more she seemed able to drink. Seeing some colour come back into his wife's wan cheeks, Phillip was cautiously optimistic.

"If she continues to improve, she might be open to receiving more visitors, which I believe would further improve her spirits," he said. "What do you think?"

Harriet's feelings were mixed. Of course Anne should have company if it cheered her. But Anne was still decidedly unwell. For herself, even if convention might limit her socialising while still in mourning, Harriet's social skills were very rusty. But Phillip looked hopeful at Anne's fledgling recovery, so despite her reservations, Harriet smiled.

"Yes, I think that's an excellent idea," she said.

Alexander became a regular caller. Then, early one afternoon, he brought with him another visitor.

Anne, glancing at the calling cards held out by Coates, nibbled her bottom lip.

"What is amiss?" Harriet asked, watching the confusion spread across Anne's face.

"Lady Porter-Hume has come to call," Anne replied. "I had no idea Mr Richardson knew her."

"Who is she?"

"She is the Marchioness of Bamford. She holds a position in her family's bank and is an active part of the board, I understand. She is – unusual." Anne rose awkwardly to look at her appearance in the mirror. She sighed. "I do not have time to change. Please show them up, Coates. And—"

Coates turned.

"Please serve tea from the Sèvres service." The butler nodded and left the room.

Harriet was faintly alarmed at the obvious effort Anne was making, and her sudden pallor. Anne took her seat and they did not speak. Harriet heard Alexander's deep voice as their guests climbed the stairs.

"Lady Arabella Porter-Hume, Marchioness of Bamford, and Mr Richardson," intoned Coates and stepped back. A statuesque woman of about forty, with curly chestnut hair and twinkling brown eyes, sporting a dashing feathered hat, arched her eyebrows while Alexander looked on.

Anne and Harriet stood and curtsied; Anne leaned against a chair arm because of her swelling belly – and overbalanced. Harriet darted across the room at the same time as the countess and they caught an

CHAPTER 15

arm each. Harriet glanced at the dancing eyes of Lady Porter-Hume as they eased Anne back onto the sofa.

Anne was scarlet with embarrassment. "Oh! I'm so clumsy in this state!" she muttered under her breath.

"Now, my dear!" chided Lady Porter-Hume, smiling, as she stepped back. "Do not, I beg you, make a meal of this. I recall my third child – I thought I'd topple over if the wind blew too hard!"

"Won't you please sit down?" Anne said, trying to recover her composure. "Harriet, would you ring for tea?"

Tea was rung for, the visitors took their seats, and hats were settled. Alexander began a tale of his previous night's visit to Covent Garden where the tenor's wig, crafted to such extravagant heights that it brushed a candelabra, caught fire on stage. The tenor, with astonishing *sang froid*, continued with the performance after a stagehand knocked off the wig with a broom and stamped on the smouldering mass. The singer was greeted with tumultuous applause at the end of the aria.

An eye on Anne's still-flushed cheeks, Harriet laughed with everyone else, but could not help feel a tinge of yearning for the concerts of the London season. Still, it was good to see Anne chuckling at Alexander's description as she gradually relaxed from her earlier stumble. As Harriet handed Alexander tea in the precious Sèvres cup, he murmured to her, "Are you well? You looked sad earlier."

She lifted startled eyes to his and then smiled. "No, all is well," she said. Her own situation was what it was; she should not bemoan it. "I'm so pleased to see Anne in company. Do you think she looks a little better?"

Alexander quirked an eyebrow at her change of topic but looked at Anne. "She does look brighter. Your doing, I presume?"

"We are trying a remedy of Margaret, one of the women on the estate. It works on some days and not on others. Anne still needs to rest a good deal, but I am hopeful that if she accustoms her stomach to drink, she may be able to take some gruel or clear soup," she told him, and he smiled.

"You are a good friend to be with her for her confinement," he said meaningfully, and Harriet shook her head, her cheeks hot.

"Lady Rochford, your tea is excellent," commented Lady Porter-Hume. "Who is your merchant?"

"Twining. They have their warehouses near Temple Bar in the Strand," replied Anne, pleased.

"Hmm." Lady Porter-Hume smacked her lips and took another sip. "I buy from Winter, Hughes and Company in Newgate Street; they have a particularly fine Hyson. But I may pay your merchant a visit."

"I'm certain they would welcome your ladyship's custom," Anne replied, smiling.

"I understood from Mr Richardson that you have been unwell," Lady Porter-Hume added after a pause.

"Ah, but my good friend Mrs Colchester has been taking such care of me!" Anne beamed at Harriet, who found herself the object of Lady Porter-Hume's bright, piercing gaze.

"It is a remedy from a woman on my husband's..." Harriet faltered and then continued, "*my* estate in Northumberland. Mrs Margaret Earnshaw has safely delivered many a babe, and I thought to write to my steward to ask her advice. The potion is all her doing.

Anne is getting stronger, certainly, but she still needs to rest."

Lady Porter-Hume nodded slowly and then said, "But how perspicacious of you to set the wheels in motion!" She turned back to Anne. "Would you feel able to drive with me tomorrow? I have a new barouche landau that I want to take for a spin."

Anne's eyes widened slightly at the invitation and the marchioness' condescension. "I should be delighted! My husband believes I should take a little more air to aid my recovery. Harriet, what say you?"

Harriet had dreaded the question as soon as the words barouche landau fell from Lady Porter-Hume's lips. She glanced at the window. The spring sunshine shimmered through the muslin draperies, enticing her to come and experience the lovely afternoon. Harriet was torn.

"You should certainly go," she said to Anne. "The sunshine will do wonders for your constitution."

Anne laughed. "I shall certainly not go without you! I know you are still in mourning, but this is hardly a riotous expedition!"

Lady Porter-Hume leaned forward to replace her cup on the tea table. "Might I ask – your husband died in November?" Harriet nodded. "Your observance does you credit, but a veil would suffice to satisfy the most traditional of sticklers when we are out of doors."

Harriet hesitated, imagining the reaction of her mama-in-law to her driving around the Ring in Hyde Park.

Alexander added his voice. "We shall not even trot if it offends your sensibilities, and of course, we will be mindful of Lady Rochford's condition."

Harriet shot a look at him to see his teasing wink. No help from *that* quarter, then! Anne cast her a yearning glance, and it occurred to Harriet that her friend had been cooped up for months, venturing merely into the garden, and only that when the weather was clement.

And Mama wasn't in London, was she? Perhaps Harriet had been too circumspect and all her fuss about a simple outing was ridiculous. She drew a deep breath.

"Yes. I, too, would be delighted," she said.

"Excellent!" said Alexander, his eyes warm.

Chapter 16

BERWICK, FEBRUARY 2023

To my surprise, it was light when I woke. I lay for a moment disoriented in the strange room before the thought crept into my head that if it was light, it was late. I glanced at my watch and gasped to see it was nearly a quarter to nine. I pushed the covers aside and stumbled into the bathroom.

To my enormous relief, the Aga was as good as Hugo had promised and the water was hot. I scrambled into my trousers and red cashmere. I was combing my fingers through my hair – sticking out a bit, I would probably need to wash it tomorrow – when there was a tap at the door.

"Gabriella, are you awake?" Hugo's voice rumbled from the corridor.

I pulled open the door. "I'm so sorry! I don't normally sleep this late. You must have thought I'd died!"

Hugo grinned at me, and I took in tousled hair, a thick checked shirt in green and ivory, and the same moss-green sweater he had worn yesterday. He looked large and vital, and even looking at him pushed a jolt of energy through me.

A client. Remember this man is a client of your employer, I told myself. I smiled.

"Breakfast?" he asked, and I nodded, suddenly ravenous.

While he made tea on the stove, I looked through the responses to my messages to Aunt Mo and Gerrard. Aunt Mo very sensibly asked me to keep in touch and urged me to keep warm. Gerrard said that he would simply close the gallery, given London had ground to a halt as it always did in snowy weather, and told me to contact him when I was booked on a train.

The text from Liam arrived while I was taking a bite of toast, covered in butter and thick with marmalade. It read:

Know trains aren't running smoothly because of snow when are u back – mum on her own & we can't get out. I've got awful 'flu and no tubes running. Confirm when u coming. L

I stood up abruptly, the chair scraped across the stone floor and Hugo glanced up.

"Problem?"

"No!" I smiled at him brightly. "Can you excuse me a moment? Am I okay to use the library?"

"Be my guest."

I stormed to the library and closed the door with exaggerated care. I sat on the sofa, only to have Mango jump on my knee. I laughed, startled out of my temper, and stroked him, listening to him purr. After a couple of minutes of this, I began to text.

I'm three hundred miles away with no trains for at least the next day or so, so unable to help. Suggest you pull on wellies and take the kids to see Mum. No power so saving phone battery. Also, call in on Aunt Mo.

Satisfied, I put my phone in my pocket and returned to the kitchen to resume my breakfast.

CHAPTER 16

Hugo flicked a look at me and picked up the teapot. "Fresh cup?" he asked, blandly. I nodded. "Everything okay?"

"I think my brother hasn't grasped where I am at the moment. He wants me to check on Mum."

"Where is she?"

"North London."

Hugo stared at me. "And he lives…?"

"About three miles away."

Hugo burst out laughing, his deep voice bouncing around the room. My sense of humour reasserted itself and I joined in.

"There are some occasions when I devoutly wish to be an only child, despite the fact that I love my brother dearly, with all his faults!" I said, wiping my eyes.

"Choose your friends, but not your family," agreed Hugo, stirring milk into his tea. "I'm surprised, if I'm honest. I wouldn't have thought you'd be guilt tripped like that."

I thought about it, uncomfortable that through Hugo's eyes, I could be seen as a doormat. "I've sort of taken control since my dad died," I said at last. "And I suppose they've got used to me doing things for them."

"Will you be able to continue with that in your new job?"

The simple question made me pause. My family had taken centre stage, and I'd tucked elements of my job around them. If I was going to take the gallery forward as I had envisaged, I wouldn't be so available. I nibbled my lip. I'd made a start, I told myself. Hugo was still watching me.

"I'll just have to wean them off me," I said, and sought to change the subject. "You have a brother and sister, I thought you said."

He nodded. "Carol is my little sister. She's in the Italian alps being a ski instructor."

"What about your brother?" There was silence. "I'm sorry, please don't feel obliged to answer; I'm too nosy for my own good," I said quickly, my stomach sinking. He shook his head.

"No, it's fine. Pierce is a PR consultant. He set up his own business a few years ago."

"Through the pandemic?" Hugo nodded. "Wow, tough gig."

"Yes, it was. And it still seems to be so." His expression was sombre, and I had the feeling there was something more to it than a bad economic climate. So, secrets in the family?

"I'm sorry," I said softly. "I imagine it's hard to see him struggling."

Hugo drummed his fingers on the table and stood up, his well-shaped mouth twisted a little. "Yes, it is. Anyway – I'm going to sort out the generator."

"Can I help?"

His brown eyes raked over me and his lips tweaked. "Not dressed like that, and I don't have overalls to fit you. So, no."

"In which case, I'll clear up here and have a look at the fridge," I said, collecting the breakfast crockery. He frowned.

"Why?"

"Because the power has been off all night, and I imagine we might need to use anything we can for dinner before it goes off. The freezer should be safe for a few hours yet."

A smile spread across his face. "Please don't feel obliged. Is this some kind of cooking programme contestant fantasy?"

"I've never cooked on an Aga and I like a challenge. And to be clear, I *can* cook. Well, normally, anyway."

"Good luck. Agas aren't for the faint hearted!" he said, and left to tackle the generator. My eyes followed him through the back kitchen window as he forced his arms into his overalls. I needed to resurrect some barriers. This was too friendly a conversation to be having with a client, despite the unusual circumstances. I'd wanted to cook to try to reduce my obligation to Hugo Cavendish in some weird calculation in my head.

I glanced at the sky, bright blue with fluffy white clouds, and sent a silent prayer to the gods for improved weather.

I turned from the window and opened the fridge.

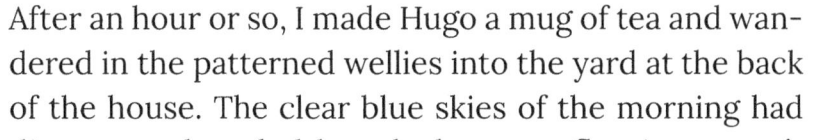

After an hour or so, I made Hugo a mug of tea and wandered in the patterned wellies into the yard at the back of the house. The clear blue skies of the morning had disappeared, and although the snow flurries weren't heavy, it was freezing.

The outbuildings were scattered around what I imagined had been the stables, but like the house, the buildings were well kept. I found Hugo cursing under his breath as he carefully poured petrol into the generator, shaking his head. I coughed softly and he looked up and saw the tea.

"Thank you. Could you put it over there, on the shelf?"

I turned, and at the very end of the workshop, saw the wooden workbench and a series of immaculately kept shelves, with square containers, all neatly labelled. As I put the tea on the bench, I examined the labels. There were screws, drill bits, nails and wrenches, plus tools I didn't even recognise, all carefully stored and easily accessible.

"Wow. This is impressive," I commented.

"I like a tidy workshop."

Silence fell and I knew I should leave. "How's it going?" I said instead. "I didn't think you'd be this long. Don't you just fire it up?"

"The diesel fuel was old, and I've had to drain it." He nodded to a tray of black greasy liquid sitting on one side of the generator.

"Oh. I knew petrol could be out of date, because I used Dad's lawnmower. I suppose I might have guessed that diesel does the same."

"You have a garden?"

"No, but Mum does. I've got a ground floor flat. I've got some pots and a bit of a patio, but no grass."

"I'd find it hard to be in London in the summer without a garden," he said, focusing on a particular nut.

I laughed. "Yeah, it can be a bit steamy. I usually jump on a train and head out to Margate or Brighton to get some sea air."

"Along with the other half of London?" he said with a twinkle.

I shrugged. "There's enough sea air to go round."

CHAPTER 16

A smile grew on his face, and I found myself responding. For a moment, neither of us spoke, and I felt the hair at the back of my neck stand up as his expression warmed. I made my excuses and hurried away.

I retreated to the library. I wandered over to the shelves to pick a book and noticed the small group of photos on the desk. There was a photo of a diminutive woman and an upright gentleman with a fine moustache. I saw a resemblance around the eyes; these were his parents. A tall, willowy blonde posed by a sports car, laughing at the camera, her white teeth small and even.

"I think you're Carol," I muttered, recognising the strong jaw, although she'd escaped the family nose, which obviously came from Hugo's mother. The final photo was of Hugo with a man with a shock of dark brown hair and a beard. The man was scowling slightly, his brows low over intense eyes. I wondered if this was Pierce, although the family resemblance was less strong. I itched to pick up the photos and look more closely, but restrained myself, and instead chose a book and returned to the kitchen.

At lunchtime, Hugo put his head around the door. I put down *Persuasion*, one of my favourite Austen novels.

"Take what you like from the pantry for lunch. Do I guess what dinner is?" he said.

"Cheese soufflé," I said smugly. "With salad and bread. Assuming I've conquered your Aga." I make a cracking cheese soufflé in normal circumstances and hoped I wouldn't fail on the new stove. His eyebrows rose and I gave him a sweet smile.

"Sounds delicious. I'll be putting the generator on in the next couple of minutes," he said, and I nodded, looking forward to proper light in the house.

The dishwasher whooshed into action as the power returned, and all the lights on the bank of coffee machines and microwaves flickered into life, each with the incorrect time.

When Hugo came down later that afternoon, I wondered if he'd given himself the same talking-to that I had given myself this morning. A layer of formality settled over our interactions. He sat at the kitchen table with his laptop, and I continued to look at, if not to actually read, my book.

When his phone rang, I jumped, just catching the mug of now-cold tea that I had been nursing.

"I need to take this," he said, and walked out, leaving the door slightly ajar.

I headed for the now-operational kettle to brew another tea and heard Hugo's exasperated voice from the library.

"What, *again*? Pierce, I've never known anyone go through money as fast as you! Do you burn it?"

I stopped dead and quietly shut the door. I picked up my book and pretended to read until Hugo returned five minutes later. His face was expressionless.

"Everything okay?" I said hesitantly.

He seemed to recover his good manners with an effort. "Yes, of course. Can I help with dinner?"

"You could chop the salad," I said.

He grinned. "I'll just finish these emails first. I'll build a fire in the library, too. It'll be more comfortable."

When he returned, I was whipping eggs. I was ridiculously self-conscious to have him watch me cook. He offered me a glass of wine. I shook my head, imagining myself knocking it over. When he sat at the table, he seemed restless.

"How did you start working for Gerrard?" he said at last.

"I worked at an advertising agency, and I was getting a bit fed up of the backbiting," I said, beginning to make the sauce for the soufflé. "Everyone was scrambling for promotion, and I got tired of being trampled in the process. It coincided with a big exhibition of David Hockney, and I was inspired by his vision of the world. I saw a tiny ad in the *Guardian* newspaper for a gallery administrator, and I could do everything Gerrard wanted, so I applied. I liked Gerrard and felt I understood him – he was like a lot of the directors in the agency, lots of vision and..."

I paused. I had been about to say, "not much practical sense", but that would have been disloyal to Gerrard. "And just needing some support in implementation," I amended.

"Right." I looked up at Hugo, whose knowing twinkle made me wonder again if he'd read my thoughts. "And he's appropriately appreciative of your talents?"

"He is," I said firmly. "He completely supports my plans to grow the use of the gallery. Could you please set the table?"

"What are your plans?" he asked as he gathered cutlery.

I told him more about the mezzanine. I had artists' talks, book launches, an entertaining space all in my sights. As we ate, I realised I hadn't talked to anyone about my work in this depth – ever. Not to Joe, not even to Gerrard, who skim-read my proposals and waved them through unless the numbers were too high. I warmed under Hugo's interest.

Nearly an hour later, Hugo put his knife and fork together. "That was delicious," he said. "I've always wanted to be able to cook a cheese soufflé, but mine turn out disasters."

I meant to say something light-hearted, but the only words that swirled through my mind were, "It's a delight to spend time with someone who listens, who's appreciative, who seems genuinely interested in me…" And they were too revealing, too intimate, too true.

So I said nothing, but just smiled, and his eyes narrowed. "I'll clear up," he said.

I nodded, and briefly his hand covered mine; the jolt that went through my system made my lips part. His eyes locked on mine. "Go and sit in the library," he said, his voice gravelly.

I fled.

Chapter 17

GROSVENOR SQUARE, LATE MARCH 1803

Anne nodded to an acquaintance of her husband who had just tipped his hat to her, before Stoneley, the short, sturdy groom, handed her into the carriage. She was a little breathless – negotiating carriage steps while nearly seven months pregnant was bound to be awkward, particularly given the bustle of Piccadilly – but she at least had colour in her cheeks. And she looked *happy*, Harriet thought as she settled herself opposite her and lifted the black lace veil on her hat.

"You look better," she observed. "Do you feel as well as you look?"

Anne beamed at her. "The spring sunshine helps! Are you happy with your purchases?" Anne nodded at the parcel of books recently acquired from Hatchards.

"Oh, yes! I can read for you this afternoon, should you wish?" Harriet replied, thinking of the volume of Scott's *The Lay of the Last Minstrel*, which would, she was reliably informed, focus them on the picturesque topic of sixteenth century Border society.

"Ah, I need to rest," Anne said, dismayed. "Phillip has suggested we use our box at the opera. Mr Braham and Mrs Storace are performing *The Clemency of Titus*. I understand she sings like an angel."

Harriet smiled to see her face. "You goose! We can read any time, but Mr Braham and Mrs Storace are not to be missed! I saw her in a comic opera in Covent Garden when I was first married and thought she had excellent timing."

"You'll accompany us?"

"Of course!"

Harriet's anticipated pleasure for the opera lasted for much of the afternoon, until a letter was delivered while she was reading in her pretty, yellow and white bedchamber. Recognising Augusta's cramped handwriting, Harriet could feel the joy draining from her body. She straightened in her chair and, her lips firmly pressed together, opened the seal.

I trust you have not forgotten the Duty you owe to John? I have recently received correspondence from an acquaintance who tells me you visit circulating libraries and go driving in the Ring. I dismissed such ridiculous notions, knowing you for the well-meaning, if not always sensible Wife of my beloved son, who would not offend convention nor denigrate the name of the family to whom she is so deeply indebted.

I have now recovered from the journey from Colchester Hall to York – such jolting roads, with peril lurking around every bend! Indeed, such was the discomfort that I took immediately to my bed, and it is only last week that Burgess allowed me to leave my chamber.

"Ah, Dr Burgess," Harriet murmured. "Always available to provide the medical advice that would enable Mama to do exactly as she wishes." The next paragraph drew her eye.

Edwin plans to return to England before the end of the season and I have given him your direction; he is much

CHAPTER 17

fatigued by his travels and intends to recover a little in Calais before embarking on the crossing Home.

Harriet's heart sank. She dreaded to think what Phillip would think of the foppish, foolish Edwin, whose will was so easily moulded by his aunt.

I sincerely hope that you will return to Colchester Hall shortly – surely Lady Rochford will be brought to bed soon? John entrusted you with the assets of the Colchester family and they must not be left to dwindle to ruin while you pursue pleasure in London.

"Ooh!" burst out Harriet, clenching her hand around the letter. "Could you not have thought well of me? That I was here for Anne, rather than for my own *pleasure*?" She paced the room with quick strides, breathing heavily, her thoughts in chaos. She finally came to a halt and forced her shoulders down from her ears, a numbness settling in her core. A quiet knock sounded on her chamber door, and Anne peeped into the room, her arms full of silk dress.

"I wanted your opinion on this dress—" Anne stopped, her eyes on Harriet's face. "What is it?"

Harriet shook her head. "I do not think I can come to the opera with you," she said in a flat voice.

Anne's soft mouth fell open. "But dearest, why? Are you unwell? Or—" Anne caught sight of the letter. "Is it bad news?"

"No, no. But – I have had second thoughts about the opera. I don't feel it's seemly to me to socialise just yet."

Anne was silent and Harriet felt her disappointment keenly. "I'm sorry," she added, lamely.

"The letter was from Augusta, was it not?" Anne said, dismissing her apology with an impatient gesture. "Don't let her sway your behaviour with outdated notions," she continued, correctly identifying the cause of Harriet's change of heart. "Phillip is a very conventional man, and he sees nothing amiss in attending the opera."

"No, Anne, my mind is made up."

"I feared it would be. You can be astoundingly stubborn." Anne sighed and then asked her opinion of the gown she was going to wear. Harriet, blinking at the change of subject, considered the rich magenta against Anne's pale cream complexion. She screwed up her nose.

"No?" Anne said anxiously.

"I think, when the baby comes and you can eat to your heart's content, this gown will be wonderful, but I feel you're a little wan for it. I love the apple-green brocade, or your jade lace – both really bring out your eyes but flatter your complexion."

"Of course! I knew I could count on you! Thank you!" Anne kissed her on the cheek and went out of the room trailing the despised magenta silk behind her.

Harriet stared at the closed door for a minute and then scolded herself for inaction. She picked up a book and lay on the chaise, where she stayed for the next half hour, not reading a word.

She was in the drawing room, grimly hanging on to her principles, when Lady Porter-Hume and Alexander arrived to take up Phillip and Anne in their carriage. On hearing the news that Harriet was unable to join them, Alexander scowled, making him look rather saturnine.

Lady Porter-Hume pursed her lips thoughtfully and then patted Harriet's hand. "You must be comfortable, of course, but do not concern yourself. I have a niece who is wild to see Mrs Storace and I will send a note. I imagine she would be happy to join us."

"At this notice?" Anne looked doubtful, but Lady Porter-Hume waved aside her concerns.

"Tsk! She shares some of my traits – can dress in a trice!"

Lady Porter-Hume scribbled a short note and then was happy to take a glass of madeira. Alexander came to sit next to Harriet and said in a low voice, "I am very sorry that you will not join us. What has caused this?"

"I had a letter from Mama—"

"Ah! All is explained!"

"She merely reminded me that I was in mourning!"

"But you are not dead, too!" Alexander stopped short, seeing her face. "I beg your pardon. I can see that my frankness has shocked you. But your conduct has been beyond reproach! A visit to the opera, with close friends, is unexceptionable, surely?"

"I do not feel comfortable and will do better at home," Harriet said through stiff lips. "Pray say no more."

"Of course," he said with barely suppressed frustration, and stood to speak to Lord Rochford.

The party prepared to leave twenty minutes later, but just as the ladies were pulling on their gloves, a footman passed a note to Lady Porter-Hume. She scanned it and smiled.

"Capital! Georgiana can join us if we can pick her up *en route*! And indeed, we can, it is but a detour of a few streets. Mr Richardson, although as her aunt I can be said to have a decided preference, I believe she is a charming girl and prettily behaved."

"I look forward to making her acquaintance," Alexander responded civilly. He turned and gave Harriet a slight bow and then walked to the carriage.

Harriet was chilled at the formality of his leave-taking, which indicated he was still cross, but kissed Anne and waved them off from the front door. She trailed to her chamber, feeling out of sorts, determined to read an improving book and feel quietly virtuous and happy doing her duty.

As it was, she slept very poorly and was heavy-eyed when she arrived at breakfast the following morning. Phillip was breakfasting when she opened the door; he rose to his feet and wished her a good morning.

"How was the opera?"

"To tell the truth, I went because Anne so loves the music – seemed a lot of vocal acrobatics to me," Phillip admitted, his grey eyes rueful. Harriet smiled as she helped herself to eggs and ham. His indifference to the performance made her feel somewhat soothed that she had missed the outing.

However, when Anne arrived a quarter-hour later, she was considerably more enthusiastic than Phillip, who kissed the top of her head and retreated to his study in the middle of her accolade.

"Did the whole party enjoy the performance?" Harriet asked.

"Oh, Miss Georgiana Porter-Hume was in transports! We were all quite taken with her; she was so amiable and pretty, although of course, very young. She is not yet eighteen." Anne took a sip of her hot potion, paused and then smiled, satisfied that she would not be unwell. "Well! I may try some gruel later today – I am feeling optimistic. Would you like more coffee, dear?"

"I have sufficient, thank you. Was Mr Richardson also quite taken with her?"

"Oh, yes! I was surprised how his manner – which can be quite stern, you know! – softened as the evening went on."

"Indeed."

"Well, it *is* high time he was setting up his nursery, Harriet – oh, are you finished? Are you quite well? You look a little pale."

"I am very well. I fancy I would like to ride today. Could I borrow a hack from the stable?"

Anne nodded absently. "Of course, please ask Coates to send a message to the stable. I'm unable to join you, obviously – you'll remember to take a groom."

"Of course."

Harriet turned abruptly to leave the room, her breathing rather hurried. She needed some fresh air.

Less than an hour later, a veiled Harriet was trotting through Grosvenor Gate to the green expanse of Hyde Park. Stoneley followed at a discreet distance. She felt the tension begin to drain slowly from her shoulders as she rode, and inwardly she chided herself for not riding more regularly. She realised that one of the last occasions she had been riding had been with Alexander, back at Colchester Hall. She sighed. Since she had been in town and in society again, the formality between them had perforce grown. She missed their easy conversation and camaraderie, which made her feel less alone.

Anne was slowly recovering her strength and a little weight, which boded well, Harriet hoped. But as Anne's energy grew, Harriet's mind turned to the next trial –

that of the birth itself. Childbirth was such a hazardous event that Phillip was additionally protective of his wife. Their obvious affection often made Harriet feel *de trop*, even if she was glad for such a strong bond between them.

Stoneley coughed and Harriet belatedly became aware that a man had raised his hat to her. She nodded and wished him a good morning. It was, she knew, a little odd for her to be riding in the Park in the morning, rather than the more fashionable hours of the afternoon, and for a moment, she tightened her lips as she turned over in her mind What Augusta Would Say. The grey mare sidled a little as she tensed, and with an effort, Harriet forced herself to relax.

"Shall we gallop?" she said over her shoulder to Stoneley, and had barely received his response when she urged on the mare and sped away.

Caught in the pleasure of her ride, she only gradually became aware of someone calling her name. Reluctantly, she pulled on the reins and wheeled the mare around to see, much to her surprise, Alexander, looking rather cross.

"Alex— Mr Richardson!" she corrected herself swiftly. "Good morning!"

"Mrs Colchester, I am glad to have caught you!" he replied, bringing his mount to a halt and sweeping off his hat. "You're so new into town, you may not know that galloping in Hyde Park is generally frowned on. I wanted to warn you."

Harriet felt her mouth drop and responded immediately. "All this space, and you can't shake the fidgets out of your horse's legs? What nonsense!"

"But you are keen to avoid society's censure, are you not? If so, you might be advised to restrain yourself."

He sounded stern. Harriet's face grew warm, and she knew she had blushed to the roots of her hair. She drew a deep breath and leaned down to pat the mare's neck. "Ah. Thank you for the advice, sir."

There was an uncomfortable silence, which was broken when a laughing voice said, "Oh, it is such a shame! You ride so well, ma'am!"

Harriet looked up to see a lovely young woman wearing an exquisitely cut habit in cerulean velvet smiling at her. The stranger had guinea-gold curls, large blue eyes and a straight pert nose, and Harriet immediately felt dowdy and every one of her twenty-four years. A maid, her mouth straight and severe, rode up behind this vision. Harriet stopped staring and remembered her manners.

"Hello, we've not been introduced. I am Mrs Colchester."

"I know. Mr Richardson said it was you when we saw you flash by us! I'm Georgiana Porter-Hume, niece to Lady Porter-Hume."

"How do you do?" murmured Harriet, glancing between Alexander, sitting stiffly on his horse, and Miss Porter-Hume, a picture on a white pony.

"I must thank you! While I am sorry you were indisposed for the opera, I was in transports! Although I feel it wasn't *quite* to Mr Richardson's taste!" Miss Porter-Hume added with a twinkle at Alexander. He smiled ruefully and Harriet felt rather ill.

"I'm pleased you were able to take my place," she lied.

A few more pleasantries were necessary before Harriet was able to make her excuses and continue with her now sedate ride. But the joy had somehow drained from the day.

Chapter 18

BERWICK, FEBRUARY 2023

I peeled open my eyelids at the tinny sound of the wind-up alarm that Hugo had dug out of a drawer for me. It was like one that Mum had to go on holiday – about four inches square and in a case that snapped shut when it was laid flat.

I was a bit groggy, disturbed by dreams of my family telling me off and laughing at the designs that I'd developed for the gallery mezzanine. I stumbled to the window and pushed aside the heavy curtains. The sunshine hit my face and I winced. After a few seconds, my eyes adjusted to see bright blue skies, glittering trees. And it wasn't snowing. I breathed a sigh of relief before remembering that yesterday began with blue skies before it snowed again.

I leaned my forehead on the cold glass, thinking about the strange tension of yesterday evening after dinner. The memory of his fingers on my hand was almost visceral, and I was in danger, I told myself, of overthinking a simple human gesture. He'd seemed to read my mind.

I would check the trains after I'd showered.

I was rubbing my hair dry with a towel when there was a tap on the door.

"One second!" Grabbing a towelling robe that only just overlapped in the middle, I tied the knot as tightly as I could and opened the door a few inches.

"I thought you might like to try on some of my sister's togs," Hugo said, thrusting a pile of clothes at me. Still clutching the robe around me, I put out a hand to take the pile, which promptly tumbled to the floor. I stammered an apology and scooped them up.

Hugo backed away and muttered something about sausages under the grill. I exhaled thankfully as I closed the door. The pile held jeans and a few shirts that I knew immediately wouldn't fit my boobs, but there were also two tee-shirts (a bit small but would stretch) and a couple of oversized sweatshirts. At least these gave me some alternatives to my red cashmere sweater. The jeans were loose on the waist but snug on the hips when I wriggled into them. Catching sight of my bum in the mirror, I wondered if they were too tight, and I hesitated.

"I'm ready to serve!" Hugo called.

No time to change into my wool trousers, I decided. I grabbed one of the sweatshirts, a glorious jade green, tied it round my neck and scampered down the stairs. Hugo was cooking.

"Thanks so much for the clothes," I said to his back.

"No problem. Did they fit?" He turned to look at me and paused, his lips parting. I glanced down and decided that yes, the jeans might be a little tight. And the tee-shirt.

Drat.

"I think your sister might be a size or two smaller than me, but I'm very grateful." Casually, I slipped the sweatshirt off my shoulders and pulled it over my head.

When I emerged from the neck, his face was flushed. He coughed and turned back to the stove, where he stirred baked beans. I made myself some tea and sat down at the table, not sure how to begin the conversation.

I took a swallow of tea and said, "I've checked the trains, and nothing is moving this side of Newcastle, so I'm sorry you're stuck with me for another day. I thought I might look through some of the newspaper archives and do a search for Harriet; she might have done something with some of her money, you know – opened a school, or other good works?"

Hugo nodded, putting a plate in front of me. "I didn't think the railways would start moving just yet. I don't even know when Harriet died," he added. "She inherited her husband's fortune and then seemed to disappear."

"I'll have a look, but do you need me to do anything before I do that?"

Hugo shook his dark blond head. "No, you're fine. I checked the weather and they're predicting more snow."

My heart sank. "Ah." I ate my breakfast. When I'd finished, I threw a glance towards the window, at the blue and white outside.

Hugo followed my gaze. "Do you fancy a walk? I know we probably won't be able to go far, but some fresh air might be a good thing."

For the first time this morning, I examined his face and noticed the slight shadows under his eyes. Had he suffered a disturbed night, too? Or was he feeling irritated by his unexpected visitor?

"Sounds a great idea," I said easily. "I'll go and get my coat, but I'd appreciate some thick socks for those wellies."

"I'll fetch you a pair."

The air was crisp and cold, a proper wake-up call after the snug warmth of the house. It was impossible to not smile as I stood on the drive by the front door, the sun sparkling off the crystalline surface, and I grinned at him as he shut the door and came towards me.

"Here," he said and handed me a pink woolly hat with a white pom-pom on the crown. I pulled a face but slipped it over my head and was immediately grateful for the warmth over my ears. His lips tweaked in a slight smile.

"What?" I said immediately. "Do I look a pillock?"

"You look about seventeen," he said abruptly, and turned to stride towards the fields beyond the garden fence. Clumsy in the flowered wellingtons boots and trying to keep upright in eighteen inches of snow, I followed.

I had a childish yen to build a snowman but wondered if that was beneath my position as assistant gallery manager. So, we walked, admired the white hills and sapphire sky, and talked about nothing much. I relaxed into Hugo's company, until my calves started to ache.

I hid a wince. My generous curves had never graced a gym, and as a Londoner, I generally hibernated in bad weather, so tramping around the countryside was a novel experience.

Hugo glanced at me. "Want to walk a little more?"

I hesitated; I didn't want to offend him, nor appear a weakling, but nor did I want to punish my burning calves further. "Yes, of course," I heard myself say. So, we walked on for another twenty minutes, and then of course it was another twenty minutes on the return journey. I could have wept in relief when he suggested we went back, cursing myself for being so polite.

"Do you play chess?"

His question distracted me from my aching muscles. "I did at school. I'm more of a scrabble girl, myself, but I know my way around a chess board."

His eyes glinted. "I'll challenge you to a game of both, if you like."

I quirked an eyebrow. "You're on."

I hid a smile as we retraced our steps to the house. I played a mean game of scrabble.

"Checkmate." I could almost hear Hugo straining to keep the triumph out of his voice.

I squinted at the board and cursed the careless loss of a knight about three moves ago that had set me up for defeat. "Nice one. Fancy a game of scrabble?"

"Absolutely. More tea? And maybe a tuna sandwich for lunch?"

"Mmm, great, thanks." I cleared the chess pieces away and laid out the scrabble board. I had just finished turning over the last tile in the lid when he returned with a tray. Mango, sniffing tuna, followed close behind.

We munched the rolls, still warm from their defrosting in the microwave. I wiped a piece of tuna from the corner of my mouth, and finally giving in to Mango's unnerving stare, gave him my finger to lick. "You must be running low on groceries," I observed.

"Milk, yes. I don't have much cheese left, but the freezer is well stocked with bread and casseroles and chicken, plus I have a larder full of cans, so we're certainly not going to starve yet. We get snow a lot here, so I've learned to be prepared." He tickled Mango behind the ears and rose to put another log on the fire. I watched the flames greedily lick the wood.

"Do you have a dictionary?" I asked. He stared. "Don't look so surprised; the New Oxford Dictionary is the arbiter of all disputes."

"Of course. I had no idea you took it so seriously," he said slowly, his eyes narrowing. "Why do I get the feeling I'm in for a pasting, suddenly?"

I jumped up and searched for the dictionary, hefting it down from the shelf. "Don't be ridiculous, Hugo. It's just a game."

An hour and a quarter later, he flung his hands up in disgust. "You're kidding me! Who knew 'aardwolf' was a thing?"

"I think you'll find it's 'a nocturnal, black-striped African mammal of the hyena family'," I said smugly, calculating my score. "Stop making such a fuss; it's not even that many points!"

He shook his head. "You knew you'd beat me, didn't you?"

"What, and you didn't think you'd thrash me at chess?" I retorted.

He threw back his head and laughed, while I smirked. "Fair enough."

I opened my mouth to speak and then stopped as the noise of an engine sounded outside the window. Hugo frowned and moved swiftly to look.

"It's a tractor," he murmured. He left the library swiftly and I followed.

CHAPTER 18

He threw open the front door, and around his silhouette, dark in the glare of the snow, I glimpsed a tall, thin man in a parka coat climb down from a farm tractor, fist bump the driver and drag a rucksack over his shoulder. He turned to see Hugo standing at the door.

"Hey, Hugo! How's it going?" the man said in a light, pleasant voice.

"Pierce. I'd have thought you were better staying in Berwick," Hugo said, and I found it impossible to decipher how he was feeling. Pierce threw back his fur-trimmed hood. He was bearded, with a shock of dark brown hair and thick eyebrows.

Pierce stepped forwards into the porch. They were obviously brothers – they shared the same nose and brown eyes, but where Hugo's were dark, Pierce's were light brown.

"I thought I'd come and see how my big brother was doing, and Dave offered the tractor; we'd never had made it otherwise... Hello, who's this?" Pierce caught sight of me, and those thick eyebrows shot up. I forced myself forward, holding out my hand in greeting.

"Hi, I'm Gabriella Sullivan. I've been landed on Hugo because of the snow."

"Really? How did you come to be here?" He shook my hand, and I managed not to wince at his grip.

"She was delivering a parcel for me," Hugo said, closing the front door. "Did you want to leave your stuff in your old room?"

Pierce smiled. "Sure. Could I have a coffee? Cheers."

He brushed past me and took the stairs two at a time; there was an uncomfortable pause as Hugo watched Pierce's lanky, retreating form. Tiny creases of stress had appeared between his eyes that hadn't been there before.

"Shall I put the kettle on?" I asked hesitantly, and Hugo snapped back into the present.

"Not at all. I'll make us all a drink."

Pierce reappeared twenty minutes later in a black tee-shirt and loose jeans, and I suddenly wondered how it must appear to others, me being here with Hugo, alone. I had cleared away the games before Pierce came to the library, feeling as if I'd been caught in *flagrante*. Although that was ridiculous; I was just making the best of a bad job while the trains were disrupted.

Pierce threw himself onto the sofa beside me, and it was all I could do not to shrink up against the cushions away from him. Mango, seeing Pierce arrive, flicked up his tail and stalked away.

"So, what's this parcel you delivered? And who are you, Gabriella Sullivan?"

"I'm assistant manager at Gerrard Williams – it's an art gallery in London."

"You don't look like the average art gallery employee," he said carelessly. I flushed, knowing exactly what he meant. I wasn't very glossy, like many of the gallery assistants I'd seen in rival galleries. Not thin enough, my accent not cut-glass enough. "How fascinating," he added.

"Yes, isn't it?" I replied coolly and he laughed. Close up, his face held more lines than I'd initially seen, and I almost revised my idea of his age. But wasn't he the younger brother?

"Sorry, I didn't sound all that sincere, did I?" he said with a chuckle. "But I am in PR, so it's second nature."

"I'm sure it is. I run the gallery day-to-day, arrange new work to be hung, that kind of thing." I glanced at the door to the library, wondering where Hugo was.

"And deliver parcels? What did you deliver?" He leapt to his feet and started looking around the room, a sharp, restless edge to his energy. He strode to the table, where the miniatures were propped up on their stands. "Was it these paintings?"

"Yes, the person in them is apparently distantly related to you."

"Fascinating." He picked up one of the miniatures and I tensed. "How much did he pay for our ancestor, then?"

"I wasn't part of the negotiations." That at least was true. He spun to look at me, his lip curling slightly.

"Hmm. Assistant gallery manager, you said?"

When Hugo elbowed open the door with the mugs, I breathed out. Hugo glanced at his brother and quietly asked him to put the miniature back in the case. Pierce shrugged and then came to sit down again and slurp his coffee.

A silence fell, and it was almost a relief when a text came from Gerrard. "If you could excuse me a moment, I need to give my boss a call."

I trotted to the bedroom and closed the door. The text from Gerrard was innocuous enough: *Are you okay? Snow melting in town; when do you think you'll be back?*

My watch said a quarter past four. The gallery closed at five on weekdays – it was Friday today, wasn't it? I'd lost all track of time. I dialled and Gerrard picked up on the second ring, his voice rushed and sounding anxious.

"Gabriella! How are you? Is everything all right? Are you still at Cavendish's house?"

"Hi, Gerrard. Yes, I'm fine. Mr Cavendish has been very hospitable, and at least we have power back, so it's quite comfortable. The trains are running south from Newcastle now, so hopefully I'll be on one back to London soon from here! I'll have to see Justin another time."

"It must be a bit awkward for you, I'm so sorry."

"No, he's been a perfect gentleman."

"Keep me posted. And Gabriella – check he doesn't have any further commissions!"

I laughed ruefully as I closed the call. Once a dealer, always a dealer. I dithered about returning downstairs; they might be having brother-to-brother chats, and I didn't want to be in the way. But my drink was downstairs, so presumably I could just go, collect it and then come back up to the room?

As I walked down the staircase, I noticed the rain against the long window and my heart fluttered. It would melt the snow. I could go home.

Chapter 19

GROSVENOR SQUARE, LATE APRIL 1803

Gradually, day by day, Anne declared herself to be stronger. The April weather had improved in London and all kinds of outdoor amusements were available to her, so she became restless.

"You must conserve your strength!" protested Harriet in vain as Anne catalogued her hats and bonnets one afternoon, tossing out those that no longer appealed. "Do think, my dear!"

"But I cannot just lie abed; I will go mad!"

And to be fair, Anne had progressed to gruel and from there to soup, and although she did not always keep these meals down, she believed herself making good progress. Eggs were her next challenge, she had decided.

To make Anne even less amenable to the idea of rest, in a visit one afternoon, Lady Porter-Hume confessed that she had always followed the advice of Lady Emily FitzGerald, who had given birth so many times that visiting during her confinement was almost an annual part of the Dublin social calendar.

"My own mother told me that Lady FitzGerald exercised as usual right up to the time she was brought to bed, and even drove around in a carriage to 'shake things up' when she was near her time," she declared. "Nineteen children and only lost one!"

Hearing this, Harriet closed her eyes in despair. She had no doubt that Emily FitzGerald had also possessed the constitution of an ox, while Anne was still too slender.

But Anne eagerly gathered up this advice, and soon, no entreaty would prevent her heading out to Hookham's Circulating Library, or walking in the Ring at Hyde Park, although Phillip forbade her to ride, or to visit Astley's Royal Amphitheatre.

"The crowds might prevent your leaving, and you are too near your time, Anne," he said firmly.

While Anne might meekly follow her husband's instructions on this, she knew her mind on one thing and nothing would budge her. Dr Thomas was dismissed and instead, a midwife who had waited on Lady Porter-Hume was engaged. Anne had originally wanted to send for Mrs Margaret Earnshaw, but Harriet had gently dissuaded her. Mrs Earnshaw would be needed at the Colchester Hall estate.

Other preparations for Anne's lying-in were enthusiastically supported by the new midwife, Mrs Janes, including advice passed from Dr Charles White, who encouraged exercise, light and plenty of fresh air for the mother-to-be.

"Indeed, I recall as a young child that Mama seemed to be giving birth in a tomb," whispered Anne to Harriet while Mrs Janes organised new curtains for the windows. "I fear now that that might have been prescient, as three of my brothers and sisters died soon after being born."

CHAPTER 19

Harriet read aloud parts of John Locke's *Thoughts on Education*, which eschewed the use of tight swaddling and pins for newborn babies, all of which stung as she considered her own childless state. At one stage, Anne interrupted her reading.

"Are you certain all – all *this*—" Anne gestured to her belly and to the new hangings at the windows, "is not too painful for you?"

Harriet smiled tightly. "You are my dearest friend. I can bear any amount of pain for your sake."

Anne gulped and dashed a tear from her eye. "Then I am indeed blessed, but perhaps we can put Mr Locke down for a while. I should like to hear more of *Belinda*."

With relief, Harriet went in search of the novel.

At dinner, a week later, Anne had just put her lips to her glass of ice water when she gasped. Harriet looked up to see her turn red and then very pale, lips parting. Anne had complained of discomfort throughout the week, feeling pains in her back and lower abdomen.

"What is it?" Harriet said at once.

"Oh! That hurt! I think the baby is coming!"

Calmly, Harriet stood up and rang the bell. Coates arrived and then gawped as Anne doubled over with a groan.

"Coates, please send for Lady Rochford's maid, and then send for Mrs Janes. Also, we need a footman to fetch Lord Rochford. He is at White's tonight, is he not?"

"Yes, ma'am. Will you need assistance with my lady?" Coates looked doubtful, as if Anne might bite.

Harriet huffed with impatience. "No, she's going into labour, not drunk!"

Coates turned and left speedily with a sigh that sounded to Harriet like relief. Suppressing a smile, she took Anne's arm. "Come, my dear. Let us get you to your bedchamber."

Anne clutched her hand. "You will stay with me, won't you?"

"Wild horses couldn't tear me away."

Mrs Janes arrived by the time Harriet had helped Anne from her gown. The midwife beamed as she was shown into the room.

"Excellent, my lady! But you may wish to walk a little, rather than lie abed, at least for a while. Fetch more candles, so we can see what we're about," she said to the maid, who scuttled away.

Anne valiantly tottered around the room, clutching Harriet's arm; Harriet winced with every contraction as Anne's fingernails dug into her flesh. The door flew open, and Phillip almost fell into the room, flushed and with his normally immaculate cravat askew.

"Anne!" he cried as he staggered towards them. Anne looked up with dismay, taking in her husband's appearance with a glance.

"Oh, Phillip! *What* a time to be foxed!"

Phillip, who was indeed in his cups, looked forlorn, and Harriet advised that he might retire to the library where Coates would serve him coffee. "I'll send for you when you're needed," she added and he nodded, walking unsteadily out of the door.

Harriet and Anne exchanged looks and burst out laughing, until another contraction made Anne gasp.

CHAPTER 19

As the hours wore on, Harriet began to worry that Anne's strength would not last. Early on in the evening, she urged Anne to sip iced water, and between contractions, she was able to take small mouthfuls of soup. For a first labour, Mrs Janes said, my lady was doing very well. Anne, drenched in sweat, scowled at this.

It was just past four o'clock in the morning that the baby's head crowned, and Anne gave a mighty scream of pain. Harriet dashed to the door to call Coates to fetch Lord Rochford.

He appeared at a run, much sobered, and immediately went to Anne's side. Anne gripped Phillip's and Harriet's hands on each side while Mrs Janes shouted encouragement from the foot of the bed.

"That's it, one more push, my lady! You're doing splendidly! And here comes baby!" Mrs Janes reached forward to pull the tiny, bloody, scrap into a towel. There was a moment of quiet and Harriet looked up quickly, holding her breath in sudden fear. Then a thin wail rose into the room and Harriet closed her eyes in a silent prayer.

"You've a lovely son, my lady!"

Anne sighed and closed her eyes while Mrs Janes cut the cord. Phillip clasped the baby and Harriet immediately began to chafe Anne's cold hand. Mrs Janes, narrowing her eyes, shouted for more hot water.

"Anne, my love!" said Phillip, his eyes full of tears. "Look at our son! Stay strong for our son!"

Anne's eyes flickered open and she smiled as the baby was laid on her breast. "He is beautiful, is he not?" she murmured. Then she closed her eyes.

"Rub her hands, Mrs Colchester," Mrs Janes commanded. "Keep her warm. She's not bleeding, so that's a good thing. Wake her if you can, while I rub her with hot towels. My Lord, go to the head of the bed and talk to her. Girl," she said to the maid, "take the babe and wash him gently, water not too hot. Then dress him and wrap him in a blanket, not tightly. Then get the wet nurse."

For another two hours, Anne drifted in and out of consciousness. Harriet scolded her, patted her cheeks and mopped her with hot flannels, rubbing her briskly with warm towels. Their efforts met with limited success. Both she and Phillip were beginning to despair, and at nearly five o'clock in the morning, Anne gave a sigh and closed her eyes.

Harriet moaned in anguish and Mrs Janes reached over to pat her hand.

"Hush! All is well," said Mrs Janes. "Look at my lady's face."

Harriet peered at Anne to see her cheeks gently flushed and her chest softly rising and falling.

Anne was asleep.

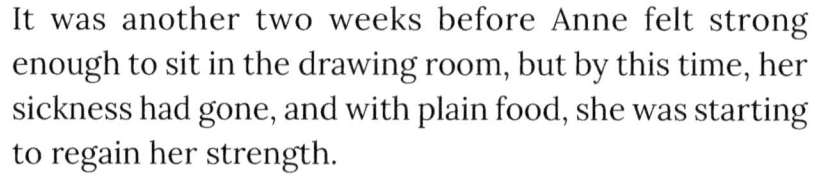

It was another two weeks before Anne felt strong enough to sit in the drawing room, but by this time, her sickness had gone, and with plain food, she was starting to regain her strength.

Following Anne's descent to the drawing room, and with baby James in fine fettle, visitors to the Grosvenor Square house increased. With Lady Porter-Hume now came Lord Benborough, a slender, attractive man with pale blond hair and a sweetness of expression that warmed Harriet's heart. They were joined by Miss Georgiana Porter-Hume, who was as kind as she was beautiful, however hard Harriet tried to dislike her, and of course Alexander. A number of Phillip's friends also paid their respects, and Anne declared that a day barely went past without visitors.

Harriet therefore saw Alexander often, but she noticed how far reserve had crept into their previously cordial exchanges. She was surprised to discover how much she missed their previous intimacy and watched with a jaundiced eye as Georgiana seemed to charm him from his stern demeanour.

One afternoon, Miss Porter-Hume was talking about a recent visit to the painter Thomas Lawrence in Greek Street.

"I saw his portrait of Lady Caroline Lamb and liked it prodigiously!" she said. "Ma'am, will you commission a portrait of you and baby James?"

"Of course, although I do not know whether James will lie still long enough!" Anne said, smiling. "Although a miniature may be the answer! Mrs Colchester, do you remember when you sat for that very strange-looking creature when you were first married?"

"Richard Cosway," Harriet supplied, recalling that the portrait had taken the painter only two hours. "He was very gifted. John treasured it." She smiled, fondly remembering John's delight.

"You must surely have changed since that time; you might sit again," commented Lady Porter-Hume.

"A wonderful notion!" said Lord Benborough, hazel eyes sparkling.

Harriet laughed. "I am not so vain! I see enough in the glass every morning!"

"Oh, but Mr Cosway managed to capture such a spark of you!" Anne insisted, and Alexander nodded.

"I agree. It was a rare portrait," he said in his deep voice. "Your friends insist you repeat, it, Mrs Colchester, if only to see how gracefully the years sit on you."

Harriet looked straight at him, feeling a blush touch her cheeks. A moment passed when it could have been only the two of them in the room. Something loosened in Harriet's chest and she took a deep breath.

"Yes. Yes, it might be amusing. I will enquire," she said.

Given all the discussion of the proposed portraits, one of Anne's first excursions was to the Royal Academy.

But they were a little late and the rooms were already crowded. The party had been obliged to wait for Lady Porter-Hume, who had business at the family bank that morning.

Harriet was a little taken aback. "But how is she involved?" she said in low tones to Anne. "I never heard of such a thing – I understood banking was solely the preserve of gentlemen."

"She was left shares in Hume Bank when her mother died, and is therefore a senior partner," Anne replied. "Phillip says she even attends the Fleet Street premises regularly and reviews the accounts!"

"How extraordinary!" Harriet murmured, but as she turned the matter over in her head, she realised that she had been reviewing the accounts of Colchester Hall since she was nineteen. A smaller enterprise, she had no doubt, but still, her efforts used at least some of the same skills. She was left wondering what else she might do, as a female with a large fortune.

CHAPTER 19

When Lady Porter-Hume finally arrived, richly dressed in dark green brocade that made her chestnut hair glow, Harriet looked at her with different eyes. Lady Porter-Hume, in turn, regarded Harriet thoughtfully. When the party alighted from the carriage, she put her arm through Harriet's and pulled her to one side.

"The galleries on the first floor will be a bear-garden," she said, comfortably. "I have a yearning to see the sculpture, if you will indulge me."

The exhibition of sculpture was disappointing to Harriet's eyes, though she would be the first to admit she knew little about the art form. Lady Porter-Hume was undeterred, however, searching through the twenty or so exhibits in the cramped, dark, ground-floor room with a handful of other visitors.

"Hmm. An undistinguished display," Lady Porter-Hume said with a sniff. "But this is what I wanted to see." She stopped in front of a terracotta bust and peered at it. "Ah. Yes. I see what Horace meant."

A tall, stately woman walked from the side of the room. "Pardon me, ma'am – did you mention my godfather?"

Harriet stared at the woman. She had dark curly hair and a long, clever face. She was dressed very plainly, and although the fabric of the gown was fine, it sported no lace, no frills, and was almost masculine in cut.

Lady Porter-Hume turned sharply, and she beamed at the stranger. "You are Miss Damer?"

The lady nodded her head. "Anne Seymour Damer, ma'am. And who do I have the pleasure of addressing?"

"I am Lady Porter-Hume, and this is Mrs Colchester. I knew your godfather some years ago, and I'm sorry for your loss."

Miss Damer put up her sharp chin. "Thank you. Although it is nearly six years ago, I miss his counsel."

"And his conversation, I imagine," Lady Porter-Hume replied dryly. Miss Damer laughed.

"Indeed. He was a man of rare intelligence. Are you pleased with my terracotta bust of Princess Caroline, Mrs Colchester?" Miss Damer turned to Harriet

"It is charming. Will you render it in bronze?" Harriet said, a little out of her depth.

"I will. Are you a fan of sculpture, ma'am?"

"I hesitate to answer, given that my lack of knowledge would likely embarrass me, but I like your exhibit, Miss Damer. It seems a fine piece to me."

Miss Damer smiled. Lady Porter-Hume hunted in her reticule and withdrew a calling card.

"I should be pleased to receive you, Miss Damer, should you be passing Portland Square."

"I should be delighted," Miss Damer said, taking the card. "You must see Mr Turner's painting. I was on my way to look at it; it has caused much comment."

The three women made their way up the stairs and eventually found Lord Porter-Hume, Alexander and Georgiana. Anne was sitting on a chair, fanning herself. Harriet shouldered her way through the crowds and knelt by Anne's chair, grasping her hand, concerned.

"I am well, just a little tired. You must see the *Calais Pier*," Anne said with a smile. She glanced at Miss Damer and her eyes widened at her clothes. Lady Porter-Hume stepped forward and made the introductions, identifying Miss Damer as an artist and sculptor. Georgiana smiled prettily and suggested they battle with the crowds to see the picture.

"I have seen it," Alexander said, his gaze narrowing. "I'll remain here with Anne."

Reluctantly Harriet pushed through the mass of people, all speaking in excitement in front of the painting, which was hanging opposite the entrance to the Great Room. Harriet, eyes round, stared at the scene, the swirls of paint, the ragged people.

"What is your opinion, Mrs Colchester?" asked Miss Damer.

"It is immediate, almost overwhelming," Harriet said, thoughtfully. "But it seems – different. New, almost. I can imagine it causing a stir."

"Bravo, Mrs Colchester. The Academy has very mixed opinions. Some think it brilliant; others dismiss it as inappropriately radical. I am in the former camp."

"But are you not a radical, Miss Damer?" Harriet said, thinking that sculpture was not traditionally a woman's art form.

Almond-shaped eyes gleamed at her, and a tiny smile lifted the wide mouth. "Some say so, I believe."

Harriet paused, hearing something under the words. When Georgiana joined them, it was to say that Anne was now ready to leave. Harriet bade Miss Damer farewell, still curious.

As they returned to the chair where Anne was sitting, Harriet was surprised to see a small group of ladies clustering around Alexander, including a number of richly dressed matrons and what looked like their daughters. Harriet counted seven or eight women and bent to Anne.

"Who are all these people?" she whispered to her.

Anne giggled. "Mr Richardson is becoming quite the catch! Calling Lady Porter-Hume a friend has indicated his wealth and enables the good matrons to pass over his lack of a title." Anne glanced at Harriet's face and patted her hand. "You must agree; Mr Richardson is a handsome man."

Harriet was at a loss for words and turned to find Lady Porter-Hume, who had overheard Anne's comment, watching her.

"You look almost wistful at the mention of marriage, Mrs Colchester. Perhaps we need to consider finding you a husband," Lady Porter-Hume said, and Harriet was startled.

"I am not yet out of mourning!" she exclaimed. Lady Porter-Hume put her head on one side and said nothing, and Harriet continued airily, "And I find myself enjoying my independence."

"Ah, indeed. But would you relinquish your fortune for love?"

Harriet laughed. "I have yet to fall in love, ma'am."

Alexander raised his head and his gaze caught hers, his face still. Harriet hurried to follow Anne to the carriage.

Chapter 20

CENTRAL LONDON, FEBRUARY 2023

London had returned to greyness by the time I rolled into Kings Cross station the following afternoon, with drenched pavements and piles of dirty snow at the side of the tracks as I stared out of the window.

After Pierce arrived, the restrained, but nonetheless comfortable atmosphere that rested between Hugo and me had changed to something much spikier, as if one wrong word would cause a bomb to detonate. The evening after Pierce's arrival, we dined on beef pie and frozen veg from the freezer, and I forced myself to sit with them in the sitting room, rather than the library. This was a bigger and more formal room that took longer to make cosy with a fire. It was then that I noticed that Hugo didn't possess a television and, God help us all, we were forced to talk to one another.

I made an unfortunate observation. "It's interesting to think that Sophia and Harriet would have had to make conversation, rather than be entertained."

"Who?" Pierce asked, looking up from a large whisky.

I frowned. Hugo hadn't explained more about the miniatures? Bum. Oh, well. It wasn't really my problem. I was just the courier. "Sophia is the sister of Harriet Colchester, the lady in the miniatures."

Pierce turned his gaze to Hugo. "Are they by anyone famous?"

There seemed to be an edge to his voice. Hugo shrugged. "I bought them for their relevance to our family history, rather than being concerned about the artist."

"Right." Pierce seemed to lose interest, and I kept my mouth shut. Obviously, Hugo thought it was none of Pierce's business.

It was a tense evening, despite Pierce's humorous stories of client demands and PR cock-ups. Checking the trains passed fifteen minutes, and it seemed as though the rail company were hopeful that journeys would resume the following day. I agreed that I would check the website in the morning, and Hugo said he would drop me at the station in Berwick in the Land Rover if there were no cabs to be had. We shared a few rueful anecdotes of journeys where trains were missed or stops passed through inattention.

But all in all, I was glad to bid them both goodnight.

I closed the door to the sitting room, and on impulse, walked to the library to pick up my book. But as soon as I flicked on the light, my eyes were drawn to the portraits, resting on Hugo's desk. The elder Harriet eyed me steadily, and I could have sworn I saw her eyebrow tweak as if to ask me what on earth was happening.

"Beats me," I muttered to her and picked up the copy of *Persuasion*. But having collected the book, I lingered, looking again at the miniatures. I was startled at how sad I was to lose sight of them and, pulling out my phone, took more pictures. Then I went to bed, feeling as if my shiny heart had been dulled.

CHAPTER 20

In the morning, the first train I could catch was at two-fifteen. I insisted on calling for a cab, and to my relief, a driver agreed to pick me up. Although the drive up to Cavendish Lodge was still laden with snow, the main roads had cleared somewhat. Hugo spent the morning clearing a path from the front door to the drive. Mango supervised from inside the porch.

Pierce waved a careless hand at me from the kitchen when I'd pulled my coat on and then disappeared. I was left with Hugo at the front door, while the driver executed a nine-point turn among the piled-up snow to take me away.

"Making a right pig's ear of that, isn't he?" Hugo observed, and I laughed.

"I don't care, as long as he can take me away!" I said and Hugo looked askance. I launched into apology mode. "I didn't mean that as it sounded! You've been so kind!"

He laughed, the first natural sound to come out of his mouth since his brother had appeared. I made to speak again, and he shook his head.

"No, don't say anything else! You're very welcome, Miss Gabriella Sullivan, and I apologise for being so prickly when we first spoke. You make a wonderful cheese soufflé, and it's been a pleasure to get to know you a little."

The cab finally faced back down the drive. But now I was reluctant to leave.

"I'll be in touch if I discover anything else about Sophia or Harriet," I promised, and his dark eyes glinted.

"That would make us quits, Gabriella."

He shook my hand, his grip warm and firm, his palm smooth. I climbed into the cab and didn't look back. I spent the whole train journey in a kind of numb silence.

There was no getting away from it – I felt strange, a bit irritable, a little lost. Gerrard had been delighted to hear I was on my way back, fed up with fending off the builders who had been waiting to speak to me about the mezzanine. Joe had promised me fish and chips as a coming home present. With the sole exception of Aunt Mo, there had been no response to the WhatsApp message I'd sent to our family group that I was returning from the wilds of Northumberland.

That stung. It hurt that Mum hadn't responded, and a slow anger began to build in me. Had I been in their position, I'd have been on the phone daily to check how I was. Hugo Cavendish could have been an axe murderer, or a womanising seducer. Obviously, he wasn't, and Gerrard had known where I was but...

As I passed the newsagents in the station, a bold black and yellow book cover caught my eye.

The Gentle Art of Saying 'No' – and Meaning It

How to reclaim your life and stop arranging other peoples'

I stopped dead. This was what I needed. I needed to say no to my family more often. I slipped inside the store and bought a copy.

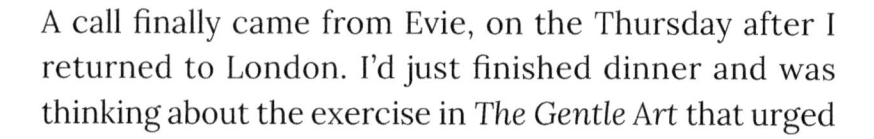

A call finally came from Evie, on the Thursday after I returned to London. I'd just finished dinner and was thinking about the exercise in *The Gentle Art* that urged me to use the broken record technique to anyone who wouldn't take no for an answer.

"Hi, Gabs. Are you back, then?"

"For a few days now. Didn't you see my post on the family WhatsApp group?"

"Gosh, really? Mind you, I've been frantic. Anyway, I'm glad you're back. I'm ringing you about the twins' birthday..."

No, it wouldn't be to ask how three days snowed in in the house of a complete stranger had affected me, would it? I sighed. The twins' birthday was right at the beginning of March. Their birthday party was an explosion of sugar and food colouring, and I remembered last year...

"... it's just that she's told me she now can't make it, and I wondered if you could step in?"

I snapped back to the conversation. "Sorry?"

"I know it's a bit short notice, but you're so good at these things, and I certainly don't want to end up taking them to MacDonald's or Pizza Hut!"

"Back up a bit," I said, swinging my legs off the sofa and sitting up. "Who can't make it?"

"The caterer – didn't you hear me?"

"How many kids are coming to this party?"

"About twenty-five, plus some parents of course."

I stood up and breathed in slowly through my nose. "Can I just check? You'd like me to cater for probably forty-plus people at your children's party with two days' notice?"

"Well, yes, but you've done the catering before!"

I had, and it had taken weeks to completely clean the jelly from the inside of my fridge. I took a deep breath, preparing to try out advice from *The Gentle Art of Saying*

'No'. "I'm not free, I'm afraid, so I can't do this for you," I said, firmly. Keep saying No. Over and over again.

"What?" Evie sounded horrified. "But – but they're your nephews!"

"And they're your sons," I returned, reasonably. "Find another caterer. Ask people to make a dish and bring it. Or take the day off and raid Marks and Spencer."

"But you did it last year!"

"Then I was available. Now I'm not."

"What are you doing that's more important than Sam and Jasper's birthday?" Evie asked.

"Going to a work conference," I said promptly.

"Can't Gerrard go?"

"No, *I'm* going, I *want* to go, I've *paid* to go and therefore I won't be available to prepare the catering for Saturday. You'll have to find someone else."

"I can't believe this!"

"I'm sorry you're disappointed, but I'm just not available." I was proud of how calm I sounded. How many times was that I'd said no?

"Just wait until Jasper and Sam hear that their Aunty doesn't want to come to their party!"

"I would like to come; I'm just not available to cater for it."

Evie hung up. I was suddenly assailed by a vision of Jasper and Sam in tears, and I almost called her back. Instead, I called Aunt Mo.

"Of course you're not being unreasonable, Gabriella!" she snapped at me after I told her the story. "It's about time you stood up for yourself a little more and said no to some of your family's frankly outrageous requests!"

"I know! But – what if they won't let me in to see Jasper and Sam?"

CHAPTER 20

"Don't be ridiculous. I don't think they've hired bouncers."

I laughed, suddenly calming down. "Thanks, Aunt Mo."

"Anyway – tell me about your trip to Northumberland," she said. "Was it very uncomfortable, being marooned with a total stranger? I've been dying to ask you about it."

I hesitated. "It was fine until the client's brother arrived, and then there was something I couldn't put my finger on. After that, I was pleased to get away!"

"Oh?"

Just that short, interested word, and I was on the phone for an hour, describing the house, its owner, the cooking and the library. And the game of scrabble, the walk, the log-carrying, and the seeming rift between the brothers.

"So now you've come back to London, the miniatures of Harriet and their new owner are out of your life?" Aunt Mo prodded thoughtfully.

I took out my phone, thumbing to the images of Harriet. She looked enigmatic, teasing. As if she was daring me to discover more about her and her sister.

Well. Challenge accepted, Harriet.

"No. I was thinking of doing more digging, and he's asked me to send any info I find."

"Excellent. Keep me posted," said Aunt Mo, and I could hear the smile in her voice.

The following day at the gallery, I opened the web page of the British Newspaper Archive and typed in what I knew about Harriet and Sophia, including the date of John Colchester's death. There was little more about Sophia and as previously, it brought up details of John's death notice. After a little more clicking, I found an advertisement for a teacher in Harriet's parish with reference to Colchester Hall, after John had died.

"Hmm. Did Harriet Colchester set up a school? Interesting..." I murmured. Then my eye was caught by a headline about a Miss Jennings, from Lancashire.

An elopement to Gretna Green was lately prevented when a young lady, possessed of a considerable fortune, at the age of 17, who resides in Preston, had formed a passionate attachment to a young gentleman. Her father held this suitor in great aversion. The young lady was in the regular habit of taking a walk before dinner, and on the day of her flight, her lover had a chaise ready at the end of the lane, leading to the North, in which he was waiting to carry her off.

I paused, thoughts jostling one another as I recalled Hugo's words. "Miles should have married in the family chapel, but I've searched the Berkeley records, and I can only find dates for the christenings of their children. So, wherever they got married, it doesn't seem to have happened in the normal way."

I felt my pulse jumping in my throat. If Sophia and Miles Berkeley had eloped, their wedding wouldn't have been registered in Miles' parish – it might have been registered in Gretna Green, or another parish in Scotland. I quickly changed my search and spent another half hour going around in circles, until I hit on the

CHAPTER 20

Collection of Gretna Green Marriage Registers. I typed in the name Miles Berkeley and pressed enter.

And there it was; Miles Grantley Fitzharding Berkeley, married to Lady Sophia Chudleigh, 14 September 1795. The two witnesses must have been people pulled off the street. The marriage was officiated by Mr David Lang. I sat back and breathed a huge sigh of satisfaction. Hugo would be delighted to know this and it made the fate of Harriet even more intriguing. Even from my scant knowledge of history, Sophia would have brought disgrace to her family, eloping.

I printed screenshots of the information and drafted an email to Hugo. I was smiling when I pressed send. I was curious to see if, or how, he would respond.

I called Gerrard and asked him to take over while I went out to buy a sandwich. I wondered when I would speak to Mum. She'd sent me a thumbs up when I texted her directly that I was back, but there had been no other communication.

I was paying what seemed an extortionate amount for a ham and cheese roll from our 'artisan bakery' and wishing I'd had the forethought to bring in my own lunch, when my mobile rang.

"Hi, Gabriella, it's Hugo," said the chocolate voice. I nearly dropped my sandwich.

"Oh! Oh, hi. I take it you got my email?" I said, grasping my lunch more firmly and trying to edge my way out of the shop and put my debit card away at the same time.

"I did. I'm going to be in London later this month – shall we meet to discuss?"

I stood in the street, feeling my tummy do a somersault. He cleared his throat, and I wondered if he was as nervous as I was.

"That would be great," I heard myself say.

Chapter 21

GROSVENOR SQUARE, MID MAY 1803

Peters' latest missive gave the mistress of Colchester Hall little to be concerned about in terms of managing the estate and business, but Harriet fretted nonetheless. Now baby James was here, growing into a plump, lusty member of Anne and Phillip's family, there was little reason to linger in London. Yet Harriet did linger, and, alongside the entreaties of Anne not to leave her so soon, she sought additional excuses to delay her departure to Northumberland.

One such excuse was the portraits. Anne had declared that Harriet was to keep James entertained while a portraitist called John Hoppner immortalised them on canvas. "As Phillip has demanded a full portrait, it will take much longer than a miniature, and I depend on you to distract both James and me!"

Mr Hoppner was charming, and very good with James, and the portrait progressed well. Harriet watched fascinated, as the artist sketched her friend with her baby, and the portrait took shape between his brush strokes. But Mr Hoppner thought it might take two weeks, particularly as Anne would only sit in during the first half of the day, when the light in the morning room was bright and clear. James, who was generally placid and gurgling, would begin to squirm after an hour or so, and the wet nurse would whisk him away, which also delayed proceedings.

Anne sagged with relief as the artist smiled and suggested they might finish for the day. Nuzzling James' neck, she handed him to the wet nurse and rose to her feet, smoothing the primrose silk of her dress.

"I do not wish to complain, but James can feel *very* heavy after an hour!" she said laughing.

Harriet glanced up from her needlework and began to fold away her silks. "Would you mind if we visited Madame Monique? My black crepe needs taking in. I can go with a maid if you are engaged elsewhere."

Anne examined her face. "Are you ailing for something, Harriet? I thought you looked a little gaunt!"

"I am well enough."

This was not quite true; Harriet felt restless, on the verge of crossness, her normal even temperament high one moment, low the next. She dismissed it as part of the grieving that she must endure. She knew that this was not the complete story, but she dared not speculate further.

Anne put her head to one side and said nothing for a moment. "Let me change my dress and I'll be happy to accompany you. Will Mr Cosway be calling this afternoon?"

Harriet nodded.

Anne beamed. "Then we must amuse you sufficiently so your lovely smile is in evidence!"

Harriet was in the hall when Anne tripped down the stairs in a dark blue pelisse and a new bonnet, much animated. "Harriet! Lord and Lady Porter-Hume are holding a private ball! We are all invited!"

CHAPTER 21

Harriet smiled, but then her expression faltered. She could not wear black to a ball. Anne, catching sight of her face, wagged a finger at her. "Ah, no! The ball is in two weeks, and to my calculations, you will be in half-mourning by that time, and I may have recovered my strength sufficiently to dance. So we should visit Madame Monique for some new gowns, my love! Come, come!"

Harriet found herself pushed into the carriage, and she felt excitement threading through her veins.

"If you could just remain in that position, Mrs Colchester, I would be so grateful," Richard Cosway said, smiling. Harriet was reminded of his reputation as a womaniser. Her lips curled at the corners as she surveyed his flamboyant coat of puce, lined in deep blue silk with red roses, and his shoes with pink heels. Some things had not changed even after five years.

"Lovely, Mrs Colchester," he purred and made a mark on the ivory.

There was a pause, and then a soft knock at the door heralded Anne and Alexander. Harriet felt her heart swell; she had not seen Alexander for a week or more.

"Forgive me for not greeting you, Mr Richardson," Harriet said.

"No apology necessary," he replied with a bow.

Anne sat with a flurry of pale blue sprig muslin and clasped her hands in her lap. "This seems so strange! It must be five years since we made your acquaintance, Mr Cosway!"

"Indeed, Lady Rochford. But Mrs Colchester has merely matured like a fine wine, and it will be delight to capture her expression – and beauty – again."

Alexander's eyebrows shot up, and Harriet stifled a giggle. At least he hasn't likened me to cheese, she thought, and glanced downwards in an attempt to keep her countenance.

"Indeed, Mr Colchester loved the portrait; is that not so, Mrs Colchester, Mr Richardson?" Anne said, glancing between the two of them.

"I believe it was one of John's most treasured possessions," Alexander said, moving behind the painter to look at the work in progress.

"At least your portrait will be completed more swiftly than mine!" observed Anne.

"May I enquire who the artist is?" Mr Cosway said. When he was informed, he sniffed. "Ah. His work is very traditional, often echoing Lawrence. But I have heard that his depictions of women and children have great charm."

His praise was so lukewarm, Harriet's eyes danced, and a slow smile spread across Alexander's face. Anne looked as if she should be offended but could not identify what Cosway had said that was objectionable.

"But what is your news, Mr Richardson?" Harriet said in an effort to stop giggling.

"I have an engagement at Lord and Lady Porter-Hume's ball at the end of the month," he said. "I trust you will be there, Mrs Colchester?"

"Oh! I had not thought… I… yes, I will be there," Harriet stammered, the thought flying into her head that she had not expected Alexander to attend. But why not? She had seen him dance at the assembly in Berwick, and he was a skilled and graceful partner.

"Mrs Colchester has promised me faithfully that she will be present!" Anne said, and Harriet flushed as she recalled how she had changed her mind about the opera.

"But I will not be dancing," Harriet stressed.

"But she *will* be there, and in half-mourning, too!" Anne responded. "It will be lovely to see you in something other than black crepe, dearest!"

"Yes, you have hidden from the world long enough," Alexander said quietly.

Harriet felt her cheeks heat and raised her chin. Richard Cosway narrowed his black eyes; he surveyed Alexander thoughtfully. "Perfect, Mrs Colchester! I feel another half-hour should suffice!" He began to paint furiously.

There was no doubt about it; the lavender silk overlaid with a fine black gauze became her considerably more than had the black. Harriet was secretly very pleased with Madame Monique's design, which emphasised the roundness of her bosom and showed her slender, pale arms to advantage. The skirt was straight, as was the fashion, the waist high. Anne's maid had drawn back the hair from Harriet's face and pinned it higher than was her custom, and a black and lavender feather curled over one ear, giving her a dashing air.

Perhaps the feather was too much? She dithered for a moment, but was concerned that if she removed the feathers, her hair would be ruined. The carriage went over an uneven flagstone and she jolted back into reality. She focused on Anne's artless chatter and Phillip's light voice responding, and scolded herself for being so absorbed by her appearance. She could not dance. She would watch, and converse with the more elderly of Lady Porter-Hume's guests.

Phillip handed her down from the carriage, and she stood, looking at the impressive facade of the Portman Square mansion, its stone golden with the light from the wall sconces.

Anne tucked her hand into Phillip's arm on one side and into Harriet's on the other, and together, they walked to the entrance. Harriet handed her evening cloak to a footman. From the ballroom, she could hear music and her heart beat a little faster. She swallowed, wondering if she would pass muster, recalling the cut direct she had received from many after Sophia's disgrace. She pushed away her thoughts. She had the love and affection of Anne and Phillip, and she waited in the receiving line gathering her fortitude.

She caught sight of Alexander in the crowd and her breath caught. He looked elegant in his pale knee breeches and white silk stockings. His coat was rich navy, and Harriet smiled to herself, knowing that the colour would flatter his blue eyes. As he walked around the room, he put her in mind of a tiger she had once seen at Astley's Circus, all strength and power, caged. He was not taller than all the men in the room, but he drew her eyes.

As she watched, he approached Georgiana. His previously stern face lit with a smile as he led her to the dance floor. Heart sinking, Harriet pulled her gaze back

CHAPTER 21

to the line of guests and she heard their names announced.

Lady Porter-Hume beamed as she dropped a curtsy, and to Harriet's enormous surprise, kissed her on the cheek. "I'm so pleased to see you! I thought you may not come, but I see you have moved into half-mourning!"

"I depend on you to lend me countenance, ma'am!"

"Oh, pooh – be off with you and enjoy yourself."

Lord Porter-Hume winked at her, and drawing a deep breath, Harriet walked down the shallow stairs to the ballroom with Anne and Phillip. Anne turned to her husband the moment they reached the floor.

"I have not danced for many months, so you are not to disappear to the card room, Phillip!" she said. Phillip looked sheepish. "We will be over by that pillar while you bring us refreshments!"

Harriet grinned, and arm in arm, she walked with Anne through the great room, made hot with candles. Their light was reflected from glittering mirrors that adorned the walls, and great swags of flowers draped across the doors leading to the terrace. The music floated down from one of the balconies that overlooked the dance floor; an orchestra of twenty players was tucked into an alcove above the swirling figures. On the other balconies, guests leaned over the railings to watch the couples below.

Harriet was delighted by it all, but as her attention turned from her surroundings to the people around her, she was aware of some disapproving looks from one or two of the matrons. She tensed. Anne obviously felt Harriet's hand tighten in the crook of her elbow and patted it.

"Head up, my dear," she murmured with a bright smile on her face, and Harriet's chin rose. "You have done nothing wrong, and you have nothing to be ashamed of."

They reached the pillar and waited for Phillip to join them. A few gentlemen bowed to Anne, and after introductions, they nodded to Harriet. Harriet, with the best will in the world, could not stop the colour from staining her cheeks.

"I can't tell if they are disapproving of my sister's conduct or mine!" she said in low tones to Anne when they were alone.

Anne turned to her in surprise. "Goodness! That was nearly eight years ago! People have better things to think about!"

Phillip returned with two glasses of lemonade, and Harriet's nerves began to subside. Settling herself in a chair, she waved Phillip and Anne away to dance and tried to make herself as unobtrusive as possible. She was succeeding admirably until the rotund shape of Lady Altringham, a crony of her late mama, came over and raised her lorgnette.

"Is that Harriet?" she demanded, the glass magnifying a slightly bulbous pale blue eye. Harriet curtsied.

"Lady Altringham, how do you do?"

"Well! I heard you married at last! Is your husband here?"

"He died, ma'am. Last November."

"Did he? Very irregular. And who has escorted you?"

"My friends, Lord and Lady Rochford."

"Hmm. Well enough people, I suppose. So, you're looking for another husband? You'll have your work cut out. You were never the match of Sophia."

CHAPTER 21

Harriet looked at the malicious face peering at her, and decided she'd endured quite enough. "I don't believe my future is anyone's business but mine, ma'am."

Lady Altringham reared back and bared yellowing teeth in a scowl.

"Judith, how delightful to see you. I doubted you would come because of your gout," Lady Porter-Hume interjected smoothly, appearing over the dowager's shoulder. "But I see you are *still* sprightly! How wonderful."

Lady Altringham, faced with her hostess, muttered something unintelligible and stalked away. Lady Porter-Hume watched her fleshy back disappear into the crowd. "The conduct of your sister should not be visited on you," she said thoughtfully.

"I have lived with her disgrace as though it were my own," Harriet said bitterly, releasing a long-held hurt. She made herself smile. "But my friends have not disowned me, and as a widow, I have an independence only money can buy! As long as I stay single."

Lady Porter-Hume regarded her narrowly. "Do you remember Miss Damer?" Harriet nodded. "An unusual woman and a fine artist, but she can only sculpt because of an agreement with her late husband before she married, which guaranteed her an income," she continued. "Our sex is limited by society's expectations and by the law, but the law, applied correctly, can also help us."

"With the deepest respect, ma'am, a woman of your wealth will have a very different perspective from the majority!"

Lady Porter-Hume laughed. "Oh, indeed, but you must not think that I plan to simply play the man's game! I already use my position at the bank to encourage talented women – Miss Damer is protected by her family's foresight, but I hope to use my financial acumen to support others who would be made powerless by marriage. Ah, Rochford!"

This last was said to Phillip, returning with a rosy-cheeked Anne, delighted to complete a country dance without needing to rest.

They talked of the music, the crowd and how hot it was. Harriet, catching sight of yet another beautiful young lady whirling around the floor with Alexander, felt almost overwhelmed with a longing she identified as a yearning to dance. Desperate for some air, she excused herself, and headed for the terrace.

Chapter 22

NORTH LONDON, MARCH 2024

I could hear the noise from Liam and Evie's house from twenty yards away. I imagined the parents, crammed into the kitchen, necking wine. I walked down the front path and glimpsed the tent in their back garden. I paused, and texted Aunt Mo.

A few minutes later, the door flew open and Aunt Mo, resplendent in scarlet and clasping what looked like a large gin and tonic, ushered me in.

"It's complete chaos!" she muttered, and I grinned as I took off my coat and hooked it over the banister at the bottom of the stairs. Raindrops clung to the fabric.

"Don't you like your great-nephews, Aunt Mo?"

"I certainly couldn't eat a whole one."

I pulled my fingers through my hair to straighten it, and Aunt Mo squinted at me.

"You look lovely with the new hair," she said, eyeing my outfit of leggings, boots and a fitted jacket. Her finger stroked the lapel. "Have I seen you wear this before?"

"Oh yes – just not with these trousers. Joe helped me put it together."

She nodded approvingly.

"What's the food like?" I asked.

"More e-numbers than you can shake a stick at," Aunt Mo replied gloomily, clasping a hand to her chunky necklace. "The kids will be on the ceiling for hours!"

I hoisted the twins' birthday presents in my hands, both books. A book was my favoured pre-bedtime activity. I'd look forward to reading *The Kringleset Chronicles* and *The Swifts* with them.

"I think Sam and Jasper are in the garden," advised Aunt Mo.

I slipped out of the patio doors, nodding to a few adults along the way, and picked my way down the brick path to the marquee. Evie had certainly pushed the boat out, with a wilting conjurer tying balloons into animals and producing chocolate coins from behind small ears, and a trampoline, currently out of action because of the rain. A pile of towels by the entrance to the marquee told me someone – probably Liam or one of the other dads – would be wiping it down soon. I peeked inside.

Six or seven other children were throwing modelling clay around, and a couple were sitting at a low table, drawing on rolls of blank paper with felt tip pens. The twins were hitting each other with some inflated sausage-shaped balloons that had somehow escaped their dog incarnation. From the mutinous set of Sam's mouth, I guessed that tears weren't far away, and I stepped into the tent quickly.

"Hello, Sam! Hi, Jasper! Happy birthday!"

The pair of them dropped the balloons and raced towards me, enacting a pincer movement around my thighs with their hugs. I dropped to my knees and hugged them back, noting the stickiness on their faces and in their hair.

CHAPTER 22

"Have you brought us a present?" Jasper demanded, his gaze glued to the brightly wrapped books.

"Might have done," I said. "Depends how nicely you ask me."

"Have you brought us a present, *please*?" said Sam. "Is it a Space Explorer Pack?"

"It's better than that," I said airily, handing over the parcels. "It's something we get to read together!"

"Good!" Sam grinned at me and tore open the paper, almost ripping one of the book pages in his haste. Because they were lovely kids, they thanked me, and I carefully picked up the books to put them back in the house. I was gathering the shreds of wrapping paper when Liam's voice addressed me.

"Returned from your work conference?"

I stood up. "Yes, it was great, thanks for asking," I replied evenly.

"Liam, the conjurer says – oh! Gabs." Evie trailed off and I turned to find her standing with my mother, who was wearing heels, a cream skirt and a navy chiffon-like top. Perfect for a party with a set of six-year-olds, I thought, fleetingly.

"Well," my mother said. "I wasn't expecting to see you – I thought you were too busy."

"She's just too busy to cater for the party," said Aunt Mo, coming up behind her. There was a silence as we all looked at each other, and she huffed in exasperation. "Don't be ridiculous – you're all acting as if Gabriella has committed a crime. All she did was dare to be occupied when you wanted her to be available for you."

"It wasn't quite like that—" Evie protested.

"And you did it last year!" interrupted Liam. "We thought that you'd be delighted to be part of your only nephews' birthday party!"

"We'd have paid you!" Evie put in, and I swung around to her.

"I don't *want* your money!" I snapped and Sam looked over uncertainly. I lowered my voice. "Even if I had been available – and I *wasn't* – I resent the automatic expectation that I can drop everything just to do your bidding like some on-call genie!"

"Were your 'plans' as important as your family?" said Mum, twisting her hands. "It's like you no longer put us first, Gabs. I used to feel I could trust you with my life, particularly after your father died. But then you changed after you got the flat."

"Perhaps Gabriella would rather you weren't quite so helpless," Aunt Mo said, and Evie looked outraged; Liam put his arm around her. Aunt Mo rolled her eyes, muttering. "Not *just* you, Evie, for goodness' sake! All of you!"

My mother stiffened, and Aunt Mo gave her a meaningful look.

A man with flushed cheeks wearing a stained polo shirt walked towards us and then checked as he saw our faces.

"This isn't the place for this conversation," Liam said in a tense tone, and in this, at least, we were in violent agreement.

"We'll talk when you have time," Mum said, sniffing, as if washing her hands of the matter. "Evie, come and talk to the magician."

CHAPTER 22

They walked away and left me with Aunt Mo. I swallowed, feeling a mix of rage and desolation. Aunt Mo's hand on my arm made me want to cry.

"Don't they understand I have a life?" I said in a low voice, watching Sam and Jasper create a snake from clay.

"Not when you're always available. If they have to manage without you, they'll discover how much you did for them, and be a bit more appreciative. It's your father's fault, in part," Aunt Mo said, looking very uncomfortable. "He did too much for Theresa…" She trailed off and then clasped my shoulder with her bony fingers. "But you'll need to let them come to you, you know."

Jasper yelled at me to see his snake and my heart contracted. I went to get multi-coloured clay under my nails and to wonder when I would get the opportunity to read their birthday books with them.

A week later, the discussion with Mum and Liam still hadn't happened. There was nothing directed at me on the family WhatsApp group, and I gritted my teeth.

Joe was brilliant when he heard the ridiculous tale, sweeping me off to a drag cabaret with Steven. A riotous Saturday night was followed by a boozy brunch on Sunday, so by the time I was back in the gallery, I was glad of a break from the alcohol. Aunt Mo sent robust, supportive text messages telling me to stand my ground. I caught up with old school friends, saw a lot of Joe and Steven, and dug in.

I had just finished a meeting with the builders about the mezzanine and was tidying my papers when Gerrard tapped lightly on the door of the office.

"Busy?"

"Not at the moment – what's up?"

He sat and played with the signet ring on his finger. "I was thinking of taking a bit of a holiday," he said slowly.

"Aren't you off to California in September?" I leaned back in the chair and scanned his face. It might have been a trick of the light, but he looked younger, I noticed.

"Yes, but I need some time off now."

"Is everything all right? Are *you* all right?"

He beamed at me. "I'm wonderful, Gabriella. I've met someone."

My eyebrows rose in surprise, and then I checked myself. Gerrard was in his mid-fifties. He'd lost his partner, Jonathon, five years ago, and although he dated regularly, the affairs were light, joyous fizzles of fun, soon over.

I smiled, encouragingly. "And who is the lucky man?"

"Peter Foster," he said, a blush staining his cheeks. "He's an architect. He's only just come out and he's free for three weeks starting mid-March…"

My eyes widened – that was only a week away – and he held up a hand. "Before you begin to panic, I've talked to Antonio, and he's proposed that Helena come in while I'm away."

Antonio Torres was the owner of another gallery down the street, and Helena was his assistant with the glossiest hair and nails I'd ever seen on a woman. We were polite, but she always stared at me as if I'd wan-

CHAPTER 22

dered in from the street by mistake. Oh, no. That would never do.

"No, Gerrard," I said firmly. "If you're going to pay someone to be around to help me, I'd rather I chose them. Helena and I have..." I searched for words that wouldn't be too critical. "We have very different styles. I know most of our customers, and I'm capable of handling three weeks in the gallery alone, if I have a temp to sort out the administration. You're paying me for additional responsibility – give me some."

"What about the mezzanine?"

"The builder is waiting for some materials to come in and thinks he'll start in a week or so. We've agreed that they'll seal off the mezzanine with plastic, and that they'll work over the weekends. We'll need to close the gallery for a day to rehang the art, but I've lined that up with the installers. It's all under control."

Gerrard stared at me for a long moment and then made a face. "Are you sure?"

"Very."

He laughed and nodded. "I'll leave it in your capable hands, Gabriella!"

When I finished for the day, leaving Gerrard to lock up, my mind was churning. I was proud and excited, particularly about getting rid of Helena, but I'd thought I might feel... something more. Tutting inwardly, I made my way to the bus stop and was waiting in the creeping dusk when my phone rang.

"It's Hugo. I'm in London. Are you still available tomorrow for lunch?"

A tingle ran down the length of my spine at his voice in my ear. I breathed in.

"Sure. Where shall I meet you?"

"I'll text the details; it's not far from the gallery. About one o'clock?"

"I look forward to it," I said, a smile curling my mouth.

"Me too," he promised.

Perhaps the week was looking up, I thought, as I seemed to float onto the bus and home.

I smoothed my black skirt down my thighs as the maître d' took my coat, giving me an appreciative once-over. I'd never been to this elegant restaurant before, and even with my increased salary, I hoped this would be on Hugo. The place was clad in dark wood with pale yellow and silver accents and shrieked expensive. I glanced in the mirror above the bar and pushed my fingers through my hair. I nodded to myself. Still okay, I thought.

"This way, please," said the maître d' and led me to a table by the enormous, mullioned window where Hugo was frowning at a menu. The faint sun, shining through the golden coloured glass, warmed his skin and made his hair molten.

"Hello, there," I said huskily, and then cleared my throat. He looked up and his dark gaze seemed to flare; then he got up and offered his hand, which I shook.

After the business of ordering, the flapping of napkins, and the shuffling of chairs, I finally sat back.

"How are you?" Hugo said, his eyes curious. "You look – different, somehow."

I smoothed my hair again and half-laughed. "No, I'm just the same as always. Although I'll be running the gallery for a few weeks, alone."

CHAPTER 22

"Oh? Sounds interesting; tell me more."

I told him just the basics – it wasn't fair to discuss Gerrard's love-life – and he asked me about the mezzanine. I explained about the design and the builder, the dust sheets, and the rehanging – and then I was halfway through the main course.

"Good grief, listen to me rattle on! I'm so sorry!" I apologised, shocked.

He laughed. "No, you're so passionate about it – and there's nothing more interesting than a woman on a mission about her work." I looked at my plate. "But well done about finding Sophia's marriage," he said after a tiny pause. "I'd never have considered an elopement."

"And I've had another thought about Harriet," I said, leaning forward and just saving my sleeve from the red wine sauce that had accompanied my beef. "Bum. Sorry," I muttered and leaned back in my chair. Hugo grinned. "No, what I thought was perhaps we could look at the painter, Richard Cosway. Might he have had correspondence, invoices, even a diary?"

Hugo gazed at me, and the world seemed to go quiet. I swallowed.

"Brilliant. It's a brilliant idea, Gabriella. Where do we look?"

"The archival collections of the big art galleries like the Getty, although Gerrard recommends we start with the Tate; they have a good collection of miniatures," I said promptly. "If we get lucky, there might be a bill of sale, perhaps a letter that mentions her. Some of it might be online, but we'll need to make enquiries and see what we can get to look at. I pulled together a few contacts..."

I drew out a list from my bag.

Hugo threw back his head and laughed. "You're amazing!"

I took in his smile and warm, dark eyes and managed to stop myself melting into a puddle.

The waiter came to clear our table and I shook my head at the offer of a pudding.

"Have coffee," he urged.

I glanced at my watch. "Love to, but I ought to be getting back."

Hugo signalled for the bill, and I hesitated. He shook his head. "I'll get this. Don't argue."

"I'll make a few calls to the Getty and let you know how I get on, if you try the Tate," I said, fighting the urge to earn my lunch.

"Perfect, as long as you have time."

"I'll make time," I said, and he paused and stared at me, his gaze seeming to draw me to him. I broke the spell with a quick smile. "After all, I'm a woman on a mission!"

Chapter 23

PORTMAN SQUARE, MAY 1803

Harriet breathed in the cool air of the terrace and felt her muscles unlock a fraction. She ought not to be out here, alone, but the heat of the ballroom and the urge to dance had excited a great longing to scream. She turned along the terrace and tucked herself into a stone alcove, her mind turning over Lady Altringham's nasty comments and Lady Porter-Hume's conviction that the law could be used to protect women and enable them to enrich their lives. Her nose wrinkled. Lady Porter-Hume was heiress to a huge fortune and might make it so; Harriet was a widow with a scheming mother-in-law who constantly reminded her of her family's scandal. Harriet doubted that the law would be so benevolent to women like her.

She could still hear the music. There was a pause as the dance came to an end, and then the orchestra started up again. The country dance they played was one of her favourites.

She looked around. She was quite alone, and the moon was not so bright that it illuminated the terrace. In her lavender gown, she might be imperceptible.

Harriet stood, bowed to an imaginary partner and danced the first few steps, holding down the giggle that bubbled in her throat at her folly. She had just completed the first figure when Alexander stepped from the shadows and held his hands out to her.

Harriet stumbled and he caught her. Even though his hands were gloved, she could feel the warmth of his skin on her bare arms. He laughed softly.

"You dance charmingly alone! Would I spoil it if I were to join you?"

She drew back from him, her mind a blank. They should not be here. He should remove his hands from her arms, immediately. His smile dared her, and after a few seconds, she nodded.

He stood opposite her and bowed. They had stood up together many times. John had not been a good dancer, and he had released her willingly to Alexander, who had laughingly teased him for his two left feet. All those times crowded into her head, and when they came to clasp hands for one of the figures, the movement had a sense of rightness, familiarity.

As they danced, Harriet relaxed and began to enjoy herself. She had always loved dancing and the exercise was exhilarating. She registered the firm clasp of his fingers, the warmth beneath the fabric of his gloves, and saw the sparkle in his eyes even in the dim light. Her heart began to thrum.

Too soon, the dance ended, and with a breathless laugh, Harriet dipped a curtsy to her clandestine partner.

Alexander, who was also breathing rather fast, raised her hand to his lips, and for a moment, Harriet could not have moved for all the world.

CHAPTER 23

"You need to spread your wings Harriet," he said in a low voice. "Allow me to assist. Please accompany me to the opera next week."

Harriet stared at his dark brown head and fought the urge to draw her fingers through his hair. She said nothing.

"Well?" Alexander straightened but did not let go of her hand.

"Yes." Harriet heard the word come out of her mouth. She blinked and then cleared her throat. "Yes, I'd like that."

Without speaking, he led her back to the ballroom.

"What do you think? Is it a good likeness?" Harriet said rather anxiously as she, Anne and Phillip considered the miniature that Mr Cosway had delivered to the house. It was resting on the table in the drawing room and the three of them were gathered around.

"Of course it is, you goose!" Anne chuckled and gave her friend a nudge with her elbow. "You look splendid! And, if you'll forgive the comparison, a good deal livelier than your previous sitting!"

Harriet examined the portrait with her head on one side. The new style that Anne's maid had suggested to Louise did seem to flatter her face, and somehow the black crepe hadn't drained her complexion as it normally did. And the expression in her eyes was... lively. Certainly, Augusta would consider it unbecoming to a widow. Particularly the slight smile, which Harriet herself did not remember.

"It is most satisfactory," declared Phillip. Harriet was gratified. She looked through the paper that had wrapped the painting.

"He has not left his account," she said, frowning. "Such a nuisance! I shall have to send to him."

"No need," said Phillip. "This seemed an appropriate way to demonstrate my appreciation and thanks for all you have done for Anne. I have paid his bill."

Harriet flushed and stammered her protest, but Phillip, and eventually Anne, would have none of it.

"Do cut line, my love!" she said fondly, pulling her to sit on a sofa. "It is done. Give me your thoughts on this hat."

Anne pointed to a page in the *Ladies' Monthly Museum*; Harriet agreed that the bonnet was indeed an elegant affair, and of course, as Anne resumed her place in society, a new hat was necessary.

"That reminds me," Anne said. "You are going to the opera this evening, are you not? In the dark lavender dress you had from Monique? I have something you may want to wear other than your jet beads."

She rose and left the room, returning a few minutes later with a string of black pearls and a pair of earrings. Their black-green lustre was sufficiently restrained for them to be perfect for a visit to the theatre while in mourning.

"Oh! They're glorious! Are you sure?" Harriet said, her hand to her throat.

"Of course; I should not have offered them otherwise. I have a perfect set of cabochon amethysts, but Phillip thought they may be too showy, so I thought the pearls would be just the thing."

"It is just Mr Richardson," Harriet said, feeling a little uncomfortable that she would think so much of her appearance.

"Hmm," said Anne, picking up her embroidery. "Is it Lady and Miss Porter-Hume who will also be accompanying you?"

Harriet nodded, with rather mixed feelings about Georgiana's presence. Since the ball, it had seemed as if Georgiana and Alexander were inseparable, and there was no doubt that the young lady, always so sparkling and brilliant, made him smile often. They were always chaperoned, everything was perfectly proper, but Harriet had overheard a few whispers that the pair would make a good match.

She tutted inwardly and picked up her book. Georgiana was too young, surely, for Alexander? Perhaps not so much in years, but experience, she thought. And, now she reflected on Alexander's background, there was a further obstacle to any long-term relationship – Georgiana was from a titled family; Alexander, despite his many, many qualities, had made his fortune as a manufacturer and latterly, a gentleman-farmer.

"You seem distracted, dear," was the mild comment from Anne.

Harriet looked up, startled. "Am I?" she paused, searching for a suitable response. "I suppose I am a little nervous about the opera, given my welcome from Lady Altringham."

"Pah!" Anne dismissed the dowager with a shrug of her shoulder. "She is a rather bitter lady, I fear. You were merely first in line for her tongue; I hear she almost reduced one of the footmen to tears."

Harriet was shocked, but not surprised. She was thankful when Anne continued with her embroidery, and Harriet continued to pretend to read.

Harriet glanced across the box. Georgiana was quiet as she watched *Don Giovanni*. The young woman, so full of laughter and liveliness away from the theatre, became another person listening to opera. Harriet was surprised and then scolded herself; who was she to judge this lovely girl for her looks alone? Georgiana was obviously as intelligent as her aunt.

After the performance, Georgiana returned to her usual demeanour, and declared herself enchanted by the performance. Harriet watched as Alexander joked with her and helped retrieve a wrap and a fan that had somehow slipped to the floor.

Outside, waiting in the cool night for the carriage to draw closer, Lady Porter-Hume turned to Harriet.

"Mrs Colchester, I wonder if you would be kind enough to accompany me to a breakfast on Thursday? It's a small salon run by a frighteningly well-connected woman called Miss Mary Berry, and I thought you might enjoy it. You seem *au fait* with public affairs and well read."

Harriet was a little startled. "I'm likely to disappoint you if the rest of the company are bluestockings, ma'am!"

"Don't be unnecessarily modest, Mrs Colchester," Lady Porter-Hume said with an arch of her brow. "You're intelligent and the discussion will be about travel – Miss Berry has agreed to speak about her trip to the Continent with her sister. I felt sure I had heard you say how much you wished to travel."

Harriet swiftly rearranged her itinerary for the week in her head. "Oh, yes! I'd love to attend."

"Excellent. I daresay we will see Miss Damer there too – she is a dear friend of Miss Mary Berry."

"Miss Damer is an – unusual woman," ventured Harriet as the carriage drew up. Lady Porter-Hume laughed.

"My dear, she is indeed an original! But I liked her; did you not?"

"I did," she replied firmly after a thoughtful pause. "I thought there was something rather noble about her."

"Excellent! You will enjoy Thursday. Come to my house at eleven."

The drawing room at the Misses Berry's modest house in North Audley Street was crammed full of people and the room was so hot, someone had thrown open a window. Miss Mary Berry, a diminutive woman in her mid-forties with a prominent nose, welcomed Lady Porter-Hume and Harriet very prettily and waved a hand at the crowded room.

"I declare, I had not expected so many people, but please, Arabella, Mrs Colchester, take a seat!"

As Harriet and Lady Porter-Hume seated themselves, Harriet looked with interest at the other attendees. She spotted Miss Damer, who, astonishingly, was dressed in what looked like a man's greatcoat, open to display a snowy shirt, and a hat that would not have looked out of place on Phillip's head. No-one seemed to care much, Harriet thought, and one part of her was secretly thrilled at Miss Damer's complete unconcern.

A footman offered tea and Harriet drank it gratefully. Lady Porter-Hume pointed out the people she knew – here a politician, there an author. Harriet drank it all in. At long last, Miss Berry clapped her hands and the buzz of conversation fell away.

"As you know," she began, "I have often spoken of my desire to *shake* out of English ways, English whims and English prejudices, which nothing but leaving England gives one." There was a warm chuckle of appreciation from the room. "But, given the precariousness of the Peace, I am, I suppose, fortunate to be back among friends. I have been pressed to speak of my travels, and I shall endeavour to do so."

It flashed through Harriet's mind that Edwin would be forced to abandon his travels if the Peace looked in danger of disintegrating, but then Miss Berry began to speak again.

She had not progressed in the usual manner from Calais to Le Havre before heading to either Paris or Basel, but instead spoke lovingly of her time in Rotterdam.

"I have always looked back to those weeks as the most delicious of my existence," she declared. "I received the greatest number of new ideas, and felt my mind expanding every day, while at the same time my imagination could not be but delighted with the charm and novelty in everything I saw."

Harriet was entranced, even more so when Miss Berry began to describe her visit to the Acropolis. To her astonishment, a couple of questions in the room indicated that the Misses Berry had even been presented to Napoleon Bonaparte, and as additional comments came from around the room, she found herself thinking what a dull creature she was, how poorly travelled, and how insipid a reader.

Lady Porter-Hume, eyeing her shrewdly, murmured in her ear. "*You* could travel, my dear. You would need another female companion, but all is possible."

Harriet stared at her. Yes, all *was* possible, was it not? She had wealth and knew how to go on in society. She might fulfill her dreams. She glanced again at Miss Berry, now deep in conversation with a man sporting splendid whiskers and a virulent green waistcoat.

"Miss Berry and her sister are completely alone, aren't they?" she mused.

"They are. But Miss Mary Berry has a large coterie of women friends who are only too happy to travel with her, should her sister prefer to remain at home."

"And does she prefer to remain at home?" Harriet turned to Lady Porter-Hume with a disbelieving smile. Lady Porter-Hume burst out laughing.

"Why no, I believe she is as eager to shake out of English ways and customs as her sister."

As her amusement died away, Harriet was thoughtful.

"What is it?" asked Lady Porter-Hume gently.

Harriet looked down at the empty teacup in her hand and hesitated before speaking. "I believe that duty – duty to my parents, duty to my husband and to my husband's family – has been my master for years. Despite my deep affection for my sister, Sophia, I refrained from contacting her, out of duty to my husband and his family. I believe Mama wishes me to marry my cousin to continue the line. It is my duty. I hope I do not sound ungrateful, but I grow weary of it."

"Then our time here has not been wasted!" replied her companion, searching for her reticule. "Come! Let us go somewhere where people are not discussing antiquities *in Greek*."

Harriet arrived back at the Grosvenor Square house after one of the most stimulating mornings she had spent in years. It was then she found the note from Augusta, informing Harriet that she was at the Grillon Hotel, and would she be so good to call on her at her earliest convenience?

Chapter 24

CENTRAL LONDON, APRIL 2023

I put down the phone with a satisfied smirk. That would bring in a healthy chunk of revenue to offset the building work, I thought, looking at the requirements for our first event for an insurance company. A bit of a party for their high performers. I wondered if Gerrard would consider me a high performer and buy me dinner?

A bang and a smothered curse caused me to look upwards at the mezzanine. I was pleased with it, the clean, industrial lines, concrete floor and earthy colours, all in line with the mostly modern art that we sold. I was going to add some plush sofas in ruby velvet to soften the space, although the pale golden lighting would also help. Gerrard had been gone two weeks and I was thrilled at the progress we'd made.

A ping sounded on my phone, and it was Aunt Mo.

Anything yet?

I sighed and texted back. *Not a sausage. Have I been divorced, do you think?*

Not by me.

It was good that the gallery had kept me occupied, otherwise, instead of feeling a bit flat, I might have been very low indeed. Susan, the mouse-like but frighteningly efficient administrator I had hired to support me while Gerrard was away, needed to be shown only a few of the gallery ropes before she sailed effortlessly through the work. Although a tiny woman with short grey hair and wire rimmed glasses, she only had to fix you with her clear grey eyes before you began to wonder if, indeed, you'd got it all wrong. I'd seen the builders working on the mezzanine clean up their language and turn off their radio when she steadily climbed the stairs.

And Joe and Steven had taken me under their wings, while Aunt Mo was consistent in her offers of supper, so my evenings and Sundays were spent with other people. But, alongside the films I saw – including the one I'd missed because of my styling session – catching up with some old school friends, and finally managing to clear out my storage cupboard, I missed Mum and the twins.

My enquiries at the Getty, always a long shot, had drawn a blank on Richard Cosway's correspondence, but it seemed that Hugo's enquiries with the Tate had been more fruitful, from his last phone call.

I paused, thinking of his voice. As if conjured by my thoughts, Hugo rang me at that moment.

"How are you?" His chocolate voice filled my ears.

"Oh, I'm fine. Getting on with the mezzanine."

There was a pause. "Are you okay? You sound a bit low. Not working too hard?"

I paused, wondering what in my bright response had given me away. "I've got the opening next Thursday with a big event for an insurance company," I said at last. "The CEO is one of our biggest customers, so it has to go well, or Gerrard will have my head on a plate!"

"Are you worried?"

CHAPTER 24

I wasn't. I was a detail girl, and everything had been checked to the last appetiser. "No, it's all in hand. Had to argue with one of the caterers who wanted to add an astonishing surcharge to take the food up to the mezzanine floor, but no, all's well."

"You sound as if you need cheering up," Hugo said. "So let me tell you, the Tate has found a mention of a Mrs Harriet Colchester in Richard Cosway's correspondence, and they've told me I can come and look at the documents if I want."

"And do you want me to go to the Tate?" I asked. He chuckled.

"No, Gabriella, I'd like us *both* to go to the Tate and then I can take you to lunch again and hopefully cheer you up."

I was silent, feeling my stomach flip over. So, this was how it felt to have someone think about what was going on in my life.

"Unless you're unavailable?" Hugo added, suddenly a little distant.

"God, no!" I almost shouted down the phone. I coughed and lowered my voice. "It would be wonderful to see you again." Oh, lord – too pushy? "And I'd love to go to the Tate with you," I added hastily. "I'm so intrigued to find out more about Harriet."

And now I was babbling. The warm chuckle came down the line again, turning my insides squishy.

"When's best for you?"

I thought. The builders would leave in two days' time and then we'd need to get the gallery cleaned, because dust sheets or not, the work had made a lot of mess. Then we'd need to hang the paintings again, so we could reopen. I blew out my cheeks. It would need to be next week.

"Monday? Late morning?" I hazarded, thinking that I could slip out for a few hours and leave Susan in charge.

"It's a date."

There was no other word for it; my heart soared as Hugo opened the gallery door. He was wearing a yellow-gold sweater that reflected amber glints in his dark eyes. I gave him a wide smile. And it might have been my imagination, but I thought his face lit up as he saw me. For a second or two, I was tongue-tied. So was he.

As a result, it was Susan who spoke. "Please feel free to walk around our exhibits," she said in her quiet voice. "We have a particularly fine piece by Chloe Johnson that has just arrived, a landscape of the York moors."

Hugo seemed to come to himself, nodded, and explained he was here to collect me. Susan's grey eyes swept over me, and I thought her eyebrow tweaked, but then it was gone, and she nodded. After grabbing my coat, we were on the street, heading for the Oxford Circus tube. Other than asking how we were and how his journey from Northumberland had been, we didn't speak much in the twenty-minute ride, both of us struck, it seemed to me, by shyness.

It was almost a relief to get to the Tate, where a rather sulky archivist with a tight blonde chignon briefly introduced herself as Adriana and led the way to the reading rooms. She treated us with the air of someone who had other things to do, and my hackles rose.

CHAPTER 24

"Was this what you were looking for?" she said, gesturing to several pieces of paper and a thick book on a huge table. "These are the accounts from 1790 to1805. Please don't handle the book, but you may turn the pages if you wear gloves. And I've identified some of the correspondence, which mentions the lady you're looking for."

Hugo thanked her gravely and I readied my pencil (no pens allowed) and notebook. He took the gloves from Adriana and leaned over the books. The archivist looked at us curiously.

"I'm not quite sure why you wanted to see the originals," she said, and glanced at her watch. "I understand my colleague did say that many of these pages, including the ones you're looking for, are online. You didn't have to come all the way from Northumberland…"

I stared at her and then at Hugo, who reddened slightly. Then he shrugged and laughed self-consciously and it was my turn to feel a bit hot and bothered.

"I was coming down anyway," he said in an offhand way. "And isn't the original always better?"

"If you say so." Adriana nodded dismissal, still puzzled, and sat in another part of the library within sight of us. Pushing away conjectures about Hugo's presence in London, I drew up a chair. Hugo sat a few inches away from me and I fixed my gaze on the elaborate handwriting in the account book, not able to look at him. After a moment, I cleared my throat.

"It's difficult to decipher, isn't it?"

"Yes, but at least the ink is still dark – astonishing after more than two hundred years." Hugo threw a quick glance towards me and then took a deep breath. "So – where are you, Harriet…?"

Scanning the page over his shoulder, I pointed my finger towards a line. "Isn't that her?"

Hugo focused. "Hmm. Yes, 'Mrs H Colchester, watercolour on bone, 25 guineas. Received' – I think that's what that means; what do you think?"

I leaned over, conscious of the warmth of his body as I squinted at the writing. "Yes, I think that's right." I moved away, the faint scent of his aftershave haunting my nostrils.

"So – this is interesting, then," he said, not noticing. "It says 'Received from Lord Rochford, 20th May 1803.' So, Harriet didn't buy the miniature. It looks like Rochford bought it for her!"

"I wonder how he was involved? Was he another admirer?" I recalled the portraits and wrinkled my nose in thought. "It's ridiculous, but I hadn't thought Harriet would accept gifts like that."

He nodded. "We'll have a look at Lord Rochford, shall we? Perhaps he paid for a portrait for himself, and this was a job lot? But I wonder why he did it. It couldn't be the money – Harriet was very rich indeed."

"Well, he must have been well heeled to pay 25 guineas!" I said, scribbling in my notebook. Hugo moved to one of the letter pages on the other side of the desk and began to read through it. I moved to the others. I was just beginning to get the hang of the typography when Hugo gave a low whistle.

"What is it?"

"Come and have a look at this bit of the correspondence. 'Mrs HC had an unremarkable face until the arrival of Mr Richardson, a manufacturer, who brought a pretty flush to the lady's complexion.'"

"Oh? Who's this person, making her blush?"

CHAPTER 24

"No idea. And later, he says, 'Lady Porter-Hume is one of the lady's intimates – an excellent connection indeed, and as Mrs HC has a straightforwardness about her that cannot but please, it was an excellent commission.' So, our Harriet is mixing with a banking legend!"

"Who? Lady Porter-whatsit?"

"Hume. She was the earliest woman bank director, I think. I heard of her when I used to work in corporate banking; she inherited a fortune from her father and her family bank shares from her mother. The banks use her these days to show that banking is not a male monopoly."

That families had their own banks was news to me, but Hugo was jubilant. "If Arabella Porter-Hume is involved, perhaps there's correspondence! If they are, as Cosway writes, intimates, Arabella may have mentioned Harriet. I know a few people in banking. We can ask them where to find copies of Arabella's letters."

I scribbled some more – Arabella Porter-Hume, Mr Richardson (whoever he was), and also peered at Adriana. "If she was a big shot and the first woman in banking, I imagine someone will have written something about her, studied her?"

"Good thought. Perhaps we can ask the archivist for some ideas?"

Privately, I thought Adriana was highly unlikely to put herself out for us, but nodded. Hugo walked over to her, and even from across the room, I could see her erect the barriers. After a few minutes of Hugo's chocolate voice, however, Adriana relaxed, and soon after that, she nodded and smiled.

Hugo thanked her and shook her hand, and we left. Adriana gave me a faint smile, and Hugo was whistling, obviously well pleased. I had not allowed my thoughts to stray from Harriet and researching her, but once we left the Tate, I remembered that all this could have been done online by the tall man beside me. Who, instead of staying at home on the internet, had taken a four-hour train journey to do his research in person.

And see me. Don't forget that, Gabriella. To see me. I swallowed and Hugo glanced at me.

"If you can give me your notes, I'll type them up and share," he said, casually. "Then we can decide what to do next. Unless you don't have time," he added, his eyes darting to me.

I looked at the concrete path that headed towards the tube. "No, of course I've got time, Hugo." And I looked at him. He stopped walking and my heart seemed to hiccup.

The roar of London was suddenly muted as I gazed at him, as if imprinting his face on my memory. We stood for a moment, just staring at one another.

A man with his attention firmly on his phone nearly walked into Hugo and changed course a split second before he cannoned into him. It broke the spell that had wound around us, and as if to emphasise the point, my stomach rumbled.

"Lunch?" I said. He grinned and tucked my hand into his arm.

Chapter 25

GROSVENOR SQUARE, MAY 1803

When Harriet returned Augusta's call at the hotel in Albemarle Street, her mother-in-law was out, and Harriet was only slightly ashamed of the relief she felt. She left a note suggesting that as she would be at home the following afternoon, she hoped for the pleasure of seeing her mama then.

Anne felt sure that Augusta's heart would be melted by James. Harriet was doubtful that her mother-in-law had a heart to be moved but smiled and agreed. Thus poor baby James was dressed and prepared, ready to be sent for at a moment's notice, putting the nursery maid under a great deal of strain in ensuring he was pristine, rather than having vomit down his front, or in his hair.

At precisely two o'clock, Coates arrived with Augusta's card. Smiling, Anne asked him to show in their visitors. Augusta entered, sneering as she cast quick glances around the drawing room. Behind her was a pale wisp of a female in an ill-fitting dress who Harriet recalled as one of John's distant cousins, Emily. Emily had obviously been dragooned into the position of Augusta's companion, and from the hangdog look on her face, was finding little pleasure in the role.

Harriet kissed Augusta's cold cheek and shook the limp hand of Emily. Augusta managed a curt nod for Anne, while Emily had sufficient manners to curtsy. They took their seats and several long seconds passed before Anne enquired after Augusta's journey to London and her lodgings at the hotel.

Augusta sniffed. "The roads are dreadful, and the journey nigh shook my bones to pieces! The hotel is wickedly expensive, and I would not have come had the need not been urgent."

Anne's smile froze and she swiftly rose to ring for refreshments.

"Why urgent, Mama?" I asked.

"The estate is falling to ruin!" snapped Augusta. But Harriet was having none of it.

"You have been misinformed, Mama," she said calmly, crossing the room to find Peters' latest letter on the writing table. "Peters tells me that all the works on the estate are proceeding as planned and that the lambing has been especially good this year."

"It was not long since Peters was in short coats! He needs careful watching!"

"I have every confidence in Peters, Mama."

"You're naïve and should be at home!"

"Ah, Coates, thank you so much," said Anne in relief as the butler came in with the tea.

Augusta closed her mouth tightly. She took her cup with a curt nod. Emily, who had kept her eyes on her lap previously, fixed her gaze on her tea and sipped as if her life depended on it.

Coates left the room, leaving a silence so thick it could be cut with a knife.

CHAPTER 25

Anne leapt into the conversational void. "I have been so grateful for your daughter's presence, Mrs Colchester. She has been a great comfort to me and was with me all the way through the birth. Would you like to meet James?"

"Who?" replied Augusta.

"My son," Anne said, smiling mistily and reaching again for the bell. Coates reappeared. "Can you ask Miss Lloyd to bring James to us?"

"How old is the child?" Augusta asked in chilly tones.

"Nearly a month old, and I swear I never saw such a sweet boy!" replied his doting mother. "Had it not been for Harriet and her enquiries for my sickness, I might never have been strong enough for the birth."

"Shame she couldn't put as much effort into her own attempts to conceive!" was the response, and Anne's eyes widened.

Into such an atmosphere came James, who, with baby senses, recognised that all was not well with the world and began to squall as soon as Miss Lloyd brought him in. Anne, torn between the anguish of her friend and her son, knew not who to comfort first.

Defiantly, Harriet went over to Miss Lloyd and took James in her arms, rocking him and speaking nonsense until he subsided. She turned to Augusta.

"I think you must have other calls to make," she said quietly. Augusta's thin face heated with colour.

"Now the baby is here, you are no longer needed! You must return to Colchester Hall!" she said between gritted teeth. "I've been hearing how you dishonour the memory of my John, gadding around to balls and such like! Anyone would think you were looking for a husband!"

Lady Altringham's meddling. Hiding her flash of anger, Harriet bent her head to James and replied sweetly, "But how *nice* it is in London! With people who are pleasant and courteous! What say you, James?"

He gurgled and Harriet rubbed noses with him, his sweet, milky scent pulling on her heart. How she wished she could have had this with John.

Then Coates arrived again. "Mr Richardson, ma'am," he said to Anne. "Shall I say you are not at home?"

"By no means!" Harriet intervened before Anne could speak, feeling the blush spread up her cheeks as she answered for the lady of the house.

Anne twinkled at her. "Indeed! Mr Richardson is an old friend; of course we are at home!"

Augusta seemed to swell in indignation, and her lips thinned as she made way for another guest – and one she didn't care for, to boot.

Alexander's step paused only briefly as he saw Augusta sitting rigidly on Anne's sofa. He seemed to read the room in a second. He bowed his head to Anne, then Harriet, nodded to Emily and finally shook hands with Augusta.

"How are you?" he asked. Augusta's eyes snapped dangerously, and he hid a smile. "But I need not ask – you are always in the best of health, are you not?"

"I'm well enough!" was Augusta's icy response. "What are *you* doing here?"

"I've come to ask Harriet if she would honour me with her company for a ride in the Park."

Harriet, relishing that the use of her first name indicated an intimacy that might be misread, patted James on the back and then handed him to Anne, who was soon lost in adoration.

CHAPTER 25

"Riding in the Park?" Augusta's glare switched between her daughter-in-law and Alexander, and Harriet could see the calculation in her face regarding the state of affairs between them. James, disliking the shrill voice, set up a wail of complaint.

"Well!" said Anne, finally annoyed. "He's not used to raised voices. Miss Lloyd, could you take him? I'll be up later." She rose to her feet and Augusta, recognising her dismissal, scowled and gathered her reticule. Harriet also stood and turned to Alexander.

"Mr Richardson, I am afraid I am engaged this afternoon, but I should like to drive with you later this week, if that is convenient?" Alexander raised an eyebrow, but smiled and bowed his head. Harriet then spoke to Augusta, who was watching the exchange very closely. "I shall remain here until the end of the season. As I do not 'gad about', as you say, I am not often to be found in society, so we may not see much of one another. Good day to you."

Augusta put her thin nose in the air and marched out.

As soon as they heard the front door close, Anne clapped her hands. "Bravo, Harriet!"

Later that week, on a fine, sunny day, Alexander handed Harriet into his curricle. While he climbed in and took the reins, Harriet ran a critical eye over the two glossy chestnut horses. Alexander, seeing the direction of her gaze, informed her that he had bought them at Tattersalls the previous week and felt he had a bargain.

He called over his shoulder to the tiger. "Ready, Henry?"

"Yes, sir!" replied the groom, perching on the back of the curricle.

Alexander slapped the reins. They moved off smoothly and soon had turned through Grosvenor Gate and into the Park. Harriet, conscious of the sun, opened her parasol and kept quiet until Alexander had navigated through the other carriages on the Ring. The Park was crowded with matrons and their preening young charges and gentlemen showing off their riding and driving skills with varying degrees of success.

"Have you recovered from Augusta's visit?" Alexander asked her as they settled into a sedate trot.

Harriet smiled. "I have – although Mama is not one to give up so easily! She has invited me to dinner on Thursday and I expect I shall be subjected to a series of rants and entreaties to return home!"

"You will go?"

"She can hardly kidnap me! I'm secure in my determination to remain at least a little longer."

Alexander slowed the curricle to nod at a group of ladies and wish them good day, so it was a moment before he replied. "I'm not sure why she wants you to return. John had excellent business sense, and if he put his trust in Peters, I don't see what she has to say about it."

Harriet agreed. "I think she's concerned about me forming an attachment," she added, admiring a hat on an attractive woman leading a greyhound.

Alexander's face was all displeased astonishment. "An attachment? But you are not yet out of mourning!"

"No, indeed!"

"Where did she get that idea?"

"Augusta has sufficient connections to ensure that, should she wish, my every outing is observed!" Lady Altringham for example, she thought darkly. She wondered if the matron had seen her dancing on the terrace with the man beside her.

"Do you have a partiality that someone has observed?" His voice sounded cool. "Has she cause to think you dangling after a new husband?"

Harriet was startled. "Sir, you insult me!" A couple of gentlemen on the path turned around, and she lowered her voice. "What makes you think I would 'dangle' after any man? Particularly – as you said some months ago – given the fortune attached to me? No, sir, I have no plans to marry anyone, but intend to enjoy my inheritance!"

Her voice was brittle, and it occurred to her that she was close to tears, without knowing precisely why. There was a silence.

"Of course. I beg your pardon," he replied in a stiff voice.

A devil on Harriet's shoulder drove her to continue. "But we should be speaking of you, sir! Anne said you would soon be thinking of setting up your nursery. How goes your endeavour?"

She dreaded to hear him speak of Georgiana, but some masochistic urge wanted to know his intentions. And with the sheer impudence of her question, she felt as if she had crossed from her safe, ordered life into another, less predictable existence. Her pulse was pounding.

This time it was Alexander's turn to stare, and he pulled up the horses and faced her. He looked uncomfortable. "I – I am astonished you should quiz me thus!"

Harriet felt her face burn with embarrassment. Shaking his head, Alexander picked up the reins again. The conversation seemed to die between them, despite Harriet wracking her brains for a safe topic other than the weather.

She looked down at her tightly clasped hands as Alexander turned the horses back towards the exit to the park. Harriet was glad of her veil to hide her face. She was unused to this awkward atmosphere. The journey back to Grosvenor Square seemed to take forever and yet was over in a trice.

"Henry, help Mrs Colchester down," Alexander said, sounding irritated. "Good day to you, ma'am." Henry offered his arm, but Harriet jumped down unaided.

"Good day, sir," Harriet managed, and hurried into the house, cross and miserable. As she marched up the stairs, she was convinced that making contact with her sister and travelling the world were two fine ambitions. She could do either of *those* without a husband.

Chapter 26

CENTRAL LONDON, APRIL 2023

As if to make up for our previous silence, we both talked non-stop as we picked sushi dishes from a conveyor belt. When the topics of Harriet, the various clues to her life, and who was researching what next had been exhausted, Hugo asked about the gallery and the opening of the mezzanine.

Once again, I found myself enjoying the attention of someone who asked intelligent questions and was genuinely interested in the answers. He asked if he could pop in one night and see the gallery, and I eagerly agreed. Partway through my description of the first event, his phone rang. It was on the countertop, and I saw that the name on the screen was Pierce, his brother.

He gave it a cursory scan and switched it to silent. I paused and raised my eyebrow. He grimaced.

"We're not seeing eye-to-eye at the moment," Hugo said.

"Oh, I know about *that*!" I picked up a prawn and dipped it in soy sauce.

"Oh?"

I hesitated. Did I want to expose my family's behaviour to Hugo?

He chuckled. "Chatham House rule," he said, and I made a note to see what that was, later. "I'll go first. My brother is bright and innovative but can't seem to control his expenses. He's exhausted his good will at the bank, and he's now coming to the family to bail him out. My sister, Carol, has flatly refused, so I'm his target."

"Why don't you just tell him?"

Hugo shrugged. "Carol is much harder headed than I am and ignores his calls when he's on the scrounge. Mum and Dad died within twelve months of one another five years ago, and while we were all devastated, Pierce has just never been the same. And now I'm head of the family and have the Lodge, he thinks I'm loaded and all he has to do is ask."

I put down my chopsticks. "Hmm. Lots of similarities," I said thoughtfully. "As I told you in Berwick, I always wanted to be useful, and I suppose that my family has just grown to expect it, over the years. They don't think I've got an important job – after all, it's just pretty pictures, isn't it? – and so they think they can call on me any time and I'll just drop everything and be there."

I listed my nearest and dearest and enumerated all the ways in which I was useful – everything from tax returns and masterminding planning applications to babysitting. Hugo began to look appalled. "There's also Aunt Mo, but she's incredibly independent, so she only asks for help when she truly needs it."

He shook his head. "What's happened that you're not speaking?"

"They wanted me to cater for twenty kids for the twins' sixth birthday party with two days' notice."

Hugo choked on a piece of chicken and the assistant behind the counter started towards him, but Hugo grabbed his water, took a swallow and waved him away. "They really *don't* think you work in a responsible position full-time, do they?"

I smiled ruefully. "Never occurred to them. To be fair, I don't think – other than being a doctor, maybe – it would matter what I did! Mum told me I'd chosen work over family, and I haven't spoken to her since. Or Liam and Evie. If it wasn't for Aunt Mo, I'd have no contact with any family at all."

"That sounds really tough." Hugo's voice was soft and gentle.

I shrugged, trying to lighten the mood. "Aunt Mo says they'll come round without water."

He laughed. "But in the meantime, you need some support to stick it out and keep your nerve."

I smiled, glad he understood without me having to elucidate. There was a pause while I regrouped my emotions. "But that's me and my family. What are you going to do about Pierce? What's stopping you from telling him you won't help him, and he needs to sort it out himself?"

"Nothing, except guilt. He's the youngest of the family, and as I said, was hit hard when our parents died. But you're right. I've perhaps been a bit *too* supportive."

"Talk to him."

He smiled. His eyes were warm on my face and with a bit of a sparkle I hadn't noticed before. "I will. But now, I think we need to pay and get you back to the gallery."

Saved by the bill, I thought wryly.

The gentle buzz of conversation and the odd burst of laughter demonstrated that the fifty executives attending the insurance company high-potential employee event had drunk some excellent wine and were relaxing nicely. Some of them had even looked at the art on the ground floor, and I saw the CEO, Bill James, pause by the new Chloe Johnson landscape, a majestic, atmospheric painting of the Yorkshire moors. I hoped he would consider purchasing.

The catering company's young student waiters and waitresses threaded their way through the groups with trays of finger food and glasses of wine, champagne and mineral water. They were ably directed by a stout lady called Liz, who sported steel-grey hair and an equally steely expression. Our tiny office kitchen had been completely emptied, and the caterer's trays, cutlery and glasses set out in military lines to maximise the two-by-one metre space.

I snatched a look at my watch. Bill would do his speech in fifteen minutes, then give some awards. I smiled, satisfied. I was only slightly peeved that Gerrard, extending his holiday by another two weeks, meant he couldn't witness my endeavours.

A figure at the front door caught my eye as I looked over the balcony of the mezzanine.

Hugo. What was he doing here?

I ran downstairs and Hugo gave me an apologetic grimace. "I'm sorry, Gabriella, I'm such an idiot! I forgot your event was tonight. I was going to surprise you and whisk you away for a drink!"

"I hope to be finished by nine-thirty, if you want to hang around," I said, looking back at the mezzanine.

CHAPTER 26

"Yes, I can wait at a bar or something. I'll make myself scarce." Hugo looked over my shoulder and I turned to see Bill James striding towards us.

"Hugo Cavendish!" he said, beaming. "What are you doing here?"

"I came to talk to Gabriella about a commission," Hugo said as they shook hands. "But I'll come another time."

"No, no, why not join us for a drink? I've been meaning to look you up anyway, as I think we've got some issues in one of our departments you could help us with. If Miss Sullivan is fine with you joining us?" Bill turned to me, his craggy face enquiring.

I spread my hands. Who was I to interfere with the smooth running of the wheels of commerce? "Not at all! I'm sure we can spare one more glass of bubbly!"

They wandered off and I went to check on the level of champagne. By the time I returned to the mezzanine, Bill was beginning his speech. Reflecting the man, his speech was expansive and probably a couple of minutes too long. The award-giving began and there were hoots, catcalls and genuine applause for those who won, including a tiny woman with glossy black hair who winked at the crowd as she collected her statuette and an envelope with what I imagined was a bonus cheque.

"And before I end this part of our evening, I'd like to thank Gabriella Sullivan, who not only masterminded this whole event, but also the redevelopment of this mezzanine, which I'm sure you'll agree is a wonderful space. As many of you know, I collect art, but in that I've been guided by Gabriella and her mentor, Gerrard Williams. Gabriella was the first to remind me that art might be a good investment, but a true collector buys what they love, not only what is valuable, because as we all know – the value of investments can go down…"

"As well as up!" the audience chorused. There was laughter; Bill began to applaud me, and so did everyone else. My cheeks were hot with embarrassment, but I smiled.

I skipped down the stairs to check with Liz about the next wave of food. That done, I made my way back to the bottom of the mezzanine stairs to find Liam staring at me as if I'd grown another head. He was wearing what looked like a very expensive suit, but it pulled over his paunch.

"What are you doing here?" I asked stupidly.

"I've only just arrived. I'm joining this firm," he said, still staring at me. "I was invited by my future boss. I mentioned it, I'm sure I did."

"Right." I possibly hadn't been listening. I stopped, wondering what to say next. The best I could come up with was, "Are you having a nice time?"

"Yes, of course – but – is it right what Bill James said? That you organised all this tonight, and you advise him on his art?"

"You think he wasn't telling the truth?" I gritted my teeth.

"No! I… I just…"

"Yes. I organised the whole event. I also project managed the redesign of the mezzanine, hired the builders, completed on time and under budget. This company is one of three coming into the mezzanine. And finally, yes, I do advise your CEO on his art collection."

Liam gawped at me. Then he shook his head. "Right. Right, then. It's impressive."

CHAPTER 26

"Thanks. Perhaps you'll believe me, the next time I tell you I'm busy at work," I finished coldly.

He nodded and, mumbling, walked away. I went to the loo. It took ten minutes for me to calm down.

I returned to the mezzanine and found Hugo searching for me. His dark gaze sharpened when he saw me.

"Everything okay?" he said quietly.

"Yes, I'm fine. Liam's here, finally discovering what I do for a living."

"Ah. Surprised, is he?"

"Staggered," I returned dryly, feeling better all at once.

"Can you have a drink?"

"I'd give the world for a gin, but I'd better not," I laughed. "What do you think of the mezzanine?"

"It's a terrific space, extremely stylish, and I think it'll be incredibly lucrative. I'm already thinking of the clients of mine I can tell about it."

I grinned. "Thanks. Now, I'd better find Bill James' secretary. She runs him with a rod of iron and can tell me when he's going."

After that, time seemed to speed up, and before I knew it, people were slowly leaving. Some were gently inebriated, although not raucous. I was quietly congratulating myself when there was a loud voice from the back of the mezzanine.

"I said I hadn't finished, you plonker!" I closed my eyes. Liam was never great at holding his drink. Quickly, I crossed the floor to find a young waiter eyeing Liam with dislike.

"I beg your pardon. I didn't hear you," he said.

"Idiot! Where did you learn to wait on people? Some motorway service station?"

"That's enough, Liam," I said quietly.

"Or what?" Ah. Liam was at the belligerent stage of drunkenness.

"I'll tell Bill James what a wanker he's hired," I said without missing a beat. "How dare you insult my staff? Please leave."

He tossed back his remaining wine and stalked unsteadily towards the stairs, with me close behind him. I wanted him in grabbing distance if he missed a step; I could do without him breaking his neck on the way down. As he headed towards the entrance, I leaned round him to pull open the door. He swivelled too quickly and fell over, dragging me with him. As we landed in a heap, Liam began to giggle and I sighed, feeling the bruises on my backside beginning to form. Then a pair of well-polished brogues arrived in front of us, and Liam was dragged unceremoniously to his feet.

"Get your hands off her, you lout," Hugo growled. I scrambled up as Hugo hauled Liam by his collar until they were nose to nose – and given Hugo was a good eight inches taller, that left my brother dangling on his toes.

"Thanks, Hugo, but I've got this," I said, pulling on his arms. Reluctantly, he let a squirming Liam down. I grabbed my brother and dragged him outside. Once on the pavement, he shook off my hand and straightened his jacket. Without a word, I flagged a cab and bundled him inside.

"When you're sober, you can apologise," I said, closing the door on his cursing.

I watched the cab disappear and wearily walked back into the gallery. An *almost* perfect evening, I said to myself, straightening my black dress.

CHAPTER 26

Hugo glowered at me when I walked in. "Who was that idiot?"

"My brother." Hugo swore and started to apologise, but I cut him off. "Don't worry about it. He slipped; he wasn't wrestling me to the floor. I very much appreciate you coming in to bat for me, but it was under control."

He looked at the floor. A warm feeling of being protected washed over me, and although I hadn't needed it, it was great to have it offered.

Even in heels, I was much shorter than he was, so I went up on tiptoe to kiss his cheek. Unexpectedly he turned towards me and our lips met.

Fireworks exploded in my head.

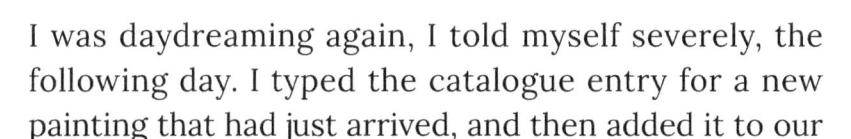

I was daydreaming again, I told myself severely, the following day. I typed the catalogue entry for a new painting that had just arrived, and then added it to our insurance. I forced myself to concentrate.

After the kiss, which had lasted all of – perhaps – two seconds, I had pulled back reluctantly. You're at a corporate event, I told myself, while all the time wishing I could grab his broad shoulders and lean into that firm, warm mouth. He stared at me, and for a moment, neither of us spoke. I cleared my throat.

"Sorry, missed your cheek."

He too cleared his throat. "No problem. Right, then. Are you up for a drink, or are you too tired?"

My stomach fell. He'd given me an out; perhaps he'd gone off the idea. Just at that moment, Liz called my name, and I accepted the inevitable.

"Hugo—"

"No, you're right, you've had a big night, and my timing is lousy," he said with a tight smile. "Shall we take a rain check? I'll be back again in London soon and I'll let you know, rather than just spring it on you."

I muttered something incomprehensible, and he nodded and made his way out into the night.

And today, he would have taken the train back to Northumberland. I sighed, glad that I would be closing the gallery in a few hours and then I could go and talk to Aunt Mo and untangle my thoughts.

I'd been surprised to get a message from Liam with a stiff apology. I'd replied, asking about his head, and he'd sent me a green-faced emoji.

I drifted off again, reliving the kiss. When my phone rang, I almost jumped.

"Hugo?" I said, trying to sound casual.

"Gabriella, can you talk?" His voice was urgent, upset.

"Of course! What's up? You sound rattled."

"The portraits have been stolen."

Chapter 27

GRILLON'S HOTEL, MAY 1803

Harriet shrugged off her wrap in the parlour that Augusta had hired for dinner. She was unnerved to see that there were three places set at the mahogany table, but then recalled that Emily had to eat, too.

The minutes passed and Augusta did not appear. Harriet wandered around the comfortable room, brightened with cream and gold striped wallpaper, and sat on one of the rather hard leather sofas. She wished she'd had the forethought to bring a book. She was just about to pull the bell to make enquiries when Augusta arrived, dressed severely in black crepe with a black lace cap. Harriet recognised the dig; Augusta was still in full mourning, while she, John's wife, had grieved enough to move into half-mourning.

Harriet glanced down her pale grey Italian gauze, trimmed with white ribbon. It was perfectly respectable, her jewellery subdued and simple. She looked up to find Augusta examining her closely.

"I see you've wasted no time spending John's money on new gowns," she said curtly.

"Good evening, Mama," Harriet responded, pressing her lips to a thin cheek. A movement at the door caught her eye, and to her horror, Edwin walked through the door, sporting a coat of such a virulent puce that Harriet winced. The points of his collar were starched so heavily, he moved as though he had a stiff neck. He raised his quizzing glass to gaze at her, and she was hard pressed not to giggle.

His mid-brown hair was brushed into the Brutus style, imitating Lord Byron, which on Edwin looked less romantic than messy. His silk waistcoat was a lighter shade of the coat, embroidered with gold daisies. He was indeed glorious to behold.

"*Buonasera*, cousin," he said, sketching a low bow. "Aunt Augusta."

Harriet curtsied. "Good evening. I thought you were still abroad."

"Returned two days ago," he said, his tone on the verge of sulky. "Boney's making a lot of noise." He strode to a small table in the corner of the room and helped himself to port. Harriet flicked a glance to her mother-in-law, wondering if Napoleon, rather than Augusta's demands, had engineered his return. But now he was here.

Harriet was no fool; this was to be a concerted effort to get her back to Colchester Hall, as Augusta wanted. While she marshalled her thoughts, a waiter arrived to serve dinner. She sat through the asparagus soup, refused the suckling pig that was the first remove and ate a few mouthfuls of the fricassee of rabbit. It was not that the food was not well cooked, or delicious; Harriet was too intent on listening for Augusta's opening sally.

Attempting to steer the conversation away from the inevitable, Harriet pressed Edwin for tales of his tour, and he responded with his adventures in Germany and Venice, although these seemed to focus on the wine he consumed and the amount of money he managed to gamble away. Harriet, so far denied the opportunity to travel, was bitterly disappointed – where were Edwin's thoughts on the excavations at Herculaneum and Pompeii? What were his views on the astonishing wealth of Italian art and sculpture?

"Did you not also travel to Naples?" she asked, and he reddened. He seemed about to reply when Augusta cut across the conversation to criticise the food they were eating, and Edwin was silent.

More food arrived, and once more, Harriet only picked at her orange soufflé and nibbled at some cheese and nuts. She noticed that Augusta had fallen quiet, and Edwin drank a lot of wine until Augusta threw him a look.

"You could use Edwin's experience abroad to guide you on your own travels, Harriet," Augusta said, and Harriet frowned, confused. "You have always wanted to travel, have you not? I have never understood it, myself – nasty foreign places full of bandits and charlatans, looking to fleece unsuspecting tourists! I declare I barely had a sound night's sleep while Edwin was away!" Augusta looked down her nose at the table.

Harriet did not know what to say to that, and Edwin nodded sagely.

"In short, my dear Harriet, I know that you will travel, eventually, regardless of the effect on my nerves, but if it is to be so, I pray you take proper precautions against the dangers."

Harriet was curious. "And how should I do that, Mama?"

"Why, with Edwin to protect you!"

Harriet laughed out loud. "You would make me the talk of society, Mama, to travel with a man, even a family member, unchaperoned!"

"Not if we were married," muttered Edwin, his brow damp with sweat. The smile fell from Harriet's face.

"It's an excellent idea," Augusta agreed, dabbing the corner of her mouth with a napkin. "This way, you are kept in the family's bosom, safe from fortune hunters."

Harriet forced herself to remain calm and took a fortifying sip of wine. She leaned back in her chair.

"Out of the question," she said, proud that her voice was steady. "I have other plans for my future, and they don't include marriage to Edwin." He gave a soft sound of relief and she smiled at him. "Don't be a gudgeon! We should never suit. I would murder you within a month."

Augusta's eyes gleamed. "So high and mighty!" she sneered. "Do your plans include marriage to anyone else?"

The image of Alexander flashed into her mind, swiftly banished. Harriet stood and retrieved her discarded wrap. "That is none of your concern, Mama. I am of age. I may do as I choose, and that may mean I remain a widow. Do not think that I'm some green girl of seventeen to be taken in by any fortune-hunter that heads my way."

"But the will is very irregular," Augusta said, almost conversationally. "I've discussed it with several lawyers who say it will be straightforward to challenge. And should you decide not to accept Edwin's offer for your hand, I will do so."

Harriet was silent, looking at the ageing, bitter face of her mother-in-law. She might have guessed. Augusta had no feelings for her as John's wife. She was merely the possessor of his fortune.

"You must do as you see fit," she said and turned to leave. There was a gasp of fury.

"All I needed of you was to provide an heir!" Augusta spat out, rising from her seat and knocking over her wine. She thrust her face close to Harriet's. "I thought the task simple enough even for a chit from a disgraced family who needed our wealth, but no, you failed!"

Anger rose so quickly in Harriet that she almost pushed the older woman away, but she caught herself in time and stepped back. Edwin was standing by the table, his mouth agape.

Had Sophia felt like this? Bullied and castigated – unless you submitted. Harriet recalled her own mother's rigid face and implacable words and then compared the memory with the face of Augusta.

Harriet drew a deep breath. "John must be turning in his grave at your treatment of me. You ought to be ashamed."

She walked out of the door.

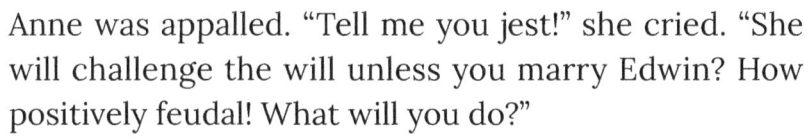

Anne was appalled. "Tell me you jest!" she cried. "She will challenge the will unless you marry Edwin? How positively feudal! What will you do?"

Harriet, who had risen early and was pale from lack of sleep, waved a letter that she had just completed in the sunny morning room. "I am writing to John's lawyer, Mr Bessiwick. I asked at the time of the reading whether the will could be challenged – after all, even I know it is an unusual legacy, to leave everything to the wife—"

"But not unheard of," commented Phillip, standing by the fireplace. "Especially – and I do not wish to cause you pain here, Harriet – especially if there are no children."

Flinching at the reminder of her childlessness, Harriet took out a wafer from the writing desk and sealed the short letter to Mr Bessiwick. She apologised for the journey he would have to make to London but requested him to call on her at his earliest convenience.

"You need some protection, Harriet," mused Anne, her chin in her hand. "Have you thought of marrying someone else?"

Even in her anxious state, Harriet laughed. "No, my love! I want to find Sophia, remain independent and travel the world with a companion!"

Anne's eyebrows shot up her forehead. "To stay a widow, alone? Surely not! Oh, Harriet, no!"

Phillip, seeing that his wife was about to enumerate the benefits of a loving marriage, thought it best to retreat to his study. He picked up the letter to Mr Bessiwick and closed the door softly behind him.

"My dear Harriet, you are so young!" Anne said, almost wringing her hands. "Surely you miss – well – you miss the *tender* side of matrimony?"

Harriet remembered John's loving – efficient, vigorous and occasionally pleasurable. She would be lying if she said she had not missed the sex since he had died – the gentle touch of a hand, skin against her skin. She recalled the dull pulse of desire that had caught her in the marital bed. But as for the heavenly transports that she had heard mentioned in whispers by other women – no, she was firmly grounded. She smiled to herself, and an imp of mischief prodded her.

"Well, I may take a lover!" she said casually.

The colour drained from Anne's face and then flooded back. "Oh! Oh... Well, I know that many women do, I just never..." She stopped.

Harriet laughed. "It is infamous of me to tease you!" she said, patting Anne's hand. "My reputation is still spotless, and it will remain so."

Anne fell back on the sofa and fanned herself with her hand. "Thank goodness! I myself would not be without the pleasures of the marriage bed, but I imagine there are other ways in which you might...?" She trailed off and once again flushed.

"Yes, Anne," Harriet said with a wink at her dearest friend. "I know some of these other ways."

Anne nodded and scooted away from the topic with obvious relief. "But – if you are not to marry, what can we do to prevent Augusta from pressing you?"

"I don't know. Perhaps Mr Bessiwick can provide me with some ideas." Harriet paused. "Or Lady Porter-Hume."

"Lady Porter-Hume? But how?"

Harriet recalled her conversation at the Porter-Hume ball. "She spoke to me of Anne Damer and told me the lady is able to pursue her sculpture because of a legacy she had written into her marriage contract. Lady Porter-Hume said the law, applied correctly, can help us if we know how to wield it. It may be that she has some strategies to prevent Augusta from challenging John's will."

"That is a capital notion!" Anne agreed.

Harriet wrote to Lady Porter-Hume, requesting an audience on a matter of personal importance, and called Coates to have it delivered. Not an hour later, Lady Porter-Hume sent a messenger with a response.

Of course. I am available at your convenience.

Chapter 28

CENTRAL LONDON, MAY 2023

I was startled into silence. Then the words tumbled out of my mouth.

"What? Both of them? From your house? Was there any damage? You weren't in the house, were you? Are you hurt? Have you called the police? Did—"

"Gabriella," Hugo interrupted me. "Both of the pictures are gone from my house. There's a bit of damage around the window and it happened while I was in London, so no, I'm not hurt, but thanks for asking. I've called the police and they're on their way. Did I leave anything out?"

I burst into tears.

"God, Gabriella," he said urgently. "Sweetheart, don't cry. I'm fine!"

After a few sniffles, I folded my lips and grabbed my control. My thoughts were running around my head as if they were in a cartoon.

"I'm so sorry," I said, finding a handkerchief and blowing my nose. "I don't know what came over me."

"Are you okay?" his voice came softly down the phone.

"I'm ashamed that at this precise moment, you're asking if I'm okay, rather than me asking you. But oh, Hugo!

Harriet's lovely miniatures! I'm gutted for you!" I threw the tissue into the bin in disgust. He chuckled.

"I'm gutted too, and possibly heading for a long, stiff whisky at the end of tonight. But, as well as telling you, I wondered if you kept any records that would help the police? Speed things along a bit."

"We have our bill of sale to you, but you have the original transaction details from when Gerrard bought the miniatures from the private collector. I placed then in the case—"

"Ah."

My heart sank. "You didn't store them in the safe?" I said, trying to keep the incredulity from my voice.

"Of course I did. But the safe was also opened. The documents and some cash were stolen." There was a grim edge to his voice that made me pause.

"Wow," I said slowly. "Someone knew what they wanted."

Hugo didn't answer me, and for a second, I wondered what was really going on. "Do you have a burglar alarm?"

"Yes. It was disarmed."

"I hope you won't be offended at me saying this, Hugo, but it sounds like an inside job." Another silence. "Hugo?"

"Yes, it does sound like an inside job," he agreed wearily. "But I don't think it is."

I narrowed my eyes, unable to place his tone. Hmm. Time enough for Sherlock Holmes when we'd got the details to the police. "Well, I have my photos of the miniatures and I can let you have a copy of our bill of sale. You're insured, I take it?"

"With a house like this? Yes, I'm insured to the hilt."

"The police probably know about the Art Loss Register, too," I said, clicking on my browser to find the number. "They have a database of stolen art and collectibles. I can give the ALR the details of the miniatures too, and they'll let us know if anyone searches for Harriet's pictures."

"What use will that be?" Hugo sounded a bit testy. I forgave him. He must be under a lot of stress.

"If serious buyers want to buy art, they check this to make sure the item they're buying isn't stolen. Galleries buying pieces also check it regularly," I explained patiently.

"Oh. That's a good idea, thank you."

Another pause. "You sound really shaken up. I'm sorry this has happened. If you think I can do anything else, please just ask – I want to help," I said softly.

"I appreciate that. You were the first person I thought of when I found them gone. I knew you'd understand."

I remembered his lips, firm and smooth against mine, and went a bit warm. I swallowed. Hugo coughed.

"Well, I suppose I'd better make ready for the police when they come." He hesitated and seemed reluctant to ring off. I waited.

"Gabriella…"

"Yes?"

"The other night…"

Oh, no. The last thing I wanted was an inquest into our accidental kiss. Or his awkwardness after it. I could feel myself starting to cringe.

"Last night, I wish we'd been able to continue our conversation over dinner."

The words bounced around in my head, and my spirits rose like a kite taking flight.

"I think you mentioned something about lousy timing," I said with a smile.

"And I think my timing is continuing to be lousy," he sighed. "The police have just pulled up. I'll have to go – but can we talk later, after you finish work?"

"Of course. You can tell me what they find," I said.

He gave a tut of exasperation. "I don't *just* want to talk about the paintings, Gabriella! I'll call you later."

I closed the call and smiled at nothing.

Susan came up behind me almost noiselessly. "Good call?" she asked dryly.

I fell to earth with a bump. "Actually, no – some low life has nicked two miniatures we sourced for him. The police are there now."

Susan's eyebrows, plucked to a fine line, rose past the rims of her glasses into her grey fringe. "That's dreadful!"

I nodded and pulled out the laptop from under the counter. "It is. Just let me send our copy of the bill of sale to him."

"I'll do that, shall I?" Susan said immediately. "I've completed the invoicing and was only going to tidy up the office."

"Star! The miniatures were sold to Hugo Cavendish in January. It's an invoice for sixty thousand pounds; you should find it easily. His details are on the client database. Send the copy over as soon as, will you?"

She nodded and returned to the office, her diminutive figure almost skipping away. I pulled out my phone, had a brief conversation with someone at the Art Loss Register and forwarded the details we had.

After the call, I stared into space. I was gutted for Hugo, and for the miniatures, which had been ripped

CHAPTER 28

from their rightful home. The theft seemed off to me. A disarmed alarm. An opened safe. Not much damage to the house. Hugo conveniently out. I was no detective, but surely that was an inside job.

And the only suspect that sprang to my mind was Pierce.

When Hugo called at about eight o'clock, my head was starting to ache from all the conjecturing I'd been forcing my brain to go through – about the kiss, about Harriet, about the paintings and about Hugo's brother, who was desperate for money.

"Hi," I said, hoping to produce the right mix of support and optimism.

"Hi." His voice flowed down the phone, and I wondered if there would come a time when the dark honey tones didn't affect me. Focusing with an effort, I asked what the police had said.

"They weren't terribly helpful. Sucked their teeth a bit and dusted for prints. They've taken the documentation you sent – thanks for that, incidentally – and they say they'll send me a crime reference number."

"Will they contact the Art Loss Register?"

He grunted. "To be honest, until I mentioned it, they didn't seem to have heard of it."

"Perhaps there's not much art theft in Berwick-upon-Tweed."

"Then I'm the lucky one? Brilliant." His glorious voice sounded flat.

I tried to reassure him, but I knew that we'd need to get very lucky for the portraits to re-emerge quickly; much of the art on the ALR had been on there for decades. Pining victims hoped that someday, dodgy owners would forget that the Matisse on their wall had fallen off the back of a lorry and try to cash in their investment with a reputable auction house. Then it would be flagged on the system, the police would be informed, and it stood a chance of recovery. There were successes – but often art changed hands quietly, under the radar, and art and legitimate owners were never reunited.

I asked what else the police had said. Hugo was short.

"They think it's an inside job – hell, even I'm under suspicion! They'll probably want to speak to you to confirm I was in London."

"They think you'd steal your own paintings for the insurance?"

"That's about it."

"There are no other suspects?" My question was gentle, but Hugo's response was cold.

"No. My brother's in Newcastle seeing clients who can vouch for him. Carol is in France. Birdie is in Eastbourne with her sister."

"Ah."

But Newcastle wasn't miles away from Berwick, was it? I examined my nails as I wondered how to phrase the next thing I was going to say.

"If the person who stole them doesn't know what they're doing, the miniatures might appear again," I said carefully.

Hugo was silent. "But the person who stole them *is* likely to be an experienced thief, aren't they?" he said at last, equally carefully.

"Maybe. Certainly, experienced enough to get into your house, disarm the alarm and crack the safe," I replied, with a tinge of sarcasm. "But that doesn't mean they know what to do with stolen art."

"What are you saying?" Even through the phone line, Hugo sounded tense.

"I'm saying that yes, the person might either be experienced – or incredibly lucky – to be able to break in as they did, but unless they have a lot of contacts, they're left with the pictures. And if they're wanting cash – and if they nicked that from the safe, they may well do – they'll want to sell them. And if they haven't sold stolen art before, they won't know how it all works. So, they may slip up."

The silence on the phone told me Hugo was thinking.

"Which would be great, wouldn't it?" I pressed. "You'd get the paintings back!"

"Yes, yes, of course." Hugo sounded almost absent, as if he was considering something else.

That was as far as I dared go. Hugo refused to believe that Pierce could be a suspect, and nothing I'd said had influenced him. I also considered the chances that Hugo would warn his brother about the Art Loss Register, in the guise of a simple update: 'Hi, just had a word with the police and they say selling to a dealer will trip the alarm...'

I drew a deep breath. "Anyway, if I can do anything else, you only have to let me know."

"I know, Gabriella, and I'm deeply grateful." He seemed to refocus. "I've got some enquiries of my own to make, but otherwise I've done everything that I can about the miniatures. I'll have to leave it in the hands of the police."

I was incredibly curious about what those 'enquiries' might be but didn't say anything. I had the impression he wasn't being completely open with me. And why should he be? We didn't really know one another, had just bonded over the portraits and shared a bit of family history. Perhaps I'd been wrong about our connection?

I heard him breathe in and imagined his broad chest rising and falling.

"But how are you, Gabriella? Have you spoken to your brother?"

Brothers, I thought absently. The cause of all earthly strife? Discuss. "We've exchanged texts," I said.

"And what about your family?"

Nothing from Mum, nothing from Evie, and after the texts, Liam probably believed we'd sorted our differences. Aunt Mo had headed off to see the Birmingham Royal Ballet with a chum, and Joe was on a modelling assignment in the South of France. Consequently, I'd been left with my thoughts, and since the news earlier today, my suspicions about who had stolen Harriet's pictures.

"I'll sort it in my own time," I said, aware I sounded a little stiff.

A brief silence on the end of the phone told me Hugo had detected it. "I need to spend some time at home, but I have a meeting with Bill James later this month, so I'll be returning to London," he said. "Perhaps we could have lunch, or dinner? And—" he coughed, "um, continue our discussion?"

However cool I was about Hugo's lack of openness, I was not impervious to the implied promise in that velvet voice or the uncertainty I heard in his voice. It was strange without the family constantly making demands, but that should be no reason to gravitate to Hugo. Not that he was hard to gravitate to – tall, broad, handsome, intelligent – I should jump at him.

But he was also a client, and that complicated things. And the mystery of who had stolen the miniatures was yet another mess to add to the pile. I felt as if I was on a switchback with my thinking – this, but that, but then, the other... It was exhausting.

"Um... it would be great to hear if the police have found anything," I said. Silence. "And," I continued softly, unable to stay quiet, "it will be great to see you again."

I heard him release his breath. "Wonderful. I'll call you when I have a date."

I stared at the wall of my sitting room for a good five minutes after he'd rung off. Then I sent a text to Gerrard.

Is it okay for me to go through your little black book of dealers? I can explain when I see you.

A few moments later, Gerrard responded.

Of course, I trust you. I'll be back tomorrow and you can tell me then.

Chapter 29

GROSVENOR SQUARE, MAY 1803

Mr Bessiwick peered over round spectacles at the assembled company of Harriet, Lady Porter-Hume, Phillip and Anne. He stroked his chin.

"Mrs Colchester, I think the will is sound," he said, and Harriet relaxed a little. "But if you recall, I said when I had first the pleasure of making your acquaintance that all wills may be challenged."

"But does a challenge have a realistic chance of success?" enquired Phillip, frowning.

Mr Bessiwick shrugged slightly. "If you were to ask my personal view, I have my doubts. It is not as if Mr Colchester left his other dependents penniless. Mrs Augusta Colchester has a generous stipend and the house in York, and he had no other immediate family. I am not sure on what grounds the lady would challenge it."

"Well, then—" began Anne.

"However," Mr Bessiwick interrupted patiently, "those who have funds will often turn to the law for redress against an imagined wrong. Sometimes the judge will listen. Unfortunately, there are many areas of grey in the law."

"And attorneys make their living through arguing over these grey areas?" asked Phillip, echoing Harriet's

CHAPTER 29

thought. Mr Bessiwick bent his head in acknowledgment with a slight smile.

"Some of us are still aware of the difference between right and wrong," he murmured. "Not all in my profession rejoice in the purely academic pursuit of an argument."

"Bravo, Mr Bessiwick!" said Lady Porter-Hume. "I like your style, sir. If you would be so good to call on my lawyer, I would be indebted. I hope you might share a sight of the will with Mr Wilkins, of Lancaster, Wilkins and Son, and then your advice will benefit from *two* legal minds."

She held out a card. The attorney's eyes widened as he realised he was being asked to consult with one of the most influential legal companies in London. He glanced at Harriet, who nodded. He swallowed.

"I should be honoured, ma'am," he said, his voice sounding a little thready. He tucked the card into his jacket, patting it for safety.

Harriet stood and shook his hand. "Thank you for coming all this way, Mr Bessiwick."

He bowed a little jerkily and strode from the room. Harriet thought the diminutive, portly man stood a little taller than he had at the beginning of their interview.

"I am unsure what to think," she declared, taking her seat again. "It seems to be somewhat of a lottery to take a case to justice!"

"But nonetheless, I feel we must go to court, if Mrs Augusta Colchester persists," Phillip said. "She cannot be allowed to dictate your life in this way."

Lady Porter-Hume's eyebrows drew together. "I understand that Mrs Colchester's mama is attempting to take her fortune, but is this what you refer to as dictating her life, Lord Rochford?"

Phillip immediately looked contrite; Harriet had not shared all the details of Augusta's conversation with Lady Porter-Hume. Harriet quickly explained that Augusta's threatened challenge to the will was a result of her own refusal to marry cousin Edwin. She blushed as she saw Lady Porter-Hume's expression of horror, which quickly turned to disgust.

"Truly? I am saddened to hear that women are so prepared to act against their sisters in this way!" she declared. Harriet hung her head and Lady Porter-Hume patted her hand. "I shall keep our conversation in the strictest confidence, Mrs Colchester. Tell me of this Edwin. I had not heard of him in our discussions before."

"Mr Edwin Beaufort, the eldest son of Mama's sister and thus my cousin by marriage. He has been on his Tour while the Peace was in place," explained Harriet. "Edwin is younger than I and he is a little..." she searched for a word that would illustrate, but not damn Edwin. "Pliable," she decided would do, "in Augusta's hands, but then she does seem to give him a great deal of money."

"Does she now?"

"Yes, Edwin's mother and father live in Staffordshire and are not at all fashionable. Mama has tried to bring him up to snuff."

Anne made a noise of frustration. "Allow me to say what Harriet cannot bring herself to," she said briskly. "Edwin is indulged by his parents, spoiled by Augusta, and can be rather sly to get his own way. He is also a bully – as I saw when the family gathered at Colchester Hall when Harriet was first married. Whatever town bronze he may have acquired in Europe, I doubt he has changed overmuch."

Harriet protested. "To give him his due, he looked rather reluctant to offer me marriage and unflatteringly relieved when I refused him!"

"And Mrs Augusta Colchester holds the purse strings – is that correct?" Lady Porter-Hume asked, and Harriet nodded. There was a silence, and Lady Porter-Hume looked thoughtful. "Do you know roughly when he was in Italy?"

Harriet racked her brains and offered some dates that seemed to stick in her mind. Lady Porter-Hume pulled out a pocketbook and scribbled.

"Why are you interested, ma'am?" Anne said.

Lady Porter-Hume smiled. "Oh, I know Lord Ware, the British envoy to the court at Naples," she said breezily. "It will be good to know a little about this Mr Edwin Beaufort and what he is like. You are certain you do not wish to wed him?"

Harriet could not but laugh. "Lord, no, ma'am! We definitely should not suit, and he would run through the Colchester fortune in a trice! He has expensive and frivolous tastes!"

Lady Porter-Hume nodded and stood. "I should go; I have other calls to make." She shook hands with Phillip and smiled at Harriet. "Chin up, my dear! When your Mr Bessiwick and Mr Wilkins meet, and have deliberated, we will plan from there."

She left in a flurry of emerald green silk.

Harriet sat rather heavily on the sofa, close to tears.

"What is it, Harriet?" Anne exclaimed, clasping her hand. "I had thought you would be happy at this plan!"

Harriet gave her a watery smile. "I am happy! It's nonsensical that I should feel so moved by all of your support, but I am!"

"I will call for tea," Phillip said hastily, and disappeared.

As she composed herself, Harriet reflected that her sense of isolation had been of much longer standing than John's death. She had felt alone since Sophia had left their family. In fact, perhaps only Alexander had been between her and abject misery.

John had not been unkind – far from it – but they'd had so little in common. Alexander had been the visitor with whom she could discuss her reading, who shared her sense of the ridiculous.

She missed him, she realised, and thought back to their last conversation. She must send him a note and not allow their awkwardness to continue. Cheered at the thought, she dabbed her eyes.

The tea tray duly arrived and so did Phillip. As she sipped, Harriet felt a warm glow of affection for her friend and her husband, who had taken up her cause so enthusiastically.

"I feel I could walk around the Park a little," she said to Anne, replacing her cup. "Would you care to join me?"

Anne cast a glance in the direction of her husband, and Harriet noticed a touch of pink on her cheeks.

"Would you excuse me? I need to… see Miss Lloyd about a particular matter for James."

Harriet frowned and then her brow cleared. James had been a little grizzly of late. "Of course! I will take Louise."

Anne beamed at her.

As she got up to leave, Harriet noticed that Phillip had arched a brow at his wife, looking positively devilish.

CHAPTER 29

Light flooded Harriet's brain, and with an incoherent mutter, she fled upstairs to change.

Harriet was still a little hot-cheeked as she alighted from the carriage with Louise, her maid, in tow. How stupid she was! Of course Anne would want some time alone with Phillip. An ache she recognised from her married life took hold of her core and she swallowed, pulling the veil over her face lest anyone see her expression, which she would wager expressed her longing.

She tutted. This was no way for a lady to behave! She spent the first five minutes of her walk deep in thought, wondering if she should absent herself more often from the Grosvenor Square house. Louise, skipping a little to keep up with her, gasped.

"Ma'am! I'm fair sorry, but could you slow your pace a bit?"

Harriet checked her stride, and the maid thanked her breathlessly.

They proceeded at a more leisurely pace, and Harriet pushed aside thoughts of Anne and Phillip. As it was a fine day, pearly clouds scudding across a sunlit sky, the Park was bustling with promenaders and carriages. Two ladies and a gentleman she recognised from the Misses Berry's breakfast acknowledged her and she exchanged a few words with them.

The sun warmed her face through the veil, and she longed to fling it over her hat and feel the rays on her skin. But she clamped down on such an impulse. Instead, she twirled her parasol and mused how fortunate she was in her friends. That Lady Porter-Hume would take up her cause, that Phillip and Anne were so steadfast in their support was heartening, warming.

But she ought to speak to Alexander. He was a treasured friend and would be offended not to know what was happening. And he would tell her that he had warned her against Augusta's mischief-making.

She was approaching the Ring and, glancing at Louise, thought that the maid might welcome a dawdle among the trees, away from the sun. As she turned towards the copse of trees, she glimpsed a familiar tall figure.

Alexander was walking slowly with a young woman, who a second later, Harriet recognised as Georgiana. Louise caught her arm as Harriet almost stumbled.

"Steady, ma'am!"

Harriet was dumb for a moment, watching the pair from a distance. She noticed that Georgiana's maid was a little distance away, discreetly looking in another direction. Alexander said something. Georgiana laughed, and Alexander's expression turned a little sheepish, before he too, smiled. He bent over her hand and kissed it, while Georgiana looked on with an indulgent smile on her lovely face.

A lump rose in Harriet's throat and she noticed that her hand was holding her parasol so tightly her knuckles showed white through her black lace gloves. She spun around, almost cannoning into Louise, and began to walk back towards Grosvenor Gate, her mind in turmoil.

Had he offered for Georgiana? It would appear as if she had accepted him, from her smile.

"Oh!" she moaned under her breath, her sentiments at last clearly visible to her.

CHAPTER 29

"Ma'am?" Louise said breathlessly, trying to keep pace with her short legs. "Are you well?"

"No, Louise. I am not," Harriet said grimly, swallowing to keep the tears at bay. She hurried back to the carriage waiting by the entrance to the gate. She pressed her lips together and was silent on the journey home. Once in the house, she headed to her bedchamber and locked the door, dismissing Louise and rejecting the offer of a cordial.

She pulled the ribbons on her hat and flung it onto a nearby chair. She sank into the chair before her dressing table, staring at the pale face reflected back at her. Then she dropped her head into her hands.

How could she have been so blind to her own feelings?

She unbuttoned her spencer, feeling as if her heart would burst from her chest, so much did it hurt. Her head began to throb, and she closed her eyes, her mind filling with memories of Alexander, his rare smile – less rare with Georgiana, she reflected bitterly – his tamed energy as he strode into the drawing room, his gentle touch, the feel of his lips on her hand. His abrupt, but always honest manner.

And now, his engagement to a Beauty of society. Her breath caught on a sob, and she gripped the edge of the dressing table to steady herself.

He would tell her soon. Or Lady Porter-Hume would announce it and Harriet would need to keep her countenance, remain calm, smile and congratulate him. Harriet bent over, feeling sick. Beads of moisture gathered on her upper lip, and she dived for the chamber pot, gagging.

After she had wiped her mouth, she fell back onto the bed. What had happened to her? When had she fallen in love with Alexander? Or had she always loved him, but had been blinded by her duty? And what of John? She groaned and rolled onto her stomach, burying her face in the coverlet.

Minutes passed, and she heard a gentle tap.

"Ma'am?" said Louise uncertainly, muffled by the door.

"I shall be well presently," called Harriet. "Please fetch me some tea."

Harriet heard the soft agreement and wiped her fingers over her face. They came away wet.

This was madness! She turned over, staring at the plasterwork on the ceiling. What was done was done. The best she could hope for was that Alexander would remain her dear friend. And that this sudden yearning for him would pass, that she could control it. And she must fight for her independence so that the loss of him might be assuaged by finding Sophia and travelling the world.

She heaved herself from the bed and checked her appearance in the mirror.

"It will be enough," she said with gritted teeth, gazing at her tear-stained cheeks.

Chapter 30

CENTRAL LONDON, MAY 2023

"That's fine," said the police officer as he closed his notebook. "We obviously needed to check that Mr Cavendish was where he said he was. Thank you for your confirmation."

I murmured that it was no problem and refrained from asking how the investigation into the theft was progressing. The officer left the gallery and I sighed.

Gerrard, finally returned from holiday, came up behind me. He was brown from the sun and with a new haircut that took ten years off him. "That looked intense."

"Hugo is a suspect unless he can prove he was out of the Hall, and he came to the gallery on the night of the theft. They needed me to confirm."

Gerrard shot me a glance filled with speculation. "You looked quite worried."

"Well, it was important!" I protested. The idea of Hugo under suspicion was unnerving.

Gerrard continued to look at me, and then with a slight shake of his head, he asked, "Have you finished calling our contacts?" I nodded. "No-one's heard anything, I take it?"

"Not a whisper."

He sighed heavily. "That's a lot of money to lose." I didn't reply. For me, I missed the portraits of Harriet, who inspired me in a strange way. I kept taking out my phone to look at my photos of the miniatures, hoping they would materialise in reality.

"The new pieces from Chloe Johnson will arrive on Thursday afternoon and I'd like you to oversee the installation," Gerrard said, changing the subject and opening a file on the computer. "This is the layout we discussed, but one of the pieces is not coming now; she's replaced it with a smaller oil painting. I thought it could go on the left wall. If there were sufficient small pieces, of course, we could put them in the mezzanine."

I focused with an effort. Chloe Johnson was a new artist, discovered from a hint passed on from Gerrard's contact in York, and her pieces were large, atmospheric and impressive. We had one in the gallery already, and I had every expectation that Bill James would buy it.

We were in the middle of discussing where the largest pieces would go, when the phone rang.

"Gerrard Williams, Art Dealer, Gabriella speaking. How can I help you?"

"Gabs?" said my mother. I started in surprise to hear her voice, slightly more fragile than I recalled. "It's nice to hear you answer the phone occasionally while you're at work," she added, and I felt my stomach sink. I forbore to mention that this was the gallery phone and naturally I would answer.

"Hello, Mum. How are you?"

"Fine, thank you." A long pause followed, and I gritted my teeth.

"What can I do for you?" I finally asked.

"Liam thinks it's time we all caught up," she said distantly. "I'm going to see them all on Thursday. You could join us after you've finished work."

I closed my eyes. "I'm really sorry, Thursday is difficult. I'm getting the gallery ready for an opening, and I'll be here quite late."

There was the sound of an indrawn breath. "I see. Well, that's that, then. I'll tell Liam you're unavailable."

"Mum! What about—" The line went dead and I was left staring in disbelief at the receiver.

"Are you okay? You look a bit stunned," Gerrard said.

"Mum hung up on me!"

I perched on the stool behind the counter, caught between fury and a longing to see everyone, my nephews in particular. This was the longest time since the day they'd been born that I hadn't seen them. My throat closed.

"Breathe, Gabriella," Gerrard advised, after I relayed the conversation. "And don't do anything rash," he added.

I nodded. He was right. It was impossible for me to go on Thursday, not without a great deal of reorganising to find someone else, and the family should understand that. No, I wouldn't just fit in with them – I'd concentrate on my job and rearrange with the family.

I turned to Gerrard. "Right – where were we?"

Aunt Mo was scathing when I called her at lunchtime to tell her about Mum's phone call.

"I had once thought my sister-in-law was an intelligent woman, but sadly, every interaction these days proves how much of an optimist I am," she said crisply. "What rubbish! No compromise, no discussion. Ooh! I lose patience with her."

I laughed weakly. She continued. "But how are you after that, Gabriella? Are you okay?"

I paused. Deep down, I knew I wasn't okay; I was struggling with this self-imposed isolation from Mum and my brother.

But I needed to be more Harriet, more devil-may-care. More full of joy, more daring, independent from others. I cleared my throat. "I want us to find a way back to one another – but more on my terms."

"Hold fast, lovey. I'll do some digging with Evie."

I laughed at that. "Don't scare her! She's frightened of you, Aunt Mo!"

"Yes, I know that," Aunt Mo said complacently. "I'll be gentle. You're still coming round for supper tonight, aren't you?" I was. "Good, we'll talk later."

I had just taken a bite of my sandwich when my phone rang again, and I saw from the screen that it was Hugo. I quickly put down my lunch and answered the call, still chewing.

"Hi! Sorry, you caught me mid-chomp," I explained, trying to swallow my mouthful. "Have the police found anything?"

He chuckled. "I could get jealous of these paintings," he said mildly. "I call to ask you to dinner and there's no 'How are you?' but you cut straight to the miniatures!"

"Hugo, how are you?" I promptly replied, wiping mayonnaise from my lips.

CHAPTER 30

"Ah, don't give me that. I know you only want me for my art."

His voice dipped lower as he spoke, and a shiver ran down my spine and did circles in my core. I laughed. "Sorry. Let me try again. How *are* you, Hugo?"

He sighed. "It's a bit grim, and I was hoping you would come to dinner to cheer me up."

"Delighted to. If you let me pick the restaurant, I'll even pay."

"Definitely a date then," he said, sounding pleased. "I'm in London next week. I'll confirm which day tomorrow. It will be great to catch up. And... Perhaps we can pick up where we left our conversation?"

Be more Harriet, I thought, and drew a breath. "Definitely. I'll look forward to it."

I stared into space for a minute after he'd gone, and then shook myself out of my reverie. I wished Joe was at home, because I needed a second opinion on the new dress I'd just decided I was going to buy.

I checked my to-do list, decided that the rest could wait until tomorrow and asked Gerrard if I could take a couple of hours off to go shopping. He raised an eyebrow but agreed, and I headed to Oxford Street to tackle the department stores.

Aunt Mo arched an eyebrow at the dress; a demure navy in a fine jersey with a deep square neck that I thought showed off my collarbone and the curve of my shoulders.

"It's quite clingy," she commented. "Of course, that's no bad thing – you have a lovely figure, so you ought to show it off. At least the stylist you went to – what was her name? Francine?"

"Mmm," I said smoothing the fabric down my hips.

"Well, she certainly steered you right," Aunt Mo said with satisfaction. "Thank goodness you're not wearing so many baggy jumpers and shirts – they completely swamped you, you know."

I grinned at her in the mirror. Today, she was dressed in a tartan pinafore with a raspberry pink shirt and black loafers. Like Mum, she was very slender and carried it off perfectly – I couldn't have worn the pinafore with my boobs. I'd have looked like I was carrying a shelf.

"I know. I feel liberated – but also a bit scared," I admitted. "I feel very out there, if you know what I mean."

"And who is this delicious purchase for?"

I dropped my eyes and reached over my shoulder to begin unzipping the dress. "No-one. Me." Aunt Mo looked sceptical. "Oh, all right. I'm going to dinner with Hugo next week. I wanted to make a good impression. We had a bit of awkwardness over his brother..."

"Oh?"

I gave her a brief recap of the theft.

"So, it's an inside job, you think Pierce did it and Hugo won't hear of it?" Aunt Mo said.

"Yup. About the size of it."

"And what would you say if someone accused Liam of being a thief?" she asked, fixing me with a stare. "Would you automatically consider it, or automatically deny it?"

I paused. "But the rest of the evidence..." I started.

"All circumstantial."

CHAPTER 30

I stared at her, not sure what to say. She sighed and spun me by the shoulders to unzip the dress. "Theresa would kill me if she knew I'd told you this – but did you know your dad went to prison when you were a baby?"

"No!" My mind went blank. "What for?"

"Step out," she said, and automatically I stepped out of the dress, which she put back on the hanger. "Someone thought he was defrauding the company he worked for."

"My God! Was he?"

"No. Your dad thought he was being set up by someone, so he persuaded your mum to take out all their savings and employ a lawyer to appeal the sentence. He was inside for a couple of months, three maybe, before the appeal succeeded and his sentence was quashed."

I sat heavily on the sofa, shoeless and in my underwear, stunned into silence.

"But your mum didn't completely believe he was innocent," Aunt Mo said, with a distant look on her face. "It almost broke the marriage, regardless of the result – that she hadn't trusted him, hadn't believed him. When he came out, there were huge rows and he threatened to leave. To try to prove that she did trust him, she put everything into his hands. And your dad did it all. He dealt with all their finances, he planned the holidays, even wrote her shopping lists. At least until you were old enough to start doing things, then he passed it all to you."

I remembered the moment as soon as she mentioned it. I'd been twelve, and he'd asked me to go to talk to our local butcher about the Christmas turkey. Liam would have been fifteen but was stuck in front of his Nintendo, or something. I went, feeling proud of the responsibility Dad had given me.

When I returned, he'd taught me to cook Christmas lunch.

My life since then suddenly made a kind of sense that it hadn't before – I'd been picking up Dad's tasks ever since, and when he died, Mum likely didn't have a clue about how to run her life. Liam had taken his cue from Mum. And here I was.

"I've been trying to find a time to tell you this," she said with a sigh. "I'm not sure even now that I should have shared it, but at least you'll understand Theresa's dependence on you a bit more."

"She's done nothing since I was a baby?"

"No. And now things have changed so much, going online and stuff, she's terrified she can't. So she asks you to do everything. In lots of ways, it's not her fault – she just abdicated everything because she felt that was the only way to prove to your Dad she trusted him."

I was silent, digesting this. Aunt Mo continued.

"And as for Hugo, surely you see that the act of believing Pierce's guilt would have a huge impact on their relationship."

I thought for a moment, still struggling to settle everything in my head. "But if he *has* stolen the miniatures, isn't the relationship already damaged beyond repair? I'd no sooner steal from Liam than I would cut off my arm."

"You're right, of course," she replied pursing her lips. "But people in desperate situations do desperate things, don't they? Who knows what's going on for this Pierce?"

I was silent. And a bit uncomfortable. I reached for my shirt and trousers and struggled into them, to give myself time to think.

"Have I done right, telling you?" Aunt Mo asked, unusually nervous. I turned to her with a smile.

"Of course you have! I know you're only telling me for my benefit, and you've certainly given me a lot to think about," I said as I hugged her.

On the bus home, I took out my phone and composed a text to Mum. I gave her a list of dates I would be around next week and the week after. Less than two minutes later, she responded, saying next Wednesday would be good. There was even a kiss. I felt better. I put my phone away and stared into the darkening streets as we travelled.

Chapter 31

GROSVENOR SQUARE, LATE MAY 1803

Coates entered the room and solemnly announced that Mr Edwin Beaufort had called and were the ladies at home?

Harriet cast a startled glance at Anne, who looked at her enquiringly. Harriet shrugged helplessly, not knowing what to think or say. Anne took charge.

"Thank you, Coates. Please inform Lord Rochford of our visitor and request his presence," Anne responded calmly. "And show Mr Beaufort up."

Harriet clasped her hands tightly together and Edwin strutted through the door. Belatedly, she hoped he would do nothing to put her to the blush. She rose and dipped a curtsy, and Edwin bowed from the waist, obviously something he had learned from the continent. He did likewise to Anne, who was trying to hide her smile at his pretension.

"How do you do?" he said in that drawling way that Harriet had always hated. It also signified that Edwin was out to impress, although his efforts were more likely to convey sulkiness than bored sophistication. She sighed and settled back in her seat.

CHAPTER 31

Edwin took a deep breath. "I know we have already spoken, but I trust you will give Aunt Augusta's proposal due consideration."

Harriet was appalled. He had obviously been persuaded by Augusta to press his offer of marriage, despite seeming relieved at the time. Her chin rose and she refused to reply.

The tea tray arrived with freshly made biscuits, and despite everything, Edwin's eyes lit up. He had always liked his food, and Harriet judged that although his gold and red brocade waistcoat was already straining at the buttons, he would eat several.

Anne, not at all impressed so far, maintained a chilly silence, other than asking him if he wanted milk. As Harriet had predicted, he grabbed several biscuits. The silence continued, and then, to Harriet's relief, Phillip arrived, looking severe. Edwin almost spilt his drink in his haste to rise to his feet.

Phillip looked Edwin up and down. To Harriet's fascinated view, a tide of red flowed up Edwin's neck and into his face. His bow was stiff.

"Beaufort, isn't it?" Phillip said slowly.

"Yes, my Lord."

"You were with Lord Gordon at White's, were you not?"

"Yes, sir; he introduced me."

"Playing pretty deep, I think."

"Not beyond my means, sir," managed Edwin, darting a fleeting look at Harriet. Harriet's heart sank. This would be where Augusta's money was going; on Edwin's gambling habits.

"Hmm." Phillip made no other comment and shook his head as his wife offered him refreshments.

Coates arrived again. "Lady Porter-Hume, my lady."

Inwardly, Harriet groaned. Anne nodded and Edwin jumped to his feet again, this time dropping a biscuit. Harriet rolled her eyes at this, just as Lady Porter-Hume swept through the door. Her gaze travelled around the room and narrowed as it fell on Edwin, brushing crumbs from his waistcoat.

Introductions were made and a fresh biscuit was found for Edwin. Lady Porter-Hume turned to him with a smile. Everyone looked on with amazement as she began to charm him.

"I don't believe I have made your acquaintance, sir. Have you only recently come to town?"

Edwin, after such a chilly welcome initially, needed no further encouragement to talk and launched into a slightly incoherent monologue about his Grand Tour. Lady Porter-Hume nodded and asked the occasional question as Edwin gave what Harriet imagined was a very scrubbed version of his travels.

"You were presented at the Naples court, I take it?"

"Yes, ma'am. I was most heartily welcomed," he said, his chest puffing and his features softening. "I believe that Italian ladies are accounted the most beautiful in the Continent."

"Well, I know how welcoming the ladies of the Naples court can be," commented Lady Porter-Hume neutrally, and Edwin smiled a little wistfully. At this, even Phillip's eyes widened. He cleared his throat and Lady Porter-Hume steered the conversation to more sober topics. After a few minutes, Edwin groped for his hat and stood.

"I must be off," he said, sounding rather subdued, Harriet thought. He nodded to Phillip, Harriet and Anne

CHAPTER 31

and dipped in a deep bow to Lady Porter-Hume, telling her that it had been a pleasure to meet her. She nodded indulgently and drank more tea.

There was a short, uncomfortable pause as the door closed behind him and Lady Porter-Hume looked around the room.

"What a ridiculous young man," she pronounced, wrinkling her nose. She pulled her notebook from her reticule and began to write. "Still, such as Mr Edwin Beaufort will always give in to the temptation to talk about themselves, and even allowing for his inclination to boast, his conversation gives us valuable information."

After a tiny pause, Phillip chuckled. "Aye, ma'am. Now I see what you were about."

"Surely you did not think I tolerated him for any other reason? No, Mr Beaufort has been most informative."

"Do you think that there's something in his conduct that we can use as leverage?" Phillip asked.

Lady Porter-Hume fixed him with an enquiring look. "Lord Rochford, without wishing to put you to the blush, I beg you to consider your own Grand Tour, before you married. Some gentlemen acquit themselves properly, but the opportunity to run a little wild, away from the confines and expectations of English society, is one few can resist. Mr Beaufort does not strike me as a man with much willpower."

As she spoke, Phillip flushed a little, particularly as Anne turned curious eyes on him. Lady Porter-Hume's lips twitched, but she continued. "Now – to business! I have heard from Mr Wilkins, who has examined your late husband's will, Mrs Colchester. He believes it sound, although he also says that the courts are often inclined to keep, as far as possible, family land and money together. Your mother-in-law's insistence that you wed your cousin by marriage may receive a positive hearing."

Harriet's heart dropped to her stomach, but Phillip spoke before she could marshal her thoughts.

"Therefore, we might need additional incentive for her to withdraw her claim?" Lady Porter-Hume beamed at his understanding and nodded.

Phillip dragged a hand through his brown hair, a sign Harriet recognised. Phillip was thinking.

"I might make discreet enquiries among the clubs," he said. "I've only seen Beaufort gambling at White's, but he might also have had an introduction to Brook's. I'll ask."

With those plans in mind, Lady Porter-Hume took her leave.

Harriet spotted Lady Porter-Hume a week later at Hookham's circulating library on Old Bond Street and approached her with a smile.

"Good day, ma'am," she said with a curtsy.

"Mrs Colchester! Good day to you too! What are you reading?" Lady Porter-Hume said, squinting at the book Harriet had claimed.

"*A description of Latium* by Mrs Knight," Harriet said, her hands leafing lovingly through the pages and pausing on one of the etchings. "I was inspired by the Misses Berry about their travels, and this was recommended to me. Mrs Knight writes so beautifully, I could almost feel myself on the hills surrounding Rome! And you, Lady Porter-Hume – what books have you chosen?"

Lady Porter-Hume looked over her shoulder shiftily. "I admit to a penchant for Gothic novels," she said a little guiltily. "I have read and re-read Mrs Radcliffe's *Udolpho*, but now I am tempted by Mr Summersett's *Leopold Warndorf* – have you heard of it? Perhaps a little too strong for society's taste, but that may be attractive for me."

Harriet hid her surprise. Many Gothic novels were on the edge of scandalous, but of course, that added to their appeal. And while Lady Porter-Hume did not look like a woman who read sensationalist literature, Harriet was charmed by this little, private pleasure that told her more about the impressive lady in front of her. It was, she thought, on a par with her own weakness for the finest chocolate, however indulgent.

"I expected to meet Georgiana here, but as usual she is tardy," continued Lady Porter-Hume. "Shall we walk a little? I daresay we will bump into her soon."

Harriet would rather not have met Georgiana, given what she had witnessed in Hyde Park, but there was nothing to be done. If she was to remain friends with Lady Porter-Hume, she would need to bear the sight of the young girl who had stolen Alexander's heart. The thought ran through her head that it would be required if she was to remain friends with Alexander, too. He was invited to dinner this evening, she remembered with a start. Oh God, she thought, closing her eyes for an instant. How would she greet him? Talk to him?

"I have not seen Miss Porter-Hume for a couple of weeks," she said finally, daring herself to be resilient and raise the topic. "Is she well?"

Lady Porter-Hume looked a little coy. "She is exceedingly well. I cannot say more at this time, but I am expecting a happy announcement shortly."

"How wonderful," Harriet said faintly. So it was true. Of course it was. Alexander was so handsome, so steadfast, so wonderful; why would Georgiana turn him down?

Harriet immediately wished to go back to Grosvenor Square, finding the teeming library oppressive, airless.

"Are you well, my dear?" Lady Porter-Hume said, her sharp eyes fixed on Harriet's face. "You look a little green about the gills."

"I – I am feeling a little odd," Harriet said, which was, she thought, only the truth. "It is the heat in here. Would you excuse me? I am sorry I can't stay longer."

"Go, go!" Lady Porter-Hume looked around for Louise. "Take your mistress home. She is not feeling the thing." Harriet mumbled her gratitude incoherently. "Hush! Send me a note when you are recovered," Lady Porter-Hume said, patting her hand.

Harriet stumbled from the library and headed towards Grosvenor Square, her mind blank with misery.

The day did not improve. While she was resting before dinner, the footman brought a note from Mr Bessiwick's hotel, begging leave to inform her that Mrs Augusta Colchester had instructed her attorney to serve papers for her challenge to the will of the late John Colchester. Augusta would start proceedings at Chancery Court,

CHAPTER 31

and the case was likely to come before the judge the following month. What were Harriet's instructions?

Harriet swung her legs from the bed and straightened her dress. A glance in the mirror told her she was pale and her eyes huge in her face. That would never do for the drawing room, but she should respond to Mr Bessiwick before attending to her appearance.

She sat at her bureau and stared at a blank page for a couple of minutes. Then she dipped her pen in the ink pot and wrote one line.

Refute the challenge, Mr Bessiwick, and fight for my late husband's wishes.

Chapter 32

NORTH LONDON, LATE MAY 2023

I looked at my watch again and then back at the text Mum had sent. Yes, I wasn't losing my mind. Right date, right time, six o'clock. But there was no-one in.

I took a brief look down the street and then bent to the letterbox and pushed open the flap as far as I could. The hall looked as it often did: a few toy cars for the unwary walker, a scarf draped over the newel post, a single trainer at the bottom of the stairs. But it was completely silent.

I stood up, sighing with impatience. What had happened? Why hadn't anyone told me? I stood on the doorstep and began to compose an appropriately stinging text to the family WhatsApp group when someone shouted, "Oi! What do you think you're doing?"

I jumped and looked upwards. Nigel, Liam and Evie's ancient and incredibly nosy neighbour, poked his balding head out of his upstairs window and glared down at me.

"Hi, Nigel, it's just me."

"They're not in!" He coughed for a few seconds after this pronouncement.

"Yes, thanks, I can see that," I said patiently. "But I was expecting someone to be home. Do you know where they are?"

"Ambulance came and took Sam away," he wheezed, leaning on the windowsill.

I stilled. "What? What ambulance?" My heart rate sped up.

"The one that took Sam away, about twelve this lunchtime," he repeated.

"What happened?"

"Sam fell in the garden. Loads of crying and screaming – it was a right racket. I was trying to watch *Escape to the Country*," he said with a whine.

I hung grimly onto my temper. "Do you know which hospital they went to?" I said slowly and clearly.

"No idea. Evie went with the lad in the ambulance; your mum and Liam and Jasper followed in the car. I don't know who made the most noise – Sam when he fell, or his mum, who was panicking. It was all go, I tell you. Fair disturbed my afternoon, it did, what with the sirens and the crying. And now you're banging at the door. This used to be a quiet neighbourhood, you know."

"They *all* went?" I asked, and then rethought. Mum had massive FOMO. There was no show without Punch, despite the fact that the sensible thing to do would have been to stay at home with Jasper and wait.

Nigel said something, but I had stopped listening. I called Evie and got no response. The nearest accident and emergency department required an Uber. I looked at my app and hailed a cab. The nearest was ten minutes away, so I would need to endure Nigel for a few moments more.

"Did you see what happened?" I asked, knowing that if anyone was in the back garden having a good time, Nigel would be looking over the garden fence, scowling.

He spread his hands out. "Well, the little lads were out of control in my opinion – too much sugar, I always say. Not like when I was a kid—"

"What did you see?" I asked again, slightly louder this time.

"He fell from the top of the slide," he replied with relish. I gasped. "They were both fighting to go down the slide first and Sam got there first. Jasper pushed him out of the way."

"Was Sam conscious?" I choked out.

"From the din he was making, oh yes, he was definitely conscious. It'll just be a bit of a bruise; no need for all that screaming and crying-"

Thankfully, the Uber pulled up.

"Thanks, Nigel, you've been very helpful," I said, grabbing for the handle of the door. "If they come back, could you ask them to ring me?"

"Go on, then. Good job I'm such a good neighbour."

"It is," I agreed and slammed the door.

I rushed to the lift and pressed the button to the fourth floor as directed by the patently uninterested hospital receptionist. The lift stopped at every floor, but finally I reached a pale turquoise corridor and headed for reception.

In my mind were all the memories I'd stored carefully since the twins were born. Their initial words. Their

CHAPTER 32

early months crawling, trailing disaster in their wake, videos with yards of tape draped across the furniture. The time I found Sam munching through a bag of frozen onion rings. Jasper climbing into the washing machine and attempting to shut the door.

And then the fresh, washed smell of them just before bed. Wide eyes while I read their bedtime story and the half-moons of sooty eyelashes drooping as they fell asleep.

I slid to a stop as I rounded the corner and saw Mum, a white-faced Evie and a tearful Jasper sitting on hard plastic chairs. Jasper caught sight of me and cried, "Gaaabeeee!"

Mum's face lit up and Evie leapt to her feet. "Thank God you're here!" she said. I hugged her.

"How's Sam?" I asked softly in her ear.

"Broken his arm, but it's a clean break and the doctors don't seem concerned," she said, her eyes filling with tears. I sent a silent prayer of thanks to the heavens.

Mum looked at me apologetically. "I clean forgot. You came to Liam's, didn't you?"

I sat down and hugged her, and she buried her face in my shoulder. "I did, but at least I was able to get the details from Nosy Nigel. It's not a problem; we can rearrange."

"I'm so glad you're here," Mum mumbled into my shirt. I squeezed her shoulders.

"God, that man!" tutted Evie. "At least Nigel's nosiness was useful this time!"

I hauled Jasper into my arms. "Hiya, menace. How are you doing?"

He mumbled something I didn't hear and flung his arms around my neck before wriggling free and going back to Evie.

"You've been here hours," I commented. "Where are Sam and Liam?"

"Getting his arm set," Mum replied, tearfully. "Sam was asking for you earlier."

That struck a hammer blow to my heart, and I swallowed. "Well, I'm here now," I forced out.

"And to be fair, we should have texted you," added Evie, eyes closed, looking exhausted, her head against the wall. "In all the chaos, it just went out of my head."

Mum was about to speak when Liam walked in carrying Sam. My nephew sported a partial cast and a bandage sling. His cheeks were pink, his hair on end, but he looked cheerful enough.

"Hello, baby!" Evie cooed and cradled his cheek in her hand. "That's a big, grown-up cast you've got there."

He nodded and turned to me. "Auntie Gabs, look at my arm! Jasper broke it!"

"Not on purpose," I said gravely, walking up to him. "How do you feel?"

"Hurts a bit," he told me. "But Daddy says I'm a brave boy and that people can sign my arm soon!"

"Yes, when the plaster hardens," I agreed. "But you are a brave boy; he's right there." I kissed his cheek, feeling it hot beneath my lips. I glanced at Liam and patted him on the back.

"Good to see you, Gabs," he said in a gruff voice. I nodded.

"Right, well, we need to get home," Mum said. I fought the urge to take charge. This was the new me.

"What do you want to do, Liam?" I said after a second.

CHAPTER 32

Liam looked nonplussed for a moment and then pulled himself together. "Right. It's a shame you didn't stay at home with Jasper, Mum."

Mum looked mutinous and I almost laughed. No way was Mum going to be left at home while doctors mauled her grandson about.

Liam continued. "Evie, you'll need to get a cab home with Jasper. That way, Mum can sit in the back of our car with Sam, and we'll have plenty of room for coats and things to rest his arm on. I'll have to drive slowly so I don't jar it. Are you coming back with us, Gabs?"

"It's a bit late," I said.

"Then you'd best go with Evie, and she can drop you off at a tube."

"Good idea," Evie agreed and took out her phone.

As we walked towards the hospital exit, Mum said awkwardly, "We need another date to talk. How about tomorrow?"

I nodded, an idea beginning to form in my head. She patted my arm and then climbed into Liam's battered Volvo. Tomorrow night I was supposed to see Hugo. Perhaps he could pick me up from Liam's, and this way, they'd know I had things going on in my life.

I sat on the sofa in Liam's house and looked sternly at Sam. "Wriggle your fingers!" He wriggled them, pathetic pink things at the end of his cast, and then dashed off to find Jasper. "Goodnight! And don't run!" I called after him.

"God, he's enough to give anyone nightmares," Evie said as she brought in the gin and tonic I'd asked for. "I'm petrified he'll fall and break something else."

Mum followed her into the room. She perched in a slim-fitting skirt on the edge of the sofa.

"I can see Francine's advice has been useful," she said, examining my navy-blue dress with the square neck. "You look so different, I barely recognised you. Oh my God!" She said suddenly, looking horrified. "I owe you money for that, don't I?"

The early evening visit had been a little strained, eased only by Sam and Jasper, who had now gone to bed. I hadn't wanted to stay for food because I was going to dinner, and Mum, who thought food healed all family rifts, looked askance. I had other things to do that were taking me away from the family.

Nothing of note had been said. So, up to me. "How's the new job, Liam?"

"You know about that?" asked Evie, surprised.

Liam shifted in his black, overstuffed leather chair. "One of the events I attended before I started was held at the gallery that Gabs works at," he said, uncomfortably.

"You never said! Did you see one another?" Evie said, frowning.

I put my head on one side. "Oh, yes. He saw me at my work; this work that everyone thinks isn't very demanding. What did your boss say at the event?"

Liam examined his fingernails. "Bill James, my CEO, told everyone that Gabs had organised the whole event, and supervised the building of the place we were holding it in. And that she advised him on his art purchases."

Mum looked astounded.

"And what did I say to you?" I asked, determined to get it all out of him.

"That you had finished the build on time and under budget. And that if you said you were busy, you probably were." He sounded ashamed.

The silence in the room was absolute. Mum stared at me, and I wondered if this might be the first time in ten years that she had really seen me. "If you'd lived at home, I'd have known all this," she said, her fingers pleating her skirt. "You seem to have disappeared from our lives."

I turned to her in astonishment. "Sorry? Disappeared? Did I imagine booking your bloody holiday this year? Or arguing with the bank over your overdraft? God above, I practically did all your Christmas shopping last year, *and* I cooked lunch – as I have done for the past twelve years!"

Liam frowned. "I thought you cooked Christmas lunch, Mum."

Mum had the grace to look away and I rolled my eyes. "No, Liam! And if you'd been more awake, you'd have seen Mum propping up the counter with a sherry! But you sat and watched telly instead. I was lucky if you laid the table!"

"Gabs—" Mum said testily, and I lost my temper.

"My name is Gabriella! For once, call me by the name you gave me and that I've asked you to call me since I was a kid!"

Evie made a soft sound of distress and my mother's mouth opened in shock.

Then Jasper pushed open the sitting room door, his hair tousled. I wondered if our argument had woken him and immediately felt guilty. Evie exclaimed and gathered him to her, asking why he was up.

"Sam's snoring!" he exclaimed in disgust. "He sounds like Daddy!"

"He's got to sleep on his back because of his arm, sweetie," Evie hid a smile.

Jasper nodded and snuggled into her. Then he turned to face me and said clearly, "When are you coming to visit again, Auntie Gabs? I want to read your book – Dad's rubbish."

"Well, thanks a lot, son," Liam muttered.

I swallowed. "Soon, I hope. And don't diss your dad." Jasper screwed up his face.

Evie looked at me, her eyes swimming. "Liam, can you take him up?"

Liam heaved himself out of the chair and carried Jasper away. No-one said anything for a moment. To my astonishment, Evie came and sat by me. "They miss you. And you miss them, I can tell," she said, taking my hands. "I'm sorry for my part in this – taking you for granted – but I'd like to change things so the twins can see their favourite aunt again."

"Their only aunt," I reminded her, trying to keep my emotions under control.

Mum shook her head. "I had no idea you had such an important job, Gabs – Gabriella."

"The job isn't important," I said wearily. "I just want you all to acknowledge that I've got my own life as well as being involved in yours!"

Evie smiled uncertainly. "Perhaps we can meet for coffee and a proper chat."

The doorbell rang. Hugo, come to take me to dinner. I squeezed Evie's hands and stood.

"That will be my dinner date."

"I'll get it!" called Liam.

CHAPTER 32

Hugo dwarfed the room, and Liam was scowling, obviously recognising the man who had hauled him to his feet in the gallery. For the second time that evening, Mum was speechless, Evie flustered, as Hugo wished them a good evening in his glorious voice.

We got onto the pavement outside the house. Hugo's eyebrow arched at the three faces at the window. "We have an audience," he murmured. "Shall we underline the idea that you might not be so available in the future?"

He drew me close and tenderly kissed my forehead.

CHAPTER 33

GROSVENOR SQUARE, LATE MAY 1803

Having survived five years of relentless bullying from Augusta, Harriet knew how to fashion unconcern and paste a smile on her face. So she had herself well in hand when she met Alexander that evening, her hard shell safely wrapped around her.

She saw that Anne cast her several concerned glances, but Harriet had not unburdened herself to her friend about her new-found feelings for Alexander, nor their origin. No announcement about any engagement had been made, and Harriet could not spoil what would be Georgiana's moment.

Alexander also considered her with a slight frown between his brows as dinner continued. Harriet ate what she could of the food, which had been lovingly prepared by Anne's new French cook – venison, beef, turbot *a la Francaise*, all manner of delights. When this dinner had been proposed, Harriet had relished the opportunity to dine with her closest friends and spend more time in Alexander's company. But now, her glimpse of the scene in Hyde Park sat at the table with her, like an awkward fifth guest.

CHAPTER 33

"Mrs Colchester – have you informed Mr Richardson of Mrs Augusta Colchester's latest exploits?" Phillip asked.

Alexander looked hard at Harriet.

"No, my lord," Harriet said easily to Phillip. "I have not had the opportunity."

"What is afoot?" Alexander said.

"I received a note from Mr Bessiwick to inform me that Augusta has filed her complaint against the will at Chancery Court. I believe the date for the hearing will be in a month."

"The devil it is!" burst out Alexander and then apologised for his language.

"We hope to get the claim dismissed," Harriet explained. She took a sip of wine. "Of course, there is precedent, I understand, for keeping the land and wealth together. That is Augusta's main argument. That the Colchester fortune should remain in the Colchester family."

"But are you not family?" Alexander asked.

"No, I know you have heard Augusta tell me that I am merely a woman who was supposed to provide an heir, and failed," Harriet responded, attempting to keep the acid from her voice.

"My dear, I can hardly believe that!" Anne protested.

"Mr Richardson, can you bear me out?" Harriet appealed to Alexander.

"I believe that Augusta's perception of you is warped by her own disappointment, but I also know another truth – that John loved you, and held you in the highest esteem," he replied tightly. "He would be appalled to see what Augusta is about."

Harriet blinked at his words. Thankfully, Phillip jumped into the conversation after a brief pause.

"And I sincerely hope that this will be one of the arguments put forward in your case, Mrs Colchester. How distraught your husband would be to have his final wishes disregarded!"

Harriet looked down at her hands, surprised to see they were trembling. Alexander had seen that John loved her, when she had been oblivious to his sentiments. She thought wryly that she made a habit of this – blind to her husband's affections, blind – until recently – to her own feelings for Alexander. Perhaps she was walking through life in a haze of unknowing?

"But we have a plan!" Anne announced with glee. "Lady Porter-Hume has offered the services of her own attorney to work with Mr Bessiwick, and we are also making enquiries into the conduct of Mr Edwin Beaufort."

"Edwin? What has that whelp to do with anything?" Alexander asked. There was a short, embarrassed silence.

"Oh, dear," Anne said, red-faced.

Harriet smiled at her, shaking her head. "Please do not concern yourself; we are among friends, here." She turned her gaze to Alexander. "Augusta has made the challenge to the will because I would not agree to marry Edwin."

Alexander's eyes widened and she could see from across the table that his fingers tightened around the stem of his glass. "I beg your pardon?" he said quietly. Harriet repeated herself and saw him draw a deep breath, swelling his chest. "I beg your pardon again, but your mother-in-law should be flogged!"

CHAPTER 33

Harriet took an unreasonable amount of comfort in his words and smiled.

"What can I do to help?" he demanded.

"Perhaps we can discuss that later," Phillip said, nodding with satisfaction at Alexander's response. "I am making enquiries through the clubs about Edwin. We hope to build a dossier that might dissuade Augusta from her legal action."

Alexander perked up and Harriet wondered what his new fiancée would think of his actions.

Anne suggested they left the men to their port.

As soon as tea had been delivered and the doors closed, Anne said, "What is troubling you? You seem very distant in your manner to Mr Richardson. Has anything occurred?"

Harriet dropped her fan and made a great performance of searching for it on the rug, to give her time to consider her response.

"There!" she exclaimed, sitting back on the sofa. "How clumsy I am! Nothing is amiss. I am a little tired tonight, Anne."

Anne regarded her quizzically, but made no reply. When the gentlemen joined them, she drew Phillip to one side and Alexander took his seat next to Harriet.

"Why did you not tell me?" he said, quietly. "I am deeply wounded that you did not take me into your confidence."

Her heart seemed to squeeze in her chest, but Harriet stayed calm. "Sir, I am sure you have many other concerns at the moment. I did not want to burden you with mine."

He will tell me now, she thought, her gaze fixed on him. He will tell me that there is an announcement to be made soon. Alexander stared at her, his blue eyes searching her face.

"I have told you that you can rely on me always," he said slowly. "I do not understand why you chose to keep me in ignorance of this wicked move against you. Surely you know me well enough to trust me?"

And what of you? The question ran through Harriet's mind. Why are you keeping me in ignorance of *your* news?

She forced a smile. "Mr Richardson, I have been truly grateful for your support when John died. I will never forget your kindness. But Lady Porter-Hume, who understands my position better than you can, has offered to help me to protect myself and my future happiness, and so my confidences have all been to her."

"How does the lady understand your position better than I?" Alexander looked most displeased.

"She is a woman!" Harriet stared at him, amazed. "She understands that it is only as a widow of independent means that I have any authority! With a fortune, as you once told me, I have an entree to society that, if I were poor, would be denied me! Indeed, without it, the only other option open to me is marriage!"

Alexander's eyes flared, and Harriet continued quickly. "But that would deny me the thing I most desire!"

"What is that?" he asked after a pause.

"Freedom," she responded promptly. "As a woman, I cease to exist if I marry. And although marriage is what we are taught to believe is our purpose, I have suffered enough invisibility in my life. If I can keep my fortune, I will remain a widow."

He was silent for a long moment, expressionless as he stared at her. Then he stood, made her a stiff bow, and walked away.

The following day, Louise remarked on her pallor and counselled some rouge. Sighing, Harriet accepted the hare's foot brush, but as soon as Louise had left the bedchamber, she scrubbed her cheeks with a handkerchief. The veil would hide her face well enough for her promenade.

Anne was uncharacteristically quiet, and Harriet too sunk in her own misery to cajole her into conversation. So wrapped up were they in their thoughts, they both started as Georgiana addressed them.

"Lady Rochford! Mrs Colchester! You both look so glum! I hope all is well?" she said, anxiously.

"Miss Porter-Hume! How do you do?" Anne said, rousing herself and smiling at the young woman. "But do I need to ask how you are? You look radiant, my dear!"

Georgiana beamed, her eyes twinkling, and the white feather in her jaunty hat seemed to nod in agreement. She brimmed with excitement and happiness. "I am well, indeed!"

"Oh?" Anne said, her curiosity sharpening as she cast a glance at Harriet, who attempted to smile.

Georgiana put her finger to her lips and looked mischievous. "I am sorry to tease you, but I cannot say just yet! I promise it will all be revealed soon!"

After five minutes' conversation in which no-one said anything very much, Georgiana bobbed a curtsy and moved away. Harriet, her legs leaden, continued to walk beside Anne. The encounter had stirred Anne to conversation that Harriet would rather avoid.

"She is about to announce her engagement, is she not?" Anne said softly. "How wonderful! I wonder who the suitor is?"

"I am sure I do not know," Harriet replied. Anne looked at her sharply but said nothing, and they resumed their thoughtful silent walk.

Approaching the house in Grosvenor Square, Harriet grasped Anne's hand. "I do beg your pardon! I have been a bear all morning! Please forgive me! How pitifully I repay your kindness and support."

"Of course! I can only imagine how confused your thoughts must be!" Anne replied thankfully, squeezing her hand.

Harriet glanced at her, unsure how she had betrayed her feelings for Alexander.

"How I loathe this business with Augusta!" said Anne, scowling. Harriet, distressed as she was, breathed more easily.

"But is this the primary cause of your unhappiness?" Anne continued. "There is nothing else?"

Harriet hesitated. "Everything else pales by comparison!" she said finally with a wry smile. "I will call on Lady Porter-Hume this afternoon to see what schemes she might suggest to protect me."

Lady Porter-Hume was indeed at home, but not alone. Miss Damer, startlingly dressed in a man's coat of chestnut brown, was sprawled on the sofa, although on Harriet's entry to the room, she straightened. Harriet quickly schooled her face and smiled as Miss Damer nodded a greeting.

"You remember Miss Damer, do you not?" asked Lady Porter-Hume, gesturing Harriet to a chair.

"I do indeed. Was your exhibition successful? I know little about it, but you appeared to me to have a great deal of talent."

Miss Damer grinned, her sharp chin making her look kitten-like. "You have excellent taste, Mrs Colchester."

"I believe I speak as I find," Harriet said serenely. She turned to Lady Porter-Hume and began hesitantly. "I hoped we might find an occasion to discuss my recent circumstances. Obviously, today is not appropriate—"

"Please, I was just about to leave for my studio," Miss Damer said immediately, and rose to her feet. "Do not, on my account, delay your conversation, Mrs Colchester, but I beg you will honour me with a visit to my studio very soon. Your face is not at all in the common way. Perfect for sculpture."

Surprised, Harriet said nothing, and Miss Damer turned to Lady Porter-Hume. "Ma'am, I shall see you at the Misses Berrys' soiree?"

"You will, my dear," Lady Porter-Hume nodded, and with a swirl of dark brown superfine, Miss Damer departed.

Harriet had to catch her breath when the sculptor had left. She felt as if she had been in a gale, such was the strength of Miss Damer's personality.

Lady Porter-Hume eyed her with amusement as she passed Harriet some tea. "A force of nature, is she not?"

Harriet smiled. "I am sorry! Was I so transparent? I like her very much, but she is so... different!"

"In more ways than one," Lady Porter-Hume said enigmatically. "But how can I help you, Mrs Colchester? I have not yet heard back from Lord Ware, but of course, his correspondence may be delayed because of Napoleon."

"Yes, I suspected it was too soon," Harriet agreed. "No, the purpose of my visit was to discuss my plans after the case. I recall you saying to me once that the law, used in the right way, might protect women such as I. Regardless of the outcome of the case, I should like to be more protected."

"Bravo, my dear, for your forward thinking!" Lady Porter-Hume gave her an approving glance. "Sadly, I feel it is depressingly straightforward. Should you win, all remains in your gift – at least until you choose to marry. But if you lose the case, you will *need* to marry."

"I hope that if I lose, I will at least be granted a competence," Harriet said, dreading the thought of living in reduced circumstances, but trying to be realistic. "In any case, my prospects with only a small portion and my advanced age do not recommend me as a wife."

"Advanced age? Do not talk such twaddle!" Lady Porter-Hume scolded.

"You are kind, but this is the way of the world, ma'am. I wanted to know how I might protect what money I have – whether that be a large amount or a small jointure."

"So, you will not marry if you win?" Lady Porter-Hume said in an odd voice.

"No, ma'am. I said the same thing to Mr Richardson last evening – I have been invisible much of my life, but John's fortune gives me choice. I am reluctant to relinquish that. If I keep my fortune, I will remain a widow."

"You said this to Mr Richardson?"

Too late, she realised that Mr Richardson was about to marry into Lady Porter-Hume's family, and her topic of conversation would not be tolerated when he was wed. She felt the heat of her blush.

"I have known him all my married life, and he and I are old friends," she forced out. "I recognise that this intimacy will change…"

When he marries. She could not bring herself to say the words.

Lady Porter-Hume gave her a shrewd glance. "My dear Mrs Colchester – I have great hopes of the rebuttal of the case, but if we lose, I give you my word that we will use the law to protect what you have, *should* you wish to marry again. If Miss Damer can craft a pre-nuptial agreement to keep her in comfort after her marriage, I'm sure you can, with the right advice."

Relieved, Harriet smiled. "Thank you, ma'am. That's what I want."

Chapter 34

NORTH LONDON, LATE MAY 2023

I sat across the table in the small Italian restaurant in Crouch End and tried to regain my equilibrium. My mind was still scattered from that gentle kiss in front of Liam's front room window.

"I read about this place," Hugo said, looking around the restaurant. "Don't the soap stars come here regularly?"

I grinned. "Not to mention a previous Dr Who! Crouch End is rammed with actors."

"How far away do you live?"

"Just a bus ride away," I replied, picking up a fork and turning it over on the pristine tablecloth. "When I bought my flat, I had to have bars fitted on the windows, the area was so rough. It's got heaps better over the past couple of years, a lot of gentrification going on. But I was lucky to buy it when I did. I couldn't afford it now."

"Did it need a lot of work?"

I relaxed as I went through the huge to-do list of replacements, rewiring, replastering and redecoration. Hugo laughed as I detailed my triumphs and disasters, broken nails and backache.

CHAPTER 34

The waiter took our order and arrived with a bottle of red wine and a bread basket. I sighed deeply in appreciation. Bread was my downfall.

"You look fabulous, by the way," Hugo said with a glint in his eye as he lifted his glass in a toast. "The dress suits you perfectly."

I swallowed a throwaway comment, like, 'Oh, this old thing?' and thanked him nicely. We clinked glasses, I took a big mouthful, and we ordered.

"How did it go with your family?" Hugo asked. "You looked completely stressed when I arrived, so I wanted to give you chance to unwind before I asked."

"Thanks, I appreciate that." I laughed, remembering. "God, their faces when you walked in! And Liam...!"

He chuckled. "Yes, it was a treat to see your brother's face, after the gallery event. After we left, he looked like a landed fish."

After the kiss. Hugo obviously shared my thoughts. A slow smile made its way across his face, and I paused to watch it. I could feel my nipples harden under the dress and I crossed my arms.

"So – what did they say?" he said quickly, and I had the impression he was trying to keep his attention in order. "And what did *you* say?"

I told him about the visit to the hospital and finding the whole family there. While I spoke, my tense body finally relaxed. Then I gave him the bones of the conversation tonight, ending when Evie had come over to hug me.

"It was strange. They looked at me as if I was someone they'd never really met before," I mused. "And I said almost everything that was on my mind, and that turned out to be more than I expected. My mum in particular

– well, you'd have thought I'd grown another head or something!"

Hugo nodded. "You sound like you were very brave."

I laughed. "I don't know about brave, but I tell you, it was very emotional! It was all I could do to stop myself from bursting into tears!" I said, leaning back to let the waiter put my burrata and tomato in front of me.

"When I first met you, Miss Assistant Gallery Manager, I wouldn't have thought you so... sensitive."

I peeked at him through my lashes. "Well, you live and learn, don't you?" I murmured. His eyes widened. I took another sip of wine and began to eat.

"Anyway – how are you? Have you heard anything from the police?" I wrenched the conversation onto more impersonal matters.

Those dark eyes flickered and narrowed, and he took a bite of calamari before responding. "No news. The insurance company is being difficult, though. They want to see all the police reports."

They also think it's an inside job, I thought. I nodded and said, "Well, I daresay they want to give the police an opportunity to find the miniatures. Has this put you off finding out more about the miniatures? About Sophia and Harriet?"

He grimaced. "To some extent – it's rubbing it in to discover more about a sitter whose portraits I no longer have!"

I looked sympathetic and got out my phone, thumbing quickly to my photos. "Look – I took these pictures of the miniatures at your house. I look at them a lot, when I'm worried things won't change. The portraits prove to me that even in the bleakest times, they will."

I held out my phone, expecting him to take it. Instead, he clasped my hand and pulled it closer, ostensibly so he could look. I couldn't take my gaze from his lips. I could feel his pulse, throbbing in his thumb. My breath came faster, and he opened his mouth to speak—

And then the waiter arrived. I saw a muscle twitch in Hugo's cheek and we both sat back. I put my phone away, and by the time the waiter had delivered our main course, the moment was well and truly gone.

I told myself my professional relationship had been saved by the pasta, but that didn't cheer me up. I took little comfort from the speed that we ate, refused pudding and coffee, and asked for the bill. As agreed, I paid, and Hugo gave me a tight smile.

"Are you catching the bus home?" he said in a distant voice, I stood for a moment and regarded him. He wasn't trying to pressurise me. I could catch the bus and he'd go for the tube. He drew a hand through his hair, and I realised suddenly that he was nervous.

What would Harriet do? In her second portrait, she looked as if she would dare anything.

"No, I thought I'd walk off all this pasta."

"I'll see you home, then."

"Thank you, I'd appreciate that," I replied.

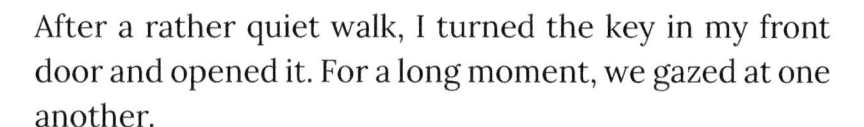

After a rather quiet walk, I turned the key in my front door and opened it. For a long moment, we gazed at one another.

"It's difficult. You're a client," I said, finally.

"I am. I'm also a gentleman and I'm happy to leave you if that's what you want," he said in a strained voice. "But just so there's no misunderstanding, I don't think I've ever wanted anyone as badly as I want you at this moment."

My jaw dropped. In the corner of my eye, I saw him stuff his clenched fists in his pockets.

"Would you like me to go?" he said softly.

I paused, on the edge of what seemed like a very tall cliff. "No," I whispered, and he reached for me, cupping my face with his big hands, tipping my chin so he could kiss my mouth, my temples, my throat. I moaned softly and backed into the door, pulling him inside. He kicked it shut.

As he continued to kiss me, I pushed the jacket off his shoulders and it fell unheeded to the carpet as he shrugged it away. I tried to steer him to the sofa, but he growled and raised his head.

"I've been dreaming of you for months. I don't want a quickie on your sofa," he muttered. "Where's your bedroom?"

I kicked off my high heels and took him by the hand. My mind was racing, one part of it wondering what state I'd left the bedroom in, the other thinking about Hugo's big, warm body and what it would look like naked. I opened the door and faced him. My arms went around his shoulders, and he lifted me off my feet, fitting my legs around his waist. My dress rode up my thighs and the heat of him scalded my skin. I groaned. He walked to the bed and sat down, nuzzling what he could see of my breasts.

"I knew I liked this dress," he murmured. "But I'd like it better off."

CHAPTER 34

I laughed and wriggled from his lap, his hands on my waist while I stood up. He gently turned me around and drew the zip down slowly, planting kisses down my spine. I began to squirm with pleasure and stepped out of the dress, my hands going to his trousers, pulling out his shirt and running my fingers through the dark silky hair on his chest. He closed his eyes as I licked one of his nipples, and soon, discarding other bits of my clothing on the way, we were on the bed. I reached to pull the covers down so I could get in, but he stopped me.

"You weren't thinking of sliding this glorious body under a duvet, were you?" he purred, and I felt my cheeks go hot. However fabulous the dress was, I was still the short, plump woman in it. I raised my hands to cover myself and he pulled my hands away and gazed at my breasts. "God help me, Gabriella, you are the most luscious creature. Don't you dare hide from me."

I lay on the bed watching him as he slowly undressed, slipping the shirt from broad shoulders and pushing trousers down taut muscled thighs. I stopped caring about my belly and fixed my avid gaze on the planes and curves of his body.

He drifted fingers over my hips, stomach and back up to my breasts, which he suckled gently as I gasped for breath. I pulled on his shoulders, but he grinned and resisted. "Not yet, Gabriella. Don't you want to take things slowly?"

Then he ducked down my body and ran his tongue over my inner thigh and I squeaked, almost jumping off the bed. His head came up.

"Don't you like this?" he said at once.

"I— er, God yes, but you don't have to—"

"But what if I want to?"

My head fell back against the pillows, and he continued lapping at me until I thought I would explode. I groaned in protest. Rising, he looked at me intently.

"Shall we stop here? We can do lots of other things...?"

"Are you having me on? No, I don't want to stop!" I said, my eyes wide.

He grinned, making him look a little boyish, and he found a condom from his pocket before kneeling on the bed. Taking him off guard, I pushed him onto his back and straddled him. I plucked the condom from his grasp and slid it down his length. Then I raised my hips and took him into me. He gasped, I moaned. I sat astride him, and with eyes gleaming like ebony, he cupped my breasts as I began to move.

"You are beautiful, Gabriella," he said, as I began to tense. He thrust his hips upwards and I spun off the edge of the world.

Waking up with a new lover was not the embarrassing experience I had feared. Hugo woke me the next morning with tea, already showered and with one of my biggest towels around his waist. I threw an automatic, panicked glance at the alarm clock.

"Don't worry, it hasn't gone off yet," he said smiling. He kissed me gently and I wondered what it would be like to wake up like this every morning. "Tea," he said, and gestured to the mug on the bedside table.

"What wonderful service," I said in a voice husky from lack of sleep and a lot of moaning. "You must come again."

"I intend to," he shot back with a wicked grin. "If invited, of course."

I took a sip of tea and then stretched luxuriously, noting with intense satisfaction that his eyes locked on my breasts.

"You have to go, don't you?" I said regretfully.

He rolled his eyes. "I do, I'm afraid. I have a meeting in the City at eight. But I'll be around at lunchtime?"

At this, my heart lurched. "I should be free," I said as casually as I could, and he grinned.

I thrust my legs out of bed. "Let me jump in the shower and then we'll have breakfast."

A mere ten minutes later, he was kissing me while my ancient toaster hummed and clicked. Only the bread popping up made him raise his head. It was vaguely unreal, buttering toast for this gorgeous man in my kitchen while he looked at me hungrily.

"What's in your day?" he asked.

"A couple of new artists coming in to speak to Gerrard and he wants me there. I've got some accounts to sort, and then I've got a meeting with someone who may want to hire the mezzanine. And I'll probably call Evie."

"Why?"

"She wanted to meet up for coffee, and I'll ring her to set it up," I said, hunting in a cupboard for peanut butter.

"I hope that you're not going to let one conversation with your sister-in-law undo all your good intentions."

"No, of course not!" I protested, rising triumphant with the jar. "But I felt awful when I saw Sam with his little cast, in the hospital. And last night Jasper asked me when I'd be around to play with them again! I felt incredibly guilty!"

He put down his toast. "I know you don't have children, but didn't Liam and you get into scrapes when you were younger?"

I thought. "Well, I was often reading and Liam was too lazy to climb trees. Or always on his computer."

"Wow, lucky you! I can remember Mum taking one or other of us to hospital regularly for one broken bone or another!" He smiled at me and continued eating. "Could you have stopped Jasper pushing his brother off the slide? You're not his mother. And he's fine, isn't he? You need to put it into proportion, otherwise the family may guilt you back into the way you were."

I frowned. No, Sam and Jasper weren't my children. But they were my monster nephews, and I loved them fiercely.

"I'm not sure I have got it out of proportion, Hugo," I said quietly. He shot me a glance from dark eyes.

"No? This is a lot of drama for a broken arm."

"He's six!" I exclaimed. "I don't want to do *everything* for my family, but they are still my family and I care about them!"

"Of course you do!" he said. "But your family has taken a lot of liberties. You need boundaries – you should decide what's acceptable and what's not."

Looking back, it may have been the lack of sleep, and my nervousness at this new emerging relationship. "Kettle, pot, black?" I said, eyebrows raised. "You've got your own issues with Pierce, haven't you?" He stared at me. "Frankly Hugo, I know he's your brother and you think the sun shines out of him, but I'm astounded that you don't think he had anything to do with the theft of the miniatures! It's bloody obvious to me *and* the police that he's involved!"

CHAPTER 34

He looked at me stone faced and I remembered all too late what Aunt Mo had said. Hugo stood up, his lips – so recently nuzzling my neck and belly – thin and pinched.

"I see. So, my brother's a thief in your estimation, is he?"

"Hugo—"

He swung his jacket from the chair and shrugged it on. "Perhaps we shouldn't do lunch and you can use the time to see your sister-in-law."

I heard the door slam.

On the bus, I relived the scene in my mind. He'd wanted me to be all brave and tackle everyone, sort things out. But he couldn't do it himself.

As I travelled nearer to work, I wavered about texting him. Perhaps it was a good thing we'd had this disagreement. I didn't want to swap one family with issues – mine – for another one – his.

I looked at the sky, at the slate-grey clouds gathering. It was going to rain. Perfect.

Chapter 35

GROSVENOR SQUARE, JUNE 1803

Harriet stared, stunned, at Lady Porter-Hume. Lying limp on her lap was the long, long missive from Lord Ware.

"I – I am astounded at these revelations," she said faintly. Phillip asked permission to read the letter and she passed it to him. He flicked out the tails of his coat and sat in one of the brocade chairs that graced the blue drawing room.

Harriet watched in silence as Phillip's eyes glanced down the pages, his eyebrows rising higher and higher the more he read. At one stage he let out a low whistle.

"Good God, what a mess!" he said. "Your cousin might well serve for a character of Mr Hogarth!"

Harriet hung her head in shame. Edwin had done the usual thing for most gentlemen on the Grand Tour – gambled a great deal, drunk a great deal and whored a great deal. But where Edwin had transgressed most egregiously was to have seduced an engaged lady of the Naples court, who was now with child. The lady's betrothed, the Comte di Cermillano, had apparently agreed to continue the engagement after Edwin produced a considerable sum of money, but, with Edwin's departure from the court, had withdrawn from their agreement. The young lady was banished from the court and was now residing with a distant cousin.

"So the Contessa di Basilio is disgraced while her former fiancé makes merry from a bargain he did not keep, and the seducer escapes without punishment!" Phillip said in disgust.

"Not quite," commented Lady Porter-Hume. "Read on. It would appear that Edwin was set on marrying the Contessa, but his parents refused their consent. He is not yet twenty-one, if you recall. The payment to the fiancé was very much the second option, Lord Ware says."

"But why refuse consent?" Harriet cried. "It would have been the honourable thing to do, and Lord Ware says that the Contessa was from a wealthy background! She would have had a good portion."

"Not as significant as yours, my dear Mrs Colchester," the lady responded wryly.

Harriet could have kicked herself. Of course. Edwin was refused permission to marry because Augusta was planning for him to marry Harriet. "Oh, the villain!" she muttered.

"Is he?" asked Phillip. "According to Lord Ware, he was most anxious to wed the lady, but prevented from doing so by his parents."

"I was not speaking of Edwin," she said between gritted teeth. "I was speaking of Augusta."

Phillip stroked his chin thoughtfully. "By Jove! I think you're right. It would have been Augusta who paid off di Cermillano. Well, the devil!"

Unable to sit still any longer, Harriet rose and strode around the room, twisting her handkerchief in her hands. Her rage at Augusta's scheming threatened to overwhelm her. She thought of the Contessa, alone and frightened, with child and unwed, and wondered if Sophia, cast out from her family, might have suffered in the same way. At least Sophia had been with Miles.

"But with respect, ma'am, Lord Ware's account is but one." Phillip looked at Lady Porter-Hume, frowning. "Will revealing this be enough to force Augusta's hand?"

Lady Porter-Hume drew out another packet of papers. "I thought you might say that, so when I wrote to Lord Ware, I asked him to provide other evidence. He has done so in style, although it makes miserable reading. I have here signed testimonies of other court lords, servants – all, indeed, that you need to bring scandal onto Edwin's name."

"But what of Augusta?" Harriet demanded, hands on her hips. "She should not escape censure!"

"Why not ask Mr Beaufort if he has her letters about the money?" Lady Porter-Hume asked calmly. "I imagine he still has them. I would, if I were in his shoes."

Harriet paused in her stalking around the room. Yes, she would be surprised if Edwin hadn't kept the letters – always a lad with an eye to the future, she thought grimly. "Would you excuse me while I write a note?" she said. "I will ask if he knows how the Contessa does."

Phillip offered his arm to Lady Porter-Hume. "Perhaps we can entertain you with a spot of luncheon while we await a response?"

Edwin's response was gratifyingly swift, and he waited on Harriet within the hour. Harriet had decided that it would be prudent for only Phillip to be present with her. She felt that Edwin would not wish to confess his misdemeanours with such a member of the *ton* present, so Lady Porter-Hume was sitting in Anne's cosy parlour, and – much to Harriet's surprise – entertaining James with finger puppets.

Edwin arrived a little sweaty and with his necktie askew. Harriet greeted him civilly and they sat down, Phillip sitting further away from their conversation.

Now he was in front of her, Harriet was unsure where to start, but Edwin burst into speech.

"I loved her! I am desolate without her! It has been torture to leave her behind!" He wiped his brow with a handkerchief. Harriet put her head on one side.

"Why don't you tell me what happened?" she said, and out it all came. Lord Ware had the particulars correct; Edwin had been presented to the Contessa, and over the three weeks that he had been at court, she had charmed him.

"She is not beautiful, like some women," he said, looking wistfully into the distance. "But she was perfect to me! I adored her. It— what happened was only a natural progression of our relationship."

"What of her fiancé?" Harriet tried and failed to keep the judgement from her voice.

"I know, I know!" he said, despairingly. "She should not have been the object of my affection. But – oh, Harriet, if you could just meet her! She is the sweetest creature in the world!"

"Then why, Edwin, have you offered for me?"

He was silent. "Aunt Augusta persuaded my father to refuse consent to marry Maria," he said at last. "I know you see me as – and indeed, I am! – a weakling, but I thought if I couldn't marry Maria, it didn't matter who I married! And with your fortune, I could try to bring her out of Naples so I could support her."

"You could wait until you are twenty-one," Harriet observed, simultaneously revolted by the idea of John's hard-earned money being used in this way, but with a grudging admiration for Edwin for his scheming.

"I am in not in control of the purse strings!" he replied bitterly, biting a nail. "My parents are so swayed by Aunt Augusta, and they remind me all the time what she has done for me – the Tour, the allowance she gives me – they quite bend my ear! But now she is starting to drop hints that she won't sponsor my sister on her come-out if I am not sufficiently grateful! And I know you don't care for me, but I cannot put my sister's future at risk!"

"But your parents – they are not penniless, are they?"

He looked shamefaced. "I have run through the blunt most abominably," he muttered. "Lord Rochford saw me attempting to recoup some of my losses at White's."

"You didn't, did you?" Harriet said wryly. He shook his head.

Harriet didn't know whether to laugh or cry. In the end, she pitied him, a weak boy, caught in the machinations of a determined aunt. He wasn't blameless, she decided, but he was rather witless. She sighed.

"Edwin, did you write to Mama to ask for help when you were in Naples? And what happened to the Contessa?"

His face hardened, and for a second, Harriet caught a glimpse of the man Edwin might be when he grew up. "Aunt Augusta only offered the funds on the condition I leave Italy and return home. The best thing I could do was to ask Lord Ware to negotiate on my behalf with

CHAPTER 35

that blaggard of a fiancé, Cermillano, to keep Maria safe. He promised that he would honour their engagement, and I thought I had done the best I could for my love – in the circumstances." He got up quickly from the sofa and, much agitated, paced around the room. "I had just returned to England when he wrote to me, saying he was breaking the agreement as he could not dishonour his family in this way. He would take the money and sue me for adultery if I objected. When the Peace fell apart, I was desperate – how could I remove her from Italy if I had no money? As an Englishman, I could certainly not return, I would be arrested and imprisoned. It was then I agreed with Augusta that I would ask you to marry me. I would support Maria and the child as soon as you and I were wed. It seemed the only way."

"Do you have Mama's letter?" Harriet asked softly, watching him closely.

"I do," Edwin said, reaching into his jacket and placing a fragile envelope on the table. "It is only one letter, but her intent is quite clear."

Harriet looked at it on the burnished mahogany table as she might a snake. "Are you content to give it to me?"

"I do not know what you intend to do with it, but if it offers me a chance to get out of her clutches, take it and welcome!"

She thought a moment. "If my plan to release us both is to work, Edwin, you must not tell her of our conversation." He nodded. Harriet patted his shoulder. "I hope all will be well," she said.

Once Edwin had left, Phillip exhaled gustily. "My God! What a story! I'll fetch Anne and Lady Porter-Hume."

After hearing Harriet's account, Lady Porter-Hume picked up Augusta's letter between finger and thumb and cast her eyes over the contents.

"She is a masterly strategist, I'll give her that," she murmured. "Our Royal Navy could usefully employ her, I'm sure." She put the letter down and looked at Harriet. "Well, my dear, what do you want to do?"

Harriet experienced a strange rush, and for a moment, she did not recognise the sensation. She had, potentially, the ability to change things. She could help bring the Contessa di Basilio and her unborn child from the Continent, and support Edwin, idiot boy that he was. She could secure her independence, reconcile with Sophia and make the most of her life, now Alexander was to be married to someone else.

"I will instruct Mr Bessiwick to write to Mama and Edwin, saying that I have certain documents in my possession that would ruin her, Edwin, and therefore the family name. I will undertake not to publish them if she withdraws her challenge," Harriet said in a voice that sounded a little loud to her ears. "If we are successful, I will bring the Contessa and the baby to England so Edwin can marry her."

"Bravo, my dear!" Anne said, tears in her eyes.

Lady Porter-Hume nodded in great satisfaction. "I think this calls for something stronger than tea!"

The letters had been sent, and what followed was a deathly silence from Augusta. It was a full two days later that Harriet and Anne sat in the drawing room, trying to read, and not seeing a word on the page. However, when Coates announced Alexander, it was with mixed feelings that she greeted him.

"How are you, Mrs Colchester? You have been constantly in my thoughts," he said in a gruff voice, bending over her hand and brushing his lips on her skin. The tingle Harriet felt was so powerful, she snatched her hand away.

He stilled, and she managed to laugh. "I beg your pardon for being so jumpy. We have written to challenge her but not had a response. I am sure you can imagine the state of my nerves, sir."

"Indeed. What will you do?" He looked at her, his gaze intent.

"Nothing, if she withdraws the challenge. If she continues, and wins, I imagine I will be living rather frugally."

"And if she loses?" Alexander asked, his gaze intent.

"I will travel the world!" Harriet said gaily, not meeting his eyes.

"You are still determined to remain a widow?"

"I am." This time she looked at him directly. "Remaining unmarried is the simplest way to secure my independence."

He frowned and almost made to speak, but then thought better of it.

"Come and sit beside me, Mr Richardson!" Anne demanded, catching sight of his expression. "Tell us all the news and distract us!"

He did his best, Harriet thought as she watched him launch into a story about a recent visit to Astley's Amphitheatre with Miss Porter-Hume and Lord Benborough.

"You are keeping exalted company, Mr Richardson," said Anne, admiringly. "Lord Benborough is considered the catch of the Season."

He smiled. "I know nothing about that," he said easily. "He is a charming fellow. Miss Porter-Hume was delighted with his company."

Harriet's chest appeared to have a stone on it; she found it difficult to breathe. Alexander's position in society was certainly gathering weight. Soon he would forget he had ever known her, moving in completely different circles. She swallowed against the tears that sprang to her eyes – God, what a fool she was! Thankfully, before she could lose herself further in such maudlin thoughts, Coates arrived with a message.

It was from Mr Bessiwick. Harriet tore open the seal. She gasped.

Anne started to her feet. "Harriet? What is the news? Oh, my dear…" She stared at Harriet in gathering dismay.

Harriet shook her head, smiling through her tears. "No, you misunderstand – she's withdrawn the case! I have won!"

Chapter 36

CENTRAL LONDON, MID JUNE 2023

"Gerrard Williams, Art Dealer, Gabriella speaking. How can I help you?" I said, the phone tucked under my chin as I unwrapped a parcel of our new catalogues for distribution to our clients.

"Hi, this is Benedict Adam-Smith from the York Gallery," said a rich voice.

"Oh, hi! You recommended Chloe Johnson to Gerrard, didn't you?"

"I did."

I smiled, dumping the programmes on the desk. "What can I do for you, Mr Adam-Smith?"

"Benedict, please. About an hour ago, I had someone in reception who was asking if anyone was available to look at two miniature portraits that he'd inherited."

I froze. "Were these two miniatures of a lady, about three inches across, painted by Richard Cosway?" My voice was a squeak, and I took a deep breath.

"Yes, my assistant believes so, although he didn't have a lot of time to examine the pictures carefully. Joel – my assistant – asked if he could just check something and came looking for me. By the time I arrived, the seller had disappeared. We've got his image on CCTV, but he was wearing a hat, so the image isn't very good. I thought something might be up – after all, this is not rational behaviour – so I checked the Art Loss Register. Which is how I found you, Gabriella."

I closed my eyes in frustration and swore under my breath. I'd put money on it that it was Pierce – but I couldn't ask, without getting everyone into a tangle involving the police. Which Hugo would hate.

"Shall I inform the police and the Art Loss Register?" Benedict asked, and I hesitated, not knowing what to do. In the end, I decided to gather more information.

"Can you hazard a guess where this man might have gone next?"

"Hmm." Benedict paused. "I think, if he lost his nerve here, he wouldn't try a reputable gallery again. Where are the paintings from?"

"Northumberland."

"What are they worth?"

I told him. Another short silence on the end of the phone started to stretch my nerve endings, and I fought the urge to tap my fingers.

"There's an auction the day after tomorrow, just outside York," he said thoughtfully. "It's described as a country house sale, but quite a few 'inherited' items find their way there. The police watch it when they've got the time, but lately, that's not often. Your miniatures might end up there."

"Can you give me the details?" I said, scrabbling for a pen and paper.

As I was thanking him, the clouds outside the gallery cleared and bright sunlight fell on Chloe Johnson's latest landscape, hanging large and impressive on the wall. Her oils had attracted a great deal of attention and I told him.

"Ah, Chloe Johnson," he said, a smile in his voice. "Incredibly talented, now just beginning to get a name for herself. She runs a B&B, you know."

"Really? She's not full time as an artist?" I asked, momentarily diverted from Hugo's saga.

"I think she didn't really believe she could survive as an artist until recently," he replied. "The B&B is a family thing and she's reluctant to let it go. But we shall see. She's a lovely girl, probably trying to please too many people."

He rang off and I was left contemplating the wildness of the Yorkshire moors in greys and deep blues, ochre and sage green. I shook myself free from its magic. I picked up my phone and dialled Hugo's number.

The dark chocolate tones told me he wasn't available and to leave my name and number. I left a rather stilted message that my call wasn't about our disagreement, and that someone was trying to sell the miniatures, could he contact me. I left him to his own conjectures about who was schlepping from gallery to gallery, trying to flog them.

By the end of the day, I still hadn't heard from him, and I made my way home, sad and frustrated. I'd just taken off my coat when there was a knock at the front door. For some absurd reason, my mind leapt to the conclusion that because I had been thinking of Hugo, he had miraculously appeared.

My face fell when I saw Joe, lightly tanned from the French sun and freshly barbered, standing at my door with a bunch of roses.

"I turn up with flowers and you look like a wet weekend!" he declared. I shook my head, found a smile and invited him in. "What's up, Gabriella? You're looking amazing, by the way."

I cast my eyes down my new leather skirt and silk blouse. At least something was going right for me.

"Come on in. If you have time, I could do with someone to bounce this off," I said, heading to the kitchen to put the roses in water. I returned with a bottle of wine and two glasses.

"Ah. I see this is going to be a long story, so shall I order pizza?" he said, a gleam of understanding in his eye. He whipped out his phone, ordered my favourite and made himself comfortable. "Tell me everything, every single detail."

Twenty minutes later, he was patting my shoulder. "Wow. That's quite a conundrum. The man of your dreams, his brother who may be the thief, and you, stuck in the middle. What would happen if the paintings were returned?"

"I'd remove the miniatures from the Register. Hugo would need to repay the insurance money, if he's received any. I'm not sure what – if anything – would happen to Pierce."

"Are you so certain it's the wastrel younger brother? Could it be anyone else?" I gave him what Aunt Mo would have called an old-fashioned look, and he chuckled. "Okay, got it. I agree, the evidence is a bit overwhelming, but your Hugo refuses to entertain the idea."

"I imagine that even if I caught Pierce with the miniatures in his rucksack, Hugo wouldn't believe it. Nor press charges."

He sipped his wine. "Then what would happen?"

CHAPTER 36

"I dunno," I said. "I expect the police have better things to do than try and prosecute without a case."

"So really, what you need to do is get hold of the pictures, right?" Joe said. The doorbell rang. "That'll be the pizza." He got up and went to answer the door.

I pondered on his words and stared at the wall, unseeing. When he came back, Joe eyed me shrewdly.

"You've made up your mind what to do, haven't you?"

I laughed. "You know me so well. Yes, I'm going to see if they're listed in the auction – Benedict might be wrong, and I might be on a wild goose chase. But if I'm not, Hugo can bid to get them back."

I put down the phone, my heart thumping. A call to the auction confirmed that the miniatures 'of an unknown lady' were indeed a lot. Trying to be calm, I tapped a pencil on my teeth, thinking about my next move. Another call to Hugo, this time with the full details, had gone unanswered, so I left another message. I was starting to feel panicked. Without someone there to bid for the miniatures, they might be lost forever.

Gerrard noticed my abstraction. "What's got into you, Gabriella?"

I explained and watched his eyes widen. "We should tell the police," he said, firmly.

"That's what Benedict says," I said gloomily. "But the auction is *tomorrow*! It took the police nearly two weeks to interview me to confirm Hugo was in London at the time of the theft. I've left a dozen messages for him!" I said, raking my hand through my hair. "If someone doesn't bid for the miniatures, we'll probably never see them again!"

Gerrard was thoughtful. "We do need to tell the police, but I'll do it, maybe leave a message – then we're covered. You need to find a train to York."

"Why? Are you giving me the company credit card?" I said with a laugh.

"Don't be an idiot. I'll have to come with you to make sure they are genuine. No, don't hug me – this suit is silk and creases easily!"

I gave him my police contact and went to book the train tickets before he changed his mind.

We arrived at the auction very early to get a look at the lot, as we'd missed the pre-sale. I gasped as we saw the miniatures, propped up inexpertly against the leather case, behind a cage. I looked at them avidly, my eyes flicking over them to check for damage. I could see a scrape on the leather case. Harriet stared back at me, as though asking where the hell I'd been. I almost apologised.

Gerrard pulled on his gloves and gestured towards the security men, indicating that he would like to look at the miniatures. One walked over, unlocked the cage and stood close by while Gerrard examined them.

Satisfied, he thanked the man and took off his gloves.

"Relax. The case has been knocked about a bit, but the miniatures are unharmed," he murmured as we walked away. "We should register and then take a seat and appear generally uninterested."

CHAPTER 36

So, after Gerrard picked up his bidding paddle, we stayed quiet and unobserved in the barn-like room, which was more like a warehouse than an auction room. The other bidders seemed to be amateur collectors, young men in too-sharp suits and plump retirees, hoping that a lifetime of watching *Antiques Roadshow* was enough to equip them to spot a Fabergé trinket. There were also some genuine enthusiasts, whose keen eyes and knowledge enabled them to spot the false from the authentic.

There were also a couple of rather large bullish men with bald heads and jackets buttoned too tightly over their chests. They had earpieces and looked for all the world like bouncers. Gerrard considered them thoughtfully.

"Good job my credit is reliable," he said.

The auction room swiftly filled, and I cast an anxious glance at my phone. I'd called Hugo again, and this time, I'd told him where I was, and what Gerrard and I intended to do. Could he *please* return my call?

By the time the auctioneer took to the stage, half an hour later, the place was packed with people, many standing around the sides of the walls. I was so tense, I felt as though I had concrete in my shoulders.

A few lots went through, and after the bidding on one vase, Gerrard chuckled softly.

"What's the matter?" I asked in a low voice.

"It's a fake," he murmured, and I stared at him. "Certainly not Delft and not that age – pattern is all wrong." I shook my head, and the auctioneer gave us a sharp look. Gerrard smiled blandly.

About three quarters of an hour later, the miniatures of Harriet came up. I straightened immediately and then deflated as Gerrard nudged my knee.

"Uninterested, remember?" he whispered. I sank back against my chair.

"And now we have two exquisite, signed miniature portraits of an unknown lady, one conjectured to be when she was in mourning," intoned the auctioneer. "The artist is Richard Cosway, a leading English portrait painter of the Georgian and Regency era, noted for his miniatures. The portrait is framed in a bone and wood inlay oval-shaped frame with a fine gold textured border. The miniatures are signed bottom right: Cosway. Who'll start us off at ten thousand pounds? Thank you, sir, do I hear eleven thousand?"

I looked down, unable to watch as the bidding began, and concerned I would look simply too eager. Gerrard waited for the smaller bids to come in. When he heard the auctioneer say, "Twenty thousand, five hundred, gentleman at the back," Gerrard raised his paddle. The auctioneer nodded at him. "Twenty-one thousand, five hundred, against you, sir. Do I hear twenty-two thousand, five hundred?" The auctioneer nodded towards the rear of the room.

"Back with you, sir at twenty-two thousand, five hundred." The auctioneer looked again at Gerrard, who again nodded. "Twenty-three thousand, five hundred. I have twenty-three thousand, five hundred; do I hear twenty-five thousand?" The auctioneer raised his head.

There was a curse and I started. I knew that voice. I made to stand up to see who it was, but Gerrard grabbed my arm. "Do not look at the other bidder!" he hissed. "They'll think you're trying to intimidate him!"

CHAPTER 36

"If it's who I think it is, he tops me by at least a foot!" I hissed back, but subsided.

The auctioneer gave me a dirty look and focused his attention on the back of the room. "Sir, your bid."

"Twenty-five thousand pounds," said a velvet voice from the back of the room and I clutched Gerrard's paddle before it rose.

"I hope I'm not wrong, but I'm pretty sure you're bidding against Hugo Cavendish," I said urgently.

"What?"

"Do I have twenty-six thousand?" asked the auctioneer, looking at Gerrard, and after a moment's hesitation, Gerrard shook his head. The auctioneer scanned the room and banged his gavel a moment later.

"Sold! Now, onto lot two hundred..."

The room seemed to exhale; the auctioneer handed a sheet of paper to an assistant, and bidding continued.

"Now can I stand up?" I asked, and Gerrard sighed.

"I think you'd better check it is Hugo Cavendish! I'll see you by the exit."

I was already out of my seat and heading towards the back of the room. Sure enough, in a casual sweater and black jeans, Hugo was checking his phone and frowning. His gaze fell on me, and his eyes widened.

"Gabriella, what the hell are you doing here?"

"Bidding on the miniatures! *Please* tell me that you won them!"

"That was you?"

"Of course it was me – well, it was Gerrard! Where the hell have you *been*? I've left loads of messages! Were you ignoring me?"

He stared at me, and completely unexpectedly, I burst into tears. He bit off a curse and pulled me into a hug, kissing the top of my head and murmuring nonsense. "Sweetheart. Don't cry. I'm sorry, my blasted phone fell into the sink, and I've had to use a replacement while they fixed it. I'm so sorry."

I sniffed and pulled away from him while I grabbed a handkerchief to scrub my eyes. "I might have known! But what are you doing here? How did you know the miniatures were here?"

He went very still and pulled me to an alcove, away from the curious eyes of onlookers. "Because Pierce told me," he said in a low voice.

"What?"

He shook his head. "I have a lot to tell you, but long story short is that I went to tackle him two days ago about the miniatures. He admitted taking them."

"Why didn't you just pull them from the auction? They're stolen goods!"

"Shush! Keep your voice down! Pierce owes money to some rather unsavoury characters, and this was the way he'd get money to pay them back. He thought if he pulled the miniatures from the auction, they would hurt him. So, I came to bid. This way, they get money and I get the portraits back." He grinned at me. "And I have to say, I was doing quite well getting them on the cheap until this other bidder cut in!"

"You've spent more money recovering your own property!" I stared at him, astonished. "That's just crazy!"

"I didn't want to put him in danger," Hugo said seriously. "This was the easiest way I could think to do it."

I folded my arms. "If you'd have told me-—"

"Oh, do be quiet," he said, and kissed me. A few moments later, he let me go and I buried my face in his sweater. "Gabriella, could we start again?" he said, and

CHAPTER 36

his voice was a low rumble in my ears. "I'd like to see if we can have a proper relationship. I'm happy never to be a client again, if that would make it easier."

"God, Gerrard will kill me," I muttered. I looked up at him, noted the faint stubble and eyes that hadn't slept as well as they ought. "But what about the police? And your insurance company?"

"Insurance hasn't paid up anyway yet, and I'm not going to press charges against Pierce no matter what, so I planned on telling the police that it was a huge misunderstanding, and as I now possess the miniatures again, there's no case."

"Can you do that?"

"Worth a go." He grinned at me and then the grin faded. "But what about us? What do you want to do?"

I thought for a nanosecond. "Well, we have research to complete," I said airily. His slow smile warmed me to my toes.

"I have to get back to Pierce, who's in a proper state," he said gravely. "But I'll book a hotel and come down at the first opportunity."

"No, don't book a hotel," I said. "You can stay with me."

Chapter 37

PORTMAN SQUARE, MID-JUNE 1803

Miss Georgiana Porter-Hume sparkled like sunlight on water; so much so, the lady was almost difficult to look at. Accordingly, Harriet turned away and glanced down the ballroom to see Lord Benborough and Lady Porter-Hume deep in conversation.

She sighed. This ball was to mark the end of the season, and Lady Porter-Hume had urged Harriet to privately celebrate her good fortune. There was certainly a need for distraction, the Peace in Europe now at an end. Harriet cursed Bonaparte for disrupting her travel ambitions.

She was sure the news of Georgiana's engagement would be a worthy distraction. Harriet took a glass from a passing footman and sipped at it. This was her second – or her third? She couldn't remember, but the champagne served to alleviate a little of the numbness she had felt for the past week.

She leaned against a pillar and patted back into place a flounce of her new lavender gauze. In half-mourning, she did not look so wan, but, she decided, a pretty dress couldn't brighten how you felt on the inside. And inside, she felt very dismal indeed.

"Why are you hugging the walls?" a familiar voice said in her ear, and she jumped.

"Alex— Mr Richardson, you almost made me spill my drink," she scolded, and he smiled, his eyes tracing her body. She felt rather hot and took another sip of champagne.

"That would have been a travesty. You look lovely," he said obligingly.

"Pooh," she said dismissively. "Why are you not dancing?"

"Because I am talking to you."

She made a noise of frustration, emptied her glass and began to look for another.

Alexander lifted a dark brow. "Steady on, Harriet. You don't want to be in your cups, my dear, victory or no victory!"

"I am a wealthy widow," she announced. Were her words a little slurry? She dismissed the thought. "I can do what I want."

He looked carefully at her, blue gaze narrowed. "Travel? See the world? Build schools? Buy a house in town?"

"Exactly."

"Take a lover?"

Harriet gulped, and stared, wide-eyed. "W-what?"

Alexander leaned on the other side of the pillar and admired the whirling dancers. "You are dead set against marriage, but as you are still so young, you must surely wish for companionship, even love. Do you not?"

Harriet swallowed, and wished she could stop the room from spinning. "I had not thought so far," she managed. Alexander nodded, and like him, Harriet contemplated the dancers. Neither spoke for a few minutes, and then Harriet said, almost defiantly, "This is a most improper conversation, but as an old friend you must have an opinion – do you have someone to recommend for the position?"

Alexander slowly levered himself from the pillar to stand in front of her, his face very still. "I do indeed, but much as he desires you, he would much rather marry you."

Her lips parted for a second at his expression and she saw the fire flame in his gaze as he looked at her mouth. Every thought in her head was chased away.

The music stopped and Lady Porter-Hume, resplendent in burgundy satin, stepped onto a raised dais. Harriet felt her heart pound as she realised what was about to happen. She grasped Alexander's arm. "Should you not be over there?" she whispered urgently.

Puzzled, he shook his head. "Why?"

"Isn't this your announcement?" Harriet said, her head beginning to ache. She pushed him forward, but rock-like, he resisted.

"Ladies and gentlemen, could I have your attention?" Lady Porter-Hume said, beaming at everyone. "Lord Benborough?"

The gentleman offered his hand so Lady Porter-Hume could step down, and then climbed easily onto the dais. Lord Benborough was immaculate, gold lace at the throat and cuffs of snowy linen, lifting the black evening coat. His face was handsome, there was no doubt, but in Harriet's mind he was also a boy, rather than a man. He cleared his throat.

"Thank you, ma'am. Ladies and gentlemen, I have some news, and I wish you all to share in my happiness," he said. His voice was clear and light and Harriet could not help but compare it to the deeper, often gruff voice

CHAPTER 37

of the man beside her. Lord Benborough grinned. "I have asked Miss Georgiana Porter-Hume for her hand in marriage, and she has accepted me."

There were gasps and oohs and applause and Georgiana blushed rosily. Harriet also gasped, but with shock. She swung to face Alexander, reaching for his hand.

"Oh! But – ! I'm so sorry! Are you all right, Alexander?"

"Perfectly," he said with a puzzled grin, but holding her hand tight. "Georgiana looks radiant, does she not?"

"I don't understand," she replied, snatching her hand away. "I thought *you* were going to announce your betrothal to Miss Porter-Hume. I've been expecting it for weeks!"

Alexander stared at her, astounded. "But why?"

"I saw you in the Park! You seemed so intimate, I could not imagine another outcome!"

He laughed and she stamped her foot. "Curse you, do not mock me! Are you saying you were never attached?"

"No, whatever made you think I was?" Their conversation was beginning to attract attention. He pushed her gently towards the terrace doors.

"You were always with her!"

He opened a door and allowed her to go before him. "But so was Lord Benborough! And it is he that Georgiana has developed a *tendre* for! I was sworn to secrecy, otherwise I would have shared this with you!"

She stepped backwards through the door, her mind whirling. "So that's why you could not tell me!" She rubbed her hand on her forehead, cursing an over-active imagination. "No, of course – you would not dally with a young, impressionable girl if you were not serious! You are too honourable for that!"

"But you are sadly mistaken in my character," he said, closing the door to the ballroom, and shutting out the noise. She stared up at him as he stood close to her. "I am lately grown so dishonourable that I would offer the love of my life a clandestine arrangement rather than marriage, because she wishes it so."

Harriet stood stock still, his words sucking the air from her lungs. The pieces took a moment to assemble, but when they did, it was as if fireworks had lit the sky.

"A-Alexander?" she said, questioning, still unable to believe.

"Yes, Harriet?"

"Is it – is it me?" He nodded gravely and the world shifted on its axis. "Oh." It was all she could think to say.

He stood perfectly still, not reaching for her as she longed for him to do. "I have wrestled with my conscience for years," he continued quietly. "You were the wife of my best friend and I put you from my mind as best I could. But I could not resist. Even through the pain of my longing, being near you was such a pleasure! And when John died, I removed myself from you by coming to London. My hopes grew when you arrived in town, but I despaired of ever getting you to see me as anything other than a friend!"

She closed her eyes, unsure whether she could trust her ears or if this was a dream. He drew a deep breath.

"If you decide you wish us to be only friends, I shall be silent on this forever – but could we be more?"

Harriet opened her eyes and searched his stone-like face, as he waited for her response. Where to begin? She decided there was too much to say, and she didn't have the patience. She put her hands around his neck and pulled his mouth to hers. After a second's resistance,

CHAPTER 37

his arms snapped around her, dragging her tight against him.

His kiss was a revelation – his lips smooth, his mouth gentle but insistent. After the first furious embrace, his touch softened, became more subtle and intense. She leaned into his warmth, her hands tangled in his hair. She could feel the hardness of him through his evening clothes and her nipples ached as they pressed into his chest. She finally broke away, her body aching and her mouth tingling from his kiss.

"Oh, yes, Alexander – I could certainly see you as more than a friend!" she gasped, and finding herself unsteady, sat on the edge of a huge marble urn and tried to command her breathing. Alexander swung away from her with a muttered curse, his shoulders rapidly rising and falling as he too, fought for control.

The longest minute in Harriet's life went by as she waited for him to look at her in the dim light of the terrace. He finally turned. "You make me lose my head," he admitted with a wry smile.

"But please explain – you and Miss Porter-Hume were never apart!" said Harriet, ignoring the heat between her thighs that his words generated.

He laughed. "She was smitten by Lord Benborough. We have some shared business interests and she asked me to make the introductions to him. I did so gladly, although I don't doubt she will lead him a merry dance!"

The months of pain and loneliness seemed to disappear like a bubble on the top of a pond.

Harriet stared at him. "I never – I thought you were lost to me. And you had lately grown so formal I thought the engagement was a certainty!"

"You were so keen to remain a widow."

"With your new acquaintance I thought you had forgotten me."

He stepped closer and captured her hands. "Never. Are you insane, woman? I've spent the last six years trying to forget about you and failing utterly." He kissed her knuckles, then up her arm and shoulder before reaching her neck. Her head fell back, her eyes closed, and Alexander cupped her face and kissed her mouth.

It was five minutes later that Alexander raised his head, his eyes a little unfocused. "We should go in," he said hoarsely. "But drive with me tomorrow and we can talk further."

Dazed, she allowed him to lead her back to the ballroom.

Anne considered her with ill-disguised curiosity. "How did you sleep, Harriet?"

Dreadfully, thought Harriet. Her body was hot and expectant and her head full of imaginings. And decisions. "I was a little restless. It must have been the excitement of the announcement."

A small smile lifted Anne's mouth. "Ah, that must be it. Is Mr Richardson calling today?"

"We agreed to get some air in the Park," Harriet replied nonchalantly. "I believe he has a new curricle to impress me with."

Anne laughed but pressed her no more.

Harriet was ready more than ten minutes before the time they had agreed, but then, he was early. Anne observed they both seemed eager to be gone. Harriet forbore to answer, but her cheeks heated at Alexander's wink. He handed her into the curricle, and they made polite conversation about the weather while he drove them to the Ring.

Once the horses steadied into a gentle trot, Alexander cast a sideways glance at her. "You look tired," he said, not mincing words.

"And you," she replied immediately, and he chuckled.

"Indeed, I was restless all night, thinking of you."

Harriet felt her stomach dip and then swirl. Her voice, when she spoke, was a little higher than usual. "I have given some thought to your proposal – or shall we call it your suggestion? And I have decided that while it may suit me, I doubt it will suit the *ton*."

"So, what is to be done?" He sounded grave, all the amusement chased from him. "I do not want to be without you, Harriet."

"I do not know," she sighed. "It may be that Lady Porter-Hume will create the kind of legal agreement that might protect me—"

"Damn it, I do not need your money!" he snapped.

"No, Alexander, but I do!" she stressed. "You know how women are treated in our circles! And while I'm sure you are very hot for me now, that may change should I grow old and fat—"

"Old I am expecting; fat may be slightly trying," Alexander interjected. "But I interrupted you – please continue telling me why we cannot be lovers."

She paused and gripped her hands together. "I – I cannot. Whatever we feel, it dishonours us both, and John – and I cannot do that."

There was a silence as he digested this. A few gentlemen raised their hats to Harriet, and she smiled and nodded, praying that no-one would want to stop to converse. Alexander drove grimly on.

"Would you marry me?" His question was abrupt.

Harriet's heart contracted and she sighed. "There's no-one I'd lief marry than you, Alexander. But understand – I was a dutiful daughter, a dutiful wife. I have been a dutiful widow – I am tired of duty. And yet, should we marry, I am not even a person in my own right any longer!"

"Answer the question, Harriet," he ground out between his teeth, and she laid her hand on his.

"Of course. In a heartbeat. But not – like this."

"Then how?"

She looked at him and he slowed the horses. "Do you trust me, Alexander?"

"With my life."

"Then I will find a way, but you may need to accept something rather different from society's expectations. It may be radical," she warned him.

He smiled. "I'm sure it will be, but I am no stranger to radical thinking. I shall have to be strong."

He drew her hand to his mouth and kissed it, and she shivered in response.

Chapter 38

BERWICK, JULY 2023

I stood hopping from foot to foot at Berwick-upon-Tweed station, wondering why it was so full of people. Impulsively, I had offered to come to Northumberland to see Hugo, but even now, I fretted about being too eager.

My mobile rang. It was Liam and I answered quickly, fearing something was wrong. "Hi, we're having a barbecue next weekend and I'm out getting charcoal in the garden centre. Did you want a new plant pot for that camellia? They're on sale and I could get you one…"

For a moment, I was lost for words. I would put money on it that Evie had prompted him to make the call. "Um… yes, that would be great, but how big is it?"

"It says sixty centimetres. Looks huge to me."

I tucked my phone under my chin and did a rough estimate with my hands. Thirty centimetres was about twelve inches, right? "That would be perfect. I'll transfer the cash."

"If you can make the barbecue, you could pay me then. Erm, you could bring Hugo, too, if he's in London."

At this my eyes widened. I said I'd ask him, and Liam rang off. I couldn't see Hugo and Liam ever hitting it off, but perhaps Hugo could give it a try for my sake.

The man in question drew up in his glossy black car and jumped out, catching me in a tight hug before kissing me. Damn. There really was something about his kisses. Perhaps I wasn't the only one who was eager.

A car drew up behind him and tooted good-naturedly. With a smothered curse, he grabbed my holdall and led me to the car, waving an apology at the driver behind him.

When we were driving away, I looked at the traffic. "What's going on?"

"It's a new Lowry exhibition," he said, slowing to allow a van to pull out from a side street. "It's at the Ravensdowne Barracks. Lowry often came here on holiday. The Art Gallery has pulled together about forty paintings, not just of Berwick, and people are coming in hordes to see it."

I nodded, thinking it was a shame I wouldn't see it.

"We can come into town later, if you like?" he said, throwing me a glance. "I bought tickets on the offchance you might want to."

"I'd like that," I said, feeling my heart warm at his foresight. He drove the car out of Berwick and began the journey along the winding roads, the hedgerows speckled with white convolvulus and late summer daisies

At Cavendish Lodge, he slung my holdall over his shoulder and opened the front door, which looked as if it had been fitted with a new lock. I didn't say anything. Once at the bottom of the elegant staircase, he paused.

"Should I put you in the guest room?" he said, gnawing his lip.

"What do you want?"

"You. With me." He sounded a bit gruff, and I smiled.

"Then, no. I don't want to go in the guest room."

CHAPTER 38

He smiled, a slow smile full of promise, and my heart fluttered. "I'll take this up and I'll be right back."

"I'll make tea," I said, sliding the coat from my shoulders and letting him see the new ruby dress that showed off my cleavage. He looked at me and nodded appreciatively.

Kettle on, I wandered into the library to see the miniatures of Harriet, out of their case and hung proudly on the wall by Hugo's desk. Mango looked up from his position on the sofa as I moved closer to the portraits.

"Well," I breathed. "Don't you look fine?" My eyes darted between them, measuring the difference in countenance, in spirit, and I was fascinated all over again by her. As I contemplated Harriet's expression in the second portrait, I thought I saw a gleam in her eye. Almost as if she was congratulating me for being here. Hugo walked in with two mugs.

"I saw you were absorbed, so I finished the tea."

"Sorry." I turned, shaking off my fanciful imagination. "Right. What happened with Pierce?"

After shifting an indignant Mango to one side, we settled on the sofa, cradling mugs in our hands. Hugo told the long version of Pierce's story. Hugo had finally managed to find him hiding back in his flat and asked him directly if he'd taken the miniatures. Pierce had crumpled like damp paper and out it all poured. The debts, the shady people who'd managed to inveigle themselves into his life, and his terror when they suggested that they didn't just know where *he* lived, but Hugo too.

"I suppose I can only be grateful that Carol is abroad," Hugo commented, fondling Mango's ears. "After I'd seen you, I went to arrange the transfer of the funds to the auctioneer, and one of these blokes was hanging around to make sure I paid up."

"It sounds like *The Godfather*!" I said, horrified. "Why didn't you call the police?"

"I could ask you the same question."

"I knew you'd hate it," I said after a pause, and he smiled warmly.

"Exactly. Way too complicated, don't you think? I would be shopping my brother, while these guys are just collecting the money Pierce owed and had agreed he'd pay them."

"Is that the end of it? Now they've got the money, will they leave him alone?"

"I'm sincerely hoping they won't be able to find him," Hugo said grimly. "I've persuaded him to wind up the business and lie low in France for a bit with Carol."

"Then what will he do?"

"He's actually really good at corporate communication, but he couldn't run a company for toffee. And the pandemic was hardly an ideal time to start a new business. We've agreed he'll get himself together while he's abroad and look for a new job before he comes back. Or," he added, his mood lightening, "he may even like working in a chalet."

I laughed. Hugo put his mug on the table and took mine from me. He clasped my hands.

"Gabriella, I'm incredibly grateful that you made me see the truth about Pierce. He's my brother, I love him despite all this, but it was way past time for some tough love."

I flushed, my cheeks heating up. "I'm sorry I was so harsh. I thought I'd really screwed it up."

CHAPTER 38

"The only way to get through to me, I think," he said, running fingers through my hair. I leaned into his hand and, turning my face, kissed his palm.

His eyes glowed. "You are the most amazing woman," he murmured. "Incredibly competent, warm, generous…" I resisted the urge to purr alongside Mango. "With the loveliest smile and the sexiest body." I stared at him, and he laughed softly. "And the fact that you don't really know those things makes you irresistible. I think I'm in love with you."

He kissed me, and the next thing I knew, we were stumbling up the stairs, still locked in an embrace. We reached the door to his room, and he shouldered it open. He lifted his head, his eyes glazed with desire. Obligingly, I wriggled out of my new dress and peeled off tights and knickers, unclipping my bra just as his hands came around me to cup my breasts, now heavy and aching.

"God, you are just so lovely," he groaned and pulled me back against him, so I could feel his erection pressing against my back. I shimmied, and with a sharp intake of breath, he turned and pushed me onto the bed. I scooted back to lie against the pillows.

He found a condom and fell into my open arms. A moment later, he was inside me, and I was clutching his back, astounded that this was *me* he was loving, *me* in this ecstasy. A very short time later, the universe exploded, and I heard him call my name.

"I love you too," I whispered.

We finally made it down to a very late lunch two hours later, me in one of Hugo's shirts and him in joggers and a teeshirt. Mango was still haughty at being barred from the bedroom and disappeared into the garden. We snacked at the kitchen table on cheese on toast, followed by fruit and yoghurt, and Hugo admitted he'd planned a steak dinner, wine, candles, the whole caboodle for later. I wasn't sure I'd be able to eat for the excitement of going back to bed but smiled.

"Sounds fabulous," I said. I licked my index finger to press on some crumbs left on my plate and Hugo's eyes darkened. Thinking we might never make it out of the bedroom this weekend, I grinned, picked up my mug of tea and asked him what he'd found out about Lady Porter-Hume. Visibly pulling his thoughts back into order, he nodded and went back into the library. I followed.

"The bank sent me some documents, and I've found more by searching their archives," he said. "I found nothing about Richard Cosway, but I did find a mention in a letter of a Mr Alexander Richardson and also Lord Rochford – or at least I think it's him. She mentions both, look – *Mr Alexander Richardson is a worthy man, obviously deep in affection; I hope Lord & Lady R'fd can arrange the match, although Mrs C does seem content to keep hold of her fortune as a widow.*"

"Does he mean Harriet?"

"I certainly hope so."

"She definitely looks happier in the second miniature," I mused, looking beyond Hugo to the wall. "Perhaps he was there!"

"Ah, but the plot thickens," said Hugo. "I went into the National Archives and found out that Mr Richardson

CHAPTER 38

was a wealthy carpet manufacturer from Newcastle. I found some newspaper cuttings about the benefits he introduced for employees – he was way ahead of his time. His family business was established in 1732. Guess who he does business with, that I found in the accounts?" I looked blank and shrugged. "John Colchester!" he announced triumphantly.

"What?" I gasped, almost spilling my tea. "This Mr Richardson knew Harriet while she was married?"

"He certainly would have known John, and from Lady Porter-Hume's letters it would seem he was in contact with Harriet after John's death, but I didn't get further than this. I wonder if Harriet knew how he felt about her. Did she marry John and realise that someone else wanted her? And did she return Alexander's feelings?"

Hugo sat back and regarded me with intense satisfaction as I sifted through this new information. "Well, did she marry him? Or stay single?"

"Next on my list to look at."

"So why are we waiting?" I said impatiently, starting to rise.

"Because I thought you wanted to see the exhibition," he reminded me.

"Oh! Yes, of course. I ought to go and change," I said, smoothing down his shirt. He caught my hand.

"Shame, it looks better on you than it ever looked on me."

"I can wear it later, if you like," I teased him, pulling him to his feet.

"I'll hold you to that."

After we'd seen the exhibition, we walked slowly along the river walk back to his car and parked near the town walls, which I'd been astonished to discover were Elizabethan. I babbled happily about Lowry.

"I read an interview with LS Lowry once," I said, making my way carefully over the cobbles. "He didn't seem to enjoy painting much, from what I recall, but he liked detail. I remember one thing he said in the interview, that he crammed as many figures as possible into the painting so he could give the person who bought it good value!"

Hugo laughed. His arm was snug around my shoulders, and I thought I fitted him rather well. I fell silent as we drove back to Cavendish Lodge; I looked at the river across the border to Scotland and wondered if the peace that had settled in my core was just temporary. I hoped not.

"Are you up for more research?" he asked as he hung up his jacket.

"Of course!" I hid a smile as I thought I saw mixed emotions cross his face.

He caught my expression and laughed. "Damn, did I look disappointed?"

"A bit. But we ought to finish the job before you cook me dinner. And I'm not going anywhere!"

He nodded and muttered something about behaving like a randy teenager. I giggled, well pleased.

Harriet's gaze seemed to greet me as I walked into the library. Tease, I thought, and then decided my imagination was running away with me.

"So – where do we look?" he said, sitting close to me on the sofa and peering at my laptop as I booted it up.

CHAPTER 38

"We'll look in the parish registers around this area, and I thought it might also be useful to browse the Northumberland archives," I frowned at the website. "Which are here, in Berwick-upon-Tweed!" I looked at him. "Did you know that?"

He looked sheepish. "Well, yes, but I needed an excuse to come to London to see you."

I gasped and then grinned, pleased. Although long distance relationships could be problematic. Who knew how long this would last?

Hugo frowned. "What?"

I glanced at him, surprised. "Sorry?"

"What was that thought? You looked – I don't know. Sad? Scared?"

I didn't speak for a moment, my head spinning with the idea that Hugo might be able to read my mind. "It's nothing. Just wondering how we're going to keep this—" I flapped my hand between us, "going between Northumberland and London."

His gaze speared me. "Are you concerned?"

"A bit. I've never been in this position before. I – I'm afraid of being hurt."

His hand covered mine. "I can't promise I won't hurt you until I know you better, but I can promise that I will never hurt you intentionally. And I don't want to lose you." His voice rumbled in my head. No, me neither, I thought. I strove to lighten the mood and grinned at him.

"Perhaps we should give it a few months to begin with – trial run?" He nodded slowly. I looked back at my laptop.

"Right, let's see if they've got anything." I typed in 'marriage' and 'Richardson' and pressed search.

"Well, I'll be blowed," murmured Hugo as the search results came up. "They were married at St B & B's."

"Sorry?"

"St Boisil and St Bartholomew's – the parish church at Tweedmouth. It's been there since Celtic times, I think. Can we see the record?"

"No, I think you'll have to go into the archives, but the details are here," I said, reaching for my notebook and scribbling. "Alexander and Harriet were married on 30 December 1803. We should see if it was reported in any newspapers – they were both big deals in the area, weren't they?"

I scoured the sites for ages but found nothing that I could see outside the paywall. I moved into the kitchen so I could keep Hugo company while he cooked dinner. I only closed the laptop when he pointedly asked me to lay the kitchen table.

"Perhaps that's why she looks so happy in the later portrait," I said thoughtfully as I unplugged the cable. "Did she know that Alexander wanted to marry her?"

"Or wanted to marry her money," Hugo said, shaking stir-fried vegetables into a dish. "She'd be quite a catch, being fabulously wealthy. And everything would have gone to her husband."

I winced at that. I hoped that Alexander really had loved her. Harriet deserved that.

Chapter 39

LONDON, EARLY JULY 1803

Finally, Harriet was ready and sent a note to Alexander to meet her at that most unromantic of venues, Mr Wilkins' office.

Alexander was ushered into a small, neat parlour and looked enquiringly at Harriet. She smiled, trying to be reassuring, but she was nervous. He bowed to Lady Porter-Hume and then kissed Harriet's hand, frowning when he felt it tremble.

For what seemed like hours, Harriet had been sitting with Mr Bessiwick and Mr Wilkins, soaking up their seemingly endless supply of patience in the summer heat that shimmered through the city. With Lady Porter-Hume, they tested the legal boundaries that might protect Harriet's inheritance. The result, she thought, was highly unconventional, and even though she didn't doubt Alexander's affection for her, it was a solution that most gentlemen would not deign to agree to.

"Mr Richardson, thank you for coming. Allow me to explain a little about the agreement we have drawn up," Mr Bessiwick began. "The position that Mrs Colchester wanted to achieve was control of her fortune, even if she marries. Before she wed Mr John Colchester, she was what is known as a *feme sole*, or a woman alone. In law, the *feme sole* can sign contracts and own property. When she wed, she became a *feme couvert*, or someone completely under the protection of her husband."

"Or completely under his control," interjected Lady Porter-Hume. "A person who ceased to exist other than as an appendage." She wrinkled her nose in disgust. Mr Bessiwick nodded calmly, and then turned back to Alexander.

"Now she is a widow, she becomes again a *feme sole*, and can create contracts and sign agreements. She is intent on creating a trust for her inheritance. This will protect her inheritance, give her a regular income and ensure that she can dispose of her property according to her wishes."

Alexander nodded. "I see. And the trustees of this trust are...?"

"Lady Arabella Porter-Hume, Lady Anne Rochford, Lord Phillip Rochford, and Lady Georgiana Porter-Hume."

"No family representatives?" he asked, after a pause, eyebrows raised.

"None that I would depend on," commented Harriet dryly.

His eyes flickered to her, and Harriet spirits dived. She had feared he would feel insulted, or that she did not trust him. She couldn't read his face.

"How are the trustees replaced should one of them become infirm or die?" asked Alexander, and Mr Wilkins went into sufficient detail to make Harriet's head spin. But as she watched Alexander's face, she wondered how attentive he was.

CHAPTER 39

At the end of Mr Wilkins' explanation, Alexander was silent. Then he looked around the room, his blue eyes turned a cloudy grey.

"I wish for a few words alone with Mrs Colchester," he said. Lady Porter-Hume gave Harriet a sharp look, but Harriet just nodded, and after some paper shuffling, they were left alone.

"I recognise that this is the way of the world," Alexander said quietly. "Talk of settlements, agreements, legalities. But I feel I am losing you in all the paperwork. How do you feel, Harriet?"

"Nervous. Terrified, in fact," Harriet confessed. "I thought you might be concerned that I would be unable to bear you children—"

His head shot up and he looked hard at her. With a gulp, she continued, "and that you would hate all this."

He gave a soft huff of laughter. "You are correct that I hate all this. But I have always wondered whether you were to blame for your childless state. It does take two, after all..."

She blushed fiery red, and he coughed and went on. "But I was not clear. How do you feel about *me*, Harriet?"

"Oh!" A pause. "I would like to marry you, of course!" She gurgled with laughter. "This is what all this—" she gestured around the room, "is about."

She expected him to smile, and he did not. "And *why* do you want to marry me, Harriet?"

"I – I suppose I want someone to share my adventures with, to travel with," she said hesitantly.

He stared hard at her. "I see. You are still in mourning, so an engagement now would be distasteful. When do you put off your mourning?"

Harriet frowned at his brisk tone. "John died in late November, so, December, I think."

"Perhaps then we should discuss this in December?" he said, rising to his feet.

Harriet was aghast as he picked up his hat. "But – the agreement, Alex!"

"I do not like it overmuch," he replied coldly. "It reduces our relationship to a business transaction when there is no need."

Harriet, who had not slept well for days, felt the fury rise in her. "That is all very well for you to say! *You* do not cease to exist when you take a spouse!"

"And *you* do not trust me to protect you and care for you!" he snarled. "Good day, Mrs Colchester!" Then he walked out, banging the door behind him, the draught wafting the agreement to the floor.

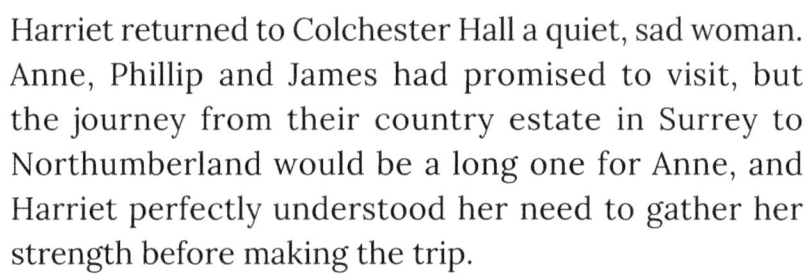

Harriet returned to Colchester Hall a quiet, sad woman. Anne, Phillip and James had promised to visit, but the journey from their country estate in Surrey to Northumberland would be a long one for Anne, and Harriet perfectly understood her need to gather her strength before making the trip.

Summer settled in a haze over Northumberland and Harriet struggled to contain what felt like a second grief. Wanting to give her thoughts a more positive direction, she wrote a long-overdue letter to Sophia. It was short:

Beloved sister – I have longed to make contact for the past six years and now I am in a position to do so. I have

CHAPTER 39

inherited from my recently deceased husband and am independent. I have followed your life from a distance, but I beg you will allow me to visit and to reacquaint myself with you and your family. It has been so long! Your loving sister Harriet

It took a little while for Sophia to reply, due to one of the children being ill with fever, but at long last, Harriet dressed in her oldest dress and took the carriage to Middleton, near Pickering.

Sophia's sharp angles had been smoothed by motherhood and genteel poverty, and both sisters cried when Harriet appeared at the door. Struck dumb at first, their tongues loosened and they gradually overcame the awkwardness of their meeting, which reflected Harriet's change of fortune and Sophia's relative poverty. Harriet was shocked at the roughness of Sophia's skin and hands, no longer the delicate beauty Harriet had known. But beneath it all, a wealth of happiness kept the sparkle in Sophia's eye. That she and Miles adored one another was indisputable. On her first visit, Harriet was armed with candied fruit and toys. On her second, she brought a bolt of cotton, a round of cheese, warm jackets for the children, a muffler for Miles and fine kid gloves for Sophia.

When Sophia and Miles came to Colchester Hall, Sophia laughed as she was shown around the house.

"How on earth do you find your way about?" she teased. "I declare I will need to trail string from the drawing room to my bedchamber, so I don't become lost!"

As the year slipped towards autumn, Harriet heard the corridors of the Hall ring with laughter as Miles played hide and seek with little Robert, Louisa and Freddie. Watching their flushed and laughing faces, Harriet could almost imagine herself happy.

In September, Alexander was mentioned in a letter from Phillip, revealing how diligently Mr Richardson had used his business associates to facilitate the removal of the Contessa di Basilio from Italy, delivering her safely to Southampton.

From Alexander himself, she heard nothing.

The Christmas yew tree twinkled with little wax candles and was adorned with sweetmeats, almonds and raisins in paper twists, fruits and toys. James clapped his chubby little hands, his eyes wide at the sight, and Harriet, holding him, smiled. The tradition of the yew-bough, introduced by Queen Charlotte, certainly set young eyes a-sparkle.

Anne chuckled at his glee. "Yes, you shall have some of the sweets after your dinner, sir. But your godmother looks weary, so come to me, darling!" Harriet relinquished James and dropped her arms, allowing the blood to flow through them again. James was a solid, growing baby.

Harriet looked around the room and discreetly stretched, her back still stiff from her long journey from Northumberland. But she was glad to be here at Phillip and Anne's country house in Surrey, among company to lift her spirits.

Pregnant again, Sophia was unable to make the journey from North Yorkshire to Colchester Hall, and so she and Miles had reluctantly refused Harriet's invitation.

CHAPTER 39

Anne had eagerly invited her to Rochford Park. Christmas at Colchester Hall, alone, would have been very dismal.

The drawing room was beginning to fill with people, but these were strangers to Harriet. There were elderly ladies, clutching shawls around their shoulders, despite the roaring fires at both ends of the room. A few children, currently awed by the Christmas bough, pointed at the sweetmeats and the small toys – stuffed poppets, wooden horses and tin soldiers. A couple of young girls, not out yet, awkward and all elbows and knees, were accompanied by proud mamas, monitoring the antics of two would-be young bucks, in glorious waistcoats and hair pomade. These lads were also surreptitiously observed by fathers and uncles to ensure they did not over-indulge in the punch and supply local gossip for the next month.

Phillip introduced her to his guests, and conversation was easy, but vapid, as they talked about the bough, the upcoming refreshments for the children and the carols to be sung.

The table, when the doors were opened to the next room, groaned with pasties and slices of pie, jellies and puddings. The half-dozen children for whom it was intended would never be able to eat it all, although Harriet thought that the young bucks would soon lend their support.

She walked towards the fire, loving its fierce heat, and fell into quiet reflection. After Christmas, Phillip and Anne were expecting Lady Porter-Hume for a visit, together with Georgiana and her new husband, Thomas, Lord Benborough.

Harriet swallowed, pushing gloomy thoughts away. After the meeting with Mr Bessiwick, Alexander had left town, and without him, the season had just limped to a close. Would there ever be a time when women could dictate their own lives, without the ornate dance of society, the marriage market? Lord, she hoped so! Although Alexander had refused her contract, perhaps if she thought this way, so would others, in the future.

She closed her eyes, trying to recapture the feel of his lips, and starting to worry that she couldn't quite recall it.

"Harriet," said Anne's concerned voice. "Are you well?"

Harriet forced a smile. "Of course! But forgive me if I can still feel every bump on the road from Northumberland to here!"

Anne's brow cleared. "You occasionally look so sad, you know," she said softly. "I wish you would return to town!"

Harriet shrugged. "I am much engaged in planning, as Napoleon makes actual travel to the Continent impossible. And did I tell you, I will be an aunt again next month? This will be Sophia's fourth child, and she is devoutly hoping for a boy. So, my dear, I am content."

"What would make you deliriously happy, rather than just content?"

To see Alexander again and feel his arms around me, she thought. To thank him for his help extracting Maria from the Continent earlier this year. "Do not seat me next to Mr Robert Johnson. Sweet as he is, I cannot deal with his clumsy attempts to appear manly."

Anne put her hand over her mouth to hide her giggle. "He is at that *awkward* age, is he not? Poor boy!"

Harriet tucked her hand in Anne's arm. "You'll have to face that trial with James, won't you?"

Anne rolled her eyes. "I trust his father will have something to suggest when the time comes!" She pulled Harriet to the sofa. "Have you heard from Edwin?"

Harriet had. His letters to her were long and repetitive, telling her over and over about the beauty of his new wife, the exquisite features of his new baby daughter, and giving endless thanks for her kindness for settling him in his modest house in Durham. Harriet was a fast learner, and she had put the money for Edwin and Maria in trust for little Consuela, administered by herself, Mr Bessiwick and Anne. This way, Edwin could not fritter away the money on gambling, although, she reflected, he seemed to be devoted to Maria and his dainty daughter.

Edwin also repeated his gratitude to Alexander. This only served to exacerbate the ache that Harriet felt in the background of all her days. She truly missed Alexander, his straightforward way of speaking, his intense energy. Anne spoke.

"What of Augusta?"

"We have exchanged chilly letters," Harriet said, staring into the fire again. "Some communication must take place, but neither of us believes it needs to be more than distantly cordial. However, I have invited Clarissa and Jacob to Colchester Hall to see if we can establish a friendly relationship. Without their bullying, they might be pleasant company."

"Your cousins? You are generous, Harriet."

Harriet's mouth twisted. "No, I am not. As they might learn."

Finally, after games, tantrums and one little girl being sick, the children left, and the house was quietly and efficiently restored to order by the footmen. The adults complimented Anne and Phillip on a splendid afternoon, and how everyone was looking forward to dinner. Anne suggested Harriet might come down a little early to secure her favourite seat by the fire.

Harriet tried to inject some bounce into her step as she went to change into her new gown. It was a rich emerald, which she thought very festive as well as becoming. The sumptuous silk was a far cry from her usual style, which tended, even after her mourning ended, to be subdued. She draped a silver stole over her arms and then immediately discarded it.

"No, Louise," she said to her maid. "I resemble the Christmas bough! Give me the ecru lace instead."

Louise wrinkled her nose but passed the delicate stole. With a satisfied nod at her reflection, Harriet went to the drawing room and tentatively opened the door. It was empty, and she walked towards the fireplace, slightly unnerved by the quiet.

A noise made her turn and she gasped. Alexander stood at the open door.

"Good evening, Mrs Colchester," he said and walked towards her. She moved her mouth but her throat wouldn't work, and so she simply drank in the sight of him. His dark hair was longer than she was used to seeing and his skin was a little tanned. He was thinner. He stopped close to her, so close she could feel the heat from his body. They stared at one another.

"I – I wondered if I would ever see you again," she whispered.

"Are you glad you have?" His tones were husky.

"Oh, God, yes!" she breathed, and she swayed towards him. He locked his arms around her, and half carried her to the sofa, nuzzling her neck.

Between tears and giggles, she scolded him softly. "Idiot! I am not about to faint!" She put her arms around his neck and raised her head. After a fraction of a second's hesitation, he lowered his mouth and briefly, tenderly, kissed her. She gave a little moan of protest as he pulled away, and he clasped her hand.

"Harriet, the rest of Phillip's dinner party will join us in a moment! Anne only gave me five minutes!" he said urgently, his gaze never leaving her face.

"I have so many questions!"

His eyes glinted wickedly. "Later, my love. But first, we must eat dinner."

Chapter 40

CENTRAL LONDON, SEPTEMBER 2023

Gerrard was calling my name, and I quickly closed the window on the internet. Even now, researching Harriet and Sophia was a bit of an obsession, and I filled my tea and lunch breaks with it.

"Ah, there you are," announced Gerrard as he walked into the gallery. "I wanted to talk to you about expanding our exhibits."

I concentrated. Gerrard had highly tuned antennae for an 'about-to-be-popular' artist.

"I wondered if we might turn the mezzanine into a space dedicated to sculpture?" he finished. "Shall we go up and have a look at what's needed?"

After climbing up to the mezzanine, I rubbed my chin. "I don't know what size of pieces you were thinking of, but it's like the paintings – we don't have room for many if people are going to have enough distance to admire them,"

Gerrard frowned. "Yes, you're right. It might be a bit cramped. And it would be more difficult to sell as a meeting space if we put the sculpture in the centre of the room. Hmm…"

Silently, I agreed. The pictures on the wall were perfect for social gatherings, as they took up wall space, not floor space. We trailed downstairs, but Gerrard had his 'thinking' face on. We weren't finished with the sculpture conversation just yet.

I perched on the stool and opened the laptop again. Hugo had sent an email to my personal address, and I opened it. It was a scan of the marriage licence for Alexander and Harriet, and the witnesses were Lord Rochford and Lady Arabella Porter-Hume.

Finally, I found it! The happy couple! Hugo had written. I clapped my hands, thoroughly satisfied at this information.

I grinned. I'd looked up a portrait of Arabella and thought she looked a hoot – glorious chestnut hair, a strong, straight nose and a wicked twinkle in her eye. The kind of woman you'd want at your wedding. Or your hen night. It was amazing what having pots of money could do for your confidence.

I'd compared Arabella's portrait with that of Harriet in mourning, and I wondered if Harriet's new-found confidence as a widow might have slowly drained away, as Alexander assumed control of her wealth. I wanted to know for sure that Harriet had had the happy ending she deserved and not married a man who wanted her only for her money. I thumbed open the photos of the portraits on my phone.

Harriet didn't look as if she would be anyone's fool. I glanced again at my email. Lady Porter-Hume would be canny too, as a director of a bank.

"I wonder if there's a record of the marriage settlement?" I said to myself. A customer entered the gallery, and I closed my computer and beamed at them. I'd have to do this at home.

It seemed I was to get no peace, I grumbled to myself as I went to answer the door to Joe, just returned from a shoot in Japan.

"I want to hear how your love life is progressing!" he grinned at me, pale green eyes gleaming from behind the kohl. I had to smile, and then blushed as I recalled Hugo's last visit. "Oho! Time to tell me everything, girl!" Joe hooted with laughter.

I packed away the idea of looking for more information on Harriet, and invited him in.

"I can hardly believe how wonderful you look! Like a changed woman!" he declared, flicking my midnight-blue velvet top. "And I take some credit for that."

"Absolutely right," I agreed, and we clinked glasses.

"But you've been dating a while! What happens next? Is he coming to live with you? You off to Northumberland to live?"

I laughed. "We've been together four months! And who knows if it will last? I've forgotten how these things work."

I'd deliberately focused on the moment, rather the future. The relationship with Hugo was so new, so long-distance, I didn't want to put too much faith in it just yet. Joe narrowed his eyes slightly and took a sip of his drink.

"Need to think about these things, Gabriella."

"Not yet," I said firmly. My phone pinged with a new text message. I glanced at it. It was from Mum, inviting me to lunch, her treat. I raised an eyebrow.

"Let me guess – your mother?" Joe said shrewdly and I laughed.

"Am I that transparent? Yes, it's Mum."
"What does she want now?"
"She wants to take me to lunch."

Joe clapped his hand on his chest. "Be still my beating heart! Your family doing things for you, Gabriella?"

"They're trying," I said with a smile. "Not always succeeding, but Mum's making a real effort. They all are."

At the end of August, I had invited Mum, Evie and Liam to the gallery for an open evening. They'd even found another babysitter for the occasion. I walked them around the gallery, talking to them about the pictures and the artists. When other people began to arrive, Evie immediately embarked on a charm offensive, chatting to everyone and giving them snippets of information she'd remembered from me.

Liam saw a business contact, and they talked sport, but not before I heard him say, "My sister practically runs this place, you know. She put in the new mezzanine and it's one of the most sought-after spaces in the area. My company, QE Insurance, held the inaugural event."

Mum clutched an increasingly warm glass of white wine, nervous at being out of her depth and knowing no-one. She'd made a special effort with her dress and hair and I felt rather proud of her. On the other side of the room, I nudged Susan, brought in to help me with the event.

"Could you refresh Mum's glass and chat to her? I've got to talk to Gerrard about the music."

"Of course. She looks a bit lonely. I'll show her our new landscapes, get her talking. Other people are bound to chip in," Susan said promptly, grabbing a bottle from the makeshift bar. When I glanced over ten minutes later, Susan, Mum and an upright, greying gentleman were pointing at bits of the landscape, engaged in a lively debate. When the evening ended, Mum dragged this man over to me. She looked flushed and happy – and not just from the wine.

"I was going to catch the tube, but Richard tells me he lives in Muswell Hill!" she said to me. "So, we're sharing a cab."

"Richard Coleville – I'm pleased to meet you," said Richard in a cut-glass accent, quickly offering a firm handshake. "I know Gerrard from our Oxford days."

"I hope you've had a lovely evening," I said as I shook his hand. He assured me it had been splendid. Tactfully, Richard added that he'd wait for Mum by the front door.

"Please text me when you're back home," I said to her, watching the straight back of Richard walk away.

"Of course!" Mum said breathlessly. "Isn't he lovely? So polite and so English!"

Good Lord, was Mum about to start dating? I was struck dumb. She hugged me. "Well, I'll just find Liam and Evie to say goodnight – I think they're off into the West End for a drink."

I nodded, thinking that the babysitter would certainly be earning their money tonight.

"It's been brilliant to see what you do, and it's run like clockwork, hasn't it?" Mum said. "Are you pleased? You should be, you've obviously worked very hard – it's been brilliant."

She kissed my cheek and beamed at Richard as he held open the door.

So, although our family relationship was far from perfect, it was improving, partly because everyone was trying.

CHAPTER 40

"And how's the detective work going?" Joe said, nodding at my laptop and bringing me back into the present.

I told him what we'd found. "But I want to see if she was *happily* married!" I burst out, surprising us both. "I want to find a letter from Harriet telling her best mate that she's deliriously in love, anything! But instead, I'm looking at the bloody marriage settlement! Anything less romantic is hard to imagine!"

"What's a marriage settlement?" He grimaced as I explained. "Ugh. Sounds cold."

"Yes," I said, picking up my laptop again. "It is. I found it in the Richardson family archive."

"What does it say?" Joe shifted from the chair to sit beside me on the sofa.

"Let's see." I clicked on the document. After a few lines, I wrinkled my nose. "Blimey. Ornate writing and legalese... You have to get your eye in." After a few more minutes, I caught the words 'in trust' and focused. "What's a trust?" I asked Joe. He whipped out a phone and began to Google.

He tapped into his phone. "Hmm. 'A trust is a legal arrangement where a trustee manages assets on behalf of the beneficiaries of the trust.' Does that sound right?"

"I see." Indeed, I was beginning to see, and cheered Harriet's foresight. "Sounds like all of Harriet's property and wealth was put in trust for herself, and following her death, one third of it would go to Alexander, should he still be living, and the rest would be for all her children equally."

"Her husband couldn't just take it all away from her?"

I squinted at the curly writing. "No, I don't think so. The trustees were Lord Rochford, Lady Rochford and

Lady Arabella Porter-Hume, and someone called Lady Georgiana Benborough. At least two women who would be on her side. Well!" I sat back, wondering who Georgiana was. With another thought, I scrolled down the document. "And Mr Richardson signed this! It sounds very progressive for the time."

"Wasn't he rich anyway?" Joe commented.

"Yes, I think so; he owned a well-established company. I wonder if he made her happy?"

"Did they have any children? Not that that signifies anything, of course."

I glanced at my phone portrait again. Yes, I bet Harriet would have barred Alexander from the bedroom if he treated her poorly. I clicked back into the archives and began to search, and it was a couple of minutes before I realised I'd said nothing to Joe. He was watching me, much amused. I apologised.

"You're really into this, aren't you?" He rose to his feet. "Look, invite the lovely Hugo to dinner again and I'll bring Steven."

I apologised yet again but was happy to hustle him out of the door. An hour later, my eyes starting to smart from the screen time, I sent a triumphant note to Hugo.

Marriage settlement entirely in favour of Harriet, keeping the fortune in her hands as much as was possible then. Alexander signed it, AND settled a portion on her! Baptism details of Harriet's first child in the link. She had seven children, lost one girl, sadly. Seems like the marriage was successful on at least two counts! G xx

CHAPTER 40

I looked again at the clock. I was due to catch the train to Berwick in a couple of hours. Susan was standing in for me for the weekend. She had hit it off remarkably well with Gerrard and I was hopeful I might get a few more Saturdays off in the future.

Gerrard joined me in the gallery, bringing me a mug of coffee. "I'd like a quick chat before you head off," he said.

"Oh?" My mind raced through my recent to-do list.

He smiled. "Relax, Gabriella. You've been as efficient as you usually are. No, I wanted to know if you'd do me a favour. Could you pop up to Edinburgh for me?"

"Of course. Do you want me to look at an artist?" I relaxed and took a sip of coffee. I hid my flinch. Gerrard liked nuclear-strength coffee. I did not.

"I'm thinking of buying another gallery," he said. "I'm very keen to move more into sculpture and we don't have the space here." He eyed me calmly as I spluttered. "Do you need a tissue?"

I patted my pockets, found one, and wiped my mouth. "That's interesting," I said, and he laughed.

"Yes, it's very interesting. I know you're settled in London, so I'm not asking you to up sticks, but I would like your wonderful organising brain to help me set it up. Would you be happy to do that for say, four months? It may be a shorter time, but I wasn't thinking of opening until the New Year. And of course, it's only an hour from Berwick."

I felt heat rush up my neck and cheeks.

"Ah, about that..." I began and then stopped. Gerrard waited, grey eyebrows raised. "I should have told you," I said at last.

"Yes, you should," he agreed. "I don't like secrets."

I winced, feeling like a schoolgirl caught behind the bike shed with a cigarette. "I'm sorry. I meant to tell you, but I thought you'd consider it a conflict of interest."

"On the basis on one commission? No. More important to me that we're honest with each other." He looked askance and a wave of guilt swept over me.

"I can go to Edinburgh this weekend, if you like, to look at the space," I offered quickly.

Gerrard smiled. "I'm thrilled for you, Gabriella. I don't think I've ever seen you this happy. Perhaps – if this all works out – you might even consider running the Edinburgh gallery for me, seeing what you can make of it." He put his head on one side and eyed me speculatively.

My immediate response was to say no – and I stopped myself. Yes, there was my family to consider. It would be a shock for them if I moved to Edinburgh for four months, let alone permanently, but they'd get used to it. It was an easy train journey, after all. And the relationship with Hugo was still very new – but a move would make it possible to see where it led us.

I thought of Harriet and wondered if I could work for Gerrard on a shared profit deal. Something to spur me on to success.

"Maybe," I said.

Chapter 41

ROCHFORD PARK, DECEMBER 1803

Harriet barely registered a word that was said at dinner. The goose and the venison came and went and she could not have passed comment on a mouthful. Somehow, she managed to maintain a conversation with the bishop beside her, who was kind enough – or oblivious enough – not to notice her distraction. She cast occasional glances towards Alexander, who seemed very merry with one of Phillip's uncles by his side, but she spotted the flicker of his cheek muscle and the tightening of his jaw whenever she caught his eye.

At last dinner was completed and the ladies rose, leaving the gentlemen to their port. Harriet, dreading the tittle-tattle of the tea tray, grasped Anne's arm.

"I must get some air! Will you excuse me?"

"Certainly, but the gardens are chilly, this time of night," Anne said, raising an eyebrow. "Try the library. There is a fire in there. I shall see you later. Or tomorrow…"

Harriet stared at her and then kissed her cheek and walked hastily to the library. The room was dimly illuminated by the fire, and she busied herself lighting some candles. After ensuring that she had enough light to at least appear as if she was reading a book, she settled to wait.

Alexander arrived only fifteen minutes later. She leapt to her feet as he carefully opened the door, and once more, they looked hungrily at one another. But this time, Harriet had gathered her wits, and with a tight smile, invited him to sit opposite her by the fire.

"Perhaps we should share our news?" she said with a shaky breath.

"Of course." He sat in the chair, his long legs stretched out in front of him, almost touching her slippered feet. A silence fell, broken only by the crackling of logs on the fire.

He put his chin on his broad chest and fell into deep thought. He finally spoke. "Lord Rochford asked for my assistance with Contessa di Basilio, and I was pleased to help. The lady was most grateful—"

"As was I!" interrupted Harriet. "You have done me a great service, Alexander, in helping Maria and Edwin."

He smiled slightly but made a dismissive gesture with his hand. "I was happy to help. I went to Ireland for a while, and returned to London in November. I thought you would join Anne for the beginning of the season, but she told me you had no plans to."

"No. As a wealthy widow coming to the end of her mourning, I grew tired of the place and the endless marriage proposals," Harriet said raising her chin and folding her hands in her lap.

He winced. "Contrary to what you might think, Harriet, I *do* want to marry you."

"But not on my terms?" She could not keep the bitterness from her voice.

CHAPTER 41

He stood up in one swift movement, towering over her. "Damn it, it seems I would marry you on *any* terms!"

She stared at him. "Then why did you leave? I spent three days putting that agreement together!"

He clenched his fists. "Because I didn't care about the agreement!" he ground out. "I cared that you didn't *love* me!"

Harriet was surprised into silence. He sighed in frustration. "All this – the agreement, the fortune – I wanted none of it. Your marriage settlement would be anathema to most men of my station, but I would have signed anything that would make you comfortable enough to wed me, because I love you. But all you said was that you wanted to marry me because you wanted a *travelling companion!*"

Harriet gaped. Of all the ridiculous... She stopped. She hadn't said it, had she? She put her head in her hands. "Oh, Alexander," she muttered.

"Well?" he demanded, seeming to brace himself for bad news. "Shall I just sign the damned agreement and merely hope we can find happiness?"

"You fool!" she said, jumping up and flinging her arms around his neck. "Of course I love you! I've loved you since we danced together on Lady Porter-Hume's terrace!" His hands tightened around her waist, and he gazed at her. "Kiss me, you numbskull," she said under her breath.

"Thank God!" he muttered and bent his head, and her memory of his kiss was magically restored. His lips demanded a response from her, and she slanted her mouth over his. A deep moan came from her throat, and he nuzzled her neck. She gasped and he nipped and suckled the top of her breasts over her decolletage and ran a hand over her thigh, sliding aside the silk of her dress to touch her skin. She pushed herself against him, and this time it was his turn to moan. Alexander took a deep breath and, letting her skirt fall, cupped her face in his hands.

"I shall take you on the floor if we continue this!" he growled, and she revelled in the sound. He picked her up and sat on the settle, trying to control his breathing. She rested her cheek on his shoulder and waited for the fire in her belly to subside, squirming with unfulfilled need.

"Be still, you baggage!"

"You are no fun at all, Alexander! I hope you will be livelier when we are married," she replied and felt him still under her thighs.

"Are we to wed?"

"I certainly hope so, otherwise I shall be pining for the one I love a long time," she said softly. "As well as feeling very uncomfortable." She wriggled on his lap to make the point and he cursed her and kissed her soundly.

When he stopped, she breathed out and stroked his face. He rested his forehead on hers and closed his eyes. "Anne has been a most useful correspondent, but I should like to hear how you have spent the last six months."

Harriet told him briefly of her contact with Sophia. "I had hoped they would be with me for Christmas, but Sophia is with child again and cannot travel from Yorkshire. So I accepted Anne's invitation. She was quite insistent, and now I see why!"

He chuckled. "Lord, it's taken an age to get here, has it not?" She nodded, but she was smiling. "I understand that among the party we have a bishop. In my pocket I

CHAPTER 41

have a special licence – will you marry me after Christmas? And before you say anything, I have sent for Mr Bessiwick to bring your blasted agreement for me to sign before we wed."

"W-what?" Harriet said, momentarily stunned. She drew back to look at him. "You were so sure of me, you dared to instruct *my* lawyer to do your bidding?" She pretended to look scandalised, but in truth was heartily glad of his forethought. To have him in the house but not in her bed would have been torture.

"Of course I was not sure of you, but I was prepared to risk your anger to ensure there were no impediments," he said, reasonably. "Am I forgiven?"

"I suppose so – I do like an organised man," she said with a smile, and he pulled her close.

"Should we rejoin the party? And announce our engagement?" he asked.

"Yes," she replied. "Yes, I think we should."

Chapter 42

EDINBURGH, DECEMBER 2023

The bells of St Giles were ringing nine o'clock. I locked the door with a sigh of relief.

GW2, the name of the new gallery, was in lights above the window, and we would be open on the eighth of January. Despite issues with the Council about the building work and the signage design, and the faintly cautious welcome from other galleries in the city, I'd made my deadline.

The past four months had been the most exhausting and the most exhilarating of my life, but now I just wanted to curl up in my bed and sleep for a week. Sadly, with Christmas coming up, this was unlikely. Thank God for online shopping.

"Need a lift?" said a chocolate voice from the car that had just pulled up beside me. I swung around.

"Hugo! What are you doing here?"

"I thought you'd be tired. Hop in."

I smiled, but was hoping he hadn't booked a restaurant, I was so whacked. I climbed into the car and sighed deeply as I sank into the leather seat. I could smell something else – tomatoes? Basil? I must be tired.

"Gallery all finished?" Hugo said, flicking a glance at me as he slowed down for the traffic lights.

"Mmm. Just. Thank God Justin managed to sort out the lighting earlier this week. It was all I could do to keep Gerrard in London rather than tearing up here to bash some heads."

He chuckled. "You've done a brilliant job. Your place?" he added.

"Please," I said. "I was going to have a pizza delivered."

"I cooked," Hugo said, and I stared at him. "Lasagna, garlic bread and salad. It's in the boot."

"You marvellous man."

He smiled and drove to the tiny flat I'd rented while I set up the gallery.

My two-foot-tall Christmas tree by the bay window twinkled in the streetlights as I opened the door. I switched on lamps and kicked off my shoes before closing the curtains. Hugo busied himself in the galley kitchen, taking out bowls and dishes. He glanced at me.

"Go and shower if you want. This will take at least twenty minutes to finish off in the oven."

I didn't need a second invitation. By the time I returned, with towelled-dry hair, jeans and a sloppy jumper, the table was set and the salad dressed. Hugo was humming, and I went behind him and wrapped my arms around his waist.

"You're wonderful," I murmured, my cheek against his back. He turned in my arms and kissed me gently.

"You look exhausted. Sit down and I'll get you a glass of wine."

We ate, talked, and the knots in my muscles unravelled as I relaxed. I was going to Mum's house for Christmas Day, and Liam and family would join us for lunch. Hugo was flying out to France to see Carol and Pierce. I felt like I'd been split in two.

After we'd cleared the table, I put on some music and we nestled among the wool rugs covering the enormous sofa. As I lay against Hugo's shoulder, I could hear his heartbeat, solid, regular, strong. I sighed with pleasure.

"I've got a present for you," he said, nuzzling my hair. "I know you're going back to London tomorrow."

"Oh! Yes, I've got yours, too!" I scrambled off the sofa and went to my bedroom. I searched in my drawers and grabbed the small flat package, adjusting the ribbon.

Hugo was on the sofa, staring into space. He clutched a parcel wrapped in brown paper. As I walked towards him, he smiled apologetically. "It only arrived this evening – I didn't have time for fancy paper."

"Tsk!" I teased him. "What are you like?" I handed his gift to him. "Merry Christmas, Hugo."

He kissed me on the mouth and my fatigue faded as libido took over. I pulled away, cursing my hormones. God, at this rate I'd never get any sleep. He grinned.

"You're too knackered, aren't you?"

"I am!" I laughed and hugged him. "But I'm also conscious that I'm not going to see you for a week..."

"Do you think I'll forget you in a week?" His dark eyes gleamed in the glow of the Christmas lights.

"You'd better not. Open your present."

He was one of those people who carefully undid ribbons and peeled off sellotape, so naturally, I became rather impatient. He chuckled. "It drives you mad, doesn't it? All good things, etcetera..." He opened the flat box and read the document inside it.

"You've bought me a cookery course?" he said, raising his gaze to my face.

"You said you always wanted to know how to cook a soufflé," I said uncertainly, wondering if I'd got it wrong.

CHAPTER 42

His face cleared and he roared with laughter and pulled me into an embrace.

"You darling girl! My God, what a memory you have! And you're absolutely right, I always seem to screw it up, so this is perfect! When do I go?"

I explained he'd need to contact the Edinburgh-based company and arrange a date. He kissed me firmly, carefully put the voucher on the coffee table and then put his gift on my lap. It felt like a photo frame; I tore away the brown paper and a card fluttered to the carpet. When I saw what was in the square frame, I gasped.

It was a small portrait of me, gorgeously executed in watercolours and ink. I blinked, surprised at the likeness, and felt my eyes fill.

"Oh, Hugo," I murmured. "It's lovely."

"Gerrard gave me a contact and I took a photo of you at the last open evening you held at the gallery. Do you like it?"

I nodded, too choked to speak.

"Look at the card," he urged me, and I picked it up. In Hugo's firm hand were the words, *Be More Gabriella*.

"You don't need to be more Harriet," he said softly. "You're terrific as Gabriella."

I put the portrait very carefully on the table, tears falling down my cheeks, and he gathered me in his arms. I turned my face to him, and he gently kissed my lips.

"I love you," I whispered.

"I love you right back," he said. "Fancy spending New Year with me?"

I nodded, smiling.

Epilogue

MIDDLETON, NORTH YORKSHIRE, MAY 1804

White May blossom was sprinkled across the hedgerows as the carriage drew up outside the rectory. The door flew open, and Freddie raced down the path to the carriage that drew up at the gate.

"Aunt Harriet! Uncle 'Sander!"

As Alexander handed down Harriet from the carriage, Freddie was talking ten to the dozen and Harriet laughed, only just able to keep up with his gabbling.

"Freddie! Yes, I can come and see your ducks, no, we're not leaving until next Saturday and yes, Uncle 'Sander will play spillikins, but pray, let me speak to your mama and papa first!"

"Freddie!" called Sophia from the door, holding a baby in her arms. "Fetch your father from the barn, please! And let your aunt and uncle catch their breath!"

"But not without a kiss first!" declared Harriet, and Freddie submitted to her embrace before wiping a slightly grubby sleeve across his cheek and racing to the barn. Sophia, blue eyes twinkling, looked rather hard at Harriet as she walked up the path to the rectory, a faint crease appearing between her brows.

Harriet bent over the new baby, Peregrine, and cooed as she saw his mop of fine dark hair. "What a darling!"

she breathed and kissed his forehead before carefully embracing her sister. Then she turned to Alexander, standing quietly to one side.

"Sophia, this is my husband, Alexander Richardson."

Sophia bobbed a curtsy, but Alexander smiled and took her hand to kiss it. Sophia laughed.

"So lovely to meet you at last! You are most welcome! Now, let us get tea before you consider us savages, with no manners!"

Putting her arm through Harriet's, Sophia drew them inside to the drawing room, while Miles' manservant unloaded their packages.

Some hours later, after a simple dinner, Harriet was delighted to see Miles and Alexander discussing William Pitt's recent return to the post of Prime Minister and laughing a great deal. She became aware of Sophia's eyes on her.

"What is it?" she asked.

Sophia smiled. "How are you feeling, sister?"

Harriet considered, surprised at the question. "Very well, I thank you! Do I look ill?"

"No, no! Did the journey here cause any nausea?"

Harriet frowned. "Not especially. I do feel fatigued, but I put that down to our journey. Why do you ask?"

Sophia's eyes twinkled and she leaned closer to Harriet and whispered in her ear. "When was the last time you had your courses?" Harriet's eyebrows flew up and she turned to her sister, astonished. "Nay, don't look at me so," gurgled Sophia. "I am never wrong. You look glowing, my dear, and I trust you will tell me the happy news when you are sure."

Harriet gaped and then slapped Sophia playfully on the hand. "Don't tease me! Five years of my previous marriage has convinced me I shall never bear children!"

"Pooh!" retorted her sister. "Don't talk fustian! I will wager my new bonnet against your gold locket that I am right!"

"Accepted!" Harriet responded with an uncertain laugh, her mind beginning to churn with dates. The talk turned to Peregrine, the twins, Michael and Sabrina, and of course, the irrepressible Freddie, who was demanding that Alexander play spillikins with him.

A month later, Sophia had just taken up yet more darning when the post arrived. To her surprise, it was a small parcel, addressed to her. Putting aside her workbox, she slit the string with her letter knife and unwrapped the parcel. A black velvet pouch lay in a box, and when she loosened the strings, a gold locket fell into her lap. She gasped and then began to laugh. There was a note, in Harriet's writing.

You win.

The End

Hang on! Don't go! Thank you for reading my book! If you liked *The Year of Yes and No*, please leave me a review!

EPILOGUE

https://www.amazon.co.uk/Year-Yes-No-dual-timeline-Duality-ebook/dp/B0DDMHPQ7R

Other Duality novels

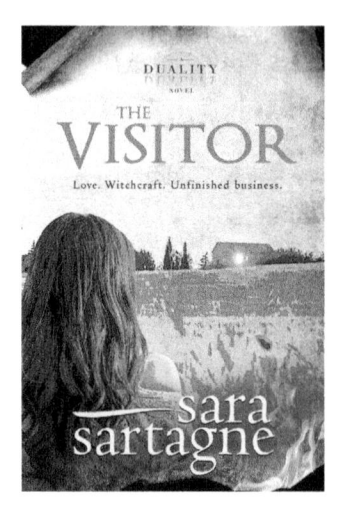

Two outsiders connected by love. Four hundred years apart.

2019. Trainee teacher Stacie Hayward is spending the summer with her brilliant, academic family. And with her ghosts. It's a strange gift that she's had since childhood – and learned to keep quiet about.

When Stacie's parents invite American professor Nate to stay, Stacie's ghosts suddenly vanish. Then Stacie is visited by the ghost of a young woman who calls her cousin and who offers to protect her. But protect her from what?

1619. Sarah Bartlett, a young healer, is suspected of witchcraft. The only person to defend her is John Dillington, the new parson. But is he in love – or bewitched? And can he save her from the flames?

Alone and bewildered, Stacie uncovers more of her past and realises that choices made long ago are rippling through time to threaten her. History may be repeating itself – but this time, it's Stacie who's in danger.

▫*The Visitor* is the first in a new series of Duality Novels that always feature two storylines, somehow connected. It is a standalone book.

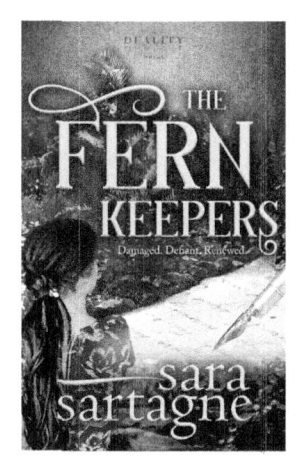

Damaged. Defiant. Renewed.

2022: Finally free from a controlling relationship, author Cat Kennedy moves into her aunt's old house. Rapidly running out of cash, she desperately needs to recreate the success of her first novel.

When she discovers a Victorian diary buried in the garden, she's inspired by the story of Emily, Lady Cleveland, and begins to rebuild her confidence – and the fernery. But somebody is watching Cat and they want to see her fail.

First, it's anonymous text messages that grow darker and more threatening. Then a carefully-designed campaign of intimidation that rapidly escalates. Is Cat's life in danger?

1862: Grieving the loss of her new-born son and suffocated by society's expectations, Emily Cleveland flees from London and the manipulative Dr Schenley, who she holds responsible for the death of her longed-for baby.

Designing the fernery in the peace of Cleveland House gives Emily new purpose, helping her recover the spirit and self-assurance she had when she was first married. But even from a distance, Dr Schenley's insidious influence over Emily's husband, James, threatens not just her rediscovered independence, but her very liberty.

As Emily fights to convince James of her sanity, and Cat battles an unseen enemy, both women need to find reserves of courage they never thought they possessed.

The Fern Keepers is a compelling dual timeline suspense novel, perfect for readers of Susanna Kearsley and Barbara Erskine. It is a standalone book.

Printed in Great Britain
by Amazon